That *Forgetful* Shore

TRUDY J. MORGAN–COLE

Bestselling author of *By the Rivers of Brooklyn*

That *Forgetful* Shore

A NOVEL

A CIP catalogue record for this book is available from Library and Archives Canada.
ISBN 978-1-55081-362-3

WWW.BREAKWATERBOOKS.COM
Breakwater Books is committed to choosing papers and materials for our books
that help to protect our environment. To this end, this book is printed on
paper from responsible sources and is Forest Stewardship Council® certified.

MIX
Paper from
responsible sources
FSC
www.fsc.org FSC® C011825

Canada Council   Conseil des Arts
for the Arts   du Canada

Canada

Newfoundland
Labrador

We acknowledge the support of the Canada Council for the Arts which last year
invested $20.1 million in writing and publishing throughout Canada. We acknowledge
the Government of Canada through the Canada Book Fund and the Government
of Newfoundland and Labrador through the Department of Tourism, Culture and
Recreation for our publishing activities.

PRINTED AND BOUND IN CANADA.

For Jamie ... In Memoriam

I can't believe I've written a book
you'll never be able to read.

For this alone on Death I wreak
The wrath that garners in my heart:
He put our lives so far apart
We cannot hear each other speak.

–Tennyson, *In Memoriam*

Prologue

"The thing you don't know about me," Trif Russell says, "is, I was one of a twin."

She has said this to many people, over the years. She has said it in the garden above Aunt Rachel's house, picking rocks from the stony ground. She has said it in the dark, turning to a face half-seen beside her in the bed. She has said it so often that it is, in fact, a thing almost everyone knows about her. Yet she creates the illusion that she is letting you into a confidence. She says it with lowered voice, with a glance to make sure there are no eavesdroppers.

She says it today over a cup of tea at her kitchen table, to the young Church of England minister, Reverend Bliss. A grand name, that, Reverend Bliss. Reverend Bliss himself shows a certain formality about the nicknames the people of Missing Point have come up with to manage their odd Biblical appellations. Ki Barbour is Skipper Hezekiah to him; old Aunt Hepsy Snow is Miss Hephzibah. He has called Trif "Mrs. Russell" since he came to town six months ago, but now, in the comfort of her kitchen, trying to get better acquainted before leading the service tomorrow, he says, "You would be named Tryphena, I suppose?"

"No," says Trif as she gets up to refill his cup. "No, you'd think that, wouldn't you? I was christened Tryphosa. You see the thing you don't know about me, Reverend, is I was one of a twin. Mother had the two of us, two girls, and I don't know if it was her or my Aunt Rachel picked out the names, but Aunt Rachel said we was to be called after the two sisters in the Bible, Tryphena and Tryphosa. *Who labour in the Lord*, as the apostle says."

"How very unusual," says Reverend Bliss.

"Isn't it?" She puts the teapot back on the stove, the big Waterloo that takes up half the kitchen. Katie Grace has been after her for years to get an oil stove. Trif has put it off long enough that now it doesn't matter any more; soon she'll cook her last meal on that woodstove.

Tryphena and Tryphosa; Peony and Posy. It explains everything, she thinks. Half of a whole, a piece torn away.

"You're a legend in these parts, Mrs. Russell," the Reverend says. He sips the last of his tea and looks into the bottom of the cup. "Like your namesake, you have laboured in the Lord. A wonderful life of service."

She is sixty-four. Does this young minister think it's her life that's over? Will he make a mistake and bury her tomorrow, thinking that sixty-four is as good as dead?

Their two teacups, hers and the Reverend's, sit side by side on the small table, framed by the kitchen window. Trif has spent more than forty years looking out this window, the two pine trees in the yard and beyond them, the Long Beach, the whole scene framed by the kitchen curtains she sews from old flour sacks. Year by year the pines grow a little taller; every few years Trif hauls down the curtains, sews and embroiders and hangs a new pair. Those are the only changes. The same grey waves roll onto the same grey rocks, as they've done for two hundred years – as they did long before that, when there was no window and there was no house, when not a soul lived on the Point to watch the waves break on the shore.

"What will you do now?" the young minister asks. The same question they're all asking. Where will Trif go now, what will she do?

She knows, but she isn't about to explain her decision to Reverend Bliss. To understand where the story ends, he'd have to know it all the way back to the beginning, and that's more of a story than she has time to tell today.

"What you don't know about me is, I was one of a twin."

It's forty years earlier – no, forty-five. She lies in bed beside Jacob John Russell, in the front bedroom where the roof slopes down above the bed. Jacob John blows out the lamp and shifts himself to face her.

That *Forgetful* Shore

They said their vows earlier that day, down in the parlour, the Church of England minister reading off from the book. Uncle Albert and Aunt Rachel stood beside Trif, and Jacob John's mother, sister and brother-in-law on the other side of him. Trif's cousins, Ruth, Will and Betty, squeezed onto the settee. That was all the people they could fit in the parlour, though half the folks on the Point came later to the kitchen to have a piece of dark fruitcake and a drop of tea.

Trif had no-one to stand for her. Aunt Rachel had tried to get her to have Ruth for a bridesmaid, or her cousin Lizzie Snow, or one of her other girlfriends – Minnie Dawe or Millicent Butler, perhaps.

"No," Trif said. "If Kit can't be here, I'll have nobody. I wants Kit standing up beside me on my wedding day, or no-one."

"It's Jacob John you'll have standing up beside you," Aunt Rachel reminded her, her eyelids lowered like blinds pulled half-way down in a house of mourning. "You'd do well to remember that."

She got through it anyway, Kit or no Kit. Put her hand on Jacob John's arm and felt the rough weave of his good suit coat, the muscle underneath. Said the vows, and silently asked God to be her witness. Now, in the dark, she turns to him and tells him her secret. She brings few enough hopes into this bedroom with her, but she tries telling him anyway.

"I knows that," he says. "I knows your mother died having twins and she lost the one twin. Another girl, wasn't it?"

The dark tale of her birth sounds blunt in his unvarnished words. "Another girl," she agrees. She does not tell him Tryphena's name, says nothing about Pheenie and Phosie.

"What else do you know about me?"

She feels the movement of his shoulders against the mattress, feels him shrug. "Only what everyone knows, I s'pose."

Then that's all you'll ever know, she promises silently. *Only what everyone knows, less if I can manage it.* Never asks herself what she knows of him, what secrets a man like Jacob John might have.

His hand on the fabric of her nightdress. "Come on now, maid," he says. "Let's get on with it."

"What you don't know about me," Triffie says, heaving a rock onto the rock pile, "is that I was one of a twin."

"You were?" Kit Saunders is supposed to be helping Trif pick over the ground before planting the garden. She was eager enough to be bazzing rocks around for the first little while, but now she's perched up on the fence railing, sucking on a toffee while Trif bends over and scrabbles one rock after another from the thin soil of early spring. "What happened to the other one, the other twin?"

"It was a storm, the night I was born. A terrible January storm," Trif has been rehearsing this story in her head for all of her ten years, piecing it together from bits of gossip, tales overheard, Aunt Rachel's pinched replies to her questions. She has never had the chance to tell it aloud before. Now this Saunders girl, newly come all the way from Trinity, is avid to hear it. Trif strings her words together carefully.

"A terrible storm, and my mother was sick. It was early – two months before we were supposed to be born. Me and my sister, my twin sister. We were only seven-month babies, and my mother went into labour."

"What's labour?"

"You know – the birth pains. Like when a woman, or a cow or anything, is going to have a baby."

"We never kept no cows," Kit says. Her father is not a fisherman; he was clerk for a merchant up in Trinity and has now moved to Missing Point to do the same job for his wife's people, the Parsons family who own the Mercantile and two schooners. Kit has no brothers or sisters; she knows nothing. "So what happened to your mother?"

"It was a terrible storm, a terrible winter storm. Aunt Rachel sent her brother out for to get Granny Morgan, the midwife, but it was too stormy. And the babies were coming, and there was only Aunt Rachel here with my mother. She borned us both, first my sister, then me. Aunt Rachel had in mind to call the first Tryphena and the second one Tryphosa. But it was too early; we were too little to live. Aunt Rachel thought we were both dead. She told my mother we were both dead, and my mother died of a broken heart. And when Aunt Rachel looked away from tending to my mother to the two of us wrapped up in the basket, sure enough, Tryphena was all blue and pale, but I let out a little cry, like a baby kitten. And I was no bigger than a kitten, either. And she took me up, wrapped me all up and put me in the warmer on top of the stove. Where you put bread in rise."

Kit's mouth is as wide now as her eyes. "And you lived?"

"Of course I lived, maid, here I am." After a moment both girls bust out laughing. Then Trif bends to her work again. She picks up two good-sized stones. Every winter the snow and ice sweep over the land and leave behind this debris of rock that has to be picked over before the potatoes and carrots and cabbage can be planted. Picking over the ground before the hard work of planting is a job for young maids like herself. She hands one stone to Kit, who hurls it at the rock pile.

"Where was your father?" Kit asks.

Trif shrugs. The missing father, a topic on which Aunt Rachel volunteers no information, has always been the least interesting part of the story to her. What is an absent father, or even a tragic dead mother, next to a ghost twin, a shadow-self that almost was?

"What would she have called you, if you'd both lived? You couldn't have two Triffies in the one family," Kit points out.

"I asked Aunt Rachel, but she wouldn't say. They couldn't have called out Tryphena and Tryphosa all the time. Not every day."

"Pheenie and Phosie," Kit suggests.

They laugh again, but Trif nods. "I thought of that," she said. "I could be Phosie. I'm almost glad she didn't live, so I wouldn't be called that. But I'd like to have a twin. It's almost like I misses her."

"Pheenie and Phosie," Kit repeats. "They could be like two flower names, almost. Peony and Posy."

"That's pretty." Trif has a hard time thinking of herself, hard, tall and angular, as Posy.

"I wish I had a sister too," Kit says. "Mom says the doctor warned her not to have no more after me. She's delicate. Come over to the Long Beach with me after you finishes picking over the ground?"

Triffie's jobs done, they walk down the North Side Road, past the new causeway linking the north side of the Point to Bay Roberts, then across the neck of the Point to the south side where Kit's family lives. On the vast pebbled shores of the beach they throw stones again, this time for fun, skipping them on the water.

"Are you staying here?" Trif asks, unable to bear the hope building inside her.

"For now. Pop talks about going away, to the Boston States, but Mom won't hear tell of it."

"Why did you leave Trinity?"

"Mom was homesick for the Point. She grew up here."

"If you stay here, we could be like sisters."

"My birthday's in February," Kit says. "One month after yours. We're almost twins. I could be Peony."

Trif nods but doesn't dare speak, afraid she might cry or say something stupid.

Kit picks up a piece of rock different from the smooth beach rocks all around. This one has a hard, jagged edge, not yet worn down by the endless pounding of the sea. She draws the edge quickly over her palm, raising a bright red line. "I heard tell of people mixing their blood," she says, holding out her hand. "So they can be blood brothers. Or sisters. It was in a book."

Trif takes her hand, though not the rock. "We don't have to do that. Aunt Rachel says your grandmother Snow was her father's first cousin." Then, seeing that Kit doesn't understand, she explains, "We got the same blood in us anyway."

And that is where the story begins.

That *Forgetful* Shore

My
Heart is
Thine

1904 – 1908

Triffie

TRIFFIE IS SCRUBBING clothes in the big wooden washtub in the kitchen – she'd rather do it outside but it's raining – when Kit raps on the window. Trif straightens up, goes to the window. She presses her hand against the watery green glass, meeting Kit's hand on the other side. Looking at Kit through a window is like looking in a strange, distorted mirror. Their dark eyes are level with each other; Kit's long dark hair is loose while Trif's is tightly braided to keep out of her face while she works. They look alike in some ways, yet though they are always together people seldom comment on the resemblance. Trif understands that this is because Kit is beautiful, while she herself is not, though studying the lines and angles of their two faces, she cannot quite grasp what makes the difference.

"Can you come out?" Kit says, through the glass.

Trif goes out the back door and circles the house to the front bridge. "I got to do the wash," she says. It's Monday, and the fact that Mr. Bishop has said the final examination results will be handed out at the school today makes no difference to washday. A light, spitting rain drizzles the girls as they stand talking.

"Won't she let you come up to school to get your report?"

"Not likely," Trif says. "She says school is done now, what odds what marks I got. Will you bring mine back for me?"

She watches Kit step off the bridge and go on down the North Side

Road. Yesterday Trif took a worn bedsheet and ripped it clean down the middle so she could sew it up again with the sides in the middle. The cotton tore neatly, dividing into two in her hands. She hears again now that clean ripping sound, tearing her from her schoolgirl life, from books and words. From Kit, who will go on while Trif stays behind.

They are two of three scholars to write Standard Six examinations in the school at Missing Point. The other is Ted Parsons, son of Skipper Wilf, who is destined for college in St. John's. Ted is still in school at thirteen, two years after all the other boys have gone fishing; his father even kept him back from going down on the Labrador this June so he could finish the school year and write his exams. Ted finished school because he was expected to, Triffie and Kit because, as Mr. Bishop says, they are true scholars. They have read half of Shakespeare's plays out loud to each other in Triffie's bedroom, huddled beneath blankets on winter nights. Ted Parsons is going on to school because his father can afford it, but Mr. Bishop had to haul Ted through his Geometry proofs one unwilling step at a time, both their faces red with frustration. Meanwhile Trif and Kit helped each other through the proofs, then passed a piece of paper back and forth. They were writing a series of sonnets illustrated with Kit's funny drawings, sonnets that Mr. Bishop would later confiscate, then smile as he read them, applauding the girls' cleverness. His clever girls.

Trif thinks about it all morning while she finishes scrubbing out stains and hangs out the wash, glad the rain shower has ended. It's as if thinking about Mr. Bishop has conjured him when she sees him walking down the road beside Kit, drawing in at the gate to stop, holding out her report to her.

Kit, beside him, stands still but looks like she's dancing, her eyes and face alight. Her hand flutters as she takes Trif's report from Mr. Bishop so that she can be the one to hand it to Trif, thrusting her own next to it.

"You took top marks in Reading, Geography, Geometry and Algebra," Kit says, "and I took top marks in British History, Newfoundland History and Composition. Between the two of us we got all the top grades."

It's no surprise. No one expected Ted Parsons to take the top scores, least of all Ted himself; the only thing to be determined was which subjects Kit would lead in, and which Triffie.

"You both should be teachers," Mr. Bishop tells them. "A year or two of college in St. John's to get your Preliminary CHEs, and you could be teaching in a school of your own the September after next."

Trif catches her breath. A sudden vista opens up before her: stepping aboard the train at Bay Roberts station, the tracks carrying her away from the Point. Sitting in a classroom in St. John's with an open book on the desk in front of her, clean sheets of paper to write on. Her own little boarding-house room with her skirts and blouses hanging on hooks behind the door. Standing in front of her own classroom, children's heads bent over their Royal Readers. Everyone in town calling her Miss Bradbury.

Kit pouts. "I'm not sure I want to be a teacher." Kit sees other vistas, other possibilities. For her, teaching dozens of children in a one-room school is a narrowing of possibilities. For Trif, there has always only been this one path, the dark tunnel that leads through Aunt Rachel's house. She will rear her younger cousins, cook dinners and scrub clothes, till the tunnel leads her straight to some man's house where she will bear her own children and do the same chores till she dies. Now, a door opens: a brief glimpse of another corridor, a different room. The door closes as quickly as it opened. "Aunt Rachel and Uncle Albert would never let me go to St. John's."

"That's why I walked up here with Kit, so I could speak to your aunt," Mr. Bishop says. Uncle Albert is away on the Labrador for the summer; any major decisions will be made by Aunt Rachel. "There's such a need for teachers, so many little coves and bays where children don't learn because there's no-one to teach them. It would be a shame if girls with gifts like yours didn't have the opportunity to further them."

His excitement is contagious and Trif finds it hard to tamp down that little flame of hope that kindles again with his words. Joe Bishop is a tall man with dark hair sprouting high up above a smooth-domed forehead that makes him look clever and distinguished. He has been the teacher at the Missing Point school for six years, which makes him the only teacher Triffie has ever known: when she reads the word "teacher" in a book it's Mr. Bishop's face that comes to her mind's eye. She and Kit secretly call him Dear Pedagogue behind his back.

Aunt Rachel appears then, coming around from the back of the house. She invites the schoolmaster to come in through the front door, used only for important guests, to sit in the parlour and have a cup of tea. Trif and Kit, excluded from the parlour, go to the kitchen where Trif hangs out the last of the wash and quickly makes soda bread to go with the fresh meat soup Aunt Rachel has put on for supper. Uncle Albert got credit for supplies from Abe Parsons before he shipped out for the Labrador with Skipper Wilf, so

That *Forgetful* Shore

the pantry is full and they're able to enjoy a change from salt fish every day.

Half an hour later, Aunt Rachel lets Mr. Bishop out of the parlour. "Kit, I'm going up to talk to your parents now," he says, and Kit joins him, going out the front door. He turns back to Triffie. "Congratulations on your examination marks, Triffie." His voice sounds sad despite the congratulations. He turns to leave with Kit, his silhouette beside hers in the doorway.

It occurs to Trif suddenly, with the early evening light slanting down off the water behind Kit and Mr. Bishop, that she has always thought of Mr. Bishop as a middle-aged man, as old as Uncle Albert or the other fishermen of that generation. Now, with the suddenly older eyes of a young woman who is no longer a schoolgirl, she sees he is not old at all, perhaps not twenty-five yet. Just a few years ago he was one of those boys finishing Standard Six, with a teacher saying, "You're a clever boy, Joe, you could go on to school in St. John's, you could be a teacher." He is ten or twelve years older than Kit and herself, a young man with no wife or children. He comes from here in Conception Bay, from some place farther up the shore, past Carbonear. He and Kit suddenly look right together, as if they are part of the same world. He lays a hand easily on Kit's shoulder as they turn to go on together into that world from which Trif is barred.

Aunt Rachel says nothing, that night or any other, about her conversation with Mr. Bishop, about Triffie's excellent report marks, about the possibility of St. John's and teacher-training. A dozen times Trif shapes words, practices what to say, but never speaks the question aloud. She and Kit talk about it, of course, as they talk about almost everything. Kit's parents have agreed that she will go to college; she is packing her trunk, making her plans.

One night, walking back from the Salvation Army meeting in Bay Roberts, arms linked and heads close together, Kit and Trif fall behind the other girls. They go to the Church of England on the Point with their parents on Sunday morning, or on Sunday afternoon if that's when the service is held, the minister dividing his time between two congregations. But on Sunday nights the young people crave a livelier sort of worship than can be found at Evensong, so they traipse off, either to the Methodist Chapel on the south side of the Point or, more often these days, across the causeway to the Salvation Army Citadel in Bay Roberts. There they enjoy loud singing and the clang of tambourines, fervent testimonies and shouts of praise. The air is heightened; it's as good as a play, or as Trif imagines a play might be. Girls and – more rarely – boys sometimes go up to kneel at the mercy seat, tears streaming down their faces. On the way home on fall and winter nights couples pair off, boys linked with girls they have admired from afar, washed up together on a sudden wave of emotion. But on summer nights the group is made up almost entirely of girls; most of the young men have gone fishing, so the delicious edge of romantic tension is missing from the air.

"I asked Pop to talk to Aunt Rachel for you," Kit says.

"What?"

"About college. About you going with me."

"She'll never let me go," Trif says.

"You never even asked her." It sounds like an accusation.

"I never had to. Mr. Bishop talked to her, and she never said a word to me about it, so I know she said no." Mr. Bishop gives Trif a sad look every time he sees her in church or on the road. She knows he pities her, the clever girl not allowed to go farther in school. "They don't have the money to send me to town."

"I'm sure if they really wanted to they could find a way. Mr. Bishop says there's scholarships and the like."

Trif says nothing, because this is one thing Kit truly doesn't understand. Kit is the only living child, beloved daughter of her father's house, the one upon whom all her parents' hopes and dreams ride. The Saunders family is not poor, and whatever worldly wealth they have will certainly go towards making Kit's path through life as easy and pleasant as possible. Albert and Rachel manage as well as most fishermen's families do, but Trif is not their daughter. She is the illegitimate niece, the unpaid help, and they have three children of their own to provide for. "They put a roof over my head and food on the table," Trif explains. "That's more than they got to do. They don't owe me no more."

"Pop's going to talk to her, all the same."

"Tell him not to, please. It won't do any good." And it might do harm; Aunt Rachel might take it out on Trif, thinking she had put Kit up to asking.

If Kit's father talks to Aunt Rachel or not, Trif never knows it. Plans for Kit's departure continue and Trif's life continues too, unchanged, the routine that will shape her days till they marry her off. She tries not to think

That *Forgetful* Shore

of Kit leaving, of the Point without Kit. Strange to think they have known each other barely three years. All of Trif's life seems to have happened in those three years.

"I wish you were going with me, Posy," Kit says. They are sitting on the rocks of the Long Beach, three nights before Kit leaves for St. John's. "I'm afraid of it all – everything will be so strange and new, all people I never met before. Townie girls with their fancy airs. It wouldn't be so bad if you were coming with me."

"Will you write me letters? You won't forget me, Peony?"

"I'll write every day. I'll never forget my Posy, my twin sister." Kit throws her arms around Trif and they share a long, delicious embrace.

This is the moment Trif wants to remember: she and her Peony in each other's arms, vowing to let nothing part them. The truth is that in after years she will have forgotten their farewell on the beach. What will stay with her always, what lingers in her mind, is the vision of Kit walking away from her on the last day of school, walking down the road side by side with Joe Bishop. It's that moment that will come to haunt her. It haunts her already, as she and Kit stand on the beach, faces buried in each other's hair, while the salt wind blows in off the water.

Kit

St. John's
October, 1904

My darling Posy,

How I wish you were here with me! How different it would be,
living in my cold, bare boarding house, walking the busy streets of
town, if Peony and Posy were again entwined in one bouquet. How
cruel of Fate (*or your Aunt*) to sunder us!

My lessons are progressing very well and I have determined to be
ready for my Preliminary exam in one year instead of two. Miss
Shaw (the finest teacher here by far!) says it is possible if I work very
hard. The other scholars are all very dull and I do not think I shall
have any particular friends. Indeed, what friend could take the place
of the One who has been *torn* from me? Peony shall be a flower that
grows alone, until we are *together* *again*, my darling.

The teachers here are very good, clever and mostly kind, though
distant. How I miss the gentle words of our Dear Pedagogue, who
would speak so kindly to me when I worked at my Mathematics!
My only comfort is that he will soon be here in St. John's too, for he

has written that he must come to Town in October, and will call on me. I long to see him, for he is my only link to the old life I have left behind.

How I longed to be out in the great world, and how glad I am to be here, yet ... how lonely I am at nights, when the moon rises over the ships in St. John's harbour (I can see it through the trees from my window) and I imagine it shining down on the calm, still waters of our cove! How grand to go on to new adventures, but how sad to have to face them alone, without the ones we love!

Ever and always your own,
Peony

For Kit, all her life, first in Trinity and then in Missing Point, "schoolroom" has meant a crowded room with hand-made benches pulled up around the stove, huddled close for warmth. Now her schoolroom at Bishop Spencer College is a large, airy room with tall windows, separate desks for each scholar, and more books than she has ever imagined. Lace curtains cover the windows, and a piano occupies one corner. The room is almost always cold and the other young women look older and more serious than Kit, who still feels like a child. Yet she knows many of them are thirteen, like she is; fourteen or fifteen at the most. Many of them come from outports, some from places smaller than the Point. There is no reason why she should feel young or ignorant in their company, why she should not have the same laughing confidence she had in the schoolroom back home. But she is severed from herself, from everything she knows. From her Posy. She has been here three weeks, and tells herself she is still finding her footing.

Kit has heard that Catholic girls who want to train as teachers, if they don't want to become nuns, must live like nuns anyway, staying at the convent and taking their classes there. Some of the outport girls at Spencer board in a house owned by the school, and surely their lives are little better than those of novice nuns. Kit boards with her mother's elderly Cousin Ethel and helps the old woman around the house in exchange for her room and board. In theory she has more freedom than the girls in the Spencer College boarding house, but what opportunity does she have to use that freedom? She eats, sleeps, studies and cleans the house. Would being a nun be any worse?

On Saturdays she has a little freedom, which she uses, if the weather is good, to walk around the city, learning her way around the winding streets. She walks down Holloway Street through the muddy bustle of Haymarket Square, then along the rows of shops on Water Street, pausing sometimes to go into a shop and browse, sometimes to look at the schooners and steamers tied up at the piers. She rides the elevator in Ayre and Sons department store, and, when she's tired from her walk down the length of Water Street, takes the streetcar back.

If the weather is bad, which it usually is, she reads, devouring books borrowed from Cousin Ethel's shelves. She is glad the old woman's late husband liked novels, for all her old favourites are there – Dickens and Austen and Scott – but she misses having Triffie to discuss them with. She writes long letters telling Trif what she is reading – which is always far more interesting than anything she is doing – but misses the immediacy of Trif's tart replies. "I don't blame Mr. Knightley one bit," Trif said when they were reading *Emma*. "She deserved a lot worse, if you ask me – he ought to've slapped her." Kit disagreed passionately, of course – Emma is her favourite of Austen's heroines – but it's that disagreement she misses, the push and pull of their debates.

One Saturday afternoon Kit receives a diversion that a novice nun never would – news of a gentleman caller down in the parlour. It does not, of course, take her completely by surprise. Joe – Mr. Bishop – wrote he would come to St. John's for a few days in October, and she has been trying not to count down the days.

She studies herself in the glass before going downstairs, praying she looks like a young woman now and not like a schoolgirl any longer. He used always to refer to her, gravely, as a young lady even when her skirts were short and her hair long. Now she walks as gracefully as she can into the parlour, her skirt almost brushing the floor, her braided hair carefully pinned on top of her head. She holds herself as straight as if she had books on her head, practising her smile.

His smile is ready, eager and open. He looks like a young man greeting an old friend, surely not like a teacher visiting a former pupil. As he holds out his hands she takes them both, moves involuntarily as if into an embrace. Then they both step back a little, flushed, embarrassed, but they

That *Forgetful* Shore

don't let go of each other's hands.

"It's so very good to see you," says Joe. Mr. Bishop. Dear Pedagogue.

He offers her his arm as they walk down Gower Street. As soon as her fingers touch the fabric of his sleeve memory floods in. His hand on her shoulder as he bent over, helping her with a difficult proof in Geometry. His hand taking hers as she turned to go, last to leave the schoolroom. Hints and suggestions. Gestures she took as promises: *when you are older, when you are out of the schoolroom…*

These are the memories she cherishes, the only memories she allows. These are her daylight memories.

The memories, those she acknowledges and those she doesn't, create a link between them. *An intimacy,* she thinks. Chooses to think of that word, its precise and delicate sound, to counteract the pulsing movement of her blood created by the sense of his skin and muscles underneath the cloth, beneath her fingers.

A stroll up Water Street on a Saturday afternoon. The shops and buildings, even the wharves, look more glamorous than they do when she is alone. She remembers to lift her skirt clear of litter and horse dung. The streets are busy, the wind off the harbour chilly, but the surrounding buildings offer a kind of shelter. It's so different from the outports she grew up in; the city is like being indoors even when outdoors. She never feels truly exposed to sky and sea and wind as she did on the Point, and has not yet decided if she likes the feeling or not.

Her Dear Pedagogue asks about her classes at Spencer, talks about the Missing Point school, where this year he is dealing with a record number of a hundred and seventeen students.

"What if I gets – if I get sent to a school like that?" Kit wonders aloud. The lively chaos of that busy, smoky schoolroom seems an ocean away from the quiet, high-windowed rooms at Spencer. She remembers Mr. Bishop's – Joe's – voice straining as it rose above the babble, quieting the little ones, leading them in the Lord's Prayer at the start of the day. "You were always so sure of yourself," she says. "All us youngsters, even the wild ones that never listened or paid any mind. Like you were born knowing what to do."

His laugh is low and husky and makes her shiver for no reason, like he's laughing as he walks across her grave. "Oh, that's very far from the truth. Very far, indeed. Truth is, half the time I'd stand up there talking away and think, Why are any of this crowd listening to me at all? Why don't they turn tail and run out the door, down to the wharves? It's a strange thing, the power that keeps a child in the classroom. A funny kind of power for a man to wield when he's not much more than a boy himself. As I was, when I started teaching."

He speaks as if he's old, but she and Trif have figured it out, pieced together clues: he is twenty-four years old. Not yet married, though surely he must be ready for it now.

Kit is ready for something, though if she pulls it apart and looks at it sensibly she knows she is not ready to be married, nor to be a teacher in a one-room schoolhouse with fifty or sixty young ones of all ages, never mind a hundred and seventeen. She is barely ready to be in St. John's, at Spencer College, studying for her CHEs. Barely ready to be away from Missing Point and her parents and Triffie, from everything familiar and loved. But she is ready for something. She doesn't know what till the walk ends and Joe Bishop says goodnight to her at Cousin Ethel's door.

He has been a model of propriety all afternoon, walking a fine line between a schoolmaster visiting his former pupil and a young man visiting a young lady he might, someday, consider courting. For that, Kit has decided, is what's happening here. She is too young, school still too recent, for Joe to court her. But he's making his interest plain. When she's home next summer, then it will be suitable. Then he will politely ask if he might come calling, and there will be more evenings like this one.

This is what she thinks, until he stops her just outside the door and stares at her so long and hard she wonders what's wrong, wonders if he's angry. Then, without a word – though with a quick glance at the window blinds, to be sure no-one is watching – he cups her jaw in his hand, tilts her face up to his, and kisses her hard on the mouth. His own mouth opens, his tongue darting inside her mouth, invading her, releasing a dark coil of something that feels a little like fear in her belly.

He's never done this – not this particular thing – before. Kissing until now has been something she has read of in books. The recoil of shock and the queer, heart-racing pleasure are almost evenly balanced as she lets her body lean against his, allows his mouth to explore hers.

Joe Bishop pulls away, steps back. "Forgive me," he says, formal and proper again. "I ought not to have …. I'll be going now. Good luck with your studies, Kit. Everyone at home is very proud of you."

"Didn't your teacher want to come in for tea?" Cousin Ethel says when

That *Forgetful* Shore

Kit is inside the hall. Kit stares out the window at Joe Bishop's retreating back as he walks down Gower Street without looking back. She tucks the memory of the kiss in with the other dark memories, the ones she doesn't pull out and examine by daylight.

"He was having his tea with his own people, at the house where he's staying," Kit says, though neither of them discussed tea.

"Well, you sit down and have yours now, it's ready."

"I'm sorry, I'm not hungry," Kit says, and goes upstairs to her room alone.

Triffie

Missing Point
November, 1904

My Darling Peony,

How good it is to hear from you and hear of school and all your doings in Town. I am sure if I could be there with you, you should never be lonely, and I should never be fretful as I so often am. I preach long sermons to myself about being contented with my lot in life but it seems I am a dull and hardhearted congregation for I never learn.

Things are the same here as always … indeed, I could think of stitching that phrase on a sampler, and it would hang in the parlour and be as true when I am an old woman as it is today. The Same Yesterday, Today and Forever. Nothing changes in Missing Point, family and neighbours and church are much as ever. Aunt Rachel continues to fret about Will, with the same troubles as I wrote you about before, but otherwise all at home are well. I saw your mother at church and they are all well too…

"Young Will is after wandering again," Aunt Rachel says.

"He's not, is he? What are we going to do about that?" Trif washes the breakfast dishes as she talks, her back to her aunt, who is sweeping the floor. Uncle Albert is out fixing the shed roof. In these few weeks between the end of fishing and the first snow, all the men are busy cutting and hauling wood, and repairing houses, sheds and boats, all the work that must get squeezed into the late fall and early spring. The children are off to school, Will looking pale and tired. Makes sense, if he's been walking in his sleep again. He's never done it before this fall, but since he started off to school he's been wandering two and three nights out of every week.

For Will this is the first fall he's had to get up and go off to school; for Triffie, it's the first fall she can remember without the comforting routine of school in the morning. She plaits Ruth's hair each morning, scrubs Will's face, makes sure the children have their books ready, sends them off with a smile and a wave. She wants to tear off her apron and run up the road after them, as if there were still a place there for her. All those classes, all those examinations, all for nothing.

She puts those thoughts away, stacks them firmly on top of the plates, lays the gravy boat on them to keep them down. This is her life. No room for regret. Not in daylight, anyway. All the thoughts she tidies away in the daytime burst out of cupboard doors at night, taunt and tease her. She lies awake for hours, with two-year-old Betty curled next to her in the bed breathing noisily. Trif watches the moon cross the sky through her window. Imagines a boat that will take her away to Kit, her Peony, to some other life they can share together.

No. No such dreams in daylight. She, too, is tired in the mornings from her poor night's sleep. Will falls asleep quickly, as she cannot, but some trouble disturbs his slumber and he pads around the cold floor on small bare feet, down the steps, sometimes even lifting the latch and going outside before some sound wakes his mother and she goes looking for him.

"This morning was the queerest one yet," Aunt Rachel says. "I never heard him at all in the night, though I sleeps right on edge. Then when I got up and went in to him, he was asleep, tucked away in his bed, and I thought, oh thank the good Lord, he's never moved, he slept through the night. Then I lifted the covers and his little feet, Triffie, you would not believe it. The bottoms of his feet was covered, all covered in mud and grass. He'd been out walking, see, and never even woke himself up, came back in and got back in his bed and never even knew he was outdoors. What do you make of that, Trif?"

"I don't know, I'm sure."

"Just the thought of him, out there in the dark, not even knowing he was out of the house. It gives me the shivers, it does."

"It does." Trif tries not to picture it but the images come without volition. Will, tiny and lost, in the yard. Asleep, walking through the cold wet grass. How many steps down to the road and across to the water's edge? What would it take to startle him awake? Would he walk right into the water, let it close over his head?

"I finds I sleeps right light, these nights," Trif says. "I should stay up, watch out for him. I can't get to sleep anyway."

"Well, it would be a weight off my mind if you did, Triffie, I don't mind saying."

Instantly, Trif shifts from concern for Will to resentment at her aunt. *Not enough I works for her every waking hour and shares my bed with Betty, now I got to be on duty through the night as well.* Then regrets her resentment, because she loves her cousins and would never see any harm come to them, especially Will.

She wonders if it means anything, that his sleepwalking started just when he went off to school. Is he having trouble with the other boys? He plays with young Isaac French next door, but what about the Mercer boys from the south side? They're a hard crowd. They seem much older, though the youngest is just Will's age. They are all big, and every one of them tough as nails. Are they hard on him?

"Aunt Hepsy says to tie a string to his ankle, tie it to the leg of the bed," Aunt Rachel says. "But I don't like the thought of keeping a child tied up, like an animal."

"But an animal don't wander in its sleep," Trif points out. "Better tied up than … lost, I suppose, or catch pneumonia from being out in the night. What about when winter comes?"

"I could get the Mister to put a new hasp on the door, higher up where Will couldn't get at it, maybe."

"You could do that," Trif agrees.

"But the rope? Do you think I should try it?"

Trif is not used to her aunt treating her as an equal, seeking her opinion. It is a tacit acknowledgement that by leaving school and dedicating herself

That *Forgetful* Shore

to the house and children, she has entered the adult world. Not the same adult world she wanted to enter, the one where her Peony grows, but the one her aunt respects and understands. The world of women and houses, food and children, worries and cares.

"I allow 'tis worth a try," Trif says now. "But talk to him first. If you don't tell him why you're doing it, he won't know what to think."

The children are home for their dinner, when Uncle Albert comes down off the roof and joins them. After they go back, Trif puts Betty down for a nap and picks up her sewing: Uncle Albert's credit from the summer's fishing allowed for several yards of blue and white gingham that she is making into dresses for the little girls and herself. At half-past three she tells Aunt Rachel she is going to walk up the school to see the children home. Her thought is that she will walk along with them, to see if those bigger boys are giving Will any trouble.

She arrives just as the boys and girls burst from the school door, hollering and leaping with the joy of freedom. Mr. Bishop leans against the doorframe, looking weary. She wonders how all that energy, all those children, can be contained in that single room, how he can keep them all in line for so many hours.

He smiles when he sees her, and after a word to Ruth and Will to wait for her, Triffie goes up to him. "You've had a long day, sir," she says.

"A long day and a hard one, Triffie. I have no such scholars as you and Kit this year. Sadie and Millicent are the two oldest, and Millicent is a good student, but neither of them is the kind of help you and Kit were with the little ones. Only now you're both gone, I see how much I relied on you. I sometimes wonder you got any learning done at all yourselves, with all the time you spent hearing the children's lessons."

"Ah well, all that practice will stand Kit in good stead now, when she finishes up her learning and starts to teach."

"Indeed, indeed. What do you hear from her?"

She likes his careful, teacherly speech, his accent tugging at the edges of his voice but most of it smoothed away, made proper, dressed up with words like *Indeed, indeed*. She feels her own language adjust itself to match his, becoming tidier and more formal than it is at home. "I had a postal and a letter from her last week," Triffie says. "She was studying for some big examination, something in her English grammar, I think it was."

"I'm sure she'll do fine, she was always good in grammar." He runs a hand through his hair, and again she sees how tired he is.

"I shouldn't trouble you, sir," she says, "only we're a bit worried at home, about Will. Seems there's something the matter, something on his mind, though he won't say what. He – he don't sleep well at nights." She is reluctant to confess to the actual sleepwalking. "I thought it might be something at school, some other boys giving him a hard time, perhaps."

Mr. Bishop shakes his head. "No, he gets on fine with the other boys – he and Isaac French and Charlie Mercer are thick as thieves, the three of them. Where Charlie's got his two older brothers here nobody dares bother anyone who goes around with Char. But you know, Will has a hard time with the lessons. He's not as ignorant as poor little Charlie, but he's having a hard struggle learning his letters. Not quick like you, or even average like Ruth. He doesn't like school because it's hard for him, and the worst of it is, I don't have enough time for lads like Will and Char, to give them the extra help they need."

It hasn't even occurred to Triffie that Will's trouble might be the school-work itself. For her, learning has always come so naturally that she forgets there are children for whom books are an enemy, rather than a joyful release. And to think her own cousin, her dear little boy, should be such a child!

"Well, now that I know what the trouble is, sir, I'll be sure to give him extra help at home."

"He couldn't wish for a better tutor. If only I could do more here at the school. The Board has promised me they will try to find money to hire me an assistant, and I don't see how I'll carry on without one."

His eyes brighten suddenly. "If the money does come – the person wouldn't have to be a qualified teacher. Indeed, couldn't be, not for the money they could pay. Anyone who had done well in school could help – you could take the position, do what you were doing in school, without the bother of your own lessons, and get paid for it. Would you like that?"

She bites back her immediate joyous assent. It's hardly the same as going to St. John's, being with her beloved Peony, studying at a college – but it would be something. A classroom is better than a kitchen, and earning her own money would be more than she dares hope for. "I don't know, sir," she says. "I mean, of course I would like to do it, but I don't know if my uncle would allow me. I'd have to ask him."

"Of course, of course. And it's all speculation, now, until we see if the

That *Forgetful* Shore

money is there. Still it would be a wonderful advantage to you, and a great help to me, if it came to pass."

She walks down the road behind Will and Ruth, thinking of Will's troubles with school, planning how she will teach him to read. Why did he say nothing at home about the trouble he was having? But then, she thinks, he did say he hated going to school. She had put it down to the laziness of a boy who would rather be out playing on the beach.

What can any adult know of what goes on in a child's mind? Trif thinks of her own childhood, how little her aunt and uncle guessed of anything that might please or trouble her. Hers was a private, stormy world, and Will's must be too. But his private world bursts into his dreams and tears him from his quiet bed.

That night, Aunt Rachel tries the rope cure, explaining to Will that it will stop him if he tries to walk in his sleep. About two in the morning Trif, lying awake, hears a crash from across the hall, followed by a howl of pain. She goes across to find Will lying on the floor bawling. He is tangled in blankets, his foot tethered to the bedpost. He's gotten out of bed in his sleep, tripped in the rope and fallen hard enough to wake himself. The noise wakes Ruth, who usually sleeps soundly in the bed beside him. Aunt Rachel, arriving right behind Trif, helps calm both children down and get them back to sleep, but the fall frightens Will as much as his earlier wanderings frightened his mother and cousin. He tears at the rope, insists they take it off, refuses to lie down unless they promise never to tie him again.

Nor does his fear lessen on future nights. He refuses to be tethered, putting up such a howl that, despite spankings, his resolve cannot be broken. Aunt Rachel tries to tie him on after he's asleep, but the same child who can wander down to the kitchen, open a cupboard, cut himself a slice of bread and butter it without waking, wakes instantly when he feels the touch of the twine around his ankle, and howls till it is taken away.

"So you think it's trouble with his lessons got him so nervous?" Aunt Rachel asks Trif one Saturday as they scrub the floor together. "Do Mr. Bishop whip the youngsters if they don't get their lessons right?"

"No, I only ever saw him use the whip on the bigger fellows if they're saucy or won't listen. The little ones gets a tap on the hand with the ruler if they can't say their lessons, but no worse than that. I 'low all Will needs is a bit of extra help like I've been giving him at home. Mr. Bishop don't have the time he needs, with all them youngsters in that one room."

Trif is feeling her way cautiously towards the question of being hired as Mr. Bishop's assistant; she doesn't want to waste too much time and good-will on it in case it never comes to anything, but if he were to come to her tomorrow and say he had the money to hire someone, she would like at least to have the ground prepared.

She writes to Kit before bed that night, making mention of Mr. Bishop's offer. She sleeps fitfully, dreaming of Kit far away in St. John's, her dreams flavoured with the usual mixture of envy and concern.

A noise wakes her before dawn, and she thinks, *I must have fell asleep after all.* She lies there awhile, drifting through dreams, something tugging at the edge of her mind. Finally she remembers: *Will.* The sound she heard – how long ago now? She turns toward the window: the sky is just graying towards dawn.

She gets up, wraps her housecoat around her and puts on slippers against the bitter chill of the room. Now that she's up she may as well start the fire, save Uncle Albert the trouble of doing it when he rises at five. She crosses the hall to the children's room and sees Will's side of the bed, the covers tumbled, empty. On the other side Ruth snores lightly.

Downstairs, everything is still and bare. Shapes of table, chairs, crockery on the table, emerge gradually from the gloom. No sign of a little boy with bed-messed hair and bare feet.

She goes through the hall, the parlour, back upstairs to check his parents' room. Sometimes he gets in bed with Aunt Rachel and Uncle Albert, though Albert always brings him back to his own room. This morning, Will is not there. His parents are both asleep and Trif hesitates a moment, wondering whether to wake them now or later.

She puts on her boots and coat and goes out into the frost-edged yard, but there is no sign of him out there. She follows the path, unwilling, down to the beach. No signs that anyone has passed this way, but what sign would his little bare feet leave on rocks? Her heart races in her throat. *Time to wake Aunt Rachel,* she tells herself. But cannot bear to, because the moment she wakes her and says, "I can't find Will," is the moment it will be real.

She goes back up to the house, looks everywhere again, still can't bring herself to go into her aunt and uncle's room. Outside once more. The sun is about to rise, a vivid line of light tracing the horizon to the east, out beyond the eastern tip of the Point. Triffie stands on the front bridge, frozen both inside and out, watching the orange disk of the sun slip up out of the

That *Forgetful* Shore

sea, even though she knows in a search like the one that will begin as soon as she wakes her aunt and uncle, every minute will count. *Please, God,* she prays. *Let him not be in the water, I'll do anything. Any vow you want me to make....* She would promise to be a missionary in India or China if she could only figure out how ... but then, that would be no sacrifice; she would love to go somewhere far and be a hero. The greatest sacrifice, perhaps, would be to stay exactly where she is, do what she's doing, and never complain again, even silently, or in letters to Kit. Even that would be worth it, if Will is not floating face-down in the ocean.

She shivers, shakes herself. How much time has she wasted standing here, watching the sun? A minute or two. But even that is too much. She turns back to the house, to alert the sleepers, to begin the hue and cry.

"Triffie! Are you up?"

Of course I'm up, I'm standing on my front bridge, you ignorant cow, Trif thinks, but does not say, as she turns to see fat Nellie French from the house next door, out in the laneway. She is clad, like Triffie herself, in a winter coat over her nightdress, boots on her feet.

"Well! You will not believe, not in all your days, what I found in my house this morning," Nellie French says, obviously pleased with herself. And though Triffie wants to burst out the answer, joy and relief make her magnanimous enough to listen through the woman's whole story.

"...and I went in, before I lit the fire, like I always do, to check on the young ones, and there in Isaac's bed there was two little heads instead of one, and the other one was fair-haired. You knows none of my crowd is fair, so I peeled back the covers and there was young Will, sound asleep. Now I knows he wanders so I wonder could it be, he just wandered right out of your house and into ours, up into Isaac's bed? Could he do that, I wonder?"

Trif is ahead of Nellie French, racing into Nellie's house, up the stairs. He could do such a thing, apparently, and did. Today Uncle Albert will have to put on that new lock, up high on top of the door where even standing on a chair – for he's capable of that – Will won't be able to reach it. He's capable of anything, if his night-wanderings can take him into a neighbour's house, a friend's bed, without ever waking.

He wakes when she picks him up. "Triffie," his sleepy voice says.

"Will! Do you know where you are?"

"In bed."

"Yes, but not in your own bed." She carries him downstairs and sits down in Nellie's kitchen, by the newly lit woodstove, while Nellie chatters away about the strangeness of it all and Trif, in the rocking chair, rocks her small cousin. His golden head fits just under her chin.

"I'm in Isaac's house?" he says, confused.

"Yes, you got right out of your bed in your sleep, went out of the house and over to Isaac's house. Do you see now why your mother got to tie you on? You could come to harm, wandering like that."

"But I didn't come to no harm. You came and found me."

"Yes. Yes," she says, soothing him. "What did you dream, Will? Do you remember your dreams?" She has never asked him this before.

"Same dream as always," he says sleepily.

"What dream is that?"

"I'm far from home, and I got to find my way back. Out on the barrens, and I got to walk back before the fairies takes me."

Though the boy is safe in her arms, another shiver runs down Trif's spine at the mention of the fairies. She knows the tales as well as anyone on the Point, stories of children who vanished on the barrens and never returned, or worse, returned forever changed, fairy-touched. Old wives' tales, Trif would have said if anyone asked her, though she carries a crust of bread in her pocket when she goes berrypicking all the same. Now she holds Will closer in her arms, till he falls back to sleep and she can carry him across the lane and put him down in his own bed.

Kit

My dearest Posy,

Oh to think of you now, in our old Schoolroom, standing by the side of our Dear Pedagogue and the little ones before you in their breeches and pinafores. How strange that you should be teaching the children while I am yet Learning, still a Schoolgirl though in a Schoolroom far bigger and grander than we ever imagined back home!

I spend my days in study and books, but I yearn for the day when I shall have my own classroom to manage, my own Pupils to <u>Inspire</u>. All the <u>hard</u> <u>work</u> I put in last year towards my Preliminary examinations has paid off, and I am finding this year much easier. Though I would like to carry on, and learn <u>all</u> <u>there</u> <u>is</u> <u>to</u> <u>learn</u>, Father says that will be enough schooling for the present, that I should take a school of my own next year.

I send you <u>kisses</u> <u>and</u> <u>dear</u> <u>thoughts</u>, all the way from gray and cold St. John's to the beautiful shores of Missing Point. I imagine the sun sparkling on the waters off the Point, though I know that if the Sun is shrouded here, it is likely foggy there too. In my memory the sun is always shining.

It is indeed a gray, windy day in St. John's. Kit finishes off the letter to Triffie by drawing a few quick pencil sketches in the margin – caricatures of Miss Shaw, Miss Babbage, rude little Nancy Ellis and a few other girls from school. She puts in a handful of pressed flower petals picked from Cousin Ethel's rosebush two weeks ago. It is late September, and the summer months at home are already receding, slipping away from her memory. Home is real when she is there, but once she steps on the train it becomes a place in a book, covers closed. She likes to imagine it as a place where nothing will ever change, where her parents will never age and the children will not grow up. Only Triffie is allowed to change, growing year by year older to keep pace with Kit herself.

This latest change – Trif assisting Mr. Bishop in the school – is, of course, wonderful news for everyone. Wonderful for Mr. Bishop, who needs the help. Wonderful for the children, who could not ask for a better tutor. Wonderful most of all for Triffie, who has so longed to get out of the drudgery of Aunt Rachel's house. Kit has behaved exactly as she should, congratulated her friend on this wonderful opportunity. She won't admit even to herself that she envies Trif, who since last spring has been standing where she, Kit, ought to be – not just in front of the classroom, but at Joe Bishop's side.

Kit has seen little of Mr. Bishop since he came to call on her here in St. John's nearly a year ago. When they meet in passing during her school holidays, he asks about her studies but betrays no personal interest, nor has he written to her. His last hard, urgent kiss is seared into her memory, but it seems to have been an end rather than a beginning.

Very well then, she will make her own beginning. Kit Saunders is not a girl to wait on anyone else for a fresh start. She makes her way in the world, creates her own opportunities. So she tells herself, every day.

Miss Shaw, the English mistress, is her new role model, her new Dear Pedagogue. Sturdy, brisk, her red hair turning gray – she must be about forty – Miss Shaw strides into the lecture room, a model of sober spinster scholarship. But when she opens a textbook a new woman emerges, a Sarah Bernhardt hidden beneath the sensible gray tweed of her skirts and jackets. As she reads Shakespeare aloud, she becomes each character in turn, creating an entire Globe Theatre with her voice and hands.

Some of the girls laugh at Miss Shaw, imitate her accents and gestures behind their hands in the common room. They invite Kit to join them with

That *Forgetful* Shore

smiles and glances, but she holds herself aloof.

What the magic of her own voice and Shakespeare's words do in the classroom, Miss Shaw attempts also to do with the Spencer College stage and a handful of awkward adolescent girls. Kit joins the Dramatic Society and wins the role of Petruchio in *The Taming of the Shrew*. She felt she had the temperament and spirit to play Kate, but tall girls who can act well tend to get the male roles. Which would be good news if they were doing *Macbeth* or *Hamlet*, but Miss Shaw says tragedies are too ambitious for schoolgirls; one needs to have suffered to play Hamlet. The older students are doing *Much Ado About Nothing*. Miss Shaw likes plays with strong female roles, even though her girls end up playing men as well, in a reversal of Shakespeare's original staging.

Having fallen in love with the part of Kate, Kit now tries to throw herself into the opposite role, to learn the lines of the proud man who wants to crush that independent spirit, bring Kate to heel like a trained lapdog. "It's impossible!" she complains to Miss Shaw in the gymnasium, flinging the book across the room.

"A very Kate-like display of spleen." Miss Shaw draws down the sides of her mouth as if she's trying not to laugh. "But this is acting, Katherine. It's not finding an excuse to play out your own little dramas under someone else's name. It's about crawling into another person's skin, seeing the world through his eyes, *becoming* Petruchio."

"But can I do it? I'm not sure I can."

"I certainly hope you can; if not, I shall have to recast the part," says Miss Shaw, and strides away to where the girls playing Kate and Bianca are practising their quarrel.

Something rises like a tide in Kit's chest. She thought she wanted Miss Shaw to do what Mr. Bishop would have done when she was a child, to say, "Of course you can do it, Kit. You're clever, you're brilliant, you can accomplish anything you set your mind to!" But this is better – this brisk dismissal with no honeyed words of praise. *Do the job, or I'll find someone else who can.* This, Kit decides, is a challenge to which she can rise.

"Very well then, let's take Act One, Scene Three, from Kate's entrance," Miss Shaw bellows a few moments later, and Kit walks onto the stage, trying to imagine how a sixteenth-century Italian man might swagger into the courtyard, confident in his right to possess and rule. She thinks what she is doing is actually a poor imitation of Miss Shaw striding into the classroom, but perhaps it will do for now. "Good morrow, Kate, for that's your name, I hear!" she announces.

The pert little thing playing Kate – Nancy Ellis from Bonavista – looks up at Kit through fluttering eyelashes. "Well have you heard, but something hard of hearing. They call me Katherine that do talk of me."

"What the – what do you think you're playing at, Nan!" Miss Shaw's voice cuts across the lines. "Kate's not *flirting* with Petruchio, she can't abide the man! She's a wild horse who won't be broken! Show some spirit, Nancy!!"

Kit remains Petruchio, does not break character, does not even listen to the voice that says *I could have done it so much better!* She is Petruchio; she will not disappoint Miss Shaw.

When the rehearsal ends, Kit goes into the cloakroom to put on her coat and hat when she hears the chatter of a group of girls just outside. "Ahh, I don't mind Shaw, she's not so bad," one girl says. "I mean, she's a bitch, but she's a schoolmistress – it's 'er job to be a bitch. What I can't take is girls who act like they're better than anyone else, and you knows 'oo I mean, don't you?"

"Oh yes, prancin' around up there like she's God's gift to the theatre," the other girl chimes in. It takes no effort at all to recognize the voice as belonging to Liza Butler, who plays Baptista. Only in that context does Kit realize the first girl who spoke was Nancy Ellis. She's rarely spoken to Nancy except during rehearsals, and the carefully cultivated stage voice Nancy uses for Kate bears little resemblance to her real Bonavista accent, which, like most of the girls' accents, sounds stronger when she's excited or upset.

"I wouldn't care so much if Shaw didn't make a teacher's pet out of her," says another – that would be Grumio, a skinny redhead whose name Kit can't recall. "Not just in the play – she's just as bad in class, calling on her all the time, reading out her themes like she's – oh, I don't know what."

"Like she's better than the rest of us," Nancy says. Kit, long since dressed for the outside but now trapped in here, hears the other girls murmur agreement. "She wants to be taken down a peg or two, is what she wants – 'oo do she think she is? Miss Kitty Saunders from God-Knows-Where, a cut above the rest!"

The other girls laugh and Kit hears them getting ready to leave, going to collect their coats from the other cloakroom. She considers, just for a moment, sweeping out of the room before they go, head held high, fixing them all with a cutting glare, and then walking past them all as if she really

That *Forgetful* Shore

is so much better than they are that their petty insults don't even touch her.

Inside, there's a Kit who can do that, who is just brazen enough to come out now. But she's lost access to that Kit, here in this place where her only ally is a teacher who is said to make a pet of her. After a year at Spencer she's not made one close friend. She was always the centre of a lively circle of girls back on the Point, though Trif was the only one she truly felt close to. Here she is a loner, and has made no effort to change that status.

If Trif was here, I could do it. I could brazen it out, I could face them all. She hears the girls leave, waits till their voices fade, then steps out into the corridor.

But worse awaits. One girl is still there, kneeling down, packing her books in a satchel. It's blonde and pretty Alice Templeman, who plays Bianca – another girl Kit has barely spoken to in her time here. In Alice's case it's not dislike but sheer intimidation: she comes from a well-off St. John's family. What acquaintances Kit does have are girls from around the bay like herself, aspiring teachers who were the brightest and best in their little one-room, outport schools. While Kit's family connections make her one of the most well-off girls on the Point, she's well aware that the St. John's merchant families are a different class of people. She has no experience of girls like Alice, who make up the majority of students in her classes at Spencer. Knowing that Alice was out there, hearing the other girls discuss Kit, makes the whole experience infinitely worse. She can only hope Alice leaves quickly, without saying anything, without meeting her eyes.

"Miss Ellis used a rather coarse word beginning with a B." Alice's clear voice has no trace of an accent that needs to be expunged. "I'd say it applies to her more than to anyone else, wouldn't you?"

Kit forces herself to meet the other girl's eyes as Alice straightens up and shoulders her satchel. Alice's small grin looks positively wicked in her pretty face. "Don't mind them," she says. "You know there's always that kind of girl that has to put other girls down to make herself feel like someone. Nancy's that kind – I've seen it in her ever since she came in here. There's a few in every school."

"I suppose so," Kit says. "Thanks."

Alice shrugs. She hasn't, after all, done anything much – she certainly didn't tell the other girls to shut up, defend Kit to their faces. But a little friendship offered on the sly is better than nothing at a time like this. "I don't have much time for people like that," she explains.

That *Forgetful* Shore

"I knew there'd be all kinds in college," Kit says, "but to tell the truth I was more worried about – well, girls like you. Townie girls. At home they always say the townies will look down on you."

Alice smiles. "So we will. Some of my friends are awful, the way they talk about the bay girls – making fun of their clothes, their accents, the things they didn't learn in school. But the bay girls are worse to each other, especially if they think anyone's getting above herself. Like lobsters – you know?"

"Lobsters?"

"They say if you're cooking a lot of lobsters in a pot, you know, boiling them alive –" Alice wrinkles her pretty nose at the idea. "– if one tries to escape, the others will pull them back down into the pot. I don't know if it's true, but you see it all the time with people. Can't let anyone rise too high, you know."

Kit goes home that night and writes to Trif about the lobster pot, and the girls' cloakroom, the nastiness of Nancy Ellis and the unexpected kindness of Alice Templeman. It would all be more bearable if she and Trif could face this together, but in the absence of her Posy she forges a sort of friendship with Alice and some of her townie friends. It makes Nancy more poisonous than ever, to see Kit walking to and from class with the St. John's girls who have been at Spencer since they were learning their alphabet. But even if few of the girls have the qualities Kit would like to see in a true friend, sitting or walking with them is like having a bodyguard – no-one dares touch her when she's in their midst.

Still, it's only when lost in a book or onstage, playing Petruchio, that she loses all self-consciousness and really loves college life. It can't be denied that the rivalry between herself and Nancy adds fire to Kate's and Petruchio's scenes: they are able to snap at each other with genuine dislike, though their eventual reconciliation and romance is less convincing. But on the night of the performance they come out together to take their bow and clasp hands as if they really were lovers, united for that one moment in the glory of performance.

It's a pity, Kit writes to Triffie the next day, *that going on stage is considered neither a Respectable, nor a Practical Occupation for a young woman. For if I had my wishes, I think that is exactly the career I should Pursue! What would my mother make of that, do you think?*

That *Forgetful* Shore

Triffie

THREE OF THEM go off to school in the mornings now. Ruth leads the way, her plaits so tight they almost stick straight out from her head, her pinafore always clean and starched. Will slouches along behind until he catches up to Isaac French or another of his friends; he seems more reconciled to school this year and rarely sleepwalks, though it's clear he'll never make a scholar. A little behind them walks Trif. Miss Bradbury, they call her once they are all inside the schoolroom, even her cousins. Back in the spring when she first started helping at the school she was in Parsons' Mercantile one day when she heard Annie Barbour say to her sister Clara, "Do I got to call Triffie Miss Bradbury now she's a teacher?"

"That one! She put on enough airs before she was a teacher; she won't be fit to live with now," Clara replied. "Too good to walk on the same ground with the rest of us." Trif was standing only a few feet away, the other side of a stack of barrels, and the Mercantile isn't a big shop. Clara knew she was there, meant for her to hear. Clara never liked Trif and Kit in their schooldays, but her insult has no sting for Trif. All she hears out of that is "now she's a teacher." She walks to the school each morning like a prisoner on the day of her release, leaving behind laundry and scrubbing, garden and house, Aunt Rachel and Betty.

In the schoolroom a different kind of chaos waits to be made into order. Boys and girls tumble through the doors, stumble over each other. Small quarrels flare and die down as children hang up their jackets and press onto the benches. Trif moves among them with authority, silencing them, straightening away books and boots to make the aisles and desktops clear. Then she sits on a chair by the stove, which is already throwing out a nice bit of warmth since Joe Bishop got here early to build it up. He takes his place behind the desk at the front of the room and the children, magically transformed from a pack of wild puppies to erect, dignified schoolchildren, rise to sing "God Save the King."

Mr. Bishop has a fine voice for leading the anthem, and Triffie joins in with enthusiasm. She remembers the day when she was ten years old, when Queen Victoria died and they had to switch from singing "Save the Queen" to "Save the King." Mr. Bishop said he had been born in the reign of Victoria and so had his father; they had never known anything but "God Save the Queen" and it truly was the end of an era. The next day he brought in a picture from *The Illustrated London News* to show them the new King, King Edward. He told them how King Edward had been called Prince Bertie when he was just a prince, and even though he was a middle-aged man now with grown children of his own he was still considered a bit scandalous for his wild ways, but he was their king now and they all must pray for him as they had done for his good mother, God rest her soul. Now it's been "God Save the King" for four years and there are children in the schoolroom who have never sung "God Save the Queen" in their lives.

When the lessons start it's the usual thing, the older ones helping the younger, but with Triffie here to take the very littlest ones through their alphabet and First Reader, Mr. Bishop has a little more time to spare for the older ones. He teaches a Geography lesson to the oldest group, while the children in the Third and Fourth Readers are reading. Triffie gathers the smallest ones, those who are six and seven years old, on the bench nearest the stove. Some of their feet don't touch the floor yet; many of them only know the alphabet and a few simple words. She reads them a story from the First Reader and writes some of the words on her slate for them to copy down.

Charlie Mercer shoves Isaac French off the bench, hoping to get in trouble and get sent outside so he won't have to write. Triffie goes to sit between the two boys, settles Isaac to his copying and then opens up the Primer for Charlie. It's a hopeless task. "The fat cat sat on the mat" means nothing to him when he sees it on the page, much less: "Lo! I am on my ox."

That *Forgetful* Shore

He laughs at "an ox, a box and a fox," but can't see the difference between the *f* and the *b*. He has learned to recite the alphabet from memory but can't recognize most of the letters: he sees no connection between the shape of *b* and the sound at the beginning of "box." Will and Isaac, who are at the end of the Primer, have to copy out sentences like "Jack is on the deck of a ship," and "I wish I had to go on a ship." Charlie, hearing these sentences spoken aloud, gives a wistful sigh.

Charlie is seven now and Triffie has her doubts about him. His mother already has one poor silly boy at home, Edward, who can't learn at all – not letters or anything else. He can't even go out in boat for fear he'll fall in the water. His brothers Fred and Harry both left school when they were ten to go out fishing; Alf, the next oldest Mercer boy, will leave this year. But at least they all got as far as the Second Reader. Poor Charlie's not simple the way Edward is, but Triffie's not sure he'll ever master the Primer.

On the other end of the bench, in every sense, is Matthew White. He has every advantage, of course, being the minister's son, books all around and both his parents being educated people: Mrs. White was a teacher in St. John's before she was married. But Trif knows well enough all that background doesn't guarantee a bright child; Matthew's older brother and sister are capable enough, but nothing special. Matthew is six, a year younger than Charlie, Will and Isaac, but he's already through the first Royal Reader and into the second. He's bored when the other children his age go through the Primer or hear simple stories, but if he's put with the older children, then Ki Barbour and Wilf Dawe and some of the other big boys tease him. This morning, while she works through the simple words with the others, Triffie gives Matthew "The Wreck of the Hesperus" to memorize, to say up front on Friday afternoon when Mr. Bishop always has recitations.

"I do not know what I would do without you, Triffie," Mr. Bishop says at dinnertime when the noisy flood of children has poured from the room.

"You'd do what you did before, Sir," Triffie says. "You always did well enough by our crowd, even though you had no-one helping you then."

"Ah, yes, but it's so much easier now. You're a gift from God, is what you are, Triffie. And you have a gift for it, a way with the little ones, there's no doubt of that. It's a shame –"

But Triffie doesn't want to talk about what's a shame. "I'm glad to be here," she says, cutting him off, "and Uncle Albert and Aunt Rachel don't mind so long as I'm bringing in a little money. It's a grand help to them."

Like most fishermen, her uncle sees little cash money from one season to the next, except in spring when he goes to the ice. Trif's pay packet is a boon to the household: she keeps none of the money but Aunt Rachel expects her to do less around the house, in honour of her status as a working woman.

"After dinner, the third and fourth book will be doing History," Mr. Bishop says, "and the older ones have some Mathematics to work on. They'll all be busy for awhile. Why not let me have a try with Charlie while you teach the other little ones their sums?"

"He's not as bad with sums as he is with his letters," Trif says, opening her lunch pail. The children all go home for dinners, but she has taken to packing two slices of bread with partridgeberry jam and having it here in the schoolroom with Joe Bishop, enjoying this little time talking about the children and their classes, feeling like a teacher.

"Sums will do him more good than letters," Mr. Bishop says, "but we must do our best to teach him his alphabet at least. If he can count, add and subtract, and knows his alphabet, that's the best we'll do by him. And all that might take him until he's old enough to go out in boat anyway."

Later in the day she passes the bench where Joe Bishop and Charlie Mercer are bent over the slate. The Primer is laid aside: Mr. Bishop has gone back to trying to teach Char the alphabet. He draws well, his little sketches bringing scenes vividly to life with a few lines. On Charlie's slate he has drawn a large curving fish, curled into a half-circle, a few quick lines delineating scales and gills, a single eye peering up. Joe traces the curving outer line of the fish's body. "That's C," he tells the boy. "C for codfish – can you see the codfish shape? When you see that shape, think of the codfish, the letter C."

"That was clever," she tells Mr. Bishop later. "Do you think he'll remember?"

Joe Bishop shrugs. "He might; he might not. The problem with teaching A is for Adam, or apple, is that half the children don't know Adam – well, from Adam. And if they've seen an apple one Christmas, that's all they've seen. A for axe, B for black bear, C for codfish – that would make more sense."

"You should write your own alphabet book," Trif says.

"If I only had time," he sighs, picking up a stack of copybooks. "Anyway, Charlie couldn't sit still for more than A, B and C, so after C for codfish I sent him out to stack firewood with the older boys. Someday

That *Forgetful* Shore

we'll have to tell him C is for Charlie too, but that might only confuse him."

"Well, you helped him, anyway. Better than I could have done."

"It's only experience, Triffie. I've been ten years in the classroom now, and I've learned a few tricks. I'll take Charlie now and then for some extra help, when I can spare the time – you can make it up by reading with the Third Reader children. You're such a good reader, you could be working with the older ones."

Triffie thinks the older children, so recently her classmates, won't accept her as their teacher. Sadie Parsons and Millicent Butler, both doing the Fifth Reader now, are the closest she has to friends now that Kit's gone; it's strange to walk home from church with them on Sunday night and then stand up in the classroom on Monday as if she were a teacher. But Trif will do whatever she can to please Mr. Bishop and help him.

By three o'clock the last lessons are finished, and Mr. Bishop ends everyone's day by reading the latest chapter of *Robinson Crusoe*. He read that aloud the year Trif and Kit were doing the Fifth Reader; before that Trif remembers travelling through *David Copperfield* and *Oliver Twist* on the waves of Mr. Bishop's deep voice, the voice that carried the children of Missing Point to shores their father's dories would never take them to. She closes her eyes to hear him read the last words of the chapter, then moves quickly into action to help the little ones with their jackets. It will be more work as the winter gets colder, when she'll have to wind them into scarves, find cuffs and mitts for small hands, put gaiters on over their shoes. They learn quickly to do for themselves, but the smallest children always need help.

Ruth and Will walk home with the other children while Trif stays back. When the children are gone and the room is tidied, she leaves Mr. Bishop to correcting compositions, making plans for the next day, and helping any older students who may need extra coaching. This year Trif has noticed that Millicent Butler is singled out as she and Kit used to be: a clever girl who reads and figures well, who has a chance of going on to school in St. John's and whose parents might have a chance of sending her. Mr. Bishop has kept Millicent behind several times this month already for extra tutelage; now, as she moves to get her coat, giggling with Sadie Parsons, he says, "Millicent, don't you want to go over those Algebra questions? We talked about spending a little more time on those, remember?"

The girl looks startled, almost guilty. "Oh, sir, I think I got all them learned; I don't need to take up no more of your time."

That *Forgetful* Shore

"If you've done them all, that's wonderful," Mr. Bishop says. "Just stay back a minute and let me look at them."

"Not today, sir, I got to help me mother," Millicent says.

"Tomorrow, then?"

"I … I don't know, sir. I'm not sure how much extra tutoring Mother wants me to do, it takes up an awful lot of time, especially now the evenings are drawing in and it's dark so early. I'll … I'll let you know." She ducks out the door quickly behind Sadie before Mr. Bishop can reply.

Trif, buttoning up her own coat, clicks her tongue and shakes her head in disapproval. She glances over at Mr. Bishop. "She's a foolish young thing, to throw away an opportunity to learn like that," Triffie says. "She don't know what's good for her. You ought to talk to her mother."

But Mr. Bishop is staring out the window, his eyes focused on something faraway. He seems not to have heard, and Triffie doesn't want to presume, so she goes on home out of it.

On Friday afternoon when the books and slates are put away, it's time for recitations. Matthew White stands up and rhymes off "The Wreck of the Hesperus" in fine form, hands clasped behind his back, his voice an early echo of his father's pulpit voice. An older boy recites a passage from the *Odyssey*. Millicent Butler, who was supposed to say the fourteenth chapter of the Gospel of John, is absent. As the penultimate performance of the day, before the recitation he always gives himself to finish off the week, Mr. Bishop announces Charlie Mercer.

Charlie clambers up on to a three-legged stool Mr. Bishop pulls out for him. He shiggles around on the stool for a minute, then crosses one ankle over the opposite knee and lays his hands on his thighs. He lifts his head and begins to sing

> *There's a noble fleet of whalers a-sailing from Dundee,*
> *Manned by British sailors to take them o'er the sea …*

His little-boy voice is thin as a penny whistle but he sings out every word clear and true, and on tune as well. His right hand taps lightly on his thigh, lining out the rhythm of the song.

It occurs to Trif that Charlie's pose is the exact copy of his grandfather, old Uncle Jedidiah Mercer, one of the best storytellers and singers on the Point. Trif is sure the old man cannot read a word or sign his name, but she, like everyone else on the Point, has sat spellbound, whether in the church

That *Forgetful* Shore

hall or in his kitchen, as Uncle Jed rhymes off some ancient song or tall tale.

Joe Bishop watches Charlie with a smile on his face. She is sure this was Mr. Bishop's idea, that he put Charlie on to the idea of learning a song by heart from his grandfather. Charlie has clearly inherited not only his grandfather's memory but his flair for dramatic presentation: he pauses, crescendos, even gestures from time to time as he sings about the *Polina*, the fastest ship in the whaling fleet.

> *For she challenged all, both great and small,*
> *From Dundee to St. John's!*

Charlie hops off the stool and sweeps a bow towards his schoolmates, who all applaud. When Joe Bishop stands up, he says, "It's almost four o'clock, and I haven't time for my recitation today – and anyway, I'd rather leave you with Charlie's song, for I couldn't do a better performance than that. All stand for prayer."

He leads them in the Lord's Prayer to close the day and then they all flood towards the door.

That night Trif finishes off a letter to Kit:

> *You are so blessed, you can't know, and I know it's a wicked sin to*
> *envy but I can't help it, tho' it doesn't diminish my love for you,*
> *which is Strong and Deep as ever it was. But someday you will be*
> *in charge of your own classroom, and be able to do as our Dear*
> *Pedagogue does, to Inspire and Educate, to find a spark of Hope even*
> *in the Dullest. Oh, if you had seen Charlie Mercer singing today,*
> *seen how our old teacher coaxed him to find his own buried Talent.*
> *How proud I was of Charlie, how admiring of Pedagogue, how*
> *envious of you, who will spend your working life in such Worthy*
> *Endeavour!*
>
> *But I remind myself: "Brighten the Corner Where You Are,*
> *Tryphosa!" I have been given this little task, to help our Dear*
> *Pedagogue with the children and to make his task lighter, and I must*
> *do it with the best will in the world. Perhaps when I have proven*
> *Faithful in a Few Things, I will, like the loyal servant – like you, my*
> *dearest Peony – be made Ruler over Many. Such is my prayer, as I go*
> *to my bed tonight, and think of you so far away, under the same sky,*
> *the same moon, the same stars.*

Kit

There is power, power, wonder-working power,
In the precious blood of the Lamb!

Shouts, tambourines, stomping feet and clapping hands carry the joyful sounds of worship up through the roof of the Salvation Army Citadel in Bay Roberts and straight to heaven. Kit mouths the words, unable to stop watching Trif dance as she beats her tambourine. Trif is completely lost in the music, lost in God. Kit will not get her back until the meeting ends, until the preaching finishes and the call comes and Trif goes up to the mercy seat, weeping over her sins, asking Jesus back again over that well-worn threshold into her heart.

How many sins can Trif have committed since last Sunday? Kit wonders. The only one she knows of for sure is the sin of envy, for this one Triffie has confessed to her. Triffie commits and confesses the sin; Kit feels the guilt and does the penance.

It's only natural that after Trif has worked for more than a year as Mr. Bishop's assistant, she will be jealous when the School Board finally agrees Missing Point needs a second teacher – one with a Third Grade certificate at least – and hires Kit. They cannot afford two teachers and an assistant as well, so to all intents and purposes Kit has taken away the job that gave meaning and purpose to Triffie's life.

"I've made up my mind I won't let it come between us," Trif said, confessing her jealousy back in June, when the fateful decision was made. "Our friendship means more than anything. Anyway, I got to think of what's good for the children – of course they're better off with a qualified teacher. You'll be more help to Mr. Bishop than I ever could."

"If I could give it up for you, you know I would," Kit said with passionate sincerity. She has no idea whether those words are true or not, but they're easy to say, since she can never be tested on them. If Kit Saunders doesn't take the job, someone else will – an outsider, someone from away. Trif would be no better off, and Kit would go off as a stranger to some other outport, some other school.

Kit misses Spencer College, misses Miss Shaw and the other teachers, even some of her classmates. Coming home feels like putting off her own life, postponing independence till some future date. But it also means coming home to Triffie and to Joe Bishop, and despite complications, these are, beyond even her parents, the two most important people in her world.

The call has gone out; Triffie and a dozen others are kneeling at the mercy seat. Two years ago, Kit and Trif used to laugh together at girls who went down to the mercy seat every week, who got saved over and over. Now Trif is one of those girls; she no longer goes to Salvation Meeting just for entertainment. Something has changed in the two years Kit has been away.

Whatever Kit's sins – and she has them, hidden, unspoken – she will never be found here, weeping, displaying emotion like a new Sunday dress. She misses the grandeur of worship at the Anglican Cathedral in St. John's, a loveliness of liturgy and vestment that has less to do with religion and more, she thinks, with poetry and art and theatre. *These are my religion*, Kit tells herself, trying out both the phrase and the sentiment for size.

Whatever Triffie has to confess, it can't be lust, Kit thinks. They walk home with Jacob John Russell, who is sweet on Kit, and his friend Fred Mercer, who is happy enough to go along and partner Trif. Fred is an easygoing fellow, not bad-looking, and would be happy enough to fall in love with Trif given the slightest encouragement, but he gets none. Jacob John gets none from Kit either, but that's not because Kit lacks passion or the desire to fall in love. She has set her sights higher than Jacob John, though so far she has little to show for it.

During her two years in St. John's, after that first visit with its strange ending, she heard almost nothing from Joe Bishop. Not even letters – just the occasional postcard expressing sentiments so general there was no need of an envelope to contain them. Wishing her well, encouraging her to make the best of her opportunity – the sort of thing a good teacher might write to any promising former student; the sort of letter Mr. Bishop writes to half a dozen young men and women who have left his classroom.

But when he wrote to say that the School Board finally had the funds to hire a second teacher, she knew the pieces were falling into place. All part of God's Great Plan, Triffie might say, or the Workings of Providence, as Kit's mother would put it, expressing the same sentiment in more formal language. Providence, Kit thinks, is a more manageable concept than Triffie's intensely present Father God, or that meddling Jesus.

But lately, she has begun to doubt even Providence. Could there, truly, be a Divine Hand at work bringing her home to Missing Point? Providence has apparently neglected to inform Mr. Bishop. There could be no impropriety in the schoolmaster coming to call on his young colleague, or in walking her home from church, could there? Yet no such overtures have been made. And considering what he did when she was still a school-girl – well, no. That must not be thought of. It makes no sense. If he were to court her, to propose, it would settle not only the future but the past; it would make sense of everything that had gone before. Until that happens, certain incidents from the past must remain forever shrouded. *Forever shrouded*. Another lovely phrase to try out, to roll around on the tongue.

"So, you likes it, being a teacher?" Jacob John asks, his question sawing into her thoughts like a blunt knife cutting into rope, unable to sever them cleanly. "You must have some patience with them young ones, is all I can say."

"They're not so bad," Triffie says quickly. Triffie is finding Fred Mercer as poor at conversation as Jacob John is finding Kit, though Kit thinks it's unlikely Fred's thoughts are taken up with deeper things. Likely he just can't think of anything to say.

Triffie, though, can talk to anyone. *She'd talk cod out of the water, that one*, Kit thinks.

Triffie says, "I had a grand time with them last year – there's some right smart youngsters in that primary class, isn't there, Kit? Young Mattie White – now he's a bright one, but there's Amelia Snow, too, hasn't got any of his advantages and yet look how quick she is."

"Smart as paint," Kit agrees. "She's already going through the Fourth

Royal Reader even though she's supposed to be in the second. She can't help it – she got the first, second and third ones all read, and half the other books in the classroom too. I wish I could get a few more books in here, for young ones like her that can't read 'em fast enough. There's never been enough books in that classroom for anyone who liked to read – was there, Trif? Sure it was even worse when we were coming up."

"There was always plenty of books for me," Jacob John says. "Ain't that so, Fred? More than enough books for the likes of you and me – sure I thought that old Fourth Reader would've been the death of me, thought we'd never get through that."

"I never did get through it," Fred says. Like many of the boys, Fred stopped school when he was ten: Jacob John lasted a year longer. Girls are more likely than boys to finish schooling in a place like Missing Point. And there are families, like Kit's, who see the value of a daughter with an education who can earn her own keep as a teacher for a few years before she settles down to get married.

"I like teaching," Kit says now. A sudden burst of gaiety lightens her mood, lightens the air around all four of them – for though they rely on Triffie to keep the conversation going, it's from Kit that they all catch their mood, somber or merry depending on her whim. Even Fred laughs when she says, "Some of the young fellows think a lady teacher won't whip 'em, or that they needn't listen to me because they remember I was in the schoolroom with them only two years ago. I suppose a few of 'em gave you the same trouble, Trif? But Peter French won't make that mistake again, not since I called him up to the front for carrying on when he was supposed to be working on his arithmetic. Well he said right back to me, brazen as you please, 'What are you going to do, call in Mr. Bishop?' And I told him, I don't need Mr. Bishop to give you what you've earned, and I made him stick out his hand. He put it out with a smirk, like nothing I could do could ever hurt him, and I let fly with the ruler. My word! I think they heard him screech all the way back home. His mother came up to me in church this morning, told me whatever I done to him it must have worked, for he's practising his sums at home and says he don't want to get in trouble at school ever again!"

That gets the boys laughing, comparing their own tales of being whipped and strapped and beaten in school. Neither of them holds the slightest resentment against Joe Bishop for the frequent corporal punishments they were given: it is, in their view, a boy's job to misbehave and a schoolteacher's job to punish. That, too, is ordained by Providence.

Providence does nothing more towards bringing Kit and Joe Bishop together as fall chills to winter, though she's one room away from him every working day, on the other side of the partition hastily erected by Joe and some of the older boys over the summer. Some days after school he takes the time to help her plan her lessons or answer the questions that pile up like snowdrifts by the end of each day. Other days, he's busy helping the upper students, and Kit puts on her coat and walks home alone, through cold afternoons that deepen to twilight as she walks.

One Friday afternoon she is nearly home, turning onto the South Side Road, when she realizes she's left behind her history book; she planned to read ahead to be sure she knew the lesson before teaching it to the children on Monday. The schoolroom will be locked tomorrow and Sunday, and it's a waste of a weekend if she doesn't catch up on her work. Tonight Triffie will come over, as she does almost every night, knitting while Kit does her schoolwork, waiting till the work is done so they can read aloud together. They are halfway through *Othello*.

She turns around and goes back to the schoolhouse.

She pauses at the door, hears voices inside. Joe must be tutoring someone after school – maybe Effie Dawe, who has nearly finished the Fifth Reader. Kit glances through the window; beyond the frost that coats the glass, she sees the shape of the girl in her desk and Joe Bishop leaning over her.

Memory slams into Kit so hard she imagines it might knock her off the schoolhouse step. She cannot see any detail through the frosty glass, cannot see how close his head is to the girl's nor where his hand rests. But she is herself, twelve years old again. Dear Pedagogue's hand on her shoulder, creeping down to the tiny curve of her little-girl breast. His hand slipped inside the neckline, beneath the petticoat, touching bare skin. Then he sat beside her, patiently working through a Geometry proof, his other hand on her thigh. Under her skirt, fingers working up the nubbed wool of her stocking, exploring the warm bare flesh between stocking and bloomers.

Kit opens the door, slips into the room. The scene is, perhaps, innocent enough. She would think it innocent if she had never sat where Effie Dawe sits now, feeling the pressure of Joe Bishop's hand on her shoulder, his breath on her cheek. He has an arm around Effie's shoulders now as he reads from a

That *Forgetful* Shore

textbook, but Effie's eyes are on him, not on the book.

Then they hear the door, and Kit's footstep, and both look up. She reads it all in Joe's face: guilt, shame, apology – though she has seen nothing but a teacher reading with a student, his arm around her shoulder.

"The extra time he takes with the youngsters – like he used to do with me and you, sure – the man's a saint," Triffie says, when Kit mentions Joe Bishop is keeping Effie Dawe behind for extra lessons.

"Yes, he used to have both of us in after school the odd time, to work on our compositions. And he kept me in for all that extra help with Geometry," Kit says. "He never used to keep you in on your own, did he?"

Trif shakes her head. "No, Aunt Rachel hardly ever let me stay, she always wanted me home working as soon as school was out. What I can't fathom is them who do have the opportunity and won't use it. Last year he tried to give Millicent Butler a bit of extra help, and I know her father would have paid for her to go to St. John's for teacher-training. But she wouldn't stay after school – just couldn't be bothered to put in the extra time or the extra work."

"Funny how it's always girls he keeps back for extra work, isn't it? You and me, Millicent, Effie …."

"Well, 'tis good of him to see the potential in young girls, when so many folks don't," Triffie says.

Kit gives up. There is no way she can phrase even the most delicate question, no way she can ask, "Did he ever …?" Trif's admiration for Dear Pedagogue is a wall that cannot be breached, and whether it's built of genuine ignorance or an inability to speak the ugly truth aloud, Kit cannot tell.

She cannot tell Triffie. Kit imagines a dozen conversations, but every one would mean explaining why she had never told before, years ago. How could you tell someone a thing you didn't even tell yourself? Things that didn't make sense didn't happen. She would grow up, and Joe Bishop would come courting. Everything would make sense then.

Now everything makes a different kind of sense. She finds it hard to look at him day after day in the classroom. He says nothing – what can he say? – but the atmosphere between them has changed, the comradely chatter of colleagues at day's end is gone now.

One night Jacob John Russell makes bold to call at Kit's house, a thing he has been threatening to do for weeks, though she has always discouraged him. The night is clear, without either fog or snow, the stars shining brilliant in a cold black sky. Kit allows Jacob John to squirm awkwardly in the parlour for half an hour while she finishes marking homework, then, with her father's permission, she puts on her gaiters and bundles up in her coat, hat and mitts to join Jacob John for a walk across the Long Beach.

She feels the young man's relief as soon as they're outside, away from the stuffy propriety of her mother's parlour. They walk down the road, empty of travellers this cold night, listening to the rush and hiss of the waves on the rocks. A light burns in Abel Morgan's storeroom where men are mending nets and telling stories. As Jacob John leads her onto the beach, Kit slips a hand into the crook of his arm, for warmth and for protection against the icy rocks. Jacob John Russell smiles, like he cannot believe his sudden good fortune.

That *Forgetful* Shore

Triffie

KIT, IN HER new suit and hat, already looks like she belongs in St. John's instead of on the Point. Standing next to her on the train platform, Trif feels dowdy, dressed in a hand-me-down of Aunt Rachel's that she has altered to fit. The dress and her boots are not the only things Trif has that are hand-me-downs; before he went down on the Labrador Jacob John Russell, who had abruptly lost all interest in courting Kit, started offering his unwanted attentions to Triffie.

Kit's father embraces his daughter; her mother dabs away tears. Mrs. Saunders can accept Kit going to St. John's to take summer classes. What she cannot accept is that Kit would throw away the advantage of living at home and teaching in the Missing Point school, for a one-room school in Trinity Bay. Kit grimaces as she meets Trif's eyes over her mother's head. She hates emotional scenes like this, farewells and tears. She and Trif have said their private goodbyes, and Triffie will not weep or beg her to stay.

To Triffie, Kit has said only that she never intended to live out all her life in Missing Point, that she wants to be mistress of her own classroom, live away from home, see the world.

"The world, starting in Elliston?" Triffie probed gently.

"The world has to start somewhere," Kit declared. She was lighthearted after the decision was made, and Triffie suspected there was more to it than just Kit's desire to strike out on her own. Sometime during the winter, the pleasure of being home palled for Kit. Trif cannot quite believe that Kit is keeping a secret from her, but when she pressed Kit to explain why she wanted to leave, she found herself facing a stone wall. The same thing happened about what Kit had done to scare off Jacob John. There might be no secrets between them, as such, but there are subjects Kit is not eager to talk about.

Trif has her suspicions, of course. She's long thought that Kit cherished a schoolgirl crush on Joe Bishop. It must have become clear to her, over the course of her winter at home, that Dear Pedagogue was not going to come courting. It would be hurtful to press her about her reason for leaving, when the topic must surely be as painful as a sore tooth.

When the moment to say good-bye comes, Triffie grips both Kit's hands in hers. "You'll write, of course," she says.

"Of course I will, my dearest. Every day."

A kiss on the cheek, a squeeze of their clasped hands – that is more than enough display. Any passionate feelings will be saved for paper, or for prayer.

She has little time to commit anything to paper, though plenty of time for prayer, as the weeks of summer dwindle away. She puts in hours working in the garden, supervising Ruth and Will, which is sometimes more work than pulling the weeds herself. She hates gardening, but knows the hours scrabbling weeds out of the rocky soil will make all the difference in the long winter months when the root cellar is stocked with potatoes and turnips.

In the evening hours, garden work and housework done, she ruins her eyesight, according to Aunt Rachel, reading by lamplight. Joe Bishop gets novels from St. John's for the schoolroom, but lets Triffie read them first. "To see if they'd be suitable for the children," he says, by way of explaining his kindness. She writes postcards and letters to Kit, saying as much about the books she reads as about her daily routine.

After books, and letters to Kit, there remains God. Trif still goes to the Church of England every Sunday morning and to the Army every Sunday night, but she needs more; her desire for something beyond her daily existence drives her to her knees in long, passionate nightly prayers. She imagines that if her family were Papists she could become a nun. No-one would deny Trif's desire for a different kind of life if she were called by God. But she's not inclined towards the teachings of Rome, only to the idea of a convent, a life of holy dedication.

She swallows long passages of the Bible, praying her way through the

That *Forgetful* Shore

nightly Psalms in the prayer book and dipping at random into the darker and stranger corners of Scripture: Ezekiel, Daniel, Isaiah, Revelation. Their wild poetry is harder, in some ways, than Shakespeare's, but while the Bard points inward, to the depths of the human heart, the Bible points upward and outward, to something so far beyond, so other, that she can never fully grasp it. When she reads in Revelation, *Come out of her, my people*, she pictures herself stepping out, moving out of the stultifying round of her existence into something larger and freer. Ezekiel's cries of a people in exile speak to her too: Trif feels like an exile on the Point where she was born, an unheeded wanderer in a valley of dry bones.

One Sunday night Captain Fifield at the Citadel gives a thundering sermon against deceivers and false shepherds leading people astray with strange new doctrines. The diatribe is far too heated to be general; after the meeting, Trif lingers to ask the Captain if he knows of any false prophets in particular.

"There's two men going around – they've been working their way up the shore, from Holyrood to Brigus and now here. They say they're selling religious books that will help people understand the Bible better. But beware of them, Triffie – they're wolves in sheep's clothing, teaching error and heresy. You watch out, now – a clever girl like yourself don't want to be led astray. Pray to the Lord to guide you, and if you should run across one of these Seventh Day crowd, you run the other way. *Yield not to temptation, for yielding is sin.*"

"Yes, sir," Triffie says. On Monday afternoon, two men who call themselves Brother Anderson and Brother Pierce tap at Aunt Rachel's front door, and Trif does not run the other way. She asks them into the parlour and offers them each a cup of tea, though they decline, explaining that tea is a dangerous stimulant.

Trif is at a loss without teacups; she has nothing to give the men except her attention, though she does scrounge up a few tea buns, hoping the name won't put them off. "Now don't be in there all afternoon jawing with the likes of them," warns Aunt Rachel, who is busy with the Monday wash.

"I'll only talk to them for a few minutes, to be polite," Triffie says.

"Well, sing out to Ruth to come help me if you're going to waste time talking to preachers."

The two young men – Americans, polite and scrubbed, with strange hurried accents unlike the long, slow tones she is accustomed to hearing along the shore – open their books and begin to talk. They are delighted to discover how well Trif knows her Bible, that when they begin to quote a verse, she can finish it.

"Have you ever wondered, Miss Bradbury, about the prophecies of Daniel and Revelation?" Brother Anderson asks.

"I ponders over them for hours," Trif says honestly, "but to tell truth I can't make head nor tail of them."

Brother Anderson takes one of the heavy, clothbound books from his satchel and reveals the title: *Daniel and the Revelation*. "This book will make a great many things plain to you, that are now murky and hard to understand."

Triffie turns the pages, skims the dense paragraphs of type, examines the diagrams. The frontispiece shows a lurid horned beast with many heads. She traces the picture with her fingers. "The man who wrote this – this Uriah Smith – he can open the books that are sealed till the end of time?"

Brother Pierce smiles. "These books are being unsealed now because this is the end of time, Miss Bradbury! These are the last days, the days to which prophecy points. Only read this book, with your Bible open beside you, and you will see how clear it all is!"

Triffie buys the book from her own small store of money. She reads it exactly as the missionaries suggested, her Bible open beside her, checking each verse and reference, making notes in the margin. For a time even Shakespeare, along with Dickens and Austen and Mrs. Gaskell, are laid to one side.

Not only the Salvation Army officers but even the Anglican minister – and, she hears by report, the Methodist preacher too – warn their congregations about these Seventh Day missionaries, who believe that Jesus is coming soon and in the meantime we should all go to church on Saturday and avoid the flesh of pigs. "If I did all you said I'd plant myself crosswise to every soul on the Point," she tells Brother Anderson, the smiling and handsome missionary, the younger of the two.

"But that is what the Lord says we are to be," he tells her. "Planted crosswise to the world, as you put it, at odds with family and friends and all the world around us, for His sake."

The idea pleases her. Trif Bradbury, a warrior for truth, at odds to all the world. One of the faithful ones who keeps the commandments and has the testimony of Jesus, who will not be shaken even in the time of trial.

That *Forgetful* Shore

Missing Point
August, 1907

Dearest Peony,

I know how you disdain what you call my "religious enthusiasms" and that yours is a Quieter Faith, yet I long to sit down with you and show you what I have learned, what I am learning, about the prophecies of the End Times.

I have envied you your opportunities for learning in the Wider World, but now I feel I am learning as much or more here on the Point, and that while you take your courses in town and prepare to venture off to your new task as the Teacher in Elliston, I too am Embarking on a new Venture, no less fraught with Danger and Possibility than yours. You know how I hold you in my heart and in prayers – oh that you would do the same for me, even though you do not share my Beliefs!

At the end of September, a Seventh-day Adventist preacher from St. John's comes out to Bay Roberts once a week to hold meetings, to reap what Brother Anderson and Brother Pierce have sown over the summer months. Aunt Rachel says she won't have Triffie going to the meetings, but Triffie simply says she must obey God rather than men, finishes her day's work, puts on her hat and gloves, and walks across the causeway to Bay Roberts.

The meetings are held on Sunday nights, and the first two Sundays Trif talks Sadie Parsons into coming with her. Of the girls her age, Sadie is her closest friend now that Kit is gone. Sadie is by no means a soulmate; she is a pleasant, silly girl, not overly bright but with a thin veneer of sophistication due to the fact that her uncle runs the Mercantile and her father is captain of a schooner. There was talk when Sadie finished school that she might go on to college in St. John's, as her brother Ted did, but once she wrote her examinations no more was said about that. She is Kit's cousin, and used to be best pals with Millicent Butler, but with Millie in service in Harbour Grace, Sadie is, like Trif, at a bit of a loose end. They are thrown together, friends more by chance than by choice.

Sadie showed no interest in the prophecy books Trif was reading, but the week before the meetings started, word came to the Point that Skipper Wilf Parsons' schooner, the *Eliza May*, lost two of her boats in a storm on the Labrador. The *Eliza May* is full of men from the Point – Trif's Uncle Albert is on her, and most of the young fellows including Jacob John Russell and Sadie's beau Jabez Badcock. The possibility that their men may have been lost paralyzes the women of the Point as they wait for news, and Sadie is driven to her knees to beg the Lord to spare Jabez's life. When Triffie suggests the Adventist meetings as a possible way to seek God's will, she comes along readily enough.

The visiting preacher lectures in a dry tone untouched by any hint of revival fervour. He talks about the end of the world the way a merchant might talk about the price of fish. Many curious people press in on the first night, but after hearing discourses on the year-day principle and the twenty-three-hundred day prophecy, many of them stop coming. They say it's because they've been convinced the Seventh-day Adventists are in error, but Triffie thinks it's because they had hoped for something more impressive – fire and brimstone preaching, perhaps. The coloured posters of the beasts of Daniel and Revelation are bizarre enough to lure a few people in, but sometime during the discussion of the Roman emperor Constantine and his nefarious plot to change Sabbath to Sunday, they drift away.

What little fire and brimstone is to be found at the Seventh-day meetings comes from the lips of young Brother Anderson, who does not preach but often gives the closing prayer. *Now that one will be a powerful preacher someday*, Triffie thinks; he has told her he is studying at college to become a minister back in the States. He and Brother Pierce go around to the homes of the few people still faithfully attending the meetings, holding Bible studies on the evenings there are no services. His prayers are condensed altar calls, urging God to act upon the listening hearts, drawing them out of Babylon and into His remnant people now – *now*, while there is yet time and hope, before probation ends and He comes to judge the earth.

In the middle of October comes the welcome news that all the men from the *Eliza May* made it safely to shore and are bound home. Soon after, the survivors themselves arrive. Some, the storytellers and braggarts, are eager to tell the tale. More taciturn men, like Uncle Albert, only say, "'Tis good to be home." Jacob John Russell comes up to Triffie on the dock where everyone has gathered to welcome the crew and stands in front of her with his hands in his pockets, bobbing up and down on the balls of his feet with a foolish grin on his face.

"What do you want?" she says.

"I might've died, Trif. Is it too much to ask you'd be glad to see me alive?"

"I'm glad you're not drowned. Now go on, and don't make a nuisance of yourself."

That Sunday afternoon, Sadie tells Trif she can't come to the Adventist preaching service with her anymore. "Jabez don't want me to," she says. Jabez is a strikingly handsome young man a few years older than Sadie and Trif, a staunch Methodist, who since his return from the Labrador, has been heard saying he means to become a minister now. "He says God saved his life for a purpose and he's going to dedicate himself to the Lord, and he don't want me being led astray by no false doctrines before we gets married," Sadie explains.

Triffie goes alone that night, walking over the causeway with the other young people who are heading, as she once did, to the Salvation Army, then going her own way to the rented hall where the Adventists hold their meetings.

When the service is over she steps outside to find Jacob John Russell, of all people, stood up leaning against the wall. "What are you doing here?" she asks, when he falls into step beside her.

"Walking you home."

"I'm after telling you a dozen times I don't need you walking me home."

"You told me that back in the spring when we were walking home from the Army," he points out. "Fair enough – there's plenty of other people coming back along the road when Salvation Meeting lets out. But there's not another soul on the Point coming across to these fool meetings, and I won't have you walking back over the causeway on your own in the dark."

"What business is it of yours?"

"It's my business if I make it mine. I knows now you'd rather have that fellow Anderson walking you home, but I don't see him trudging over the causeway to bring you back to the Point."

"You think I got my eye on him, is that it? I suppose you'd be glad to know he's got a fiancée waiting for him back in the States."

"Is that so, now? And when did you find that out?"

"A nice while back." In fact, it was only last week that Brother Anderson

mentioned the saintly Louisa, the lovely young girl who is studying to be a nurse back at the Seventh-day Adventist College in Battle Creek. When he returns from his missionary work in Newfoundland they plan to be married. Triffie will not confess – not to Kit, not to God, and certainly not to Jacob John Russell – that her heart fell a little at this news. Perhaps she had dreams – but no. Those were only fantasies. And with the end times approaching, she has more serious matters on her mind than catching the eye of a handsome young American missionary, and going back with him to Battle Creek.

"And you're still going to those meetings, even though the young missionary's spoken for?" Jacob John taunts.

"I wouldn't expect the likes of you to understand. There are some people in this world got more serious matters on their mind than courting and marrying."

"Tell me then, Triffie. What's more important than courting and marrying? Queer old pictures of buckhorned goats and flying angels? Is that worth traipsing over the causeway twice a week and turning everyone on the Point against you?"

"I don't mind being persecuted for the truth," Trif says. But she thinks of those words – turning everyone against her, or her own words about planting herself crosswise to the whole town. Is she willing to stand out, to be one of the handful of people baptized when the evangelistic meetings are finished? To worship on Saturday, forswear eating salt pork and cooking with lard, dig a chasm of difference between herself and all those she knows and loves? If she is one of the remnant, she and Kit will be forever on opposite sides of a great gulf, unless Triffie can somehow win her to the truth. Trif knows in her heart that's a long shot.

"Time for you to give up this foolishness, think about settling down, getting married, now, ain't it?"

She stops short in mid-stride, turns to face him. Jacob John is as brazen as brass, but even so she didn't expect him to be as forward as this. "What did you say?"

"Only that it was high time you thought of getting married, that's all."

"I'm not even seventeen. I'll think of it when I'm good and ready," Trif says. "You got some gall." He's always had gall, of course, but where Jabez Badcock, Sadie's young man, came back from the near-disaster on the *Eliza May* with a sober conviction that God had a holy purpose for his life, Jacob

That *Forgetful* Shore

John Russell has come strutting back like the cock of the walk, sure he was leading a charmed life and that fate would hand him whatever he wanted – even Triffie Bradbury.

"You watch yourself, Jacob John," she warns. "I'll tell my uncle you're taking liberties."

"I'll tell him myself I'm ready to take any liberties offered," says Jacob John. He walks on beside her, not chastened at all, over the causeway and up the North Side Road as far as the front gate of Uncle Albert and Aunt Rachel's house. When her hand is on the gate to swing it open, he says, "I got me own house."

"You do not – you lives with your mother."

"Yes, but before Father died he put the house in my name. It's mine when I gets married or turns twenty-one. Mother says when I marries, she's going over to Bay Roberts with Liza and Joe. So I got me own house." Liza is his older sister; there are also two younger brothers, not fortunate enough to inherit a house.

"I don't know why you thinks I'd care about the likes of you and your house," Triffie says, and goes up the walk to the front bridge, careful not to give a backward glance.

She knows the house. It's a fine sturdy old house, built by Jacob John's grandfather fifty years ago. It sits on the south side of the Point, right at the head of the Long Beach, looking out over the beach and the bay at Bareneed across the water.

Trif walks into her uncle and aunt's house, this house where she will never be more than the unpaid help, the poor relation. *I got me own house.* She tries not to dwell on Jacob John's words, for what good can come of it?

A house of one's own, even the promise of one, is not enough. She sets her face against Jacob John and his patient efforts at courting. *In my Father's house are many mansions*, she recites to herself as she goes about the round of her daily work, digging up the potatoes and turnips she weeded all summer, preparing for winter. *I go to prepare a place for you, and if I go, I will come again and receive you unto Myself.* The end times are coming, and it's no time to be thinking of marrying or giving in marriage, even if she were so inclined. She tells the minister she wants to be baptized when the meetings are finished. If she has to trust someone to help her escape her life on the Point, it's going to be Jesus, not Jacob John Russell.

That *Forgetful* Shore

Kit

My Darling Posy,

How strange your letter seems to me! As strange as those books and
charts of prophecy that you write of, as if it comes from another
land or another time. I know you have always felt closer to the
Throne of God than I could do, but to imagine you being entranced
by these Strange Doctrines, being – I want to write "Taken In" but
it is impossible to me, dearest Posy, that a mind as clear and sharp as
yours could be ever <u>Taken In</u> by any charlatan or deceiver.

You are right, of course, there is a great gulf fixed between us if you
truly believe the end of all things is near, while I think that the
world will go on <u>much</u> <u>as</u> <u>it</u> <u>always</u> <u>has</u>. And yet, forever and
ever, world without end you will always be my dearest friend and
companion, nothing shall change that. Change everything, dear one,
but not <u>your</u> <u>love</u> <u>for</u> <u>me</u>!

I suppose I ought to write about my own new <u>Voyage</u> <u>of</u> <u>Discovery</u>,
here in Elliston. The school here is not bursting at the seams like ours

*at home, but has upwards of forty students on the books, of whom
about twenty-five attend on a regular basis, with the others coming
and going more or less as they please. There is the usual mixture
of bright children, dullards and all in between. I have one boy
preparing to write Standard Six examinations, the oldest boy left
in school once all his fellows have gone fishing. His father, who is
Captain of a Schooner with one older boy already gone to college,
has great hopes of sending the lad to school in St. John's, but it will
take a* <u>*deal*</u> *of* <u>*work*</u> *to get him ready to occupy such a place.*

*I am busy from dawn till long past dusk, sitting up in my boarding-
house room muffled in blankets and gloves making plans for my
classes. Yet the greatest* <u>*burden*</u> *comes not from the teaching itself, but
from all the things the community expects of its Teacher. I promise, I
had not considered how heavy my duties might be …*

It's ironic, Kit thinks, that just as Triffie plunges ever deeper into the
mysteries of holiness, Kit, who barely knows what she believes, finds herself
expected to be a pillar in the Church. It's not enough that she teaches the
children five days a week at school; she is expected to be the girls' Sunday
School teacher as well. It is assumed that she will take an active role in the
Church of England Women's Association: the minister's wife runs it, but
latches onto Kit and enlists her help.

Mrs. Chaulk, her landlady, has expectations of the new teacher as well.
Kit pays for room and board out of her wages, but has been told that the
greatly reduced rate assumes she will take her turn at cooking and cleaning.
As Mrs. Chaulk cannot read or write, Kit also reads her letters and writes the
replies Mrs. Chaulk dictates. She reads three chapters of the Bible aloud for
her landlady before bed: "yourself being an educated girl and all."

Kit does everything she's asked. What would it mean, if the teacher put
her foot down and refused to teach Sunday School, or help plan church
women's meetings? Or, for that matter, if she refused to cook and scrub
and read the Psalms to her landlady? She is determined to give no-one in
Elliston any cause for complaint: she will be a model teacher, a paragon.
When she is gone from here, they will shake their heads and say, "We never
had a teacher so good as Miss Saunders, not before nor since."

She rises before dawn to go down and light the kitchen fire and cook porridge for her own breakfast and Mrs. Chaulk's, then packs herself a lunch so she can stay at school and work through dinnertime. She opens up the school an hour before the children come, and sometimes starts the stove herself, if the big boys don't come early with wood.

Then the dizzying reality of the school day sweeps over her, balancing the various classes and subjects, trying to give enough time to everyone while keeping order at the same time. Despite the anger that surges inside her whenever she thinks of Joe Bishop or recalls his name, she can't help calling on him as an example. His work is more relevant than that of Miss Shaw or any of her other Spencer teachers, who had the luxury of teaching a single subject at a time to groups of eager scholars.

Winter closes in. The ground turns to stone beneath her boots. Kit rises in the dark in order to get to school, to have the stove going early enough to drive the chill from the room.

One morning she climbs the hill leading up to the school and sees a tall figure leaning against the schoolhouse wall. She hesitates. She is a woman alone on a dark road. Would anyone dare lay a hand on the school teacher?

The figure steps forward: a man, tall and broad shouldered, carrying an armload of wood.

"I'd take off my cap, but my hands are full," he apologizes, "and I can't hold the door open for you neither." He speaks with a Bonavista Bay accent but his speech is careful, as if he's used to choosing words to impress people far from here. "Father told me the new schoolteacher was a woman so I thought you might want a hand laying the fire," he adds, following her into the schoolroom.

Inside, she lights a lamp while the stranger carries his load of wood to the stove. Crouched in front of the stove door, he doesn't speak again till he has a flame going.

"I'm Ben Porter, by the way," he says. "Harry and Maud's boy."

"Oh, of course," Kit says. If it weren't so early, if he hadn't startled her by appearing in the dark like that, she would surely have had the wits to guess. She knows Harold and Maud Porter's eldest son is their pride and joy, the boy who went through school in St. John's and then on to university up in Nova Scotia, studying to be a lawyer or doctor or something grand. For a man like Harold Porter, skipper of a fishing boat, this is a lofty height for his son to soar to. Captain Porter's second son, Lije, has no inclination for further schooling and is already a crewman on the *Clyde*, but Harold Porter has told Kit he hopes the younger boy, Sam, will follow in Ben's footsteps. Sam is Kit's senior student this year, the boy struggling his way through the Third Reader while sailing through his Mathematics.

"You're home for Christmas, I suppose," she says to Ben Porter.

"Yes. And you'll be leaving us soon, going home for Christmas yourself, no doubt." He gets up and moves away from the stove, closing the door, and crosses the floor to stand by her desk. He is very tall, one of the few men Kit has stood beside who makes her feel small. Lamplight mingles with the first gray light of morning leaking through the windows, light enough to see the clean strong lines of Ben Porter's cheekbones and jaw, his large nose, his full, warm mouth. He lifts his cap. "Pleased to make your acquaintance while you're still here, Miss Saunders."

"I – thank you. Yes, I'll be here for another fortnight, till we finish up lessons and have the Christmas pageant, and then I'll go back to Missing Point for Christmas and New Year's."

"That's a shame," he says, then smiles. "I mean, it's a shame for me. You'll be glad to get back to your people for the holidays."

Kit can think of nothing witty or charming to say, although he has charm enough for the both of them. "I think that fire will do fine," Ben says. "I 'low some of the boys will be up here soon with more wood – that's what we used to do in my day."

"In your day!?" she echoes. "You sound like your schooldays were fifty years ago." It's a relief to laugh, though she's sure it comes out as a nervous titter.

What does Kit Saunders know of men like Ben Porter, outside of books? He might as well be Mr. Darcy or Mr. Knightley for all the experience she has of a flesh-and-blood man, tall and handsome, a fisherman's son gone away to university. All Kit knows of men is – well, there's Joe Bishop. *Infatuation*, she calls that now – infatuation on her part; something else on his. Something she has no name for. Then there was Jacob John Russell: her word for that is *dalliance*. A brief dalliance, quickly ended. Now she needs a new word: *romance*, perhaps?

Even her words come from novels; that's all she knows. She went from an outport schoolroom to an all-girls college and now to another outport schoolroom where she plays a different role: different, but equally chaste.

The next three mornings he's there before she is, each time with a load of wood, waiting for her to open the door. His parents' house is on the opposite end of the road from her boarding house, so there's no passing each other on the way. He gets to the school, builds up the fire, and leaves before the first children arrive. She doesn't even see him in full daylight till church on Sunday.

After church, he lingers to ask if he can walk her home. She asks about university, about the things he studies – he is getting a degree in History with the intention of going on to law school – and the people in his classes. She asks where the other young men come from, what kind of people they are.

"It's not all men, you know. There's a good few girls there, getting their B.A. degrees. A couple of years ago there was even a woman from Newfoundland."

"From St. John's, no doubt," she says. Who but a wealthy St. John's merchant would send a daughter to university?

"You should go," he says. "I know what you're like, you've got a good mind. You'd fit right in up there."

"You know what I'm like? And how do you know that? You've only met me three times, and every time to build up the fire in my woodstove." The words, spoken in as light and flirtatious a tone as she possesses, suddenly sound suggestive, as if she were hinting at something improper. Or perhaps it's just his answering smile, the dimple in his right cheek, that makes her think so.

"I hear things," he says. "I hear talk about the new schoolteacher, how smart she is, the grand fine books she reads to the youngsters." Kit imagines the younger children, Sam, Tillie and Rachel prattling about school, telling tales about Teacher. She imagines Ben drawing the children out with questions, glancing away as he does so, trying not to seem too interested. Kit feels a blush creeping from her collar up to the brim of her hat, which she dips to hide her face.

Apart from filling the woodstove and walking home from church, the social life of Elliston offers few opportunities for courting. Young couples walk back and forth on the road on warmer evenings, but with winter closed in there's little of that, and Kit wonders if it's considered proper for the schoolteacher to engage in such mating rituals, anyway. In lieu of more romantic activities, Ben volunteers to help with the Christmas concert. He

That *Forgetful* Shore

comes to the school in the afternoon as Kit rehearses with the students and helps keep them in line while they wait to go on with their songs and recitations. He hangs a piece of canvas and paints a backdrop, and builds a passable manger.

After the triumph of the concert, Kit packs her bags for home. Two weeks ago she could not have imagined being reluctant to leave Elliston for the holidays. Whatever mixed feelings she has about people back in Missing Point – her parents, Jacob John, Joe Bishop, even Triffie in a way – it is her home, the place her roots are planted. She will never live there again, but she'll always go back there – and Triffie, whatever strange new religion she's embraced, is still her second self, her other half. What could Elliston offer to compete with that?

Ben takes her bag down to the wharf and sees her off on the *Ethie*. "I'll be gone to Nova Scotia when you get back."

"Yes, and if you come home for the summer, I'll be getting ready to go home again," she says.

"Ships passing in the night. I'll be sure to have my flags out when you pass by, though."

"You could write me," she suggests.

"I'm no great letter-writer," he admits. "But I may send the odd postal."

"You do that, then," says Kit. "The odd postal. The odder the better. I'll look for it."

Triffie

Missing Point
January, 1908

My Dear Peony,

Just a postal to send on the <u>Ethie</u> when she sails tomorrow – long letter to follow. How short a time you were here, yet how great a gap your Absence leaves. New friends may come and go but none fills the Void left by an Old, True Friend who is Far Away. I sit at my little table tonight and wish I could cross the water and be with you. And if I caught a glimpse of a certain Mr. Darcy, that would at least satisfy my curiosity!

"He's really nothing like Mr. Darcy," Kit had insisted when she was home at Christmas. "A bit in looks perhaps. But not in character. Can you imagine Mr. Darcy building a manger for the school Christmas pageant?"

Of course Triffie couldn't. This Ben Porter sounds like a perfectly nice, charming, helpful young man. Handsome, of course. Tall and dark, Kit has assured her. Her quick pen sketched a series of caricatures that left Triffie laughing, but Triffie can't entirely erase the idea of Mr. Darcy from her mind. The thought that Kit has an admirer whom Trif has never seen, who is entirely outside their circle of acquaintance on the Point, fills Trif with the blackest envy. She offers this sin up to God in her prayers but never manages to dispel it completely.

Before Christmas, blond and smiling Brother Anderson said his goodbyes to Trif and the rest of the small flock of faithful Adventists left behind in Bay Roberts and the nearby harbours. He has gone back to America, to Battle Creek, that town humming with devout industry. It's a mythical place in Trif's mind, filled with golden corn-fed young men like Brother Anderson, and apple-cheeked blonde maidens like his fiancée Louisa, coupled off two by two like animals going into the ark: missionary preacher and teacher; missionary doctor and nurse.

But his departure does not spell the end of Trif's newfound faith. Rather, with the American missionaries gone, she is stirred into action, keeping the little band of believers faithful by gathering them on Sabbath mornings, doing everything short of preaching sermons. A dozen times Uncle Albert has threatened to put her out of the house if she won't give up her new religion and do some housework on Saturday. But Triffie has figured out by now he's all talk; he'll never be known as the man who turned his own niece out of doors to starve. Aunt Hepsy Snow, the only other soul on the Point who continues going to the Adventist meetings now that the missionaries have gone, is a valuable ally. She is Aunt Rachel's first cousin by marriage, and is quick to defend her own and Triffie's religion when others in the family criticize. Moreover, Aunt Hepsy has a horse and sleigh that she drives to meetings, picking Triffie up along the way.

Trif's work week is reduced from six days to five, since Aunt Rachel won't hear of her doing any housework on Sunday. On Fridays Triffie bakes a double batch of bread and cooks a big pot of something – pea soup or beans, usually – that will do for Saturday's dinner. If it's pea soup, she puts her own aside in a separate pot before adding salt pork for the rest of the family, though she can't work out a way to get around frying things in lard. She turns over the Saturday jobs of blacking everyone's Sunday boots and polishing the silver to Betty and Ruth, who are old enough now to take over those tasks, and moves her scrubbing day back to Friday. Trif won't lift a finger from sundown Friday till sundown Saturday, but nobody in the house can fault her, for she works like a slave the rest of the week. Given that the blessed martyrs suffered and burned at the stake and the faithful remnant will suffer the same in the last days, Trif is hardly about to complain of a bit of extra housework.

That *Forgetful* Shore

Unlike the rest of the new Seventh-day Adventists, she hasn't heeded the call to *Come out of her, my people entirely*. She tells her fellow believers it makes things easier on her at home if she continues to accompany her aunt and uncle and the children to Sunday services at the Church of England. She can still keep an eye on the youngsters during church, though she resigned her post as Sunday School teacher before the minister could relieve her of it. She tells herself she is like Namaan bowing in the house of Rimmon.

The truth is, she wouldn't know what to do with herself if she weren't in church Sunday morning. Church is where everyone goes. It's one thing to stand bravely alone as part of God's last-day remnant, but quite another to miss out on the one major social event of the week.

By the same token, she still sometimes goes to the Sunday night Salvation Meeting at the Army, now that Adventist preaching services on Sunday night have ended for the winter. She misses the singing and clapping and tambourines at the Citadel. She's absolutely convinced of the end-time prophecies Brother Anderson showed her, and still reads Daniel and Revelation faithfully, trying to understand those beasts better – though she can never think of them now without hearing Jacob John's voice in her head saying "Buckhorned goats and flying angels." But she finds it hard to accept this one article of faith: that someone or something as vast as God can be confined in one particular room, can be the property of one group of people, and be absent everywhere else. Well, that and the business of not drinking tea. She has abandoned pork and bacon because the pig is plainly listed in Leviticus 11 as an unclean animal, but she can't embrace the Adventist idea that a cup of tea is bad for the nerves.

If it weren't for God, Triffie feels she'd have precious little to look forward to. Kit is off in Bonavista Bay, running her own school and falling in love. Joe Bishop has another teacher helping him out at the school, a young girl named Sylvia Morris from Notre Dame Bay who, despite her romantic name, is a very dull, small-minded girl with whom Triffie has been unable to strike up a friendship.

The schoolroom is closed to her now, the possibility of teaching children as remote as the chance of getting any more book-learning herself. From here on, Triffie determines, she will be self-educated. She continues on through Shakespeare, having reached minor works like *Timon of Athens* and *Pericles, Prince of Tyre*. Joe Bishop still brings her novels from St. John's to read before putting them in the hands of the schoolchildren, and she returns often to her favourite poets: Tennyson, Wordsworth, Blake. She's also working her way slowly through Gibbon's *Decline and Fall of the Roman Empire*, and with the help of the Adventist minister from St. John's, who comes periodically to preach to the faithful few in Bay Roberts, she is reading the collected works of Mrs. Ellen White, the Adventist prophetess. Given how few hours of lamplight she has these winter evenings after the supper dishes are done and the dark draws in, it's a busy reading schedule.

"How come you reads all them books?" Will asks one night. He is perched on a stool at the other end of Trif's little writing desk, sharing her lamplight as he makes his painful way through a story in the Third Royal Reader.

"Because I like it. You can learn a lot from books," Trif says. Of her three young cousins, Will is by far her favourite, but she has had no luck inspiring him with a love for books and learning. He is ten years old now, eager to put the schoolroom behind him. "Books can take you to foreign lands," she adds, looking up from *Idylls of the King*.

"No they can't," Will says. "Ships can; books can't."

"In your imagination," Trif says.

"I knows what you meant Trif, I'm not stunned. I just don't say it works. Or it don't work for me, anyway. I'm readin' this story now about the feller on a ship going to China, but I ain't going to China, I'm right here on the Point, sitting on my backside in your room, reading a book when I'd sooner be down on the beach or out in the woods."

Trif laughs. "Anybody as clever with words as you are, Will Bradbury, ought to like books. It's a sin you don't, and I don't know why, for you couldn't ask for a better teacher than Mr. Bishop. Maybe when you're older you'll find out what you've missed, and take up reading when you're an old man, too old to go fishing."

"We'll have to see about that." Will's tone clearly indicates he thinks it unlikely. After a moment more of squinting at the page he adds, without looking up, "You know what Jacob John says about you and your books?"

"Jacob John? As if I minds what he says!"

"He says if you took your head out of a book now and again, you might see what's in front of your eyes."

"Does he now." Trif draws a breath, and decides there is nothing to be gained by venting her opinion of Jacob John Russell to a ten-year-old boy who repeats everything he hears.

That *Forgetful* Shore

She lays aside her own book to pull Will's Royal Reader toward her. "Go on then, I'll read it out loud to you," she says, and the boy puts his chin happily on his folded arms. He likes listening to stories, even if not reading them. The story of Brave Bobby holds his attention once Trif reads it with the proper emphasis, since it's all to do with a ship and a sea voyage and a big Newfoundland dog like Old Jock, the dog Uncle Nate French has for hauling his wood.

In April, Uncle Albert returns from the seal hunt with both his feet frostbitten. Aunt Rachel declares he needs time to recover before going down on the Labrador in June, and Jacob John, also back from the ice but none the worse for wear, offers to take Will into the woods along with his own two younger brothers to cut wood.

The day the boys return from their overnight trip, Triffie runs into Jacob John driving over from the south side to the north side of the Point with his pony cart and a load of wood. Triffie is walking back from bringing a jar of pea soup up to poor Sadie Parsons, who has been laid up all winter. Sadie had the 'flu back in the fall but she was never able to shake it, and plans for her wedding to Jabez Badcock have been postponed until she's better. Trif wonders when that will be, if ever. Nobody says it aloud, but the cough and the rattle in Sadie's lungs have gone on too long for 'flu or even pneumonia. Her family can afford to call a doctor, but Dr. Fradsham hasn't done her a bit of good. It's not that Sadie needs Trif's soup – her poor mother could float a dory on the soup she's made, and no doubt would do so if she thought it would help her daughter. Coming over with soup or buns to tempt Sadie's appetite is only an excuse for a visit, a chance to sit down awhile and tell Sadie that her cough will clear up when the warm weather comes.

On the road back from Sadie's house, Jacob John and Will pull up alongside her with Uncle Albert's load of wood.

"You're some helpful to my uncle," Trif says, taking Jacob John's offered hand to climb up on the seat beside him as Will clambers back to sit on the wood.

"Ah, I'm the helpful kind," Jacob John says with a wink. "Anyway young Will did more than his share, he's a grand little worker. I'm glad to help out where I can – and besides, I got business to discuss with Uncle Albert."

Jacob John reins in the horse in front of Uncle Albert's gate, and Triffie hops down. "Oh, and what business is that?"

"My business," he says with another wink. He jumps down too, and begins unloading the wood with Will. When Triffie takes an armload, Jacob John says, "You go on in the house now and boil the kettle, I'll want a cup of tea when I'm finished."

"The nerve of you, placing orders like you were in a St. John's hotel."

Half an hour later, sitting at the kitchen table, Jacob John reaches for the sugar bowl. "Your tea is like yourself, Trif – too strong and not near sweet enough."

Trif shoves the sugar bowl across the table at him. She'd like to get up and leave him, go find some work to do, but it's Sabbath afternoon, her usual time for visiting the sick, so she's uncharacteristically idle. As if noticing her stillness, Jacob John says, "Off to your church this morning, were you? Jesus not come down and taken that crowd away yet?"

"If He had, I doubt you would have noticed. You'd be too busy making fun and scoffing."

"Sitting in the seat of the scornful, that's me." He grins. "You didn't think I could quote Scripture, did you?"

"The Devil can quote scripture when it suits his purposes, so I don't see why you couldn't."

Aunt Rachel comes to Trif's room that night to talk. Trif is reading the 109th Psalm and thinking of people she would like to curse.

"Triffie, I need to talk to you about A Serious Matter," Aunt Rachel says.

Already Triffie is one step ahead of this moment, past the part where she has the unpleasant conversation and onto the part where she writes about it to Kit. *As she spoke I could hear the capitals in her words, A Serious Matter, and what do you think the Matter was? Nothing less than a proposal of marriage from Jacob John Russell, who appears to have given up all hope of charming me and is trying his charms on my guardians instead.*

"It's a good match, Triffie," Aunt Rachel says. "You know we're glad to have you here, but you'll want to move on and start a home of your own someday. Jacob John is a nice young fellow, a hard worker. And he has a house of his own."

Ah, that house again – how often it seems to come up as a point in his favour! Trif writes in her mind, as she will later write on paper. *Was Pemberly such an inducement to Elizabeth Bennett, that it needed to be urged above the claims of Mr. Darcy's own personality? Surely if a man must hang all his hopes of marriage on the fact that he has a house, there must be something vital lacking in the man himself?*

That *Forgetful* Shore

The letter in her head is cooler and more flippant than Triffie herself is able to be. To Aunt Rachel she only says, "I don't fancy marrying Jacob John."

"Why not? He's always been very nice to you."

"He's saucy," Trif says, although this is in fact the only thing she likes about him.

"Well, you got a sharp tongue in your own head, my girl. With that on top of your queer religious ideas and all the reading you do, you should count yourself lucky that such a fine young man is willing to make an offer for your hand in marriage."

"He's made me no offers," Trif said. "He might think of talking to me about it himself."

"He told the Mister you never gave him much encouragement," Aunt Rachel says. "He hoped we could help you see the advantages."

"Unless you're going to put me out of the house, I don't see no advantages," Trif says. "I got a roof over my head here as good as I would there. If I'm married, I'll be doing housework and raising youngsters for the rest of my life, and if I stay here I'll be doing the same. I'm used to doing what you and Uncle Albert say; why should I get used to doing what Jacob John Russell says?"

"Don't you ever intend to marry?" Aunt Rachel says, her forehead crinkling. An unpaid housekeeper is all very well now while the children are young, but with Ruth almost finished school and Will and Betty growing up fast, it will take only a few years to move Trif from being an asset to being a burden.

"P'raps, when I meets the right one," Trif said. "But I can tell you for sure, Jacob John's not him."

"I hope you're not holding out for meeting some young man who shares your religion," Aunt Rachel says, "for you won't find many of them along this shore. And meanwhile, you'll have let a good man slip through your fingers. Jacob John won't wait for long – I think he got his eye on your cousin Lizzie if you don't give him any more encouragement than you're doing."

"Tell him there's no point in waiting, and Lizzie Snow is welcome to him," says Triffie. She is pleased with herself; this unpleasant conversation has turned out almost as well in real life as it's doing in her head. She can hardly wait for Aunt Rachel to leave, so she can write it all down.

That *Forgetful* Shore

All eyes were
on me when
I boarded
the steamer.

*All
Eyes Were
on Me*

❧

1909 – 1913

Kit

Elliston
June, 1909

Dearest Posy,

This postal comes by <u>Prospero</u> to say that I will arrive on the very next boat. The last weeks have been such a Whirlwind, with finishing the School year and making preparations for next, that I hardly know where I am. How good it will be to get home to you, my Darling Friend, and talk of all our plans and dreams!

Kit feels guilty. It will really be *her* plans and dreams they talk about, her great, impossible dream that has somehow come true, and surely that will be hard on Triffie.

Yet Trif has cheered her on all the way, telling her to apply to Dalhousie, telling her she will get in even when it seems impossible. Kit still has this final campaign to wage, going home to convince her parents that they should let her go. Her scholarship covers tuition, and she has enough savings from teaching all winter and working at the Mercantile in the summer to pay for room and board. She has enough, anyway, for the first year. After that – well, she can't think of it yet. She has the opportunity for one year of university, and if that's all she ever gets, she intends to enjoy it to the fullest.

Ben has been the other angel on her shoulder, as encouraging as Trif but with far more knowledge about how such things work. While Kit spent her second school year in Elliston, Ben was back at Dalhousie. Their paths cross only briefly, when he comes home for Christmas or for the summer, before Kit goes back to the Point. Ben brings her copies of the Dalhousie catalogue, helps her with the applications, tells her over and over that this is possible.

Kit's mother always told her that men didn't like girls who were too clever or too educated. Although, like most things her mother said, Kit disdained the advice, she has always secretly believed there is something to it. Certainly the cleverest women she knows, the mistresses at Spencer College, including her beloved Miss Shaw – who was more than happy to write Kit a glowing letter of recommendation for university – are all unmarried.

Ben Porter, having charted his own course away from a fisherman's life in an outport town, seems eager for Kit to follow suit. Yet his interests are clearly more than platonic. Their time together has been so brief over these past two years, and he spoke the truth when he said he was no letter-writer. But when he comes home, nobody in Elliston doubts that he's courting Miss Saunders the teacher.

On the night before Kit leaves Elliston for the last time, having resigned her teaching post, Ben sits beside her on the back fence of her landlady's house. The air has become warm and spring-like just in these last few days, the hard ground softening and tree buds opening into full leaf. Kit leans back against the fence, Ben perched beside her. The air between them feels like June – full of possibility.

"What if it doesn't work out?" she says, putting her fears into words. "What if my father puts his foot down and says I can't go? What if I go up there and fail the matriculation exam? Then I've given up a good job for nothing."

His fingers play with the hair swept high on her head, teasing little strands loose. His fingertips brush her neck. Shivers run through Kit's body.

"It won't happen, Katherine." He's the only person who calls her Katherine; it feels like as much a pet name as when Trif calls her Posy. "This is meant to be. It's your destiny."

Since he's already made bold to touch her, Kit dares to be a bit brazen herself. "My mother won't want me to get a university education. She thinks if I'm too educated, no-one will ever marry me."

"Oh. Well. We can put her mind to rest on that score, can't we?"

"Can we?"

Ben chuckles. "You know my intentions are honourable, Katherine. I'll write your mother and father a letter, if you like."

"They might like that. I wouldn't." She wants to keep Ben's courtship to herself, not to drag it into the harsh light of parental scrutiny. They have stolen kisses and caresses in their rare moments alone together, and Ben talks of the future as if their lives will be entwined, though he hasn't formally proposed. But Ben's greatest gift has been to show her the way to another life. Even if he never ends up proposing marriage, if he gets her out of Newfoundland and into university in Canada, he will always be the prince in her fairy tale.

On board the *Ethie*, steaming away from the wharf, she leans over the rail and waves to him, thinks of the funny postcard he sent her last winter. The picture showed a girl dressed in the height of fashion, her hat perched atop a huge Gibson Girl hairstyle, looking flirtatiously over her shoulder as she climbed the gangplank of a ship. The caption read "All eyes were on me when I boarded the steamer." On the back, Ben had written: "She reminds me of you – seems I'm always watching you sail away."

During the summer, Ben fishes on his father's boat. Unlike most fishermen, he earns cash rather than credit for his share, due to an arrangement his father has with the merchant. Kit goes back to work behind the counter at Parsons' Mercantile. The shop girl's job belongs by rights to her cousin Sadie, but Sadie is dying of tuberculosis.

A week after Kit gets home, Trif comes to the shop to meet her at the end of the day. Trif has put in a hard workday herself in the house and garden, but she has an hour to spare and now, as Kit lays aside her shop apron, they both take the lane up towards the Neck Road and then the path down to the south side.

Kit has arrived home at the tail end of the caplin scull, and it's caplin weather, misty and cool. "I'm that sick of caplin, I don't care if I never sees another," says Trif, who has been hauling buckets of the small fish up from the beach to her garden for fertilizer. This evening no-one is out catching caplin; the small fish are gone and already on a few stages around the beach

That *Forgetful* Shore

codfish are laid out to dry. A few men still fish the waters off the Point, though fishing hasn't been good here for years.

"Mother says she remembers when she was a girl, the Long Beach all lined off with fish drying, all summer long, and every man, woman and child would be working at the fish," Kit says.

"Uncle Albert says the same thing," Trif says. Now almost all the fishermen go down on the Labrador for the summer, either alone or with their families. Except for the short weeks of the caplin fishery, the beach is quiet during summer.

"Father finally gave me his permission today," Kit says after a moment's silence. They sit side by side on the smooth beach rocks, looking out at the waves. "I'm sailing on the *Bruce* at the end of August. I'm sorry. I mean, I'm not sorry, but –"

"You're sorry for me."

"Not – not *sorry* for you." She knows Trif will never want to be pitied. "Sorry you're not coming with me. I wish it was something we could do together."

"So do I. But we can't. And anyway, you won't be alone. You'll be with Ben."

Kit is sorry about that too – sorry that Trif doesn't have a Ben in her life, doesn't have anyone but the alarmingly faithful Jacob John. "I honestly thought he'd have give up by now," Trif says, when Kit steers the conversation in that direction.

"Perhaps he thought *you* would have given up by now," Kit counters. "Given up saying no."

"Well, I haven't and I'm not," Trif says. But she sounds less sure than when they've had this conversation in the past. She won't meet Kit's eyes. "Everyone keeps telling me he has his own house."

"Well, he does." They both look up at the solid bulk of the Russell house, standing sentinel across the road like the guardian of the beach.

"His mother is still in it, though. The boys are both gone – Ned to the lumber woods and Josiah to North Sydney. Mrs. Russell says she'll move over to Bay Roberts with Liza when Jacob John gets married, but what if she don't? Not much good having a house of your own if it got your mother-in-law in it."

"No, that'd be worse than keeping house for Aunt Rachel. Better the devil you know."

"I don't mind, really,"

"Don't mind what? Marrying Jacob John?"

"No! Don't mind – you know. Going on as I'm doing. Keeping house for Aunt Rachel and Uncle Albert, looking out for the young ones. I'm not saying I don't wish I was in your shoes, but I'm at peace with it. 'Tis God's will for my life, and I trust Him."

"Do you think God's got a plan for after?"

"After what?"

"After the youngsters grow up and leave home. When they don't need you so much anymore. What are you going to do then?"

"The Lord could have come by then. He's coming soon, and it's more important for me to be ready for that than to look for someone to marry with a house of his own."

"You really believe that, do you?"

Trif doesn't answer. Kit knows her friend has a kind of faith she can never approach or imagine. Trif has always had faith, but since taking up with the Seventh-day Adventists she has augmented her belief in a personal God who watches out for her every move, with a belief that Judgement Day is coming in a year or two, thus making all future plans moot. Fortunately she has not been fervent in trying to convert Kit to her beliefs. The possibility that the world might end before Kit gets to go to university, sit in classes, graduate, teach in a bigger school, marry Ben, see the world – the thought of being cut short from doing all those things is as much hell as Kit will ever need to contemplate. Kit has her heaven here on earth, all spread out like the beach rocks at her feet, every stone a possibility.

Still, Kit realizes that for all Trif's trust in the Lord, she doesn't laugh off the idea of Jacob John as she used to. Time is passing. Trif, like Kit, is eighteen. Hardly an old maid, but unlike Kit, Triffie does not have new opportunities and new possibilities beckoning. Apart from the hope of the Lord coming to pluck her out of this narrow life, her possibilities are becoming fewer. What will she be, once her cousins are raised and out of the house? A dependent relation, a burden to her aunt and uncle? No wonder Trif turns her eyes from the stones at her feet to the sky above, waiting for the Lord to whisk her away.

Jacob John Russell is no Mr. Darcy, nor even the equal of Ben Porter. And he certainly is not the Lord Jesus come riding down on a white cloud. But he is not without his appeal. As Kit has cause to know.

Kit watches and waits. There's no courting in summer. Men who fish off the Point are out in boat from before dawn till mid-afternoon; their women and children spend hours on the flakes, gutting and splitting fish, laying it out to dry. Other families are gone entirely, off to the Labrador. In many families, like Triffie's, the men are gone and the women and children stay behind, caring for chickens and pigs, tilling the gardens to grow the vegetables that will make the difference between hunger and plenty when winter comes. Uncle Albert is gone on Skipper Wilf Parsons' schooner; so is Jacob John Russell. But Jacob John's name comes up in conversation more often than it has in previous summers, and each time Kit takes note of the look in Trif's eye and the tone in her voice.

"You're going to come round, you know," Kit tells Triffie one evening. And instead of the usual denial, she hears Trif say, "I s'pose I am, after all."

"To Jacob John? Do you really think you will?"

"At least before he left in the spring he asked me for my hand instead of asking Uncle Albert for it." Trif shrugs. "I could do worse. I s'pose that's the furthest thing you could say from true love, isn't it? 'Why did you marry him?' 'I thought I could do worse.' But life's not a novel, Peony. I got to take what God gives me, and what if He's give me Jacob John?"

Kit has no words. She moves closer to Triffie – they are sitting on the bridge of Kit's house, enjoying the warm evening breeze – and puts her arms around her. "I wish it were different. I wish you were head-over-heels in love with him."

Triffie laughed. "With Jacob John? No chance. But I don't mind. I don't need love. I do need a place of my own."

Again the weight of secrets, stories untold, tugs at Kit like a tide. But what can she say? It's not a matter of spoiling her Posy's happiness, for Trif is not happy. But she is – what? Content, perhaps, or resigned at least. It's not much on which to build the hope of happiness, but she could have even less than this.

Their last outing together before Kit leaves is a melancholy one. Sadie Parsons is buried in the little graveyard behind the Methodist Church. Her father and her brother Ted are still down on the Labrador; her mother cries bitterly in the arms of Jabez Badcock, who has stayed home from the fishery to be at Sadie's side and entreat God to spare her. Jabez looks more devastated even than Sadie's mother does; his handsome young face is hollowed and grim. Kit remembers Sadie, not as the frail invalid of the past two summers but as a laughing schoolgirl. Her best chum, Millie Butler, comes to stand by Kit and Trif. Triffie reaches out an arm to put around Millie's shoulders and draw her in, and the three girls stand together looking into the grave. Jabez throws a clod of dirt on Sadie's coffin, and her mother throws another. The solid thud of earth against wood echoes with grim finality. Except for the minister, nobody has a word to say.

Three days later, Kit is on board the *Bruce*, sailing for Nova Scotia.

That *Forgetful* Shore

Triffie

Missing Point
November, 1909

My dearest Peony,

Please, I beg of you, tear up this letter and throw it away once you have read it. I sit here at the kitchen table in Jacob John's house – my house, I suppose – on my first morning as a Wife, and ask myself what have I done? I have married a man who does not share my Faith, nor my Interests, nor any of my Ambitions, a man who has courted me in his own sorry fashion for two years, yet knows me no better now than if we had just met in passing on the road.

He never said he loved me, only that I wouldn't do better than him and he couldn't do better than me. And the sad truth is, he was right. So I made my vows, without even you, my dearest Friend, to stand by my side – not that I can fault you for not being here, for you are far away, and Fall is the only season in which a fisherman will even consider a wedding.

I cannot shake the misgiving, that I have made a terrible mistake.

I said you ought to tear up this letter. Do not tear it; burn it. Burn it, and blow the ashes on the wind. And think of your own dear

Posy, uprooted and planted in a strange Garden, yet still growing all Alone.

Triffie signs the letter. She folds it, seals it in an envelope, writes Kit's new address on it. Halifax, Nova Scotia.

Her mind runs through the scenes of the day before – the crowded, jumbled hours. They were married with a handful of witnesses in the parlour of this house, her new home. Jacob John's mother looked cross, having agreed to move out but clearly not happy with it. Aunt Rachel and Uncle Albert looked relieved – that was the only possible word for it. Jacob John looked pleased with himself. God alone knows what Trif looked like.

The rest of the afternoon and evening half the people on the Point crowded into the kitchen and parlour, eating the cake and biscuits Aunt Rachel had baked, drinking her blueberry wine or, for the more abstemious, tea. The boys had something stronger, down on the beach. Jabez Badcock, who since Sadie's death has thrown over his teetotalling Methodist principles, brought a few bottles of rum, she heard, and the fellows lit a bonfire down there. Some of the girls went down and danced on the beach with them in the cold night air, but Triffie stayed up in the kitchen receiving everyone's good wishes, wishing it were all over. Hoping Jacob John had a good few drinks of that rum, that he might get too drunk to want anything from her later on.

The party on the beach broke up when Jabez started a fight with Fred Mercer, then passed out and had to be carried home. Jacob John came back to his house, his steps steady, and took his bride up the narrow staircase to the marriage bed.

The sky is dark, with an hour to go before dawn. Jacob John is still asleep upstairs. Trif thinks of waking beside him tomorrow and the next day and every morning till one of them dies.

She holds the letter beside the candle and thinks, *Why give Kit the trouble?* The trouble of reading, the trouble of burning, the trouble of knowing.

She sets the letter to the candle's flame and drops it in her wash basin, watching it flare briefly and then crumble to ash.

That *Forgetful* Shore

Triffie

Missing Point
November, 1909

*My dearest Peony – Just a note to say that the Deed is Done. Mr. R.
and I are settled in the house of our own – ourselves and no other, as
promised. How I wish you could have been with me on the day, dear
one – it was all that I wished of happiness in that fateful hour.*

*Ever your own,
Posy*

Triffie brings the postcard, along with a letter she is sending to Millicent
Butler in Harbour Grace, to the Bay Roberts post office in time to catch the
mid-week mail. It's a pleasantly crisp day for so late in the fall, the sky a
shade of blue more often seen in October than the gray end of November,
and Trif walks around the long way, not taking the causeway but going
around the Coish, past Country Path and down by Long Beach Pond, till
she comes in sight of the Russell house. Her house.

　　She stops to look at it, taking pleasure in its trim appearance, the white
paint, the green shutters. Two pine trees in the front yard, still green now
that the birch and maples are bare, frame the neat saltbox house. She opens
the gate – her front gate – and goes up the path and around the house to her

own back door.

"You looks right like you belongs here," Jacob John says to her that evening as she cooks salt fish and potatoes for his supper. He leans in the kitchen doorway, arms folded across his chest. He looks pleased with himself, to have a wife here in his kitchen.

"I s'pose I do belong here now," Trif says, though she won't give him the pleasure of turning around to look at him, to see his self-satisfied grin. He's got what he wants, and though he knows full well it's the house and the promise of a married woman's status that won her, he's as smug as if he had truly won her heart. He's not one to talk of love himself, so why should the fact that she's not in love with him give him any trouble? It's a practical arrangement, Triffie tells herself, and it should suit them both just fine.

It certainly seems to suit Jacob John fine. He glows with self-importance, enjoying his status as a man with a wife and a house of his own, though he's not yet twenty-one. He sits beside her in the pew on Sunday morning and gloats about the fact that he no longer has to seek permission to walk her home. Somewhat to her surprise, he doesn't object when she and Aunt Hepsy go over to Mabel Dawe's house in Bay Roberts on Sabbath morning for the Adventist service. He makes the odd crack about the beasts of Revelation or the prophetess Mrs. White, but he never tells her not to go to Sabbath service, nor does he mind that his dinner on Saturday is warmed over from the night before, nor that his wife does no housework on the seventh day. And when Reverend White corners Triffie after church one Sunday to lecture her about her wayward beliefs Jacob John interrupts, drawing her away with a hand on her arm. "I'll look to my own missus, thank you, Reverend," he says. "Don't the Good Book say the women should listen in silence, and ask their husbands to teach them at home?"

Reverend White, unaccustomed to hearing Scripture on the lips of young Jacob John Russell, is speechless long enough for Jacob John to bid him good-day. Triffie is speechless too, till she busts out laughing.

"So you're going to take to instructing me in Scripture at home, are you?" she says finally.

"Some chance I'd have of that," he replies. "About as much chance as there'd be of you ever learning in silence."

But he says no more about it than that. In the evenings when work is done, he doesn't seem to mind that Triffie reads instead of knitting or sewing. He often goes out in the evenings when she would rather stay home; he

That *Forgetful* Shore

visits Fred Mercer, now married to Minnie Dawe, or he goes to sit with the men in Joe French's shed, mending nets and telling stories. But he doesn't drink and he's always home by the time Trif is ready to put out the lamp and go to bed.

Bed. It's the hard part of the day for Triffie. She has always described Jacob John, to others and to herself, as "not bad looking," though "handsome" would be a stretch. He's a little man, not quite as tall as she is herself, with sandy hair and a beard he keeps neatly trimmed. His ready smile and the quick gleam in his eye draw people to him; he's by no means unappealing or ugly. Triffie simply has no interest in what goes on in the bedroom. Never has had much interest in it, to tell the truth. She and Kit puzzled out many of the basic facts by applying animal physiology to human when they were still in school, but the reality of the act remained a mystery to Trif until her wedding night and she wouldn't mind at all if it had remained a mystery forever.

Jacob John clearly has some sort of experience, though she has no desire to know where he's obtained it. He isn't rough or brutal, but neither is there anything in the whole process to make Trif see what the fuss is all about. If this is the business that drives lovers mad – if it's for these few minutes' awkward fumbling in a dark chilly bedroom that people leave their marriages and children, ruin their reputations, imperil their souls – well, Triffie simply can't see the point. Why bother?

There are moments – sitting by the fire at night, perhaps, her reading a book and him fixing the rungs on an old chair or putting a new handle on a hammer – that she feels almost fond of Jacob John. But she feels nothing close to passion, and nothing that happens in the bedroom seems likely to stir her in that direction.

At Christmas time, she misses Kit, who has always come home for the holiday before but can't afford the steamer fare from Nova Scotia this year. She and Jacob John go over to Uncle Albert and Aunt Rachel's for dinner on Christmas Day, and Triffie revels in the feeling she has every time she steps over their threshold now, the independence that allows her to come as a visitor and leave to go back to her own house. It's a wonderful thing not to be beholden to them.

She asks Will how school is going; she misses the daily company of her young cousins, though not the responsibility of caring for them. "I nearly got that hove over," he says. "I'm still trying to get through that old Fourth Reader, and Mother says I got to stay in school till we goes to the Labrador in the spring, but after that I'm not going back no more."

"He's not going down on the Labrador this year, is he?" Trif asks.

"I can't keep him back no more." Aunt Rachel sighs.

"Time for him to go," Jacob John says, chiming in to support Uncle Albert and Will. "Lots of boys goes before they're twelve and it does nobody no harm."

"And it's not like he likes school, not like you," Uncle Albert points out. Ruth, at fourteen, is also finished with school now. Trif wishes there were one other person in the family who cares about learning, who sees the wonder to be found in books.

"The only thing I'll miss about school is Trif helping me with my lessons," Will says. "And you don't do that no more anyway, Trif, now that you're married, so why should I care? I always liked hearing you read stories and poems, but I never liked reading them for myself."

"I can still read to you," Trif says. The boy often drops over to their house on the south side to hang about the kitchen or go out in the shed with Jacob John to do some small task. To her surprise, his eyes brighten a little at the mention of reading, so she repeats the invitation. "Next time you comes over our way, maybe on a Sunday afternoon or sometime I'm not too busy, I'll read something to you."

She looks at her one shelf of carefully hoarded books later, trying to pick one that might appeal to Will. He takes her at her word and shows up the first Sunday afternoon in January, a blowy, blustery day with swirls of snow streeling across the road. Isaac French is with him, and they both sit to listen as Triffie begins *Gulliver's Travels*. The next Sunday, they bring Char Mercer with them, and it becomes a routine – Trif reads to the three boys, and to Jacob John too if he'll sit still long enough to listen, through the long monotonous hours of Sunday afternoon. They all stay for their suppers, filling the house with their lively energy, and Jacob John doesn't say a word about how much they eat or begrudge them space at the table.

As winter draws in, there is more visiting in the long evenings, and Trif more often leaves her fireside after supper and joins Jacob John at the home of a neighbour or relative. One night he coaxes her up to old Uncle Jedidiah Mercer's place, just a few doors up from them on the South Side Road. She knows that evenings at Uncle Jed's always turn toward recitations, songs and stories as people huddle around the woodstove. When she and Jacob John blow in, Trif counts fifteen people crowded into Aunt Sal's kitchen. All the women have knitting to keep their hands busy though the men mostly sit still, listening while Uncle Jed tells the story of the *Greenland* disaster and sings a long song, verse after verse, to go along with it.

Over on the floor by the stove she sees young Charlie, Isaac and Will. There are two other young married couples, and several older men on their own, their wives no doubt home with the children. Jabez Badcock stands in a corner looking gloomy, as he always does now except when he's drunk. And Joe Bishop sits in a chair pulled up to the table, nodding and drumming his fingers on the tabletop along with the rhythm of Uncle Jed's song. When the song ends and a babble of chatter breaks out again in the room, Joe turns around to talk her. "You're looking well, Mrs. Russell."

She smiles at the name, still unfamiliar to her. "I am well, Mr. Bishop. Did you have any more books come in lately?"

"In fact I've got one here tonight; I brought it up thinking I might see you, or else I might have dropped it in at your door as I passed."

Triffie takes the book and turns it over in her hands. *Ivanhoe.* "A friend of mine in town sent out a box of the novels of Sir Walter Scott," Mr. Bishop said. "I wonder what you think of them for the children."

"I've only read *Waverly* – there used to be an old copy in the school-room, wasn't there? I think the boys would like this one, though," Trif says, leafing through it.

"Perhaps *Rob Roy* as well?" Joe suggests.

"I'll read this one first and tell you what I think. But if I like it, some of them might hear it from me before they hear it from you in school." She holds it up across the room for Will to see, a promise for future Sunday afternoons.

Joe Bishop laughs. "I don't mind," he says. "You're better at reading to them than I am, and the boys are lucky to have you. Young Char has already given up on school, you know, and I don't see Will or Isaac staying at it much longer, once they've gone fishing. But having you read to them is an education in itself. I wish we could still have you back in the class-room – but married life agrees with you, for all that."

"It might agree with you too, if you found yourself a woman," Trif says, surprised at her own brazenness. Being a married woman has made it possible for her to talk to a man like Joe Bishop as an equal, to tease him about his still-unmarried state. The man is well into his thirties, starting to go bald on top of his high-domed forehead, and still no woman in sight. His neck and cheeks colour a little as he laughs off her comment. "Sure, who'd have me?" he asks, as Uncle Jed starts another song.

Some lucky woman, Trif thinks, and that thought surprises her as much as her earlier bold words. She never had the schoolgirl crush on Mr. Bishop that Kit did, maybe because she never dared imagine herself growing up into a girl that a schoolteacher might court and love. And indeed, she didn't; she is a fisherman's wife, as she was always fated to be. But now that she is a wife, she allows herself a daydream of sharing a house with Joe Bishop, the both of them reading by lamplight at night, stopping to read aloud a line or two to each other, to discuss the meaning of a poem or talk about what he was teaching in his classroom.

Then she firmly lays such thoughts aside. This is not the sin of lust, exactly, but something very like it. Coveting, perhaps – not thy neighbour's husband, but a man other than her own husband.

The thoughts flit through her mind as she watches Joe Bishop's face while Jabez Badcock picks up the fiddle and plays a mournful "Barb'ry Allen." Occasionally he interrupts his own playing to sing a verse, in his fine tenor voice that was once heard leading the hymns at the Methodist Chapel.

Young Willie died for me today,
And I'll die for him tomorrow.

The fiddle plays out its last sad notes and the singer echoes the final lines:

And the rose … grew 'round … the briar.

In the silence following the song, Joe turns back to her. "Mrs. Russell should give us a recitation," he suggests. When Trif shakes her head no, he says, "The best student I ever had for recitations and poems? How can you say no?" and a chorus of her neighbours' voices joins in.

It's Will's plea that finally convinces her: "Give us that Highwayman, Trif. That's some good poem, that is."

So Trif sits up a little straighter on her chair, clears her throat and begins. *The road was a ribbon of moonlight over the purple moor…*

There are eyes on her: Joe Bishop's eyes, warm with pride; the eyes of Will and his friends, wide with interest. Her husband's eyes, but she cannot read his expression, and she turns away from his gaze, back to the boys.

The highwayman came riding, riding, riding,
The highwayman came riding, up to the old inn-door.

That *Forgetful* Shore

Kit

Halifax, Nova Scotia
February, 1910

My dearest Posy,

I am sure that when you think of my life here in Halifax, you imagine it to be one of Great Glamour, but I can assure it is Not At All as you might picture. I say this because of my own Phantasies, before I came here, of what University life must be like, and how little that accords with <u>Reality</u>.

It is true, we do have the opportunity to study with some very Learned Professors, almost all of them Male, and it can be heady stuff to hear a college lecturer holding forth upon, let us say, Hamlet or Othello. But the reality is that it is, after all, schoolwork and more schoolwork, with higher expectations than ever I had placed on me at Spencer. This week alone I have two long Themes due, and three books to read. I find myself burning the lamp <u>till</u> <u>the</u> <u>midnight</u> <u>hour</u> trying to keep up with everything, and I hope this excuses my lack of correspondence of late!

Some of these same learned men are most Condescending towards the women students, as I have discovered. The same professor who holds forth with such knowledge on the subject of Hamlet and his Fatal Indecision, has in his lecture hall some thirty-five young men, and six women. He addresses himself entirely to the men, to the extent of calling the whole class "Sirs" as he lectures – till he remembers himself, and adds with a chuckle, "oh, and ladies, of course." He was most dismissive of Ophelia, and said that she was a person of no true Weight or Substance, nor had any real impact upon the action of the play, but that her only goal was to fall in love and seek a husband – "not unlike a modern young lady attending a University!" he added, to a chorus of great laughter all around.

Yet, much as it shames me to say it, there is some truth to his condescension. Along with some of my classmates who are, like me, quite dedicated to the Serious Business of getting an education, there is certainly a class of young women, I have discovered, whose parents can afford to send them to University simply to capture a University man as a husband. I cannot think but that there must be simpler and less expensive ways for a girl of good family to meet a man of similar background. Do these sort of people not have parties and teas and dances? Do they not go to church, or visit in one another's homes?

But no, nothing must do but that Priscilla or Annabelle must be packed off to Dalhousie with a dozen fancy gowns, and aim herself for a target among the pre-medicine or pre-law students, for nothing but a doctor or a lawyer will do – one already wealthy enough that he need not work for a living, but will take up a profession, it seems, merely to further the cause of Medicine or the Law, by his own brilliance.

Oh dear, will you read this letter and think that your darling Peony has become most Sarcastic and Cynical? Remember if you do, that these seeds were planted in me at the earliest possible age, only that there is something in the climate of Canada that brings them to Germination!!

Ever your dearest,
Peony

The time it takes to write a letter severely cuts into Kit's study time. She has cut back correspondence to only the most essential people, relegating old friends from Missing Point, newer friends in Elliston, and classmates from Spencer, to the occasional postcard. Only her mother and Triffie get proper letters anymore, and never as often as they would like. But at least the letters to Trif, unlike the carefully worded ones to her mother, are something of a release.

The only two people she feels she can be honest with are Triffie and Ben, though even there she has to be cautious. With Triffie, she doesn't want to make her life sound too interesting, lest Triffie be sunk in despair and jealousy, for even college life on its worst and most crushing days has to be better than being stuck back on the Point with Jacob John Russell. With Ben her trouble is the opposite: she cannot truly tell him how tired, how overwhelmed, how insignificant she often feels in the whirl of college life, for she never wants him to regret making it possible for her to be here.

Balancing her letters to Triffie and conversations with Ben allows her to be, on average, tolerably honest: she can talk about the pleasures of her life with Ben, and the hardships with Triffie. To her mother she composes tidy little screeds that indicate that she is healthy, eating well, studying hard enough to get good marks and keep her scholarship, but not hard enough to tax her brains and lose her looks. She assures her parents she is cleaning her teeth and moving her bowels regularly, since her mother asks about these things.

She lives in a boarding house. Her life since leaving home thus far has been marked by boarding houses: first the eerie quiet of Cousin Ethel's home in St. John's, where she lived out her nun-like existence at Spencer and seldom had a conversation above a whisper. Then came her hard-working stint as Mrs. Chaulk's boarder and servant girl in Elliston. In both those cases Kit was the sole boarder; here in Halifax she is one of four young ladies renting rooms from a Mrs. Peabody, who takes in young women students although she makes it very clear she does not approve of higher education for women.

"I'm only trying to do what your poor mothers would do if they were here," she told the girls around her dining room table on the night Kit arrived. "If all was as it should be, you would be home with them, or married already, but in this day and age when young girls go wandering so far from home, as Eve wandered from Adam's side in the garden of Eden, I can only hope to shield you from the worst of temptation."

"She seems very determined we won't eat from the Tree of Knowledge, anyway," Maggie Campbell says to Kit later, recalling the Adam-and-Eve lecture. Mrs. Peabody's rules preclude staying up past ten o'clock, even in your own room making no noise: if she notices the lamp burning she raps sharply on the door. This is meant to save both lamp oil and their health, for it is not good, Mrs. Peabody assures them, for young ladies to sit up too late.

Maggie, a farm girl from Prince Edward Island, is Kit's closest friend among her fellow co-eds. She is a hearty, buxom redhead with a broad freckled face. Maggie and Kit formed an alliance in their first days at Mrs. Peabody's, recognizing their similarity in background and a shared sense of humour. The other two girls in the house are prime examples of the society daughters who so annoy Kit. Louisa Arthur is the daughter of a doctor in Saint John, while Felicity MacTavish's father owns a shipyard in Lunenberg.

Neither is empty-headed, Kit is forced to admit; Felicity is, in fact, quite brilliant, and Louisa is clever enough. Neither of them would have gotten to university if she were stupid. But the academic aspect of college life is clearly secondary to the social, in their minds. Serving on committees, meeting the right people and getting invited to various dances and teas by the right young men are their preoccupations. Louisa and Felicity dominate dinner conversation with their gossip and flirtations, while Kit and Maggie roll their eyes at each other.

Kit excuses herself from such dinners as quickly as possible and goes to her room to study. Sometimes she and Maggie study together, but Mrs. Peabody disapproves of girls gathering in their rooms and talking, even to study.

They have to be in the house by nine, which means if they want to go the library, they have to leave immediately after supper. Often, Kit will go, by herself or with Maggie, to meet Ben in the library for a few hours' study before curfew.

Despite the snobbish society girls, despite the long hours of work and the landlady who seems determined to make those hours as difficult as possible, Kit is having a wonderful time. Better than she would ever want to admit to Triffie, or to her mother. Only to Ben, in their rare moments alone, can she say, "Thank you. This is what I wanted … this is where I wanted to be."

"I know," he says into her hair, his lips tracing a path from her temple, down the line of her jaw. His fingers move as lightly, from her shoulders to her waist, pulling her closer to him.

That *Forgetful* Shore

This particular moment is being stolen in a dusty corner of the library, between tall stacks of books. Ben's courses keep him studying around the clock, and he warns her things will be even worse when he's in law school. He has promised his parents, and the great-uncle who is helping with his tuition, that he won't get married until he has his law degree.

Sometimes, Kit is grateful for this promise. She wants to finish her own degree, to teach a few more years, in some place bigger and more cosmopolitan than Missing Point or Elliston. She pictures herself as a mistress in a girl's school somewhere – not Spencer, perhaps – not yet – but she knows her teaching career will end when she marries Ben. She is enjoying this stage of life, is usually in no hurry to move onto the next.

Then he pulls her close, touches her, breathes against her skin, and she wonders how they can wait even a day, much less four or five years.

There is a way around this, of course – a way to have the delicious bliss of Ben's touch without the responsibilities of married life, just yet. But whatever might have happened in the past, Kit has no intentions of making that suggestion to Ben. He is a modern man in many ways – approving of education for women, wanting her to have her own career in the years until she's ready to be a lawyer's wife. But she suspects his morals are very traditional in most important ways. If he were to dally before marriage, it would be with some lower-class girl, some bit of fluff who meant nothing to him. Not with the woman he sees as an equal, the woman he intends to marry.

Unless she's wrong about him. Sometimes, Kit hopes she's wrong.

But it's not as if they'd have much opportunity to find out, with Kit living under the keen eye of Mrs. Peabody. College women are closely watched, and not just by their landladies, for the slightest hint of improper behavior. Some people still feel that having women in the university lowers the tone, makes immorality more likely. Modern women who seek to step out of their proper roles seem to be inherently suspect, their morals loose.

Maggie not only recognizes this stereotype but relishes it. Not that she's immoral; she's a true innocent, in many ways, Kit thinks, and certainly a virgin. But she plans to be a journalist after she gets her B.A. – "and everyone knows newspaper women are round-heeled," Maggie giggles.

"So when do you plan to start? Being round-heeled?" Kit teases.

"Oh, not till I've got a job with a real newspaper. Then I'll start having affairs with editors and politicians, sleeping my way to the top," Maggie laughs. The contrast between Maggie's apple-cheeked innocence and her brazen talk entertains Kit, but she is too cautious to join in such joking. Some jokes cut too close to the bone.

One evening, Kit and Maggie are studying in the parlour – a cold, formal and unwelcoming room, but one where Mrs. Peabody has grudgingly given the girls permission to work. Kit is writing a theme for her English class on "My Favourite Place," trying to find words that will paint a picture of the Long Beach in Missing Point for the eyes of those who have never been there. When she tries to describe the place to Maggie, whose concept of beauty has been trained by the red fields and sandy shores of another island, Kit can see she's not getting it across properly. "Rocky beaches!" Maggie shakes her head. "It all sounds so bleak – as if the sun never shines there!"

The sun does shine there – it shines in Kit's memories of the Long Beach, though she hasn't managed to convey this in words, either speaking to Maggie or writing her theme. In her mind's eye the sun sparkles on the water of the bay, the long reach of water surrounded by the encircling green arms of the Point on one side and Bareneed on the other. The round beach rocks at her feet are washed by salt water till they gleam like polished gems, and rather than the uniform grey Maggie imagines, they are each a subtly different colour, hues of red and brown and slate and pearl revealed when the waves peel back to uncover the treasure beneath.

That's what she wants to say – something that will capture the beauty of the place she was so glad to leave, something that will explain how it haunts her still.

She rereads the three paragraphs already in her composition book. Nothing she's written comes close to what she hopes to say.

Fortunately, she is spared further mental effort by the arrival of Louisa and Felicity, who blow into the room like leaves on an autumn breeze, as gaily coloured and noisy.

"Oh, working again, are you two? Do you ever stop?" Louisa has obviously practiced her laugh to make it sound like a merry tinkle, though the effect is sometimes a little shrill.

"Oh, darling, but that's unkind," Felicity says. "You know they must study, it's different when you have to keep up a scholarship, isn't it, my sweethearts? You keep right on burying your pretty little heads in the books. You'll make all the folks back home proud, won't you?" Nobody, even after years of practice, would ever describe Felicity's laugh as a tinkle; it barely escapes sounding like a donkey's bray, an effect unfortunately magnified by

That *Forgetful* Shore

her rather long face.

"Where have you two butterflies alighted this evening, then?" Kit asks, trying to keep her own tone as light as theirs. Maggie has a nasty temper and hates being patronized, and no good can come of starting a fight. It's Kit's job, as she sees it, to steer things into smoother waters.

"Oh, we've been to a little dinner party – just a few people, quite intimate – at Judge Gordon's house. You know, Bill's father, the judge?"

"Oh, is Bill's father a judge? Really?" Maggie says, the picture of wide-eyed innocence. Louisa is normally immune to sarcasm, but this is so broad even she can't ignore it, and she shoots Maggie a withering look.

While Felicity juggles half a dozen beaus and tries to decide which she likes best, Louisa settled early in the academic year on a young law student by the name of William Gordon. They have been keeping company steadily for a few months now, and while Louisa occasionally comments on Bill's fine personal qualities, she is far more likely to mention the fact that his father is a judge.

"Still, she must care about him at least a little, mustn't she?" Kit poses the question to Maggie afterwards, when Maggie creeps into Kit's room to gossip under cover of darkness.

"What, Louisa? Love Judge Gordon's son? I'm surprised she even remembers his name is Bill. I'm sure she thinks of him entirely as Judge Gordon's son, the future Judge Gordon. Which would make her, of course, the future Mrs. Judge Gordon."

"Ah well, she's the ice maiden, I suppose. No passionate affairs for Louisa."

Maggie chuckles again, a low throaty sound. "That's what she'd like you to think, but I know different. There's plenty of fire in our Louisa, just not for Judge Gordon Junior."

"What do you mean?"

"She's got a secret. A secret *beau*," Maggie clarifies, in case Kit has missed the point.

According to Maggie, there's a boy from the Island, a second cousin of Maggie's uncle's new wife, named Roddy MacCallum. He's in college on a scholarship, a hard-working farm boy studying to be an engineer. He's handsome and charming, but poorer even than Maggie or Kit.

"And he's crazy about Louisa, it seems, and too sweet to realize she's just stringing him along while she waits for Judge Gordon Junior to

That *Forgetful* Shore

propose." Maggie finishes recounting the tale she has heard through Islander gossip. "They've been meeting in secret, going for walks in Point Pleasant Park when she's supposedly studying at the library."

"Roddy's not very good at carrying on secret affairs, is he?"

There's a certain pleasure in knowing something naughty about Louisa, and Kit can't resist occasionally dropping a hint that she knows about Roddy – like smiling when Louisa takes a baked potato at the dinner table and saying, "Louisa's fond of potatoes, isn't she, Maggie? Do you think she likes potato farmers as well?"

"No, she likes lawyers. Who are going to grow up to judges, and be very, very wealthy. Isn't that right, Louisa?" Maggie's not entirely pleased to have let Kit in on a secret previously known only to a group of loosely related people from Prince Edward Island's North Shore, and gets cross when Kit drops hints about it.

Kit and Maggie become no closer friends with Louisa and Felicity as the winter term wears on, and no fonder of their boarding house and its land-lady, but apart from that Kit enjoys Dalhousie. She does well enough in her classes to hope for a scholarship that will help with next year's tuition. She joins Delta Gamma and the Philomathic Society; she makes friends. Even the four residents of Mrs. Peabody's boarding house are bonded, to a degree, by the avalanche of work that descends upon them in mid-March as they write final papers and study for examinations.

"Rotten luck for poor Louisa, getting pneumonia so close to finals," Kit says as she and Maggie study French together.

Maggie grins a smile quite devoid of sympathy. "*Tant pis!*" she says. Her schoolbook French is sometimes peppered with expressions not found in the textbook, picked up from the French villagers back home. As for Kit, her own language is becoming peppered with expressions like "rotten luck" which sound like they were stolen from English novels, and would be considered putting on airs if she used them back on the Point. What traces of her accent were not ironed out at Spencer are being smoothed away now.

"You don't feel sorry for her? You are hard-hearted."

"I don't feel sorry for her, *and* I don't believe she has pneumonia. I think our Louisa is in an embarrassing predicament."

"She's in … a what?" It takes Kit a moment to understand. "You don't mean…"

"I do mean."

That *Forgetful* Shore

"How do you know?"

Maggie smiles and lays a finger next to her nose, a gesture Kit has never actually seen someone do before.

"No, you have to tell me. Are you sure about this?"

"Very sure. Roddy told me himself. And that's a complete secret, not to be breathed to anyone."

It doesn't matter. After Louisa spends several days alone in her room with consultations from a doctor and tearful visits from Felicity, her parents sweep down upon the boarding house and carry Louisa away. Felicity goes around the house weeping and says she doesn't know if she can write her exams, she's so upset.

"Why?" Kit probes. "Has Louisa got something more serious than pneumonia? Is she going to die?"

"Of course she's not going to die!" Felicity snaps. "Oh, I wouldn't expect you to understand!"

By the time finals come around the news is all over Halifax. Louisa Arthur will not be writing her examinations, nor will she be marrying William Gordon. She also will not be marrying Roddy MacCallum, though Maggie says Roddy has offered. Everything is hushed up, yet somehow everyone knows that she has gone home for a period of nine months or so, and that once that period is over some tiny waif will be dispatched to an orphanage. Louisa's life will then continue on a different course, one plotted not by Louisa but by Destiny, if one believes in that sort of thing.

"What a little fool she must have been," Ben says one soft April evening as he and Kit walk in Point Pleasant Park and she tells him all she's heard about the sad tale of Louisa. "Going around with one fellow when she was supposed to be keeping company with another."

"Are you using 'fool' because there's a less polite word you won't use in front of a lady friend?"

"Maybe. But whatever else she was, she was a fool too, to think she'd get away with it."

It's the very sort of thing, of course, that sets tongues wagging, fodder for those – like Mrs. Peabody – who think that educating girls lowers the moral tone of society, not to mention the moral tone of the girls themselves. But as Ben pulls her behind a leafy willow and draws her into his arms, Kit finds it hard to discern exactly what lesson Louisa's tale might have for her.

Triffie

THE STEAMER IS called *Home*, but for the first time it's taking her away from home. Trif feels no sorrow over that. The Point is the place where she was born, where she has lived out nineteen years of life, but it's also the place she dreams of leaving. Standing on the deck of a steamer watching the place disappear behind her has been a favourite fantasy since childhood. It's just fate's usual cruelty that decrees that the steamer in question will be taking her to the one place she's sure she'll like even less: Labrador.

Back in the fall it had never occurred to Triffie that along with all the other burdens of marriage she was taking on a commitment to the Labrador summer fishery. More than half the men on the Point fish on the Labrador every summer; some men ship off on schooners, as her Uncle Albert always did, leaving the women and children behind from June till October. Other men take their wives along, even bring their young children, as the whole family goes north to live in a tilt for the summer, catching and making fish.

Triffie knew that Jacob John's family went to Labrador every year, until his father drowned when Jacob John was fourteen. By the time Jacob John began courting Triffie, he was well entrenched in the men's routine of summers on the Labrador, so Triffie was shocked when, during the winter, he began talking about "when we goes down on the Labrador in June."

"What do you mean, we goes? I'm not going to no Labrador."

"Of course you're coming, maid," Jacob John says, sounding mildly hurt. "A man can do a lot better for himself over a summer's fishing if he got a wife onshore to make the fish."

"I don't know nothing about making fish. Aunt Rachel never went to Labrador – I don't think any of our family ever done it that way. 'Tis always been just the men going off and the women biding home."

"Well, you're in a different family now," Jacob John points out. They are having this conversation in the kitchen on a bitter February evening, huddled close by the stove for warmth. Jacob John patches the soles of his boots while Triffie knits him a new pair of vamps. "Mother always went down on the Labrador with Father, sure us youngsters grew up going down there for the summer. I didn't go out in boat till I was eleven but I was working at the fish nearly as soon as I could walk. And it's a great life up there in the summer – the long evenings, the Northern Lights – sure, you'll love it, maid."

Triffie knows she won't love it. Once over the winter Jacob John convinced her to come in the woods with him overnight when he was cutting wood, and she spent the night in his tilt on the Hodgewater Line. *One night in a tilt is enough for a lifetime*, she thinks, and she knows from talking to other women who have gone to the Labrador that they spend their summers in thin-walled shacks no better than tilts in the woods, working from dawn till dusk.

Yet she can't deny the logic of it: a family can earn more if both husband and wife go fishing rather than the man alone. Their first married winter has been a thin one and Triffie has had to eke out her supplies: with the hungry month of March coming on she is looking forward to Jacob John going sealing because she'll have only herself to feed and he'll come back with cash in hand. If they both go to Labrador, they'll have credit enough for extra flour, extra sugar, extra tea. Extra salt pork, which Trif won't eat but Jacob John relishes. A summer on the Labrador will give them a buffer against hunger and want.

"All right then, I s'pose I'll go if I got to go," she'd said, that night back in February. Now, on a June day sitting on her trunk on the deck of the *Home*, she knows she'll live to regret this.

The voyage to Labrador, though, is almost like a holiday. There are several families from the Point on board the steamer, including some young couples like themselves: Fred and Minnie Mercer, who were married back in the fall just after Trif and Jacob John; Clara and Obadiah Snow. Trif never liked Clara much, back when she was Clara Barbour, but she's always got on well enough with Minnie and now there's a bond that draws them all together. The other two young women, along with several older ones on board the steamer, tell Trif what she can expect during the long months of summer work. There's time on board the ship to sit and talk, to tell stories and jokes – a brief respite before the busy months ahead.

Nothing prepares her, though, for the reality. The tilt is every bit as bad as the one Jacob John stays in when hunting or cutting wood: it's a single room with a bare wooden pallet for a bed. Triffie unpacks her feather mattress and quilts, a few pieces of crockery and a change of clothes, and prays God will get her through.

She has grown up in a fisherman's home in a fishing village, but because of the poor fishing around the Point and the exodus of men to the Labrador every summer she has reached the age of nineteen without ever working on the flakes. She has, of course, split and gutted a fish the odd time, but never hundreds of fish, thousands of fish, hour after hour and day after day of fish, till her back kinks up from standing and bending. The salt works itself into the creases of skin till everything, even the breath in her lungs and the spit in her mouth, tastes of salt.

She learns by watching the other women. There's a kind of camaraderie down on the flakes, although, like any camaraderie among women, it's sometimes spoiled by petty nastiness. Clara Snow, despite her brief friendliness on the boat, soon reverts to her old ways, making sly comments about how Trif Russell might be clever at books but she takes longer to gut a cod than any woman Clara's ever seen. The other girls and women are kinder, give her hints on how to work more efficiently.

The children too small to work play underneath and around the flakes, and all the women take responsibility for all the children, so that no child will toddle into the sea and drown when its mother is too busy or exhausted to notice. Despite the grim labour there is laughter, gossip, even snatches of song. Trif is glad to be treated like one of them, but she notices that the women's kindness doesn't include everyone. A young Indian woman with a half-breed baby was waiting for Jabez Badcock when he arrived. The girl does her share of the work, her baby strapped to her back, but the other women make no move to include her. Trif feels sorry for the girl but has no idea how to reach out to her, which makes her, she supposes, as bad as the rest of them.

That *Forgetful* Shore

The day begins long before dawn when Jacob John gets himself a mug up and goes out to fish in one of Skipper Wilf's dories with Alf and Fred Mercer. Trif rises a little later, has tea and bread and goes down to meet him when he comes in with his first catch of the day. Then her work begins, down on the flakes with the other women, working like navvies as the sun rises in the sky and flies buzz endlessly, constantly around, landing on her skin, greedily sucking her salty blood.

At least there's almost nothing she can recognize as housework, only the barest necessities of preparing simple food – they eat fish two, some- times three times a day – sweeping the worst of the dirt off the dirt floor of the tilt, and washing such clothes as are absolutely necessary. Niceties like laying a good table and keeping a tidy house belong back on the Point, which now glows in Trif's memory as a haven of culture and refinement.

She and Jacob John are so bone-weary that they fall onto the hard bed beside each other as soon as it's dark and are asleep often without exchanging a word. Sometimes whole days go by and she barely hears the sound of Jacob John's voice, and he usually so ready with a joke or a smart remark.

Sunday is the one day of rest and Triffie has to bend her convictions about the Sabbath for the first time since she learned of the seventh-day truth. There's simply no possibility here of taking two days off out of seven, nor of shifting the workday to Sunday and taking her Sabbath rest on God's holy seventh day. "It's not like I minds, you knows that," Jacob John says one Sunday, as they sit out in front of the tilt drinking tea. "I knows how much your Sabbath means to you, and if I could fish on Sunday and take Saturday off to spare you, you know I'd do it."

"No, you can't do that," Trif concedes. Everything ceases on Sunday; a man who went out in boat to catch cod on Sunday would probably be stoned to death upon setting foot on the shore, never mind his missus if she went down to the flake.

"I 'lows even God got to make exceptions on the Labrador," Jacob John says, slurping at the last of his tea.

Trif hopes God will. She has brought two books with her, her Bible and a book of poetry. On Sundays she reads a bit of both, and on Saturdays she prays for forgiveness for Sabbath-breaking, before picking up the splitting knife and getting to work. She's thought of her life as a hard-working one but never has she had so little time for reading, none at all for writing, and barely time to put together a coherent thought. On Sundays she sometimes manages a letter in hopes that she will be able to get it on a boat and it may end up back at the Point, where Kit is home from college for the summer, working at the Mercantile again.

Nearby, four little Frenches and two small Dawes gather around a tidal pool in the rocks, staring with great interest at something, probably a frog or a crab. "I'm not bringing no youngsters here," Trif says abruptly.

"What? Sure what youngsters have you got to bring?" Jacob John says.

"You know what I mean. When we haves children. I'm not hauling them down to the Labrador every summer. I'll come as long as it's just you and me, but this is no way for children to grow up."

Jacob John shrugs. "It's the way we all grew up, and it never did me nor any of the rest of us no harm. Family's together all year round, and the youngsters learns to work. It's not such a bad way to grow up."

"Well I grew up the other way and there was nothing wrong with that either," Trif says. Uncle Albert was a shadowy figure in her childhood, gone to the seal hunt for March and April and then gone fishing from June till October. He spent less than half the year at home with the result that Aunt Rachel was the dominant figure in the house: though nominally Uncle Albert was the head of the home, in reality his wife's authority was rarely challenged. Trif wonders if it's this, as much as her dislike of making fish and sleeping in a tilt, that fuels her determination to stay home once they have children. She will be undisputed mistress of her own house, ruling it in Jacob John's absence for seven months of the year. She had a taste of it in March of this year when he went to the seal hunt: for six weeks she had the place to herself. Yes, the house was lonely betimes, but Trif doesn't mind loneliness, considers it her natural state. She was able to keep house to her own rhythms, read as much as she liked. Of course if there were children she'd have more responsibilities, but she can't deny she likes having the run of the house.

But for now she is here, on the front step of a tilt in Battle Harbour, resting on the wrong Sabbath, gearing up for another assault on the flakes tomorrow at daybreak. Spreading out the fish that's been taken in and covered for fear of a drop of rain, then splitting and salting the next load as it arrives, forever and ever, world without end, amen.

The circle of children breaks up into tears and quarrels, and the mothers come running from the tilts to scold and slap and comfort. "Youngsters who

That *Forgetful* Shore

comes down here for the summer don't get a proper year of schooling, anyway," Triffie says, remembering Mr. Bishop's frustration at the empty desks in June and September. Jacob John believes that a summer at the fish teaches children the value of work, but in her mind it teaches them the value of only one kind of work. It teaches them that nothing but fishing matters and nothing else ever will.

"Well, maid, you know what we got to do, got to get busy makin' babies then, so you can stay home with 'em." He reaches over to pinch her bum and she squirms away.

"Some chance of that, working like dogs up here," she says. At home she sometimes complains Jacob John is always at her, but most nights up here they roll into bed too tired to do more than fall asleep. Jacob John is often snoring before she puts out the lamp.

"That's why God made Sunday, maid."

And indeed – not then, but after supper – they go to bed a little less tired than usual, and Jacob John heaves himself over her, and Triffie tries to bear it with as much patience and good grace as she can. A man has needs, even when he's worn to a rag working all hours of the day. She thinks again of staying home while he fishes for the summer, imagines months free of this tedious business.

It doesn't take long – it never does. Afterwards, she closes her eyes, ready to sleep, hoping dreams will take her somewhere far from Labrador. Jacob John gets up to go outside and relieve himself. But a few minutes later he's back, urging her, "Triffie! Trif, maid, get up!"

Her legs are over the side of the bed before the question is out of her mouth, "What is it?" His tone is so urgent she imagines a fire or a tidal wave.

"Come out and see." He grabs her hand, drawing her through the door as she wraps the quilt around her shoulders and goes out, bare feet and all.

Outside, the September night is still and clear, but it's already chilly here, chillier than at home in early fall. The sky arches huge and blue-black overhead, looking somehow larger and more empty here than it ever does at home, though the same stars shine. The moon is new tonight, barely a sliver, but what makes Triffie catch her breath is neither new moon nor stars, but the shimmer of coloured lights in the sky, like gauzy ribbons of yellow and green hung across a darkened window.

"Oh ... is that them? The Northern Lights?"

"It is, maid, it is. Brighter tonight than I've seen 'em for years. Some good thing I got up to take a piss just then, wasn't it?"

Jacob John's coarse talk is so incongruous against the backdrop of this lovely, shifting light that Triffie says nothing, hoping it will encourage him to keep silent too. Around the village of tilts others have seen the lights; here and there a door opens as people come out to watch, lifting the small children up on their shoulders, pointing out the wonder of the aurora to the little ones who, like Triffie, have never been here before to see it. A little distance away she sees Jabez Badcock with an arm around the shoulder of his Indian woman, and thinks that the man should stay here year-round; his handsome, haunted face looks more at home here than it has on the Point since Sadie died.

Triffie looks away from her neighbours and gazes up again, no longer feeling the knife-sharp night air, though she's shivering inside her quilt. Jacob John stands behind her, his arms around her, pulling her against his chest for warmth. "I was afraid you might not get to see them, but look at 'em," he says in her ear. "Is there anything finer than that?" He sounds as pleased as if he'd climbed up on a ladder and hung the lights in the sky himself, just for her pleasure. Then he has the decency to keep quiet and let her watch, till the last wisp of light fades and the display has ended, and they go back into the tilt to sleep.

That *Forgetful* Shore

Triffie

THE ROOM IS small, dim and warm, heated by the muggy weather outside. The curtains are drawn, shutting out the view of the sea that Triffie loves. The light hurts her eyes. She has been in labour for fourteen hours, since she woke in the middle of the night and felt the cramping pain in her belly.

She got up then, wrapped herself in her robe, paced the room, riding out those first shallow waves of pain. The moon rose on the water, making a path of light across the dark waves.

She delayed waking Jacob John until she cried out in pain and couldn't keep it back. When the noise woke him and she told him she'd been up for an hour he said, "How come you never woke me up?"

"There was no need," Triffie said. He should have known, should have been pulled into wakefulness as she was by the arrival of their child. It was her body, of course, but she thinks if they were connected like they should have been, linked in mind and soul, he would somehow have known.

He isn't even supposed to be here. It's the first summer in his life that Jacob John hasn't gone to Labrador. For the last three summers Trif went with him, hating every minute of it. She went last summer even though she suspected she was in the family way. She lost that baby, a boy, one hot hellish night in late August, after a day working on the flakes.

This summer she was well along, seven months by the time the steamer left for Labrador, and there was no question of her going. But Jacob John refused to go too, saying he would spend the summer fishing off the Point rather than be on the Labrador when his child was born.

"Foolish as an odd sock, you are," Trif told him. "Sure, you'll make next to nothing fishing here, and with a youngster we'll need good credit this winter more than ever."

"All the same, I'm not going," Jacob John insisted. As if he could do anything by being here! As if he was any good in this moment, when it was Triffie pitted against her body.

"Should I go for Granny Morgan?" Jacob John asked when he finally woke.

"Could be a long time yet," Trif said. "When the sun comes up, go get Kit and Aunt Rachel, and tell Granny I'll need her before the day is out."

Kit arrives moments after Jacob John leaves. "He passed me on the road, coming up to our place," Kit explains. "I woke up before dawn and couldn't stop thinking of you, thinking this might be the day. I'm glad I did – now you don't have to be alone while he goes for the midwife."

Trif, unable to speak as a contraction clenches her body, grips Kit's hand in gratitude. Jacob John, in the bed beside her, couldn't sense that the baby was coming, but Kit, all the way up the road in her parents' house, knew. "Thank you," she says when the pain passes.

The morning wears on, Trif shuffling around the house like an old woman, trying to walk through the pain. Finally Aunt Rachel makes her lie down. Jacob John hangs about, useless, till Rachel tells him to go out in boat. Birthing a child can take hours or even days, she says, and why should he lose a full day's fishing when there's nothing a man can do?

Kit sits by the bed the whole time, giving Trif her hand to squeeze during the worst of the pain. She graduated in May with her B.A. and has a good job waiting for her in September; she could have remained in Halifax with Ben for the summer, but she chose to come home because Triffie is having her first child, and Kit wants to be with her.

The day that started so clear and sharp-edged blurs into pain and chaos. The midwife arrives; Trif's water breaks. Contractions come faster and harder and Triffie, who was determined nothing could make her cry out, shrieks like a seagull. She hears Jacob John's voice downstairs, shouting, and a woman's voice replying, a soothing tone. Later, between crashing waves of pain, Trif thinks she imagined the voice. This is a woman's world of blood and birth and bawling: no room here for Jacob John or any other man.

That *Forgetful* Shore

Finally the midwife tells her to push, push, and though Trif doesn't know what that means, her body does. She's always thought she was ruled by her head, that her body was just a willing servant, but now her brain is only a spectator as her body does the work it was made to do.

When dark fills the room and Aunt Rachel lights a lamp, Triffie suckles her newborn daughter. The baby's face is round and perfect, her head topped with a thatch of reddish hair. She fumbles at first, the nipple slipping out of her little mouth, till Aunt Rachel grabs Trif's breast like it's a pillow and maneuvers it into the baby's mouth and she begins to suckle in earnest.

Lost in gazing at her daughter, Trffie pays no attention to the voices around her until Kit says, almost in her ear, "Jacob John wants to come see her. Will I let him in?"

He is not a very big man, but he looks big and rough and awkward, here in this room that feels as holy as a church to Trif. He hovers near the door, as if afraid.

"Come on in, then, and see her," Trif says. "What's the matter, are you mad she's not a boy?"

"What? No, no maid, it never crossed my mind. I'm just glad 'tis over. And you're both all right." He takes a couple of steps across the floor, still hovering, like he doesn't know what to do. He stares down at Trif, the baby, Trif's breast.

Kit finally takes the baby from Trif's arms and places her in Jacob John's. "What do you have a mind to call her?" His voice is hoarse, like he's got a frog in his throat. They have not talked about names, though Jacob John mentioned once that if it was a boy he would like to name it David after his father. With the other baby, the one she lost, they never got as far as thinking about names, and Trif didn't want to tempt fate this time by naming the baby too soon. She thought Jacob John would be sorry this one wasn't a boy. But staring at the baby girl now he looks awed, as if can't believe he's seeing this tiny living thing that carries his blood and his name.

Name. "Katherine Grace," Triffie says, because of course she's thought of it, even though she hasn't said it aloud. She and Kit vowed years ago to name their first daughters after each other. She's kept the name close to her heart, matched with her lost mother's name, waiting to see if it was a girl and the girl looks like Katherine Grace. And she does; and she is.

Aunt Rachel lifts her eyebrows at "Grace"; in twenty years she has never spoken her dead sister's name aloud. Triffie learned it from the family Bible

That *Forgetful* Shore

and from the overheard gossip of older women like Aunt Hepsy. But Rachel only nods, and Kit gasps and says, "Oh, really? Thank you!"

Trif meets Jacob John's eyes, but he only nods.

So the baby is christened Katherine Grace, only she isn't christened, because Triffie puts her foot down. Aunt Rachel, Uncle Albert, Jacob John's mother and sister all insist she must be christened in the Church of England.

"No child of mine is getting baptized by no Anglican priest," Trif says. "Baptism is a sign of a believer choosing to follow Jesus. A baby can't do that. Katie can't do that."

"Trif, I don't care what tom-fool religion you got yourself into, you cannot let a child grow up in this world without being baptized," Aunt Rachel says. "What if, God forbid, He were to take her to Himself? What if she took a fever, or – it don't bear thinking about, Triffie, but you can't put the child's immortal soul in peril."

"First, she don't have an immortal soul, second, there's nothing magic about a minister pouring a bit of water on her forehead. And third, what kind of poor excuse for a god would damn a baby just because her parents never brought her to a priest to get sprinkled?" Triffie defies Aunt Rachel with more spite than she feels. She can stand up to her own family more easily than to her in-laws, and the tongue-lashing she's already endured from Jacob John's mother has worn her down. Not to the point where she'll ever concede that it's right to baptize an innocent child who doesn't know her right hand from her left, but to the point where, if Jacob John decrees the baby will be baptized, she will go along with it. She'll begrudge it, and she'll make him pay, but she'll submit to her husband as the apostle Paul says.

But Jacob John doesn't give her the chance to submit. He sits silently by while his mother and sister berate Triffie. When she finally corners him and says, "Are you going to make me baptize this baby?" he only shrugs.

"Could I make you, if I tried? Have I ever made you do anything?"

"You made me go down on the Labrador for three years. And I suppose you made me marry you," Trif points out.

His usually pleasant face turns grim, and he looks away. "Please yourself," he said. "About the christening."

"What, you don't care what I do with her?"

"I think there's no harm in having a baby christened. It don't do no damage and for all we knows it might do a bit of good. And it makes people happy. But I don't care one way or the other. I care about rearing

That *Forgetful* Shore

her up good, putting clothes on her back and food on the table, teaching her right from wrong. I don't care much one way or the other what church pew she sits in nor what words a minister says over her. It don't matter to me, but it does to you. So it stands to reason it ought to be your decision, not mine."

"Then tell your mother and them that, when they goes on at me."

Again, he shrugs and turns away. "Your decision, your job to tell them. I'm not getting involved, one way or the other."

There's an Adventist minister in Bay Roberts now, Elder Hubley, and they're raising money to build a church of their own. Elder Hubley has started up the Sunday night preaching services again, spreading the message, and before Katie Grace came along Trif was out to every one of them, and was face and eyes into the campaign to raise money for building the church. Trif went around canvassing for donations and even organized a sale of work, but the church won't be built till next spring. Katie Grace's dedication has to be held in the parlour of Triffie's house.

It's the same kind of service the Army people have; they don't believe in baptizing babies either, so Triffie has seen this before: the family standing around, passing the baby over to the minister to say a prayer, promising to bring her up in the nurture and admonition of the Lord. No holy water; no magic words.

Aunt Rachel, Uncle Albert and all Jacob John's family refuse to come. "If it's not a proper christening, what good is it?" Aunt Rachel asks. From her house, only Will comes to watch Katie's dedication. The other Advent believers circle around to support her, and for the first and last time, both Kit and Jacob John attend an Adventist service at Triffie's side.

When everyone has gone home, Trif sits in the kitchen nursing Katie. Jacob John comes in with an armload of wood and sits down by the stove watching her. Trif hitches up her shawl to better cover the exposed top of her breast as the baby suckles.

"That was all right," Jacob John says after a long silence.

"It was fine. But your mother won't think so."

"No, maybe not. But it's none of her business." Jacob John's hands, usually so busy, rest idle on his knees. After a moment he gets out of his chair and sits next to Trif on the settee. He reaches to stroke Katie's cheek. The baby is more sleeping than nursing now, her little mouth gone slack on Trif's nipple, a milk-bubble forming in the corner of her mouth as she breathes. Jacob John touches her face with just one finger. There's dirt under his fingernail and ground into the creases of his hand.

"She's a grand girl," he says.

"She'll be a grand woman," Trif says. She glances up, suddenly fierce. "I want her to have opportunities – the ones I never had. She'll do well in school, and if she has the chance to go away, to get more education, I want to make sure she has that. Don't hold her back."

Jacob John's eyes turn from his daughter to his wife. "Would I do that?" he asks, and Trif realizes she doesn't even know the answer. "Anyway," he goes on, his voice regaining its usual saucy lilt, "you're thinking she'll be smart like you. What if she got my brains instead? That'd be a tragedy, now wouldn't it?"

"She'll be smart. I can tell. And I just want her to have a chance to use that, not be held back just because she's a girl or she comes from a fisherman's family."

Katie's sleepy head has drifted back now, her mouth open, loosing her hold on Trif's breast. Trif settles the baby more comfortably in the crook of her arm and reaches up with her free hand to pull her blouse over her breast, but Jacob John stops her, lays three fingers on her bare breast as he speaks.

"She'll have every opportunity she needs, don't worry about that," he says. "But it half sounds to me like you wants her to live your life for you – do the things you never got to do." His fingers slide down her breast, caressing it. He has never touched her like this in broad daylight, right there in the kitchen, and Trif wants to pull away or swat at his hand. But she doesn't want to wake her sleeping baby, so she watches, silent, as Jacob John's forefinger catches a drop of warm milk still clinging to her nipple. His touch, so different from the suck of a baby's lips, sends a shiver through her.

"You're only twenty-two, Trif. Just because you're married to me and we got a baby, it don't mean your life is over." He raises his finger to his mouth and licks her milk off it.

Kit

Trinity
December, 1913

My dearest Posy,

As I write this I am trying to picture you with my Namesake, little
Katie Grace. How quickly babies grow! When I left home I thought
her like a kitten whose eyes had not yet opened — small and wrinkled
and really more Asleep than Awake. Now, as your letters tell the tale
of her sitting up and looking about, reaching out to grab things, I
feel that by the time I return she will be a right little <u>Personage</u>, and
though she bears my name and the blood of the <u>One</u> <u>I</u> <u>Hold</u> <u>Dearest</u>,
still she will be, in some measure, a stranger to me.

I wish it were not so, that I could be there to help you care for her, to
see her grow and be your Companion throughout this <u>strange</u> <u>new</u>
<u>passage</u> in your life, and yet, I am more content here in the town
where I was born, than ever I could be in Missing Point. My school
at Trinity is a large one, four classrooms for nearly two hundred
pupils, and by virtue of my College Degree I find myself in charge of
the Eldest Pupils, those preparing for their Primary and Preliminary
CHEs. Also, I have all the administrative Duties that pertain to the

title of Principal, which are hardly compensated by the additional few dollars in my pay packet, I can assure you!

Despite the Paper-work, it seems a very easy job in comparison to what I did in Elliston, or what Mr. Bishop did when we were growing up in the Missing Point school. Still, I like to fancy myself someday in a city school, perhaps even at my Alma Mater, Spencer, teaching true Scholars who <u>Thirst for Knowledge</u> – which thirst, I am sad to say, is not exactly an epidemic amongst the High School students of Trinity!

Kit stops there, laying aside the pen. Her head aches and the lamp hurts her eyes; she is sitting in her classroom, working long past dark. Her pile of personal correspondence waits at her elbow, but she has precious little time for letter writing.

In addition to Triffie's latest letter, describing the rapid growth of Katie Grace Russell and Trif's own bewildered feelings about motherhood – which certainly seems an overwhelming experience – Kit also has a letter from her college chum Maggie Campbell. Maggie, unlike Kit, did not return to her own little island after graduation, but went off instead to the big city of Toronto, where she had a boarding-house room in a slum full of Irish immigrants and a job as the "society reporter" for a newspaper.

The contrast between my work-life and home-life could not be sharper, as in the morning I attend a society wedding at the St. Charles Hotel, attended by the groom's millionaire family and the bride's old society family, which has no real money but a family tree hung with English Lords and Ladies. I do not, of course, get to dine at table, but content myself with leftover scraps of the elegant wedding breakfast while I hastily scribble down notes about the bride's gown of cream-coloured satin with its court train edged with rose-leaves and pearls, et cetera ad infinitum.

From there I progress to the newspaper office, where in a smoky room full of middle-aged men who call me "darlin'," I crouch at my tiny desk and write up the report, to be laid on the desk of Mr. MacSomething. Then through the streets, which grow

progressively narrower and meaner as the babble of voices in the
streets changes from English to Italian, Greek, German and finally
English again, but with an Irish accent so pronounced I can
scarce pick out the words. Then I know I have arrived back in
Cabbagetown. Yes, it really is called Cabbagetown, and I can smell
the vegetable from which the neighbourhood takes its name, as
well as many other pungent odours.

Maggie truly is a wonderful writer; the streets of Toronto come alive under her pen. Kit sits with the two letters, one in either hand, as if weighing them. It's not Trif's and Maggie's friendship she is weighing – Maggie is a dear, and she hopes their friendship will be lifelong, but nothing will ever threaten or compare to the tie, deeper than blood, that she shares with Trif.

No, it's the letters' contents she weighs, their vivid depiction of two different worlds. For Trif, though without Maggie's journalistic training, is in her own way a vivid writer and a lively correspondent. Her letters sketch the well-known world of Missing Point, the faces and voices left behind. But lately – since her marriage, and especially since Katie's birth – there is another world revealed in her letters, one which, like the Toronto streets that Maggie describes, grows narrower and meaner with the passing months. It's hard not to contrast Maggie's life – the young career woman, forging her way in a man's world, giddy with the opportunities opening before her – with Triffie's life, married to a fisherman, caring for a baby, keeping house. Kit senses how poverty, marriage and now motherhood are grinding down Trif's ambitions.

As for Kit herself – well, here she is, poised between two worlds. She has a college degree and a job with unusual power and prestige for a woman because of that – but she is also as good as engaged, despite the lack of a ring on her finger. She and Ben have discussed it: he is in his final year of law school; next year he hopes to find an articling position with a firm either in Halifax or St. John's. Kit will spend these two years teaching, and when his year of articling is finished, they will be married.

When she thinks of Ben himself – his kindness, his humour, the touch of his fingers on her skin – two years seems far too long to wait. But when she thinks of giving up teaching, putting aside her independence and her career, and becoming a lawyer's wife – then it feels as if a trap is slowly,

slowly closing upon her. She will have opportunities, of course – as Ben Porter's wife she will be active in whatever community they settle in. She will have church and volunteer societies, but whatever she does will be done as Mrs. Ben Porter, not as Kit Saunders. She will never teach again.

The next letter is from Miss Shaw, who writes faithfully to dozens of former students.

Dear Miss Saunders,

How delighted I am to hear that you are once again a colleague in the teaching profession. I hope your new appointment brings you every happiness. I congratulate you on becoming a Bachelor of Arts. It is indeed heartening to see so many young women taking the path to higher education, and so many more of the professions opening to our Sex.

As for my own news, I have little enough, I suppose. I continue with the same courses at Spencer; this year, our play is The Merchant of Venice, which is not a tragedy, but as close to one as I shall ever likely get the opportunity to direct. This summer I travelled to Boston with my sister and had the opportunity there to see a stage production of Macbeth. Short of having seen the great Sarah Bernhardt in Hamlet, a privilege that the Lord did not see fit to grant me, I imagine there could be few greater pleasures than to see the Scottish tragedy acted out on stage. You will remember I told you of the superstitious theatre folk who will not say the name of that play aloud – so hard to imagine that one whose mind is immersed in the great works of Shakespeare, could at the same time be so ignorant as to believe that a name carries the power of a curse!

I hope you continue to read regularly and well. Novels and plays are all very well but it is important to read that which challenges the mind as well. I have recently finished a new collection of essays by Augustine Birrell, which I shall send you, if you wish. I am sure in the outports your opportunities for getting good books are limited. If you let me know your needs I shall be happy to supply any that I can obtain for you.

That *Forgetful* Shore

Reading this brisk missive in Miss Shaw's firm, rounded handwriting – her own version of the distinctive script that every schoolgirl and schoolmistress at Spencer College uses – is like opening the window in a stuffy room to allow a bracing breeze in. *This*, Kit thinks, *is the life I was born for. I don't want what Maggie wants, nor what Trif has, but I could live as Miss Shaw does, surely, surrounded by books and scholars.*

And yet – that brief sentence about going to Boston to see her sister. The sister, as Kit knows from previous letters, is married with grown children and has just had her first grandchild. Miss Shaw, by the path she has chosen in life, has been cast forever in the role of maiden aunt. Has she ever had a lover? Made love, or even kissed a man? Broken her heart, or someone else's? Little as Kit envies Trif's closed-in life of domestic duties and diapers, she knows that the barrenness of spinsterhood – even a scholarly, professional spinsterhood – will not fulfill all her needs.

Underneath the three letters is Ben's postal, already read.

Dearest One – I will come for you as soon as the <u>Bruce</u> lands me in Newfoundland on the 19th Dec – or as soon after as I can manage – and whisk you away home with me for the holidays. I won't write, out here where the curious postmistress can read every word, how very much I long to be with you again.

Today is the twentieth of December. Last night was the school pageant and today the last day of school. Kit is here tonight only to tidy away the last of her work, to make sure she doesn't return to disarray in the New Year. Then she will go to her boarding house to pack and wait for Ben's arrival. When she taught along this stretch of the coast before, in Elliston, she was dependent on the coastal steamers to come and go, but now the railway branch line extends to Bonavista and she hopes the train will bring Ben to her more quickly than a ship could. She hopes he will come tomorrow, though it might be the next day.

She's marking the last of a pile of composition books when she hears footsteps in the hall outside her classroom. None of the lower grade teachers is likely to come in today; Kit gets to her feet, startled, to see who is there. Before she can open the door it's opened from the other side and Ben stands there, smiling.

"How can you be here already? I just read your postal ... I wasn't expecting you yet –"

"Never underestimate a young man in love," Ben says. "Caught an earlier ride down from college to Sydney, so I was able to get an earlier crossing. And here I am – I couldn't have waited another day."

They are alone, the classroom door closed behind them, in perhaps the greatest privacy they have ever enjoyed in their long courtship. During Kit's four years at university they enjoyed each other's company almost every day, yet the rules of propriety and college life meant they were almost never truly alone, in a room like this with a door that could shut behind them. As Ben's lips meet hers, Kit recognizes her own need for his touch, realizes how badly she has wanted him during this fall's separation.

His hands are as busy as his lips, loosening the laces and buttons of her clothing as if he can't get enough of touching her. She doesn't even stop to think of the fact that she's allowing him far more liberties than she ever has before. She's eager for his touch, and no considerations of propriety – not the thought of her parents, nor of the school trustees, nor even of poor disgraced Louisa Arthur – cross her mind. She only wants to give herself up completely to Ben, to feel his body touch every part of hers. He doesn't ask "May I?" because he doesn't need to; every movement is her assent as he slides her shirtwaist off her shoulders and his hands move towards the buttons of her skirt.

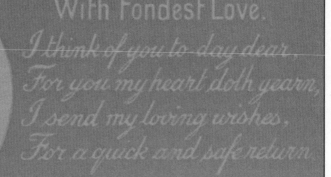

With Fondest Love.
I think of you to-day dear,
For you my heart doth yearn,
I send my loving wishes,
For a quick and safe return.

A Quick and Safe Return

1914 – 1918

Triffie

Missing Point
October, 1914

My dearest Peony,

How strangely things turn out! Years ago we vowed we would be each
other's bridesmaids, and yet when it came my time to be married you
were far away at college, and your own wedding was held in such
haste that I could not be by your side. Such are the times we live in,
and of course I understand fully why you and Ben wanted to be
Joined in Matrimony before the First Five Hundred sailed. But how
I wish I could have been there beside you, my Kit, to hold your hand
as you watched him sail away!

Imagine – a war bride. How romantic it sounds, yet the reality, I'm
sure, is far less so. Two boys from Missing Point have joined the
Naval Reserves – Alf and Harry, the middle two Mercer boys – along
with your cousin Ted, who was already in the Reserves and was
called up to report to the _Calypso_. Mrs. Mercer and your aunt,
different as they are, are both drove to distraction with the thoughts
of what might happen to the boys in a battle at sea. Meanwhile, the
young fellows – our Will, and Charlie Mercer, Isaac French and

the others their age – mere lads of sixteen and seventeen – go about
saying they hope the war lasts long enough for them to go overseas!
Can you imagine the wickedness, of wishing for bloodshed and
horror to last longer? I told Will that it was evil to say it, and cruel
to say it where his mother might hear. If Aunt Rachel were to guess
he was even thinking such a thing, I think her poor heart would give
out once and for all.

"That's young Char Mercer got Will and Isaac going on with that foolishness," Jacob John says, when Triffie grumbles. "Them Mercer boys is all mad.
They spent their whole lives fighting each other and everyone else they could
get their hands on all around the bay, and now they reckon all they got to
do is get over to France and they'll tear strips off the Huns. Kaiser won't
have a chance once the Mercer boys gets at him. Sure even Fred's going on
about it, wanting to join up, and him a married man with two little ones to
think about."

"You're a married man yourself, with a little one to think about," Trif
says. "I better not hear no talk from you about going overseas."

"Not me!" Jacob John says, and Triffie has to admit, while her husband
doesn't lack for bravery, he knows how to look out for himself. He was at the
ice in March, on board the *Bellaventure* when all those poor fellows from the
Newfoundland got stranded and died out on the ice. "Stunned buggers,"
Jacob John said when he came home. "I mean, poor stunned buggers – I
pitied 'em, Trif, anyone would, all frozen and black as they were, some of 'em
froze to death on their knees like they was praying, or with their arms around
each other to keep warm. But did you know there was a slew of them, thirty
or more, off the same crew that weren't stuck out on the ice because they had
the sense to disobey orders and go back on board their own ship? You don't
hear much about them in the newspaper reports – they're not heroes. Smart
men are never heroes. That's just what I'da done, and never mind what the
master watch or anyone else said to me. Obeying orders don't make sense if
it's only going to get you killed."

After four years of marriage, Triffie recognizes this as the code Jacob
John lives by. He would be a poor choice for a soldier. He's no foolhardy
boy spoiling for a fight like the Mercers, nor no high-minded young hero
like Kit's Ben, going off to fight for King and country. Of course, Ben is an

officer – he'll miss the worst of the fighting, no doubt. If Jacob John were fool enough to join the Regiment he'd be a foot soldier; in the Navy he'd be a common seaman. Either way he'd have to take orders from some merchant's son in a fancy uniform, orders that might well get him killed. Jacob John would never stand for that.

She doesn't believe, as so many people are saying, that it will be a quick and decisive war, over by Christmas. She believes, as do most of the Adventist faithful, that this is the beginning of something far bigger and more sinister. Elder Hubley preached all summer that Armageddon was coming as the news from Europe grew more and more ominous. Most people on the Point said it was only those Europeans up to their old foolishness, shooting archdukes and the like, and it would never come to Newfoundland.

Now the frenzy and fear over local boys going off to a war on the other side of the world has provided fertile ground for the Adventists. They can barely put out enough seats in their new little church for the people who come to the evening services. Elder Hubley preaches about how war in Europe will lead to the collapse of the Ottoman Empire, which will lead to war in the Middle East and everything will be fulfilled, just as it's spoken of in the Book of Revelation.

"There shall be wars and rumours of wars," Aunt Hepsy Snow said back in the summer, every time anyone raised the possibility of war. "The sun shall be darkened, and the stars fall from the sky. Them signs already happened, 1780 and 1833. There shall be earthquakes in divers places, like there was in San Francisco. Nineteen-aught-six. Now we got rumours of wars, and before summer's out we'll have war itself. You mark my words. You may scoff at it," she would say to the doubters, especially when the Methodist minister pointed out there had been wars off and on ever since Jesus was taken up to heaven, "but you'll see. This will be the war to end all wars – earth's final battle. New Year's 1915 is the last new year we'll ever see."

When Aunt Hepsy gets that far, even Elder Hubley tries to discourage her. He's more than willing to preach that the oncoming war is a sign of the end and Jesus is coming soon, but he shies away from setting dates for the Lord's return. Their church got its start when a preacher named William Miller attempted to do just that, and all his followers suffered the Great Disappointment. Adventist preachers now are more cautious, reminding their more enthusiastic believers, like Aunt Hepsy, that no man knows the day nor the hour of His coming. The Adventists already have one prophetess and Elder Hubley has

That *Forgetful* Shore

no desire to encourage Aunt Hepsy Snow to set herself up as another.

Trif isn't sure what to make of it all, herself, now that the war has actually started. She can see the word of prophecy laid out in Scripture and knows they're living in the end times: what more likely sign to usher in the final days than a great war? But she dislikes the pleasure some of her fellow believers take in predicting doom and disaster. Of course there must be suffering before the Lord comes, but she shudders at the thought of what war in faraway places like France and Belgium might mean to boys from Missing Point and Bareneed and Clarke's Beach.

Everywhere she goes she hears talk of war, but there's a remoteness to it, even now that boys from the Point have joined the Reserves. It's important, everyone agrees – important enough to bring people to the Adventist Church on Sunday night to learn about the prophecies of Revelation, important enough to start branches of the NPA and WPA to raise money for soldiers and for relief of the suffering Belgians. But not as important as the price of fish, which is finally on the rise. It's not even as important as the inquiries into the seal hunt after this year's disaster, for the men want to know what changes will be made in next year's hunt, whether they will be safer and have the better working conditions that Mr. Coaker fought for. Things that affect their everyday lives have a vibrant immediacy that black and white headlines about war in Europe can never have.

It must seem real to Kit, Trif thinks as she walks back from the Mercantile where she has gone to put Kit's letter in the mailbag along with the rest of her week's correspondence, and to get another sack of sugar. She's in the middle of trying to get the winter's blueberry and partridgeberry jam made before the potatoes are ready to harvest. It's hot and tiring work; she needs both sugar and a little break.

On the way home, pushing Katie and the sugar in the pram along the North Side Road, Triffie meets Joe Bishop. They stop and chat as they usually do when they meet – Triffie asking about the school, Mr. Bishop admiring Katie and asking what news Triffie has of Kit.

"You heard she's married, of course?" Triffie says.

"Her mother told me, yes," Mr. Bishop says. "Has her husband shipped out yet?"

"Yes, he went with the First Five Hundred."

"Some folk are saying our boys will never see action, that the war will be all done before they're ready to go to France."

Triffie shakes her head. "I 'low the Mercer boys'll be some poisoned if that happens. To hear them talk you'd think fighting a war was the best fun they were ever likely to have. But what do you think, sir? Do you think 'twill be over quickly, like some folk are saying?"

"I think they're a long ways off the truth, Trif. This is going to be a long war – and a costly one. Not that there are any easy wars – but it's not going to be like the Boer War, trained British soldiers fighting farmers. Germany is a great military power, even if some people don't recognize it. As for our boys, and the Canadians – well, none of them lack for bravery, that's certain. But what experience do they have with the kind of fighting they're going to see in Europe? You mark my words, Triffie, we're in for a long war."

A long war. Triffie thinks of the young boys, Will and his mates, who are hoping they'll have time to go overseas. *Two more years of war – is it possible? Surely Joe didn't mean it could go on that long. Surely the boys are safe – as safe as fishermen ever are,* she corrects herself. But isn't it better for a boy to face death on a schooner bound for the Labrador, than to risk his life on a battlefield far from home?

She whispers a prayer under her breath as she continues up the Neck Road towards home. A prayer for the safety of all the Newfoundland boys and men now in England, the boys from the Point and Kit's husband Ben most of all.

But to pray for a quick end to the war is to pray against the will of the Almighty, if war is truly a sign of the end times. Hard to think that she should welcome hardship and war and even persecution. It goes against the grain, to pray for things to get worse instead of better. Yet if that's what it takes to bring an end to this hard old world of work and worry, then won't it be worthwhile?

Cresting the top of the lane that branches off the Neck Road and curves down towards the South Side Road, Trif pauses to look out at the waters of the bay, at fishing boats and stages, houses and gardens. She imagines a little cloud the size of a man's hand in the eastern sky growing nearer and nearer, revealing itself to be a cloud of angels hovering off the end of the Point, putting an end to toil and hardship.

"Even so, come, Lord Jesus," she prays, offering up her doubt and fear and confusion. Katie, who is used to seeing her mother praying at all hours of the day – while walking, cooking, cleaning house, digging potatoes – stares up, incurious, from her pram, her wide blue eyes hinting at a world far removed from war and turmoil.

That *Forgetful* Shore

Kit

St. John's
October, 1914

My Dearest Husband,

How sweet to write those words – how horrific to have to write them in a letter, put on a ten-cent stamp, and send them far across the sea, not knowing <u>When</u> or <u>Whether</u> they will reach you!!!

How sweet those short hours we spent together before we had to part! I will tell you something in greatest confidence, sworn to the secrecy that binds Husband and Wife, else I would never commit such things to paper: I am Glad – Glad, rather than Contrite as I ought to be – that we did not allow considerations of Morality and Virtue to keep us from one another's arms in the months before our marriage. I have never found it in my heart to truly Repent of that so-called Sin, and am glad I am no Roman Catholic, forced to make Confession to a Priest. I would have to commit the sin of Perjury, either to claim I never sinned (by the Dictates of Convention), or else to claim I was sorry for it. For the truth – that we transgressed, and I am <u>glad</u> <u>of</u> <u>it</u> – is more than any Priest could bear to hear!

And yet, that truth being committed to paper, I must tell you the other half, that indeed, the embraces of the Marriage Bed ARE sweeter than those that came before. The two nights we spent in the Atlantic Hotel were such nights of bliss as I have never experienced nor dreamed of – to be Surpassed only by those I shall experience when you are safely home in my arms again. Oh, what a joyful Reunion that will be!

When will it be, I wonder? We have read the news here of the fierce fighting at Ypres, and all hearts in St. John's are heavy with the thought that this war may drag on longer than we thought, and our boys be overseas longer. Yet we swell with pride at the thought of young Newfoundland men in uniform, fighting for England, for Empire, for freedom, and against tyranny!

So I alternate daily, between hope, fear, pride and sorrow at your absence. I try to compose myself with philosophy, and busy myself with work, but neither truly takes away the pain I feel when I think of the distance that separates us, and the months that may pass before we are Together Again!

Ever your own,
Katherine (Mrs. Benjamin Porter)

Kit wasn't prepared to miss Ben as much as she does. She had, after all, barely had time to get accustomed to being married. Ben came home from law school in June with his brand-new law degree and an offer of a position articling in a St. John's firm. He came to Trinity to escort her home to Missing Point, where he formally asked her father for her hand in marriage and put a ring on her finger.

Kit applied for teaching jobs in St. John's, including one at Spencer, though she knew her *alma mater* would be unlikely to give a place to a teacher who was engaged to be married in June and thus only able to teach for a year. She was pleasantly surprised to learn that a Miss Halliday, a teacher from England, was returning to her home country for a few months in the fall. Kit was offered the opportunity to replace her until Christmas. Her old mentor Miss Shaw is now Headmistress, and anxious to have Kit on her faculty if only in a temporary capacity. Half a year's teaching at

That *Forgetful* Shore

Spencer seemed better than a guaranteed year anywhere else, so Kit accepted the offer, moved back into Cousin Ethel's house, and received her fiancé like a gentleman caller in the parlour, sitting stiffly side by side on the horsehair settee.

The declaration of war unraveled everyone's plans. Suddenly, instead of a promising young lawyer with a career ahead of him, Ben was an officer in training with the Newfoundland Regiment. In the first week of September, no-one knew how long it would take for this ragged assortment of men to be trained and equipped for service overseas. Many of the St. John's recruits and most of the officers were members of the Church Lads' Brigade or one of the other cadet groups – the Methodist Guard, the Presbyterian Highlanders, the Catholic Cadets. They had some experience of drilling and marching, but it was a huge leap to go from marching about a parade ground to practising bayonet drill, preparing for combat with an actual enemy. Yet everyone seemed to feel that it was of utmost importance to send men overseas as swiftly as possible in response to the Mother Country's call.

"It won't be long – weeks, not months," Ben told her.

"But how can you possibly be ready by then?" Ben, like every outport young man, had handled a shotgun in the woods when he was growing up, but what kind of preparation was that for going into battle in a real war, in a foreign country? They were training every day down there on the parade ground at Pleasantville, but how could they be ready in a matter of weeks for war?

"We won't be," Ben said bluntly. "But they'd rather send us over poorly trained – even without proper uniforms – than have it be said Newfoundland didn't do her part. It'll be no later than the end of September, and it could be sooner, if they get the rifles from Canada. That's what I've heard, anyway."

The recruits were signed up for a year, if the war lasted that long. Ben wanted to put the wedding off till he returned. "We would have waited a year anyway," he pointed out, "and God willing I'll be back by June. And if it should take longer, well – it doesn't seem fair to you, us being married and me overseas for so long, does it? I know you don't want to think about it, but if I didn't come back –"

"No." She wouldn't think of it, or talk about it either. The whole thing – Ben in a makeshift uniform, learning to bark commands and put boys through drill exercises while sleeping in a tent at Pleasantville – seemed like a game, a strange diversion from the lives they were supposed to be living. It would be an interruption; she would be a war bride, and then he would come home, and take up his practice, and life would continue as it was supposed to do. "I refuse to think that way. You will come home, and we'll already be married, because we'll be married before you go."

Finally they agreed. A very quiet, private wedding on the third Saturday in September. They debated writing their families, inviting their parents ("and Triffie," Kit put in, unable to imagine getting married without her, though she had not been there for Trif's wedding). It was possible their families could get there just in time.

"But then," Ben said, "we'd have to have some kind of a wedding supper, and find a decent-sized place to have it, and no matter how small we tried to keep it, it would get bigger."

"And my mother would insist on us being married in church, and then she'd want to know why I couldn't come home and be married in our church at the Point and invite half the harbour to the wedding supper," Kit pointed out, laughing.

So they were married by the regimental chaplain, and Ben was given two days' leave which they spent at the Atlantic Hotel, barely leaving their room. Then Ben returned to the base to continue his training, and Kit returned to her boarding house and waited.

On the fourth of October the *Florizel* sailed out of St. John's Harbour with the First Five Hundred, the Blue Puttees, on board. Kit was part of the crowd lining the streets as the men marched from Pleasantville down to the harbour, then she joined the crush of people on Water Street, hundreds of other wives, sweethearts, mothers and fathers, sisters and brothers, and crowds of cheering citizens. The band played "It's a Long Way to Tipperary." Kit tried not to think about what Ben had told her – how poorly prepared the men were, how little training they'd had, how the Ross rifles they were meant to shoot still had not arrived from Canada. The news from France and Belgium frightened her. On the day the First Five Hundred sailed, a headline in the paper under "War News" read: "Struggle Yet to Come Will be Long and Terrible."

After the ship sails that night, Kit goes back to Cousin Ethel's house and waits, not sure what she is waiting for. A letter from Ben? News of the Regiment arriving in England? Or something else?

She remembers reading that in olden times, when a king died suddenly,

That *Forgetful* Shore

his widow would be watched closely for two or three months afterwards, in case she might turn out to be pregnant with a royal heir whose existence would have to be taken into account in any future political machinations. The son and heir of Ben Porter, newly graduated lawyer, of Elliston, Newfoundland, would hardly have a great impact on world affairs, yet Kit hugs the possibility close during those weeks after the *Florizel* sails. She is unsure how she would feel if she really were pregnant. Does she even want to be a mother? Marriage itself holds enough ambivalence for her, though she was quick enough to hurry to the altar under pressure of being a war bride. Could she raise a child alone, if Ben doesn't return? Is it that most trite of all wishes – that she will have "something left of him" to remember him by if he is killed over there?

In any event, whatever her motive, she has nothing. Her monthlies come as usual in October, and word arrives that the Regiment has landed in England. Kit writes to her family and Ben's, telling them of the hurried wedding, and receives their good wishes. Triffie's letter sounds wistful, regretting that neither of them ever got the chance to be each other's bridesmaid. *Well, girl, who knows, we might each be married twice more, for all we know*, Kit thinks. But it's the kind of thing you could say aloud, followed with a laugh; you can't write it in a letter. Especially when your husband is at war.

Miss Shaw calls Kit into the office. Knowing that married women are not supposed to hold teaching positions, Kit fears the worst. Instead, she gets good news. With the outbreak of war, Miss Halliday has elected to stay in England, her war-torn country, where she too is about to become a war bride. In times like these, Miss Halliday writes, a woman must follow her heart instead of her head. Or so Miss Shaw tells Kit, drawing one corner of her mouth down. Her tone is reminiscent of Mark Antony insisting that Brutus was an honourable man.

"Faced with the exigencies of war," Miss Shaw goes on – she really is the sort of person who can drop the word "exigencies" into a sentence and sound quite natural doing it – "the Board is prepared to waive the usual strictures against married women teaching, to allow us to retain the services of a gifted alumna whose husband is serving his country. Congratulations, Mrs. Porter – the position is yours for the duration."

"For the duration." Kit likes the phrase, which is popular at the moment. Everything in St. John's, everything in her life, has a sense of held breath, an air of impermanence. Nobody knows exactly when and how life will continue; everyone waits for news from overseas. Nothing that happens here matters.

Ben's letters describe training in England, a grueling apprenticeship that makes it clear to the Newfoundland recruits how inadequate their hasty preparation was. Now they have their Ross rifles, and are being taught to shoot them at living men. The Allies have the Germans stalled at the Marne; both sides have dug in and will not give up any more territory. Ben reports that the boys of the Blue Puttees are anxious to see action yet frighteningly unready for it.

Kit's life rolls on. She is teaching where she always dreamed of teaching, living in St. John's. In the middle of November, Cousin Ethel quite suddenly takes a bad case of pneumonia and dies. Not surprising, perhaps, in a woman of seventy-seven. What is surprising is that her will leaves the house to Kit. Within the space of a few months Kit is an independent woman while still a wife, a homeowner as well as a teacher – an implausible collection of circumstances, largely made possible by the tragedy of war.

It is a tragedy; of course it is. She hates going to bed in the big four-poster at Cousin Ethel's house alone and thinking of Ben's body, of their two nights at the hotel, of all the wasted nights they are spending apart. She yearns for Ben, misses him, prays for him. Yet cherishes her freedom to go on teaching, and feels guilty for that.

Sometimes, walking home from her classes to that three-storey house on Gower Street that is now her home, empty but for herself and the elderly housemaid, Kit wonders if she is quite as desolate as a war bride ought to be. She misses Ben, yet she knows other women whose husbands have gone to war and they have something she lacks – or rather, she has something they lack. The other soldiers' wives of her acquaintance seem lost, as if they are empty at the core, hollow without the presence of their husbands to give shape and meaning to their lives.

Perhaps it's only that I didn't have time to get used to being married, Kit thinks. Although she and Ben kept company for six years, she was still a single woman, on her own as the teacher in Elliston and later in Trinity. Even at Dalhousie, she was a co-ed; being courted by Ben was secondary to the pursuit of her own education. Kit hasn't questioned, until now, whether there was anything wrong with that. Is she – quite – normal? Is it right for a woman always to hold a piece of herself apart, even in marriage? If Ben

That *Forgetful* Shore

were here right now, would there still be this piece of Kit that is separate from Kit-and-Ben, from Mr. and Mrs. Porter?

The thought doesn't quite leave her, continues to nudge at the back of her mind even while she corrects papers and writes letters. Something about the way other women lose themselves in marriage, give themselves up to their husbands. Especially those who marry for love. She thinks of Byron: *Man's love is of man's life a thing apart; 'Tis woman's whole existence.* Not that she takes Byron – especially in *Don Juan* – as any sort of expert on the female mind. Yet she has seen this, over and over, how love – or marriage, which is not always the same thing – becomes a woman's whole existence. And even now, when Kit loses sleep at nights worrying about Ben, she knows love is not, never can be, her whole existence.

In the bleakest part of a sleepless night, picturing Ben in the midst of the worst horrors of war, her mind returns to the question. She finds herself leaving the battlefields of France and returning to the past, to her own childhood. To the Missing Point schoolroom, to Abel Morgan's fish store, to the stones of the Long Beach.

Is something wrong with me? Kit wonders. Was something broken, damaged, early on, so that she cannot be whole, cannot give her whole self to love? So that she must always hold something back?

She doesn't want to be broken. She wants to be whole, wholly in love, reunited with a husband who returns safe and sound from war. Yet she cannot fully stifle that other part of her, the girl inside who will always be Kit Saunders, and never quite be subsumed into Mrs. Ben Porter.

She rolls over in bed, closes her eyes and tries to sleep. For now, her ability to be separate from Ben, an independent woman, is an asset rather than a liability. While it may be a failing, it defines who she is in this moment. For the duration.

Triffie

Missing Point
October, 1915

My dearest Peony,

How heavy my heart was as the train bore away this latest group of
local boys to St. John's for Points Beyond. Now that we have heard our
Regiment has finally reached the front and is fighting in Gallipoli, it
all feels so much closer. The dangers these lads will face seem far
Darker than they did last Fall when we saw our first brave recruits
sail away. With the sinking of the _Viknor_ back in the winter, and the
word that our Regiment is off to fight at Gallipoli, it has finally hit
home that this is no Grand Adventure, but a deadly business.

Or – I ask myself – does it seem more real to me, because now one of
my own Flesh and Blood has gone to that dread conflict? Perhaps I
am gay and cheerful enough when waving off other women's sons and
husbands, but – ah, though I have no son of my own to send, and
though my husband knows his duty to Katie and me far too well for
him to be lured Overseas, still I have said goodbye to one who is dear
as Son or Brother to me, and my heart misgives me.

On the platform of the Bay Roberts railway station, as Will, Char, Isaac and the other three boys put their bags on the train, Isaac's father plays the fiddle. He chooses "The Minstrel Boy to the War Has Gone." The tune, thin and tremulous in the chilly autumn air, would be mournful enough even if you didn't know that the next line was *In the ranks of death you may find him.*

Triffie was the first person Will told when he made the decision to sign up. Not that there was any great mystery to it; he and all his friends had said from the day war was declared that they would join up when they were old enough. Triffie prayed that day would never come, as did Betty, Ruth and Aunt Rachel. Will had not yet been seventeen last August; it seemed safe to hope that the war would be over within a year.

But now, in this bleak autumn of 1915, the news from overseas is grim. British troops have faced poison gas attacks and slogged through the mud of the trenches. Letters home from the boys who have volunteered are published in every issue of the Bay Roberts newspaper, each giving a brave report and exhorting other men to join up. Many more have answered the call to join the Naval Reserves or the Regiment, but no boy from Missing Point has yet appeared in the casualty lists. Triffie fears that their time is coming. Every town, every harbour, maybe even every family, will pay their debt to King and country before this is all over, she fears.

In the Anglican Church service where she prays beside Jacob John on Sunday mornings, the minister prays for peace and victory. In the little Adventist Church on Saturdays, they do not pray for a British victory, but that Jesus will come quickly, that this turmoil will truly herald His return. Only the Second Coming, Trif thinks, will redeem all this suffering, make some meaning out of the senseless suffering of boys who are barely men.

"It'll break your mother's heart," she warned Will when he came to tell her that it was all decided. He and Charlie had both had their eighteenth birthdays. They were only waiting on Isaac, whose birthday was a few weeks after Will's.

Will shook his head. "Mother's heart will be broke either way, Trif. She don't want me to go get killed, but she don't want me to stay behind and be a coward, neither."

"You're not a coward if you don't volunteer to go overseas, Will. Don't go just because you're scared of what people will think of you."

"I'm not!" He pushed a shock of blond hair out of his eyes, looking so like a child again as he did it that it wrung her heart. Going off to war? It wasn't possible. "I can't explain it, but – I got to go. I got my reasons, and I know 'tis the right thing to do."

She leaned against the rail. They were standing on the front bridge, Will sitting up on the railing while Triffie beat out the rugs and brushed them down. Now she laid aside the rug – one she had hooked herself the past winter, her own design of their house with the hill rising up behind it and the pine trees in the yard – and looked up at Will. He was a few inches taller than she, and his shoulders and chest were broadened by a man's work. He'd spent six summers on the Labrador and gone twice to the seal hunt. Half boy, half man. Like most of the soldiers over there, the boys going off to fight in a place called Gallipoli that Triffie, for all her education, wouldn't have been able to find on a map before the war began.

"Do you remember how you used to walk in your sleep?"

Will shook his head. "I only remembers Mother telling me about it. I think the last time was when I was eight or nine, but I got no recollection of it. She says I used to wake up down in the kitchen or out in the yard and not know how I got there."

"Did she tell you about the time Isaac's mother found you in bed over to their place?"

Will laughed. "Yes, Aunt Nellie musta got some shock that morning – one more youngster there in the morning than what she put to bed the night before."

It's become a story to laugh over, but what Triffie remembers is the stark terror of that morning, the cold ground under her bare feet as she looked out at the water, the fear that gripped her as she thought of Will wandering down to the wharf in his sleep. Will's dream of being taken by the fairies.

He put his hand over hers on the railing. "Don't be scared, Triffie. Don't all them prayers of yours do no good?"

"I'll be saying them every night you're over there," Trif assured him. "Mornings, too," she added as an afterthought.

The train carrying the boys to St. John's leaves on the second Monday in October, after a farewell supper and time at the church hall Saturday night. The six recruits are Will and his two friends, along with Cyrus Snow and two other boys from Bareneed who are joining the Naval Reserves. Will's sister Ruth has been keeping company with Cyrus all the past winter and summer, and the thought of losing both her brother and her sweetheart to the war has her in tears all night.

That *Forgetful* Shore

The day after the volunteers leave, Ruth sits at Triffie's kitchen table, a fresh flood of tears soaking her embroidered handkerchief. "I don't know why Pop wouldn't let us get married," she sobs. "Lots of couples are getting married before the boys go overseas. Kit did it!" she remembers. "If she can be a war bride, why can't I?"

"Kit's older than you are, she's been to college and been out on her own teaching for years. And they were engaged anyway, her and Ben," Triffie points out.

"Cy and me talked about getting married," Ruth blows her nose. "Now he'll be on the other side of the world, him and Will and all the rest."

Jacob John, who has been stacking wood out in the shed, comes in through the back door and goes for the kettle on the stove.

"Sit down, I'll get that," Triffie says. Jacob John pulls his chair up to the stove and puts his boots up on the edge, rubbing his hands together near the oven door. Triffie makes him a cup of tea and tops up her own and Ruth's.

"It's getting late – stay here for the night, Ruthie," she offers. "You can sleep with Katie – help keep her warm," Trif adds.

So Ruth goes up the stairs carrying a candle, into Katie's tiny room under the eaves. Triffie starts to clear away the teacups, but Jacob John stops her with a hand on hers.

"Cut us a slice of toast bread, missus."

Triffie sighs, not really minding, and cuts two slices off the loaf she made this morning. She puts them on a plate and Jacob John takes one on the toasting fork and lifts the front damper lid off the stove, holding the bread above the glowing coals. Trif takes down the crock of bakeapple jam and spreads a little over the first piece of toast when he gets it nice and golden brown. She hands it to Jacob John, who is now toasting the second piece, but he passes the plate back to her.

"That one's yours. I'm doing mine now," he says.

They sit together in a warm silence, eating toast with bakeapple jam, one of Trif's great pleasures. She finds herself thinking more kindly of her husband these days, with something akin to affection. It's as if she's gotten used to having him around, she thinks. They have, after all, been married six years now. Katie, two years old now, is still an only child, though it's not for lack of opportunity to have another.

Trif has to admit – to herself, not to Jacob John of course – that she is even beginning to enjoy the marital relations a bit, or at least not to mind them as much as she once did. Motherhood has eased up her mind in some ways. She is bound to Jacob John now by a tie far stronger than wedding vows; she no longer regrets having married him, or thinks how she might get out of it. She is Mrs. Russell for better or for worse, and Mr. Russell is not such a bad fellow after all, though he's no hero of romance.

Just as well he's no hero. It's mostly young single fellows like Will and his buddies who've gone off to join up, but there's the odd married man with children who takes it into his head to go off and volunteer. The very knowledge that Jacob John will never do anything so foolish comforts her, is probably half responsible for the warm feeling she feels now as he takes his plate and hers, lays them in the sink, banks up the fire and takes her hand to lead her upstairs to bed.

That *Forgetful* Shore

Kit

The Western Front
June, 1916

Dearest One,

All I can say of our location is that tired old cliché: Somewhere in France. You will know more of the news when you read this than I do, for reporters' telegraphs travel far more quickly than soldiers' letters.

I remember studying history in school, looking at maps of South Africa or the Crimea or even of ancient wars — Julius Caesar's conquest of Gaul was a favourite. I loved studying those battles, soaring above the page like an eagle flying above the battlefield, seeing the great strategic movement of armies, lines of battle moving back and forth with victories and defeats.

How different that is from being in the middle of a war! Here on the Western Front we do not soar like eagles, but slog along like the rats that keep us company in these muddy trenches. I believe there are commanders somewhere who have a sense of battle lines, and I hear that our lines are not moving much — which is bad, but also that the Germans' are not moving either — which is good. Beyond that, I do not see the movement of armies or the grand sweep of battle – only the slimy, mud-covered walls of a trench, with a bunker dug in at the end where I huddle with a few of the bravest boys I've ever known.

And they are boys, darling – at twenty-four, I feel like an old man here. So strange to think that had I stayed at home, I would be the youngest lawyer in a practice, a youngster still wet behind the ears, making beginners' mistakes and learning from my elders. Here in this trench, I'm the old man, Captain Porter, a senior soldier though I have virtually no experience of war, save that I came through the Gallipoli campaign and am one of that First Five Hundred who drilled at Pleasantville in the days when we didn't even have rifles.

How long ago it seems! And how long ago all that talk of the war being over by Christmas. Going on two years now, and no end in sight. We signed up for a year, do you remember? I've been married nearly two years, and we had two nights together as man and wife. What a strange start to a marriage. It comforts me only a little that thousands of couples are in the same predicament.

Somewhere far above this filthy trench, where that eagle soars and looks down on us, plans are being made. We hear rumours of a Big Push, but what that might involve – except for more battles and more blood – we cannot imagine. Home before autumn, the most optimistic of the boys say now ... and I wish I shared their optimism. Darling Katherine, I hope this letter won't be shredded by the censors because it betrays a hint of doubt about the war. If soldiers wrote what we truly thought, not a single letter would get through.

Hang it all, I can't end on that note. I want to say something cheerful and encouraging, and to-night's mood is hardly conducive to that. So I will say the most hackneyed and clichéd thing of all – that the thought of you, of being with you again, is all that keeps me going in these darkest hours – because it is, however trite, simply the truth.

Ever your own,
Ben

That *Forgetful* Shore

"I notice he never writes much about the fighting," Kit says, folding away the letter which she has just read out to Trif. Ben told her years ago when they were courting that he wasn't much of a letter-writer, and that was true until he went overseas. War has unlocked his pen; his letters now are long and thoughtful.

The two women are enjoying the cool of the June evening on Trif's front bridge. Trif is knitting, something she never liked to do when she was younger. Now her hands are rarely still; she has knitted more pairs of socks for soldiers than any woman in Missing Point.

"He's not much like our Will, then," Trif says. "Of course Will don't write near as well as Ben – he never was much for book-learning – but all he does write is about fighting. I thought he'd sober up pretty quick once he got over there and saw what it was like, but he's not hurt so far and he still thinks it's grand."

"Even after Alf was killed?" Kit says. Word had come during the winter that Seaman Alfred Mercer was lost on the *Alcantara* – the first casualty among the boys from the Point.

"You'd think that would bring it home to him, wouldn't you?" Triffie says. "He said Char took it some hard. But to hear Will talk about it, you'd think crawling through barbed wire, slogging up to his knees in mud, and shooting artillery shells at the German trenches was no more than skipping rocks down on the beach on a fine fall day."

"I hope he never has cause to change his mind." Kit remembers those early letters of Ben's. Ben is older and wiser than Will, but still when he first went overseas he was idealistic, believing he was fighting in a noble cause and right would be rewarded. Gallipoli knocked that out of him – seeing men he knew, boys under his command, wounded around him. He's written little about battles, it was true, but in a few sentences he could sketch what it was like to find the body of his commanding officer – a man a few years his senior, who had gone to school with him at Bishop Feild – torn and mangled on the field, his perfect blue eyes staring unseeing at the shining Turkish sky. Ben is a gifted writer – too gifted, Kit sometimes thinks. His letters put pictures in her mind she'd rather not have there. He has moved up through the ranks quickly because of the deaths of other men, many of whom he liked and respected. There is little boyish enthusiasm left in Ben after nearly two years overseas, a year of active service at the Front.

"Ah well, all we can do is wait and pray, and do what we can to help out," Trif's knitting needles fly as she speaks. "You're still going to do the recitation at the concert, aren't you?"

Trif's energy amazes Kit: she works around the house and garden all day, caring for Katie, pulling weeds from the rocky soil on the hill above the house where her vegetables grow, scrubbing and mending, baking and cooking. Jacob John is away for the fishing season, so Trif does everything. In what she calls her spare time she does WPA work, which includes not only knitting but also canvassing for money, organizing donations of clothing for the Red Cross, and now planning a big fundraising concert.

"I can't say no, can I?" Kit says. "I feel like a lily of the field next to you; it's the least I can do to help the cause."

The Women's Patriotic Association on Missing Point is officially run by Mrs. Wilf Parsons and her daughter Rebecca, and Mrs. Reverend White. But everyone agrees that Trif Russell works harder than anyone. Unlike the women of Bareneed, who couldn't co-operate and had to start two WPAs, one for the Methodists and one for the Anglicans, the ladies of Missing Point have banded together for the war effort. Even Trif's adherence to the Adventist faith doesn't exclude her from raising funds to relieve the needs of soldiers and war orphans.

Trif's religious convictions are as much a mystery to Kit as they have ever been – perhaps more. Sunday after Sunday this summer, Kit sits between her mother and father in their pew and listens to the minister pray for an Allied victory, for the success of the British army and navy in their battles, for the safety of Newfoundland boys and especially those from the Point and surrounding areas. During the school year she goes to church in town and hears the same kinds of prayers, the same patriotic sermons exhorting everyone to do their part for the cause of freedom and liberty. She cannot shake the thought that in some Lutheran church in a little German village, the pastor is urging his people to pray for German victories, for the triumph of the Fatherland, and most especially for the safety of the brave boys from their village. Both sides claim God as their leader, just as has every army that ever marched – and what does God do? Pick sides? Turn a deaf ear? Or laugh like Puck, sitting back as the chess pieces stagger drunkenly about the board and say *Lord, what fools these mortals be!*

She tries to put something of this into words, now, to Triffie. Despite Trif's fervent faith, she is the only person to whom Kit can honestly express her own doubts. Trif is never shocked by the things Kit comes out with, and

That *Forgetful* Shore

now she nods. "Jacob John says that the English say, 'God is on our side,' the Germans say, 'God is on our side,' and God says, 'Good God, what am I going to do with this crowd?'" She laughs at her husband's flippancy, then grows serious. "Honestly, Kit, if I thought God was fighting on our side like most people here seem to think, I wouldn't think much of Him either. God is above all this; He has a greater purpose."

"And what are we all supposed to do then? Sit around and wait for the end of the world?"

"Wait for it, yes, but work for it too. And do what we can to help others while the suffering lasts. I don't hold with them who says we shouldn't do anything at all to help out with the war effort, like Aunt Hepsy." Hepsy Snow has made herself unpopular of late by proclaiming that since war is the work of wicked men and God will soon put a stop to it all, His faithful people should have no part in it at all, not even to the point of knitting socks for soldiers. Kit can't imagine Trif, no matter what her religious beliefs, sitting back and doing nothing when there's a cause to support. The WPA effort animates Trif, gives her a crusade, and Trif's never happier than when she has a crusade.

"Well, I should go on and let you get some sleep," Kit says, packing up her own knitting, which doesn't take shape nearly as quickly as Trif's does. "I'll try to have my mind made up about the recitation by tomorrow. Do you want it to be patriotic, or does it matter?"

"My dear, you can recite what you likes so long as 'tis not 'Lucy Gray'," Trif says, and they both laugh. The hackneyed old poem from the Third Royal Reader is a favourite with a great many people, and in school days Trif and Kit had both been so moved by poor Lucy's fate that they had cried for hours.

The sun has set and the sky is a vivid twilight blue as Kit walks down the South Side Road to her parents' house. She finds her father sitting out on the front bridge of the house. "Mother's already gone up to bed," he tells her.

Kit sits down beside her father and they watch the waters of the bay turn gray under the darkening sky. It's a companionable silence; Kit has always been closer to her father than to her mother, always appreciated his willingness to take her ambitions as seriously as those of a son. She steals glances at him as they sit; his hair is gray now, almost white. He still keeps the books for his brothers-in-law, Abe and Wilf Parsons, and he worries about his wife, whose health has never been good and is worse this year. Kit has taken over the housekeeping while she is home for the summer.

That *Forgetful* Shore

"What will you do when I go back to town?" she says. "You know Mother's not going to be strong enough to cook and clean anymore. It's high time you hired someone to help out."

"I know." Her father nods as he looks out at the water. "Mother don't like to admit she haven't got the strength anymore, but I was talking to Aunt Sarah Dawe and she says their Ida is thirteen now, done with school, and she could come up and cook and clean for us once you're gone."

"That's good," Kit says. She is bringing back her own hired girl when she returns to town; Cousin Ethel's old housekeeper is no longer able to work, and Trif's cousin Betty, at fourteen, is eager for the chance to move into St. John's. Kit pushes aside the thought that she herself ought to stay home on the Point and look after her parents. It would be the dutiful and daughterly thing to do, but much as she enjoys the summer here she can't imagine living this life throughout the fall and winter.

On the night of June 30, the church hall in Missing Point is filled to the point of standing room only for the benefit concert. Though most of the fishermen are down on the Labrador – except, of course, those who are overseas – there are enough women, children and old men in the community to fill every seat. Two more boys about to volunteer – Ki Barbour and Wilf Dawe – are given seats of honour at the front of the room.

Kit has chosen "The Charge of the Light Brigade" to recite; she and Trif both love Tennyson, and the military theme seems to suit the occasion. Not all the evening's entertainment is required to have a patriotic or war theme: there are many good old-fashioned recitations and love songs, but sprinkled in among them are pieces like Miss Agatha Mercer singing "When the Boys Come Home," accompanying herself on the mandolin, and the Church of England choir will close the evening with "Land of Hope and Glory" followed by "God Save the King."

Kit's recitation is the last item before the choir sings. The night is warm and even with all the windows in the hall open, the press of bodies in chairs gives the room a close, sweaty feel. Ladies fan themselves with fans or with paper programs, and Kit keeps checking the clock, wondering how late the program will go. It's half-past nine now and Ada Morgan is singing "O Promise Me," a song she mastered for her sister Sally's wedding last winter. Sal got cold feet at the last minute and left Ki Barbour at the altar. Now Sal is gone off to Carbonear in service, Ki Barbour is enlisting, and Ada is bound and determined to sing her solo.

The applause is not quite as warm as the room when Ada sweeps off the stage and Kit steps on. In fact, Kit gets a larger round of applause just for walking on stage than Ada does for singing: somewhat to her own embarrassment, Kit is something of a romantic figure to her neighbours. Local girl who made good, went away to college and became a teacher in a big school in St. John's, and a war bride to boot!

Kit takes the stage and looks out at the hot, uncomfortable people crowded into their chairs, some glad for the evening's diversion and others no doubt hoping it will soon be over. She straightens her spine, puts on her recitation voice, pitched to carry to the back of the room, and begins.

Half a league, half a league,
Half a league onward …

Everyone knows the poem, of course, some of them probably memorized it in school, and all have sat through at least half a dozen recitations of it at various concerts and events. She sees lips moving, people forming the words along with her. But as she begins the second verse, the familiarity of the memorized words with their echoes of school days falls away, and she sees the trenches of Flanders, those blood-soaked, mud-soaked fields she has never seen except in newspaper reports and in Ben's letters.

"Forward, the Light Brigade!"
Was there a man dismay'd?
Not tho' the soldier knew
Someone had blunder'd.

Someone had blundered. There is a tone in Ben's letters, things he will not put into words for fear of the censor. She senses he has doubts – about the wisdom of the men above him, about the orders he gives to the men below him. What if someone has blundered? Every time she says "the six hundred" she thinks of the five hundred, the First Five Hundred. There are nearly twice that many over there now, huddled in the trenches on the Somme, waiting for the Big Push, the great advance that will shatter the German lines and secure the Allied victory they are all praying for. The Newfoundland Regiment is earning a reputation, everyone in St. John's says, for bravery, for devotion to duty. For going ahead fearlessly in the face of incredible odds. *Theirs not to reason why, Theirs but to do… or die.*

This was the wrong poem to have chosen for tonight, Kit thinks. The images tumble through her brain; she thinks of talk she has heard back in St. John's. The Regiment has suffered no great losses yet, only a handful at Gallipoli, but Ben believes – all the men believe – that their day is coming soon.

> *When can their glory fade?*
> *O the wild charge they made!*
> *All the world wondered.*
> *Honour the charge they made,*
> *Honour the Light Brigade*
> *Noble six hundred.*

Apparently no-one shares her misgivings about the choice of recitation. The hall is silent for a moment, then the wave of applause breaks over her. Kit takes her bow and leaves the stage, not even seeing the two people coming on as she walks off, blundering into them and apologizing before she realizes it's Joe Bishop and young Rebecca Parsons, going up on behalf of the NPA and the WPA to make a presentation to the two young men who are soon to go overseas. Joe makes a little speech and Rebecca, giggling, hands over a pair of hand-knitted socks to each of the boys, and gets two kisses on the cheek in thanks.

The choir ladies push past, eager to assemble under the two Union Jacks draping the stage.

> *Wider still and wider, shall thy bounds be set,*
> *God, who made thee mighty, make thee mightier yet!*

The audience joins in, everyone singing, pleading with God to make England mightier yet, and then it's the anthem and everyone goes out into the blessed cool of the last night of June. Triffie, of course, stays behind to clean up, and Kit stays with her, sweeping up garbage from the floor of the hall, taking down decorations and putting them away. Triffie hums the chorus of "Land of Hope and Glory" as she folds bunting.

"How much did we make?" Kit wonders.

"Fifty-three dollars," says Trif with pleasure. "I sent the money box off with Mrs. Parsons already."

The lamps are out now and the hall is dark; Kit follows Trif out onto the step and Trif locks the door behind her. Trif may worship with a suspect

That *Forgetful* Shore

offshoot sect, but she is still trusted with the keys to the Anglican Church hall, because she is Trif Russell, and who would deny her? Kit slips her arm through Trif's.

"It was the strangest thing tonight – when I was reciting," Kit says. "I shouldn't have picked that poem – I couldn't help thinking of Ben and all our boys – wondering where they are, what they might be facing. And what it's all for, in the end."

"It's for the best," Triffie says, with such confidence Kit wonders can she really feel it. "It's all part of God's great plan," Trif adds, as if convincing herself. Arm in arm, they walk down the road.

Kit sleeps in Trif's house that night, sharing her bed as she often does during these weeks while Jacob John is away fishing. Both women are sound asleep, dreaming their own dreams, in the long hours after midnight while the sun rises over the battlefields of the Somme. They are asleep when it is nine in the morning in France, when Captain Ben Porter and Private William Bradbury and all the rest – eight hundred of them – hear the order to go over the top, onto the fields of Beaumont-Hamel.

Back home in Missing Point, the first weeks of July alternate between warm sunshine and a cold, damp drizzle. The news from the Labrador fishery is the first thing on everyone's mind, the war a distant second now that the patriotic fervour of the WPA concert has ended. As long as no new casualty reports appear in the papers, as long as no telegrams arrive at houses on the Point, the war remains something for old men to discuss in the evenings, smoking pipes as they mend their nets, or for women to shake their heads over while they knit socks.

The news reports are slow in coming. At first they report that the great Somme offensive is a success. It is July 8 before they first see the name of Beaumont-Hamel in a newspaper story brought in from St. John's.

The fourteenth of July is a hot, muggy day, the sky threatening rain that does not fall. Kit has been helping Trif in the garden; Trif is tired; she is almost certain that she is expecting again. She sits on a rock for a few minutes, watching Katie pull at blades of grass, catching her breath.

"Don't wear yourself out," Kit says. "I can do the rest of this, you don't want to take any chances. How far along do you think you are?"

"Well, I missed my monthlies in June, and now I've missed them again, so it could be as much as two months," Trif says. "Jacob John'll be some pleased when he comes home from the Labrador, I don't mind saying. I hope this one's a boy, for much as he loves Katie I know he wants a son – every man does."

"Have you told Aunt Rachel yet?"

"I've told nobody but you, and I won't, not till I'm sure. With the price of fish so high, it's a grand year to be having a baby, and if I'm right about the times it'll be February when it comes, and I can –"

"Trif! Trif!" They look up to see Betty running down the path that crests the hill, hatless and out of breath. "Mom says come over to the house quick! Liza Dawe was down at the Mercantile and heard tell there was a telegram over at the cable station for Pop." Betty looks like she's run all the way from the north side.

"Catch your breath, Betty, what are you saying? A telegram?" Trif repeats the words as if by saying them she can slow time, fix this moment before they get the telegram, before they know.

"They must have it by now – but Mom told me to come over and get you, she knew you'd want to be there if it was – if it …"

Trif is already on her feet; she has taken off the dirty apron she wears in the garden and wiped the earth off her hands. She is the opposite of harried, frantic Betty in every way at this moment; her movements are slow, deliberate, almost majestic as she picks Katie up in her arms.

"I'll come too," Kit says, needlessly, falling into step behind them.

On the way back across to the north side, Betty keeps up her hurried pace, her frantic torrent of talk. "We're not the only ones – Liza said there's a telegram for the Frenches too – it could be Will and Isaac both. Of course Mom says not to think the worst, they might just be wounded, it might not be anything … too bad."

To this torrent of words, Trif says nothing at all, which is strange for her. Her face is cold and deadly calm, and Kit thinks of how she favoured young Will. Kit puts out a hand as they walk, to touch Trif's arm.

The walk from south side to north side of the Point takes about a quarter of an hour. All the way Betty talks, and Trif says nothing, and Kit thinks of the descriptions she has heard of the Front, of men staggering across No-Man's Land under the barrage of artillery fire, of the clouds of poison gas that carry death on the air.

Cannon to the left of them
Cannon to the right of them
Into the jaws of death …

That *Forgetful* Shore

"Look! There he is now!" Betty says as they turn onto the North Side Road near her parents' house. Young Robbie Snow, one of the cable company's messenger boys, is riding his bicycle out of the French's front gate. "He must have already brought the telegrams." As the three women draw nearer Robbie pedals faster, racing past them back down the road towards the causeway, not meeting their eyes.

Kit follows Betty and Triffie up through the yard and around the house to the back door. Inside, Rachel, Ruth and Albert – who is home this summer because Rachel said she couldn't bear to have him down on the Labrador with Will overseas – all sit around the table staring at the unopened envelope. Trif and Betty sit down in the two empty chairs; Kit is left standing, the outsider in the family circle.

"I can't – you open it, Trif," Aunt Rachel says, picking up the envelope by a corner. Trif takes it, but doesn't open it. She looks up at Kit.

"It might not be – well, they send telegrams for everything, don't they?" Kit says. "Even if a soldier's only wounded, even if it's not serious. It doesn't have to be …."

"You read it out," Trif says, handing it to her.

Kit takes it, her hands shaking. It feels wrong for her to be the one reading this private message, yet they are all looking up at her as if this is a role she has the right to play. On the kitchen wall behind Uncle Albert's head is the framed picture of Will in uniform: his eyes, too, seem to meet Kit's as if he waits with the rest of his family to learn his fate. Even as Kit opens the envelope she thinks that telegrams must be coming to houses in St. John's, too. Is there one for her, for Mrs. Benjamin Porter?

"Regret to inform you – " she reads aloud, "Number 1446, Private William Bradbury has been reported killed in action July first."

Betty and Ruth both cry out: Ruth moves quickly from her chair to kneel next to her sister and put her arms around Betty's waist. Aunt Rachel says, "Oh, dear Lord," and Uncle Albert lays a hand over hers on the tabletop. Trif doesn't make a sound, just presses the heel of her hand against her mouth. Of all the faces in the room, only the serious face of Will in his Regiment photograph remains unchanged, as if he alone is untouched by the news.

Triffie

France
June, 1916

Dear Trif,

Tis some hard to think what to wright.

I love to get your letters tho, and it don't seem fair for you to send them and never get any back. Some of the fellows loves wrighting letters and some cant wright at all. I am someware in the middle I spose.

If you promise not to read this to Mother and Father I can tell you more. About how dirty and wet we are and about the lice and the rats and how men are getting sick all the time around me. Not like when we was traning in England. That was a good laff but this is different all together. I hate to say it sence I was so flick to sign up but the truth is I would give anything to be back home right now. Isaac and Char feels the same way but they would not tell there folks either. Isaac writes to Jennie Snow from Spaniard's Bay and he always puts on the brave face for her. Remember that girl I told you about that I met over in England, Gertie? She wrights me and I tries to wright her the odd postal but its hard to know what to say. Its easyer with you Trif but you was always my easyest person to talk to.

Some of the bys are spoiling for a real fight after all the time we spent in traning. I thoht I wanted a fight too but since we been over here I got a better idea what its all about and the truth is its pretty scarey stuff. I don't know what it will be like in a big battel but no douts we'll find out soon. The bys all say we'll get orders to go over the top soon, maybe in a day or two.

I hope I don't make a fool of myself, Trif. I was brave enough in traning but a real battelfeild with real German shells coming at you is another thing all together. You keep saying those prayers for me and I'll do my best I spose. If God is listening to you at all I lows I'll be home out of this soon, back on the Point safe and sound.

I wish I was there now.

Your loving cousin,
Will

The letter arrives, as such letters so often do, a few weeks after the telegram. A ghost letter. Aunt Rachel and Uncle Albert get one too, which they read out loud to everyone, and as promised it is calmer and braver than Triffie's. Trif does not share hers with anyone but Kit. Rachel and Albert and Ruth all think they would love to have one more piece of Will, one more thing to remember him by, but Triffie honours his wishes and doesn't show them the letter. What good would it do, to know that he faced his first and last battle like the scared young boy he was?

Triffie herself reads the letter over and over. It is neither eloquent nor well-written. Will's letters have never been the kind that would be published in the *Guardian*. But its raw honesty tears at her heart as she rereads it and pictures Will, small and lost when he sleepwalked as a child, or frustrated over his schoolbooks, or a young man laughing and carrying on with his friends.

His friends. Isaac and Charlie were both wounded at Beaumont-Hamel. Isaac's injuries were minor; he is recovering in a field hospital and will be back at the front soon. Charlie has lost a leg, and will be sent home as soon as he is able to travel.

Gertie Mercer is beside herself, not knowing whether to be devastated at Charlie's loss or relieved that he is out of the war for good. With Alf drowned and Harry still at sea, she has had a hard war already. But at least she will have no more fears for Charlie – the worst has been done to him. Nellie French goes about like a ghost, horrified to think Isaac has come through the hell that was Beaumont-Hamel – for now the stories are coming out, of what it was like, of how vast the losses were – but that he will be patched up and sent back into that madness.

As for Triffie's own family, Aunt Rachel and Ruth are drawn together by grief. Betty has gone to St. John's with Kit, and the two women remaining in the house have turned to each other. When Triffie goes over to visit them she feels excluded, as if her loss is different and one she must bear alone. She sympathizes with Uncle Albert more than anyone. He goes about his work, fishing from Abel Morgan's boat, in grim silence. Trif does not talk to him about Will – nothing about her uncle encourages confidences – but she imagines that he looks at his nets and traps and wonders what it's all for. A man builds his home, his work, his life around the hope of handing it on to his son, the hope that his children will have a better life than he has had, will go a little farther and live a little easier.

Trif's own emptiness consumes her. Jacob John is still away on the Labrador and Kit has gone back to St. John's. Kit's own news was similar to what the Frenches got about Isaac. Ben Porter was wounded, but his injuries were minor and he would be back on the front line soon. More Newfoundlanders were coming, fresh from their training in England, to the Somme to replace some of the hundreds of men killed and wounded. The dance of death will go on; the offensive has failed, but the war is far from over.

Kit was Triffie's mainstay in the terrible days after the news about Will arrived. She hired a girl to help her mother so that she could be free to stay with Trif and Katie. She helped with every household chore, cared for Katie, and sat up long at night with Trif. Sometimes they sat and knitted in silence. They did not talk a great deal, for the first time in their long friendship, for what was there to say? When the silence was too hard to bear, they went back to their old practice of reading aloud. Kit read all of Tennyson's *In Memoriam* aloud. Trif has always loved *Idylls of the King* and other poems by Tennyson, but this is her first time reading the poet's lament for his dead friend. Whether it's Tennyson's words or Kit's steady voice, she draws a little comfort from these readings.

With Kit gone back to town, the world is colder and grief is harder to

That *Forgetful* Shore

bear. It will be October before Jacob John returns. News comes and goes from the boys so far away in France, yet the men fishing on the Labrador are as cut off as if they are in another world. Letters rarely come and go except in case of emergency. Triffie thinks of sending a cable to Battle Harbour but decides against it. When Jacob John comes home, he will learn of Will's death, and he will learn that Trif is pregnant again. Good news and bad news. The good will weigh more heavily with him than the bad, for though he thinks a lot of Will, a son of his own will mean more than the loss of the boy who was like a son to Triffie.

Yet when the day finally comes, when she and Katie watch Skipper Wilf's schooner dock at the wharf, she does not tell Jacob John, first, about the new baby. She lets Katie put her arms out to Papa and be swept up into his embrace. "Ah, there's my girl, there's my girl," Jacob John says.

He puts an arm around Triffie and gives her a casual squeeze. "How's yourself, missus? Keeping the home fires burning and all? What kind of summer was it? Fishing good around here?"

"Not a lot of fish, but the price is good, so people are doing all right out of it," Trif says, putting Katie back in her pram and falling into step beside Jacob John as he picks up the small chest with his few belongings and says goodbye to his shipmates.

"Lots of fish down on the Labrador," Jacob John says. "Hard old news from the Front though, eh? No bad news from any of our boys after the July Drive, was there?"

He tosses the words off so casually, as if he knows there can't possibly be bad news. The men on the Labrador must have heard how bad things were over in France, but perhaps they haven't got the scope of it. Jacob John may not realize, yet, how every corner of the island has been touched by the disaster of July 1. Surely if he knew, he wouldn't ask so lightly.

"It was a terrible day," she says. "We had – there was a telegram. For Uncle Albert."

"What?" He stops walking. "Not Will? He wasn't … was he wounded?"

Triffie shakes her head, not trusting her voice.

"Ah girl, I'm sorry." He turns and gives her the embrace he wouldn't give her on the wharf, taking her into his arms. "What a grand young fellow he was – and his whole life ahead of him. He never shoulda gone over there – none of 'em should. What a waste."

Triffie shuts out the words and lets herself relax for half a minute in her husband's arms. His chin, scratchy with a summer's worth of beard, nestles against the top of her head – not that he's so tall, but she's buried her face in his shoulder, in the smelly rough wool of his jersey. Fish and sweat and tobacco – oh, it will be good to have a man around again, someone to fill up the empty spaces in her days and in her house.

Enough weakness, now. She pushes back, away from him, and smudges tears out of her eyes with the heel of her hand.

"All summer, now, you had to bear this, and I didn't even know of it," Jacob John says. "I'm sorry I wasn't here when we got the news."

Katie, perhaps confused by the rare sight of her parents embracing, reaches up her arms from the pram. "Papa, take me up, take me up!"

Jacob John, who spoils the child something shocking, Trif thinks, lays down his sea chest and gets Katie out of the pram. Putting the chest in the pram instead, he says to Trif, "You don't mind pushing that for a while, do you?" and swings Katie up high on his shoulders, grunting a little as he does. "Ooh, you've grown since I went away, my love. Come on now, let's go home." And on the walk home Trif tells him about the baby, and he is as glad as she has imagined he would be.

Home is, indeed, easier to bear with Jacob John there. Not that his presence makes up in any way for Will's absence, or even that he is as much comfort to her as Kit was. In fact, after first hearing the news, he doesn't mention Will, except when they go to visit Aunt Rachel and Uncle Albert, and he says how sorry he was to hear it.

Still, there he is, and her nights don't seem so long. She sleeps poorly, lies awake trying not to dwell on the images that crowd her brain, tries not to see Will's mangled young body, lying in a blood-soaked uniform in the mud.

But you can get used to anything, even loss, Triffie finds. The news from France continues bad, but there are no more casualty reports of local men, until the day in October when Triffie walks over to her aunt's house on the north side and finds no-one at home. She knocks, goes inside, calls out, lays on the table the batch of date squares she carried over, and turns to go, when she sees Ruth coming into the yard.

"Oh, Mother said she thought that was you, Trif. You better come over. We're all over next door to the Frenches – well, all but Father, he's still gone cutting wood. Mrs. French got a telegram." Ruth's eyes are red.

"A telegram? About … Isaac?"

Ruth nods, and Triffie takes Katie by the hand and goes over the lane to the French house, where she finds her aunt and cousins sitting awkwardly in the parlour around Mrs. French. The telegram is on the table, telling them that Private Isaac French was killed in action on October 11 at Gueudecourt.

Triffie liked Isaac, though he wasn't family, wasn't part of her the way Will was. Yet in a way this second loss doubles the heartbreak. She thinks of the two boys, such good friends all those years growing up, both dead and buried in foreign soil across the sea. She remembers again the morning Nell French found Will asleep in the bed with Isaac. Trif thinks at least if they both had to die, they might have died in the same battle so they could lie close together again in the same graveyard. Two childhood friends; two boys from the Point.

And then there's Charlie Mercer, the third of their trio. Fall chills into winter and after the second shock of Isaac's death, the war again slips into the background for most of the folks on the Point. The Bradbury and the French families are scarred forever. Everyone else goes on about their business, reading and talking about the headlines from Europe, shaking their heads over one Allied loss after another, but getting on with the business of daily life. Then, one day in March, the same train that takes the men off to St. John's for the seal hunt brings one-legged Charlie Mercer home from the war.

He has sent word he is coming, and he is the first of their boys home from the war, so half the Point gathers at the Bay Roberts station. Nine months have passed since Beaumont-Hamel, months that Charlie has spent recuperating in an English hospital, being fitted for his artificial leg and acquiring a wife – an English nurse, the first rumours are. Upon closer reading of the letter she wrote home on Char's behalf, it turns out she's an Irish girl who worked in the hospital laundry.

At first, when he appears in the window of the carriage, there is silence, then a ragged cheer. "Charlie!" a few voices cry out, and then Joe Bishop's strong voice rises above the rest. Joe has brought the children down from the school to see the war hero return home. "Hip, hip, hurrah!" Everyone joins in on the hurrahs and then Joe and the schoolchildren sing "For He's a Jolly Good Fellow." When the chorus is done Joe Bishop shifts to "God Save the King." Everyone joins in; the men readying their bags to go on the train stop and take off their caps, and in the middle of "Happy and glorious,"

Charlie Mercer sets his one good foot on the soil of home, and his mother breaks from the crowd and throws herself in his arms, nearly knocking him off balance. His war bride, a petite girl with eyes as round as buttons, stares around the wharf as if trying to fathom where on God's earth Charlie has brought her.

He looks years older than when he went away in the fall of 1915, though he's still not twenty. He's so thin now, and his hair is cropped, and there are lines in his forehead that don't belong on a boy of nineteen. But he steadies himself, then steps forward to embrace the rest of his family and introduce his wife while the schoolchildren finish singing the anthem.

"Remember when you had him sing 'The Old Polina' for recitation day, back when he was a little fellow?" Triffie says to Joe Bishop. "I thought it was the smartest thing I ever heard of – you thinking of that, I mean, when he had such a hard time in school."

"Well, Charlie never did get the knack of schoolwork," Joe said. "But he was brave enough over there, where it mattered. He's done his bit – now the only question is, what will he do with the rest of his life?"

It is a sobering question, for a one-legged fisherman is no asset in a boat. Trif wonders if the thought troubles young Charlie, or if he is simply glad to have survived. Over the din of voices surrounding him she hears Charlie's laughter, hears him say to Jacob John and the other sealers, "Yes, b'ys, I went over there to fight for king and country – didn't realize till I got over there that the King was a bloody Englishman!"

It's hard to look at him, to hear his joking voice and the laughter which, despite everything, is still easy and boyish. Hard not to think, *Lord, if three of them went away and only one could come back, why couldn't it have been our Will?* Then she asks forgiveness for that unkind thought, and tries not to envy the blazing joy on the face of that stupid woman Gert Mercer, who was once so proud of having three sons in uniform.

That *Forgetful* Shore

Kit

St. John's
September, 1918

My Own Posy,

How strange it seems to have <u>Good</u> <u>News</u> <u>at</u> <u>last</u> from overseas. We have become so accustomed to the papers being one parade of Tragedy after another, that to hear that our boys, bolstered by the Americans, are winning Victories seems almost beyond belief.

Yet it is true. I hear sober, sensible people – those whose advice can be trusted, not those who are prone to too much optimism – wondering not if, but when, Germany will sue for peace, and what the peace terms might be, and, Most Important for <u>all</u> <u>of</u> <u>us</u>, how soon the boys will be home.

When I think of my <u>good fortune</u>, that after four years of War, Ben is going to return home safely, I can scarce believe it. He has been in hospital in England ever since being wounded at Cambrai, and now that the Regiment, so decreased in numbers, has been withdrawn from active Duty, he is being sent home. Yet I cannot speak of our Good Fortune without thinking of you, of all the women who are not so fortunate, whose Loved Ones will never be coming home.

Ben has been through such terrible things – fought at Beaumont-Hamel, at Gueudecourt, at Monchy and Cambrai. I wonder at the Horrors he has seen, how they will have changed him, how one lives after seeing so many men die all around one. He writes that only a handful of the boys he signed up with in 1914 are still in the Regiment – the rest dead, or so badly wounded they were sent home. And not all the Wounds are Bodily Wounds – Ben writes that the <u>strain</u> of what they have experienced in the trenches causes some men to <u>lose</u> <u>their</u> <u>minds</u>. And he says, most troubling of all, that he knows what such men go through.

What will he be like, when he comes home? What sort of Marriage can it be, that has begun with four years of <u>lonely</u> <u>independence</u> on my part, and four years of <u>Horror</u> <u>and</u> <u>Violence</u> on his?

Kit has come to the bottom of the page and started another. Those last two sentences stand alone on a second page, and she looks at them a long time, wondering if she will send them to Triffie. Apart from the fact that she's trying to curb her girlish habit of underlining all the important words, she fears the last paragraph is a bit too honest. To confess to worry is one thing; to doubt her good fortune is another.

Twice she picks up the second page to tear it in two, but instead she folds it and slides it inside her copy of *Ethan Frome*. On the bottom of the first page, below the words "what such men go through," she writes:

I hope for the best.

And she does. She hopes for the best on the day she goes to the harbour to see Ben's ship come in. She hopes that they will still know each other; that the pounding in her chest and the grip of fear around her throat will ease when he is here and she is in his arms. That they will still love each other.

It takes her a moment to recognize him. She's seen returning servicemen before, knows that they look aged and tired and worn beyond their years. She is prepared for a sprinkling of grey in the brown hair at Ben's temples, for the deep lines around his mouth. She isn't prepared for his voice. It has changed – or rather, she realizes after a few moments, it hasn't changed. She has forgotten the sound of his voice. His photograph has kept his face

That *Forgetful* Shore

before her eyes, letters have captured a little of his personality, his spirit. But his voice has been silent for over four years. He has a nice voice, warm and low, a little rough.

"I can't believe it's you. Really you, and not a picture," Ben says. "And your voice! Katherine, can you believe, I used to lie awake nights torturing myself because I couldn't remember what your voice sounded like?"

"You too? I was just thinking I'd forgotten your voice – I didn't realize how much I missed it."

They both laugh, and kiss. She has forgotten so much: not just his voice, but how he makes her laugh, how often their minds work together as one. It will be all right, she tells herself on the way home from the harbour. Everything will be fine.

Over the years since Cousin Ethel's death, she has been redecorating the house as much as her budget allows, turning it from its maidenly, musty gloom to something better suited to a young married couple. A young lawyer and – a lawyer's wife. The Board at Spencer has been kind enough to tell her that she can keep her position until Christmas. After that, the trustees imply, she will be expected to take up her wifely duties again.

Some wifely duties are easy and pleasant to slip back into. She asks Ben no awkward questions about French farm girls, as she knows some wives have done when the boys came home. Four years is a long time. She has been faithful, of course, but men have different needs – and more opportunities, especially in the chaos of wartime.

Night after night she's lain in bed, imagining Ben's homecoming, imagining the nights when she'll share it with him. But if slipping between the sheets with Ben, fitting her body back to his, is easy, spending an untroubled night in his arms is not. His first two nights at home go well, but on the third night she wakes to the sound of screaming. Ben sits straight up in bed, shouting at the top of his lungs.

She has tried to prepare herself for nightmares. When Ben wakes, shaking and screaming in the middle of the night, she puts her arms around him, holds him, tells him it's all right, he's safe at home now. She's not prepared for him to pull away from her embrace, shrug it off, leave the bedroom and pace the hall outside. But everyone tells her the men who've been in the trenches have a hard time, even after they're back home. You can't just pick up the threads of the old life without interruption. So Kit gets used to interrupted nights. She wonders how long this will last, if it will pass away after a few months, but she knows of no-one to ask, and Ben himself doesn't like to talk about it. In daylight, his night terrors are a weakness of which he is ashamed.

In daylight, things seem almost normal. At first. When she goes to work, Ben goes for walks, visits old friends. He says he needs a few weeks before he feels ready to visit the law firm where he was supposed to have begun work in the fall of 1914, to talk about whether there's a place for him now. If not, perhaps he'll go into practice with someone else, maybe even somewhere else. They have Kit's salary till December, so there's time for Ben to adapt. She's not surprised that he startles at loud noises or sometimes has difficulty knowing what to say when people ask about his time overseas. She leaves him to his own devices during the hours she's at work, and sometimes she works late. Things are busy at Spencer, as two teachers are off work with the influenza that's come to the city.

She comes home to have dinner with Ben at one o'clock, then goes back to work for the afternoon. When she returns at five she usually finds Ben sitting in the wingback chair by the parlour window, a book facedown on his lap, staring out through the window. Yet he often claims he didn't see her coming through the gate and into the front yard, which you couldn't miss from the parlour window. Kit wonders what he sees when he gazes out through that window with those blank eyes.

Betty Bradbury is still keeping house for Kit. Betty is nearly seventeen now, a good steady girl; the young fellow who was courting her signed up last summer and the fact that she and Kit both had menfolk overseas created a bond between them. One evening Kit goes into the kitchen after supper. "Betty, is Captain Porter home all day? He doesn't go out for a walk or to visit anyone?"

Betty's brow wrinkles and her answer comes without hesitation. "No, he don't go out at all, Mrs. Porter." Back home on the Point, Betty called her "Kit," but since coming to work in town she has been careful to address the mistress of the house properly. "I been asking myself should I say anything to you about it. The first week or two he was home, now, he'd sometimes go out for an hour or so. But now he don't go nowhere at all – just sits in the parlour all day."

Kit promises herself she will not put any pressure on him. It's wonderful just to have him back, safe and alive. She doesn't ask that he rush out and find a job, or resume his life where he left off. Only that he be here, and alive

and more or less well – that's enough. Enough for now, anyway.

But when Ben has been home for more than a month, she has to admit to herself that he seems to be getting worse instead of better – more troubled, more remote, harder to talk to. In those first days after his return they poured their hearts out to each other eagerly, telling each other everything they could remember from the last four years. Now Ben is irritated when she prods him to talk. "Give me time," he says, over and over. "I'm sorry, Katherine, I can't just walk back into the man I used to be – I'm sorry."

How much time? she wonders. If there were an end in sight – if she knew he would recover in six weeks or six months, she could bear it. Instead she is faced with the possibility that after waiting four years for Ben to come back, she has now lost him forever. A different man – a shell-shocked man, a shell of a man – has come back, and she has no idea how to help him.

There are glimpses – moments when she hopes things will soon be back to normal. One night she comes home from work and Ben is not sitting blankly in the chair, but is dressed in his best suit, waiting for her. "It's Betty's half-day off," he says. "Let's go out to dinner."

They dine at the Crosbie Hotel. The evening is a pleasant echo of the dinners they used to share together during student years in Halifax, when they could afford a rare evening out. They do not talk about Ben's time overseas, nor about the boys who never came home. They talk a little about Kit's war years; she tells him stories about the home front, about life in St. John's while the men were at the Front. Mostly, they reminisce about the past, about Elliston and about Dalhousie. And, for the first time, they dare to talk a little, hopefully, about the future. Ben says that this week he will go see Mr. Harrison, one of the partners in the law firm that hired him in 1914. "I'll write him a note tomorrow morning, and tell him I'll be calling at his office on Wednesday or Thursday," he says, decisively. "If he doesn't still have a place for me, he may have some other recommendations – might know of an opening."

That night they go home, make love, and both sleep peacefully for the first night in weeks.

It turns out to be a good thing they chose this night to go out, for in the morning the news that has been threatening for a fortnight is finally announced. With the influenza epidemic spreading throughout the city, all theatres, restaurants and other public gathering places are closed. Schools are closed as well, which means Kit is out of work and home all day.

"Makes no sense writing a note to Harrison now," Ben says. "Who knows how long this damned 'flu will keep spreading? Harrison might not be even in the office – and if he is, I'm sure he won't want callers who aren't absolutely necessary."

"But sending your card can't do any harm – that will at least remind him of you, keep your name in the front of his mind –"

"Stop nagging at me about it!" Ben stalks from the room, slamming the door. Kit gets up to run after him, then sits back down. Nothing good can come of running after him, cornering him. Nagging him.

Now that they are virtually quarantined, the big house seems too small, with the two of them and Betty in it. Moments when things seem comfortable again are punctuated with sullen silences and angry outbursts. Not all the silences, nor all the outbursts, are Ben's. Kit finds it hard to be patient with him, to be gentle in tending wounds she cannot see.

One day they have a screaming fight about Kit's decision to re-arrange the parlour furniture, and they both retreat to separate corners of the house, exhausted. Later that day, a note comes in the mail from Alice Templeman, now Mrs. Penney, Kit's old friend from her student days at Spencer. Alice is the wife of a well-off businessman now, and she and Kit have seen each other occasionally, once every few months, since Kit moved to town.

Dearest – I'm driven mad. Surely we'll die of boredom long before the Spanish 'flu gets us? Our boys are winning battles at the Front and we're here at home as bored as anyone could be in a trench. I simply can't bear it a moment longer, and am spitting in the face of Fate. I'm inviting a half-dozen couples to dinner Saturday night and we'll socialize in spite of epidemics and war and all. Will you please come along and bring that dashing man of yours in uniform? Having a veteran of Beaumont-Hamel, Monchy and all the rest, in our company, will certainly put our silly little influenza fears in perspective, don't you think?

Please do come, darling. I'm so bored, you can't imagine.

That *Forgetful* Shore

"Infectious" – the word is used, mostly these days, in reference to the 'flu, but Kit is infected with Alice's spirit as soon as she lays down the note. All of it – the ennui, the frivolity, the desire to thumb her nose at destiny. To dress up in something pretty and go out to be among people. She and Ben have seen almost no-one but each other since he came home.

"Please let's go," she says to Ben, after telling him about the party, though not showing him the note.

"It seems a foolish time to be throwing a party."

"You've risked death every day for four years and now you're afraid to go to a dinner party?"

His eyes flash for a moment and she almost hopes he'll get angry, but the mood passes in a second and he looks heavy and beaten again, his eyes empty. "It wasn't every day. People never understand that – people who weren't over there. You have weeks, months even, of boredom, punctuated with a few hours of screaming terror."

Kit suddenly feels very hard. "Fine, then. Do as you please. I want to go to a party, and I'd like to go on my husband's arm. After four years alone, waiting for you to come home, you wouldn't think that would be too much to ask, would you?"

His expression is like ice. "Are you … really … trying to make *me* feel sorry for what you've endured these past four years?"

Kit shrivels inside, like a crumpled piece of paper. He's right. Nothing she's suffered can compare to what he went through. But despite her guilt there's still that hard-edged thing inside, sharp as a blade, that makes her say, "Of course. All the suffering was yours – we can't forget that." And for a change, she is the one who turns and leaves the room. She goes up to her desk and writes a letter to Triffie, then, on re-reading, tears it into tiny pieces.

For a long time she stays up in the room she plans to turn into a library, the room with the tall bookshelves and her writing desk by the window. It's dark when he comes in, walks up behind her, places his hands on her shoulders. "I'm sorry," his voice says behind her. She doesn't turn around; he is just a voice and a pair of hands. Maybe it's better this way; maybe this is all of him she can handle.

"I'm sorry, too," she says. "I should never have belittled what you went through. You have every right – it doesn't matter how long it takes you to get better."

"What if I never do?"

She reaches up to her shoulders to cover his hands with her own. But she doesn't answer.

"I'm sorry," he says again after a moment. "I am trying. You know that, don't you?"

"I do. I know that." She stands up then, and turns to face him, and he takes her in his arms. "I know you're doing the best you can."

"I can do better," says Ben. She looks into his face, his wonderful, handsome, ravaged face. This is not the boy she married, and the love she had for that boy will have to change, grow and stretch, if it can ever fit this damaged man.

"We'll go to the party," he says. "Your friend's party."

"But – the 'flu …"

He shrugs. "You were right. I've faced worse than influenza and lived. I can't give up living now, when I've done it for so long, can I?"

She laughs a little, at last, and sits down to write a note thanking Alice for her invitation, and saying they will be there.

Kit thinks Ben might change his mind, but having promised to go to the party, he keeps his word. He is so biddable that he even agrees to don his dress uniform and his medals, which he has refused to do since coming home. So Kit gets her moment of glory, wearing a new frock, sweeping into the huge foyer of the Penney's house on Circular Road on the arm of her war-hero husband.

That is the high point of the evening; the rest is disappointing, though not disastrous. Appearing at a dinner party, in uniform, seems to be as much effort as Ben can make. He is quiet throughout dinner, making only a few attempts at conversation. He answers questions that are asked of him as briefly as possible, but refuses to be drawn into war stories. "It's still difficult for him to talk about," Kit excuses him at one point, when a particularly persistent older man wants to know the story of his Military Cross. She lays a hand gently on Ben's arm, but he moves away.

"Glad to be back on the Rock?" someone else asks Ben. "Or do you wish you were still over there, to finish mopping up the Huns?" News of the war is on everyone's lips tonight; it can only be a matter of weeks or even days before there is peace.

Ben is silent for a moment, then he says, "No man in his right mind could ever want to go back to the Front."

That *Forgetful* Shore

Only one of the men present was overseas; Frank Tuohy, who was wounded at Gallipoli and sent home. He nods in the awkward silence that follows Ben's words, but no-one else knows where to look.

Ben clears his throat. "Of course, when I was discharged, the Regiment had been withdrawn – we were sent to Montreuil, to guard General Haig's headquarters. Some people thought it was quite an honour, but –"

"Haig!" Frank Tuohy spits, and he and Ben meet each other's eyes.

"Oh, now, Haig's a good man … he's gotten our boys this far …" Alice's husband George blusters.

"Gotten them this far?" The deadness of Ben's expression changes for the first time: his jaw clenches as he turns on George. "He sent our boys, as you call them – and you're right, they were boys – into battles that couldn't be won. Used them as cannon fodder – and for what? For what? A few yards of mud that would be lost again a month later!"

Again, there's the little silence, which George Penney breaks. "But surely now, that victory is in sight –" His wife is the one this time to put a hand on her husband's arm, but it's a restraining touch, not a comforting one.

Ben says, "This victory wasn't won by men like Haig – it was won by our men in the trenches. The men that the generals were willing to throw away."

"No more war talk!" Alice says brightly, clapping her hands. "Really, it's too dreary. I've had four years of nothing but war talk, and I'm fed to the gills with it. Surely we can find something more cheerful to discuss?"

Efforts are made to introduce other topics of conversation, but with the dictum that they cannot talk about the war, the conversation naturally comes back to the 'flu epidemic, which is even less cheerful than the war. The war, at least, shows signs of ending, while the epidemic is getting worse, both here in St. John's, and abroad.

"Four new cases confirmed this week," says Violet Windsor, whose brother is a doctor. "And Miss Dickinson has died – isn't that tragic? After she was so brave, nursing overseas, to come back here and catch the 'flu while nursing the sick, and die of it? It's like something in a novel!"

"You needn't sound like you relish it so," says Alice. She was friendly with Ethel Dickinson, who was a few years her elder and went to the Methodist College rather than to Spencer.

The evening wears on, alternating between 'flu talk and war talk, neither of which does much to lift anyone's mood. People excuse themselves within an hour after dinner, and after the second couple leaves, Kit sees the mute appeal in Ben's eyes and nods. They thank Alice and George, and shake hands as the maid brings Ben's coat and Kit's wrap.

"Was that so bad?" she asks as they walk up Military Road.

"Yes," Ben says. "It was as bad as I'd imagined. But not," he adds, "as bad as facing German artillery. Not quite."

So they end the evening laughing together, and along with the day's headlines about the armistice talks, Kit sees the entire day as a positive sign, a sign that things are getting better. It will not be easy, of course. With Ben's recovery, as with the war, there will be setbacks, but surely victory and peace will come.

The next day he seems drained, as if the party has taken every ounce of energy. He is reluctant to get out of bed, and Kit encourages him to lie in and rest. She has a troubling thought as she goes downstairs for breakfast – what if he begins taking to his bed day after day, if his nerves get worse instead of better?

Ben gets up later in the day, but he's still tired and withdrawn. Kit, wishing she had work to do, reads a novel and writes letters. She will not focus on Ben's troubles; she will be positive and cheerful.

She is so fixed on being positive and cheerful that it takes her till the following day to admit that there is more wrong with Ben than nerves or melancholy or shell shock. She has become accustomed to these things, so accustomed that they blind her to the fact that he's running a fever.

"It's nothing," he insists. His eyes are glazed, and he's shivering, although he is sitting up in his accustomed chair with a blanket over his shoulders. Shivering, but his skin is hot to the touch. "A touch of cold, I think. You mustn't worry."

"Mustn't worry? Ben, fifty people have died in St. John's – and I – I made you go out to a dinner party. A party! Why didn't you talk sense, make me stay at home?"

"Katherine. Stop fretting. I've been sick before; I had a fever in the trenches one time … I was delirious, saw things that weren't there – I came through that. I'll come through – whatever this is."

Kit smiles, tries to make herself believe him. But Ben does not get better; by nightfall his fever is higher and, over his protests, she calls a doctor. The few minutes she waits outside the door while the doctor

That *Forgetful* Shore

examines Ben seem like time has slowed, as if those moments are as long and vacant as the years she and Ben spent apart, as if another four years will pass and empires rise and fall before the physician steps out of the room and says, "Mrs. Porter –" And then everything speeds up all at once.

Late that night, in the hospital, Kit tries to understand this strange stretching and squeezing of time. A day ago her worst fear was that Ben would never fully recover, never be able to work, never be himself again. That, she now realizes, was the good time, the time when things were going well, however difficult they might have seemed. Now Ben is in a hospital bed, another statistic, the newest influenza case. When she goes to his bedside and hears the harsh pull of his breath, sees the gray pallor of his skin, she wishes she could go back to the night she received Alice's note, wishes she could tear it up without ever showing it to Ben.

She takes his hand. "Be careful," the nurse says. "You don't want to expose yourself."

Too late for caution. "Ben," Kit says. "Ben, can you hear me?"

His eyes flutter open and shift in her direction, and he draws another ragged breath. "No, no, don't try to talk." Kit has already seen the effort it costs him. "It's fine, everything will be fine. You'll get through this – the doctors will help you, you'll recover, and then everything will be all right. It doesn't matter if you – even if you can't work again, I don't care. I'm sorry I've been so impatient – I really don't mind ..."

"Hush, Katherine," he says, and coughs. He looks like he wants to say more, but then just shakes his head.

Kit, too, wants to say more, to find the charmed words that will reverse the spell of his illness. If she could go back to the doubts and difficulties of a week ago, she would embrace them with the sympathy and courage a good war bride ought to show. It can't be possible, after all, that he could survive four years of war, live through the hell of the Western Front, only to die in a hospital bed in St. John's with a racking cough and a raging fever.

She sits beside him all night, watching his chest rise and fall, as if she can be certain he will keep breathing if she doesn't take her eyes off him.

In the morning, when the doctor has finished examining Ben, he turns to Kit and says, "Mrs. Porter, my dear, you're going to have to be very brave."

But I already was! Kit wants to scream. *I was brave for four years, just as I was supposed to be, and now I'm supposed to have my reward.* She turns away from the doctor, from her husband in the bed, to look out at the street through a window glass streaked on the outside with dust and dirt. She places a hand against the glass and dimly sees her own reflection press back.

And Leaves
the Wretch
to Weep

1919 – 1927

Triffie

Dearest One,

*How hard it is for me to write this letter, imagining the pain you
must feel!! I cannot grasp it, though I have felt the Sting of Loss
myself. But I think now that my loss is not to be compared to yours.
I felt I had lost a piece of myself when our Will died – for you know
I loved him – but you have lost your helpmate, your true love,
your soulmate. And what a Cruel Fate – to lose Ben so soon after
being reunited! Truly, you have been dealt the hardest blow I
could imagine, and I wish with all my heart that I could get on
to-morrow's train and come to St. John's to be with you, to comfort
you as you once did for me.*

Triffie lays down the pen. What is there to say? Words on paper are bald
and cold in the face of grief. No letter could have carried her through the
dark days after Beaumont-Hamel, and she means it when she says that Kit's
loss is far worse than hers was. To lose a husband you truly loved, one who
had finally returned after a long absence, would be unthinkable.

Trif envies Kit and Ben's love story; it has all the hallmarks of romance, and though she only met Ben the once, she saw in him every quality she could have wished for in her own ideal mate. If such a love was not to be her own destiny – and clearly it isn't, she thinks, looking across the room at Jacob John who is already in bed, snoring after a hard day's work – then she could wish nothing better for her dearest friend. To have Ben home from the war and dead on the day the armistice was signed is unthinkable.

Worst of all, Kit is not even coming home for Christmas where she might recover from the blow with Trif by her side. She is going to Elliston to spend the holiday with Ben's family, where his body has been sent on ahead to be buried in the little churchyard there.

Kit wrote:

I did not want to think of him lying in the cemetery here in St. John's, so far from his home and family, especially when I have no idea what my own Future might hold or whether I might someday lie beside him. Some days it seems that consummation is <u>devoutly to be wished</u>, and the sooner the better. Forgive me for saying such things, but I have such Dark Thoughts on these long winter nights, and to whom can I utter them if not to you?

I wish I could be with you for Christmas and New Year. What a sad New Year this will be, 1919, the year I dreamed would bring the fulfillment of all my long-held hopes and wishes! But I think it would be cruel if I did not accept Captain and Mrs. Porter's invitation. They are even more crushed than I am, for they never got to see Ben after he returned. At least they have some comfort in the news that Lije has safely completed his service in the Navy and will be home in the new year, but they held out hope of having Ben home for the holiday season. Now I will come alone, and visit him one last time in the graveyard there, and then go on to … to what? I do not Know, and <u>Cannot Imagine</u>.

"Come New Year's, I means to go into St. John's for awhile," Trif tells Jacob John a few days later.

"To stay with Kit?"

"Yes. I think she needs the company, though she never came out and said so."

He nods. "How long is awhile?"

"I don't know. I thought to take the youngsters with me, not knowing how long I'll be gone for."

He doesn't say anything for awhile, cooling his porridge, eating another spoonful. "You could leave them here," he says. "I won't be at much in January, sure. I might go in the woods again for a few days if need be, but I could leave Katie and Billy with Aunt Rachel if I do. If you brings two youngsters in to Kit's house the two of you won't have much peace and quiet. Kit's not used to young ones in the house like we are – it might wear her out more than give her any comfort."

"You're right, I s'pose, but I didn't like to leave them with you." It's good of him to offer. She won't stay in town as long if the children are at home, but what time she does have in town she'll be freer of responsibilities, more able to concentrate on Kit. Kit will be teaching, of course – now that she is a widow she's been told that her position at Spencer will be open as long as she wants it. They will have evenings and weekends together to talk, to read, to re-knit the bonds between them.

She will miss the children. Katie, who is five now, looks up at Trif with wide blue eyes on the morning she leaves and says, "But Mama, what will we do without you? Papa can't make supper."

"Papa will have to try his best," Trif laughs, although she knows Rachel and Ruth will keep them well fed and cared for while she's away. A fortnight, or three weeks perhaps – she can't be away from the children longer than that. She takes Billy in her arms for a last kiss, gives him back to Jacob John and kneels to embrace Katie before turning to board the train.

"What about me? Don't I get a kiss?" Jacob John says.

"What, in front of everyone?" Trif takes pity and brushes her lips on the side of his beard.

Kit is at work when Triffie's train pulls into the station, but Betty comes to meet her and they hire a cab to take them to Kit's house. Betty seems so grown-up, moving through the busy St. John's streets with the confidence of a city girl. Her young man, Frank Dalton, will be home from overseas soon. The soldiers are beginning to return, the survivors of war.

They reach Kit's house, which looks both large and crowded since it's three storeys tall but attached to the houses on either side of it. Trif and

That *Forgetful* Shore

Betty sit down for a good chat in the kitchen. When Betty begins to get tea ready, Trif gets up to help, but Betty slaps her hand away. "You're company now, Trif, and I'm the hired girl. You got to get used to being a lady of leisure while you're here."

The first week is everything Triffie has dreamed of for years – forever, it seems. Every time she and Kit have had a little time together in these last years, Trif has always had the pressure of family and housework and responsibility in the background. Now Kit is the one who has her work to go to each day, while Trif takes the first holiday of her life. She is free to spend her mornings sleeping late, reading, even walking about the neighbourhood as she gets braver.

When Kit is off work, in their evening and weekend hours, they are truly together, with nothing to do but talk. Betty walks the line between family friend and hired girl neatly; she lingers in the dining room to chat with them for awhile after tea, then excuses herself to do the washing up and makes herself scarce for the rest of the evening, leaving Kit and Triffie to talk alone.

Nothing is held back in those conversations: Kit pours out all her hurt and pain, the unfairness of losing Ben just when she'd got him back, her feeling of being lost and adrift. "I always thought I loved being independent, working, being my own mistress," Kit admits. "I loved it all through the war years, even while I missed Ben. I worried how I'd get used to being just a wife, giving up all that freedom, once he came home. Now I've got nothing but freedom ahead of me – years and years of it – and I wake up in the morning and think, 'What am I going to do? What's it all for?'"

Trif nods. "Of course," she said. "Before, you had a purpose. You knew what it was all going towards. But now –"

"Exactly. But now." Sometimes they don't even need words, things are so well understood between them.

Ten days into Trif's visit she suggests the possibility of taking the Thursday train to Bay Roberts. It has been a good visit – not long enough, of course, but how much time could ever be enough to spend with her dearest friend, her other self? She wants to stay longer, but is afraid it will be too hard on Jacob John and the children.

"You've never been away from them before, and you probably won't again for years," Kit says. "I won't keep you here if you really feel you ought to go, but ..."

"I don't want to outstay my welcome ..." Trif offers the one objection she knows for certain will be overridden.

As, indeed, it is. Kit throws her arms around Triffie. "Outstay your welcome! As if you could!! Do you know how huge, how empty, this house will seem when you're gone? I have a lifetime of empty rooms and empty halls ahead of me, Posy – don't make it start any sooner than it has to. I mustn't be selfish, but ..."

So they both, selfishly, decide that Trif will stay another fortnight. So often in later years Trif will look back at that decision, will wonder how things might have been different if she had gone home ten days after she came to St. John's. So much would have been different: so much lost; so much saved. At the time it seems the only people who could be hurt are Jacob John and the children, and her family will make sure none of them starve. Instead of bringing Triffie to Missing Point, the train brings a letter saying she has decided to stay a little longer.

On Saturday, Trif seeks out the Seventh-day Adventist Church and worships there. It's lovely to worship with fellow believers; good to have a few more voices to join in the Advent hymns, too, though here, in this unfamiliar setting, Triffie can't help but reflect that the stirring lyrics about the Lord's coming sound a little flat now, inspire her less than they used to.

"The truth is," she admits to Kit that evening, "when I came into the Adventist faith, it never crossed my mind I'd still be sitting here ten years later. They talked about it like Jesus was coming the day after tomorrow."

"Well, you know I never put any stock in all your prophecies," Kit says. "No offense meant, of course, but I always felt you were too clever to believe all that, Posy." She pours out tea for them both, and Triffie wonders why, when people say "No offense meant," they invariably go on to offend.

"It's not a matter of cleverness," she replies, "as you'd know if you sat down and studied it out with me. It all makes sense, all the prophecies and times and laws. When Elder Hubley used to preach back when the war started about how the Turkish Empire would fall and it would lead to war in the Middle East and Armageddon, it all seemed so clear to me."

Kit sighs. "Now that it's all said and done, I can't see how Armageddon could have been much worse."

"That's just it, Peony. It *was* Armageddon – the war to end all wars. How could any war ever be any worse than the last four years have been? This – this has to change everything, one way or another, don't it? The worst

That *Forgetful* Shore

war ever fought, and then a deadly epidemic on top of it – if that's not Armageddon, what is? If the Lord really were ever going to come, wouldn't He have come and put a stop to all this?"

"Unless there's something even more terrible ahead – unless Armageddon is worse than we can imagine."

They sit in heavy silence for a minute, drinking their tea. "No, I can't believe it," Trif says. "I can't believe God would abandon us here like this."

"Well, you've always had a lot more faith in how much God cares about us than I have," Kit says.

This is the sort of moment Trif is supposed to be looking for, an opportunity to win Kit to Christ. If she really believed in the truth of the message, and if she really loved Kit enough to want her to be saved, she would use this moment, use Kit's grief and her desperate need for purpose in her life, to ensnare her with the gospel. In fact, she leans forward in her chair, as if to begin witnessing, then sighs and sits back.

"It's harder to believe than it used to be," she confesses.

"Why not give it up? Do you really need to haul all that baggage, God and faith and everything, around with you?"

Kit's attack, after Trif has just resisted the temptation to preach to her, feels unfair – a low blow. "It's not something I haul around. It's more like – something that holds me up. The boat I ride in. Lately I think it's sprung a leak, but kicking a hole in the bottom won't help."

Kit shrugs. "What do you patch it up with, then? What do you use to plug a hole in your faith?"

"It's not about patches and plugs – it's about finding the truth. I thought I had it, but now it's – I don't know. But I picked up something today – a flyer I saw on a lamp-post, on my way back from church." She holds it out to Kit, crumpled from being tucked in her pocket for hours. A series of revival meetings begins tomorrow night at the George Street Methodist Church; the speaker is Mrs. Victoria Booth-Clibborn Demarest, grand-daughter of General William Booth himself.

Kit looks it over. "I thought you weren't in the Army anymore."

"I'm not – well, I go to their meetings sometimes of a Sunday night, because I miss the singing and the band. But this isn't a Salvationist meeting, it's just a revival meeting."

Kit rolls her eyes. "What do you need a revival meeting for, Trif? I go to the Cathedral on Sunday mornings because everyone expects it of me, and then I put it away and try to think as little about God as possible for the rest of the week. But you're always chasing after Him, and to tell the truth the whole thing makes no more sense to me than a kitten chasing its tail."

It's rare for Trif Russell to bite back words, not to say what comes to mind. But she makes the effort now. Her friend is, after all, grieving. Kit is perhaps saying more than she means, and someone has to exercise some discretion here.

"I think I'll take myself off to bed," says Triffie.

The next morning she goes to the Cathedral with Kit, for the socially necessary exercise of being seen at morning prayers. Kit flatly refuses to return the favour by coming to George Street that evening to hear Mrs. Demarest speak, so Trif goes alone.

The Methodist Church is packed with bodies, and there is enough singing, clapping, even dancing in the aisles, to satisfy Triffie's need for a livelier form of worship than she can find with either Adventists or Anglicans. It is, in fact, much like a Salvationist meeting, except for the lack of uniforms, and everyone has worked up a fine sweat by the time Mrs. Demarest gets up to speak.

A lady revival preacher! Triffie has heard a couple of women officers in the Salvation Army, and she loves hearing the gospel coming out of a woman's mouth – it's a reminder that the world is larger than the one she knows. But Victoria Booth-Clibborn Demarest is something entirely different – a performer, a show-woman, almost an actress. The Holy Spirit fills her, there's no doubt about that, but she's hardly a transparent vessel. She's more like a stained-glass window: the Spirit within only makes her colour and design shine more vividly. Her small figure at the pulpit makes the whole room glow and shudder with the presence of God.

There is nothing restrained in this preaching, nor in the response of the audience. There could be no sharper contrast to the solemn Anglican liturgy of this morning, or the lengthy, Scripture-laced Adventist study she sat through yesterday. This is pure emotion, pure Spirit – music and prayer and shouting all twined together. "Glory! Glory, Hallelujah!" people shout all around her, as Mrs. Demarest's voice rises to a crescendo. She lifts her hands above her head, shaking her fists. "Come down, oh Lord! Fill us with your Spirit! Come down, NOW, Jesus!!"

This is heady stuff, commanding God to come down and fill the room. The Adventists wait and work and pray for Jesus to return, but they know

That *Forgetful* Shore

it's ultimately His decision when He'll show up. Mrs. Demarest seems to believe one can compel God to be present, and He'll obey. It may not be the Second Coming, but the Spirit is here, right now, in this room, and it's as real as any return she can imagine with angels and trumpets.

People pour down the aisles to kneel and be saved, tears streaming down their faces, praying aloud, bursting into song. Trif kneels at the altar and feels, as John Wesley once did, that her heart is strangely warmed. God is not, after all, sitting far away on a cloud, checking off prophecies on a calendar while He waits for the moment to return, safely removed from the hell of Armageddon and Beaumont-Hamel and Monchy-le-Preux. He is here, among His people, present and alive.

Last night she felt the little dory of her faith was swamped, ready to capsize. Now she feels buoyed up, sped across the water with a fair wind at her back. Though she knows Kit will mock and be cynical, she can scarcely wait to get home to tell her about it.

Kit

St. John's
January, 1919

Dear Triffie,

I can scarce explain ...

I am at a loss for words when I think ...

It was most kind of you to come visit me in my Hour of Need,
and I feel I must apologize for ...

I regret so many of the things I said ...

It's no use. Kit has tried eight times since Triffie went home to start a letter of apology. Every time she tries, she gets angry all over again. What good is it to apologize when she's still angry?

The first part of the visit went so well. Until Triffie got tangled up in those revival meetings, and couldn't talk about anything else. One night she came home an hour later than usual and told Kit she had been to a prayer meeting after the main revival meeting where she received the baptism of the Holy Spirit and spoke in tongues.

Kit has no words to match this folly. She is still struggling to figure out what her life will be like without Ben and fighting mind-numbing despair every day. She hasn't the energy to deal with Trif in the grip of yet another bout of religious enthusiasm, babbling happily about the Holy Spirit.

Before this, she's always been able to set her doubts against Trif's faith, both of them equally sturdy, and have a lively discussion that ends with both of them still friends, still respecting each other's views. But respect is not, perhaps, most evident in Kit's tone on the night she says, "If there really is a God – something I have a harder and harder time believing – surely He could put His time and His omnipotence to better use than making a bunch of fools dance around George Street Church speaking gibberish. Perhaps He might have spared some of that power to save a few million people from dying of influenza, or perhaps stopped the war before millions of men died in the trenches? Or if that's too much for Him, I hear there are still people starving to death in the world. Maybe He could have a look over there and see what needs doing instead of making all the Holy Rollers in Newfoundland drunk, when a bottle of bootleg gin could do the same!"

There is chilly silence in the room when she finishes her diatribe, and Trif says stiffly, "I puts up with a lot from you, Kit, for the sake of friendship. But you know what the Scripture says about blasphemy against the Holy Spirit."

"Blasphemy – is that it? You really want to accuse me of blasphemy?"

"I don't want to accuse you of anything – I want to warn you."

"Warn me! Don't you think my soul is a bit past saving now?"

"Why should it be? I know you've been through a hard time, Kit, but those whom the Lord loves, He rebukes and chastens, and as gold passes through the refiner's fire –"

"I don't want to be refined!" Kit shouts. She grabs at her own hair with both hands, pulling it loose from its pins so that it falls around her face, tugging as if she would tear it out in handfuls.

"Well, you're certainly not acting very refined just now." A grin quirks the corners of Trif's mouth. It almost melts Kit – it always has before, how the same woman can speak so seriously and self-righteously about sin and blasphemy, prophecy and punishment, yet burst into irreverent laughter a breath later.

But Kit hardens her heart against Trif. She is tired of being preached to, tired of Trif's belief that there are easy, God-given solutions to every problem. She lowers her voice, not wanting to attract attention from Betty, who has gone on to bed hours ago.

"You don't know the half of what I've been through." Kit turns away from Trif to look out the window. "You think just because you lost your cousin, you've got some clue about what it's like to lose someone you love."

"I know 'tis not the same," Trif says, her voice so much calmer and kinder than Kit's own. "I've said all along that what you're going through is worse than anything I've had to bear. I know that."

"But maybe it evens the score."

Trif says nothing. In the silence Kit wants to prod further, to pick at the sores underneath old scabs. "You always envied me, didn't you, always thought I had it better? Always felt I had the easy life?"

"Perhaps. But I never wished you any ill," Trif says, still with that gentle calm in her voice. An after-effect of the Holy Spirit, perhaps, which makes Kit angrier.

"Wished or not, it's come to me now, hasn't it? I've paid for any good luck I've ever had – and paid for my sins too. For doubting God, for not loving Ben enough –"

"What do you mean, not loving him enough?"

"I never did. I was in love with him, but I can see now, looking back, that I never loved him the way he loved me. I was always torn two ways, wanting to be with him but wanting to be on my own too. I wanted to go on teaching and having a life, work of my own. I was afraid of being a married woman, afraid I'd lose myself. And it wasn't till I lost him that I saw how selfish I'd been, what a fool I was."

Again, the silence, and Kit does not turn around to meet Triffie's eyes. "You were right, though," Trif says after a moment. "Being married does

That *Forgetful* Shore

change things for a woman. At least, it did for me, and every other woman I've known. It might have been different for you, married to a man like Ben."

I'll never know now, will I? Kit rages silently. *We had forty-six days of married life together: two days of honeymoon under the shadow of war, thirty-nine days when he was mad with shell shock and despair, and five days when he was dying with the 'flu. I've had a hell of a married life, haven't I?*

She is going to say this to Trif, to speak out loud the bitterness that lies beneath her pain, to explain why her grief cannot be clean and pure. Trif will, perhaps, understand, and some of that burden will have been shifted onto friendly shoulders.

Kit opens her mouth, and instead she says something different, because that need to hurt, to wound is still there, like a serpent coiled under her tongue. "A man like Ben?" she echoes. "You envied that too – that I got a good man, someone good-looking and smart and ambitious. Jacob John Russell was never good enough for you, was he?"

Now she turns, wanting to see Trif react to the words, wanting to see the crack in her saintly calm. Sure enough, Trif's jaw clenches and her eyes narrow. "Jacob John is a good enough man," she says. "But I've never lied to you, Peony. You know I was never in love with him. You know if I wanted to be married it wouldn't have been to a man like him."

"Why – because he's a fisherman? Because you're too good for him?"

Trif takes a step back, her face like the face of a beaten child, not understanding what she has done to deserve the harsh words. But what is Kit doing that's so terrible? Only telling the truth, telling truths that have been left untold for years. Trif has always been comfortable in her illusion that their friendship is completely honest, that they tell each other everything. How many buried secrets can lie beneath the surface before they poison everything?

"I was raised in a fisherman's house. Why would I think I was too good to marry a fisherman?" Trif's voice is calm again, but not that quiet, saintly calm – it's cold now, and hard-edged, flat as a blade.

"You did, though. You always wanted something different, something more."

"What are you saying? That I had ideas – 'above my station'?" The sarcasm in those last three words can't be missed. The social gulf between them never mattered when they were girls and has been resolutely ignored in womanhood. They have chosen to be sisters, twins, so there can be no difference. But the difference has been there all along.

They always have been equal: in intelligence, in ambition, in dreams. Everything Trif has lacked, everything she's envied, has been denied her because she is the orphaned niece of a fisherman, while Kit is the only daughter of a merchant's clerk. Thus it has always been and ever shall be, no matter how many men bleed and die on battlefields for high-minded ideals like liberty and equality and brotherhood.

"I never said anything about rising above your station," Kit says. "Only that you always wanted more."

"Which is exactly the same thing, in different words," Trif says. "But if Jacob John wasn't the man I wanted, it's not because he's a fisherman. You know that. It's not the man's place in life, it's the man himself. I s'pose I had the same foolish romantic dreams most girls do, of a man I could fall head over heels for, a man who was romantic and – well, passionate." Her tone shifts to sound something like it did earlier in the evening when she talked about the Holy Spirit making her speak in tongues; it's the same longing, Kit is sure, that drives Trif to seek out odd sects and revival meetings. "Yes, a man with some passion to him. You knows what I means, don't deny it. Jacob John wasn't good enough for you; why should he be good enough for me? Did you think you could pass him on like a hand-me-down dress?"

"If Jacob John wasn't the right man for me," Kit says, "it certainly wasn't for any lack of passion. I know all about what kind of passion Jacob John Russell is capable of – probably more than you know, after eight years sharing his bed and bearing him two children."

"What do you mean?"

"I knows what kind of a man Jacob John is," Kit says, her carefully educated voice slipping back into lost rhythms and cadences, "because I had him long before you ever did. Did you think I was a virgin when I married Ben? Don't be so foolish, Trif. Me and Ben was together as man and wife for nearly a year before any preacher ever said vows over us, and before that I was with Jacob John, time and again that winter I taught out home. On a bed of nets in Abel Morgan's fish store, that's where I gave it up to Jacob John."

She never meant to say all this. It's as if one sentence drags the next behind it, like they're roped together, and she can't stop adding fact after fact, confession upon confession, as she sees the shock and disgust on Triffie's face.

"You – you and Jacob John?" A small few words in response to Kit's torrent of information, words twisted out of a mouth gone suddenly small and tight.

"Yes, me and Jacob John. Don't look so shocked, girl, it's not the end of the world. Only don't go trying to tell me that man's got no passion in him. He had it right enough when he was seventeen, and if he's lost it since then, I know whose fault that is."

"You … common … whore." Trif gives each word the weight it deserves, and Kit does not defend herself. The fight has gone out of her; she doesn't understand her own need to hurt Trif with this long-buried secret.

Trif turns to go for the stairs, and Kit thinks she will go off to bed in the guest room, turn the key in the door, and somehow, after a long and sleepless night, they will both sit over breakfast in the morning and find a way to piece this back together. Kit will apologize – only she can't do it right now.

In the morning, this demon will have left her, and she will be a better person. Not a saint, never a saint like Triffie. But a decent woman. Refined. Someone who chooses her words with care and would never dredge up a dark old secret just to hurt a friend. She knows she may have done untold damage to Trif and Jacob John's marriage. But if the older, stronger bond of their friendship can be repaired in the warm light of morning, then everything else will begin to knit back up as it should.

But Triffie stops on the third step, turns back. "Why have I been such a fool all these years?"

"You've never been a fool," Kit says. "Maybe you've been foolish about some things …"

About God, she means, about believing there's someone out there watching the fall of the sparrow, with some mighty purpose that will make sense of all our squalid sparrow lives. But Trif is thinking of a different kind of foolishness; she has her words back now, and is in full flight with them.

"…trusting you, looking up to you, and yes, you were right, I envied you. More fool me – to want anything you had, to want to be anything like you. Tying my whole life up to someone who don't know what friendship or loyalty means –"

"That's not fair," Kit says. "It's not as if I slept with Jacob John after you were engaged to him – it was long before, it was all over."

"Yes, so I could take your leavings and never know it! Some friend you are! Did you really think I'd be satisfied with Jacob John, even if I didn't know you'd had him already? You knew what I wanted out of life, knew the kind of man I would have been happy with. If you'd told me the truth, I never would have married him, and I'd have been better off!"

"I knew what kind of man would please you?" Kit repeats. "And what kind of man would that be? Someone too good for this world – the voice of Billy Sunday and the face of Mr. Darcy?"

"Don't you mock me," Trif says. "Don't you try to make a joke of this like you does of everything. My ideas weren't so high as you think. I'd have been satisfied with a good man who cared for the same things I cared for, who thought about more than what was on the table for supper at the end of the day, who enjoyed a good book. I wasn't as foolish as you seem to think – I wasn't looking for something out of this world. There are men like that. You found one, and I might have, if I'd waited."

Kit smiles slowly, cruelly. Though she already regrets what she's said, the desire to unburden the past hasn't left her. "A good man, one who likes to think and read books? You mean, a man like Joe Bishop."

Trif nods, not surprised. "Sure, a man like him. I don't mean Mr. Bishop himself – you was the one who was sweet on him in school, I recall, and I thought even after there were times you might have made fast to him. To me he was always the schoolteacher, but it's no shame to say I admired him. Yes, I would have been happy with a man like that."

"You wouldn't have been happy with him – or anyone – because you can't see past your fancies to see what's really there, what a man is really made of." Kit's angry, suddenly, on behalf of Jacob John Russell, even though she herself rejected and discounted him years ago. What is he, but a good, steady man, good looking and quick with a laugh? He was gentle and eager, for a boy of seventeen with a girl in his arms for the first time. She feels bad that he's ended up with this woman, this harridan, who will never think he's good enough just because he left school before he finished the Fourth Reader and doesn't like to quote poetry or wrangle about Bible verses. Jacob John Russell deserves better than to be compared to the likes of Joe Bishop. It's time Triffie knew that.

"Joe Bishop," Kit says, the name dipped in vinegar. "Is that your ideal man, then? And you think I was sweet on him in school – is that your version of it? Was it really just me, Triffie? Did he never lay his hand on

That *Forgetful* Shore

your thigh when he was explaining Mathematics to you, or slip a hand down the front of your dress on the sly while he helped you write your themes?"

"What are you talking about?"

"If it had happened to you you'd have known what I was talking about, or even if you'd kept your eyes open. It was me when we were in school – me that I know for sure, though there could have been others. Later on, there was Millicent Butler – did you never wonder why she wouldn't come back for extra tutoring? Of course, you thought she was a silly girl who wouldn't take a good opportunity to better herself. When really she was just an innocent young girl who didn't want a dirty old man taking advantage of her!"

"How dare you! How dare you say things like that about a man like Mr. Bishop?"

"You think I'm making it up? Ask Millicent, then. Ask Effie Dawe, or Amelia Snow. When I figured it out I made damn sure I wasn't the only one. I talked to the other girls and they all had the same story – all the clever girls, the ones with promise, once they got to be eleven or twelve and caught his eye. All those extra hours after school – this has been going on for years, Triffie. And nobody will see it or speak out because the man is like a god in that town."

"You liar!" Triffie is more enraged, even, by the accusation against Joe Bishop than by the news that her husband was once intimate with her best friend. "Why would you make up slander about a man like that?"

"The man is a saint – I know, I know. I've heard for years what a saint Joe Bishop is, all the good he does, but I'm telling you, Trif, I was twelve years old and that man was trying to get his hands up under my skirts. He made me think I was something special, just so he could do things no man should do with a young girl."

"So if this is true, why didn't you ever tell me? We used to talk about everything – tell each other everything, back then. Why would you keep a thing like that from me?"

Why? Kit has asked herself this question for years. Why she never told Trif about Jacob John is easy to figure out; why she never told her about Joe Bishop is harder. "I never knew what to think about it, how I was supposed to feel. I was ashamed, I suppose – but you're right, I did fancy him. I thought I meant something to him. It was years before I realized it was wrong, that he'd done a bad thing. By then, it was too hard to talk about it."

Trif stares at her, looking down from the height of three steps up. The hallway is dark, lit only by the lamplight that leaks out of the sitting room. For a moment they both stand in silence, eyes locked.

"I don't believe a word of it."

"You don't want to believe it."

"Something's wrong with you, Kit. You've had a terrible blow, and I think it's turned your mind, I really do. I can't think why else you'd be saying these awful things."

"What are you going to do then, go pray for me?"

"You know I will. I always have." Trif turns away, continues up the stairs. The hem of her brown homespun skirt swishes against the tread of the steps. With every step, every swish, Kit feels the gulf widen. She wants to pull Trif back, but she can't take back or change a word of what she's said. There's such power in truth-telling. The truth will set you free – but free from what? Free to do what?

"I'd think you'd care more than that, seeing you've got a daughter who'll be going off to school with that man in another year," she says. "Do you really want to risk not believing me, when Katie's the clever one, and Joe Bishop asks you can she stay behind for extra lessons?"

The swish of the skirt hem stops, and Trif stops moving, but she doesn't turn back. More silence. Finally, without turning around, Trif says, "I got nothing more to say to you tonight, Kit. Good night."

And she goes upstairs, surely to go down on her knees and pray for her wayward friend whose morals are so loose, whose brain is so infected with madness.

Kit lies awake that night. A dozen times she thinks of rising, crossing the hall to the guest room. She remembers nights in girlhood spent at each other's homes, sharing those old feather beds, their feet twining as they stretched out together towards the hot water bottle or the warmed brick at the bottom of the bed. She remembers holding Triffie in her arms in those days after Beaumont-Hamel, letting her cry out her grief over Will. How easy it had been to help and comfort Triffie; how hard for Triffie to do the same for her, Kit, in her hour of need.

There is something wrong with me, Kit thinks, lying in her empty bed, staring at the grey square of window in the blackness of the room. *I have lost my husband, and I can't even grieve properly: my world has shattered, but it's not a clean break that can heal. When my dearest friend comes to comfort me, all I*

That *Forgetful* Shore

can do is tear down her faith and throw old secrets at her, secrets that were
better kept buried.

Yet with all that, she feels a sense of relief. Not so much for the admission about Jacob John: Triffie was right about that. Kit should have either told her long ago or else kept silent forever. But the other secret – the truth about Joe Bishop, what he was and what he had done, what he was still doing, for all she knew, to young girls from the Point – it's good to have spoken that aloud. Kit wishes she had said it years ago, shouted it from the rooftops.

When morning comes, vague memories of troubled dreams are the only evidence that Kit has finally fallen asleep. She breakfasts alone, which is not unusual as Trif has been thoroughly enjoying her holiday from house-keeping and sometimes sleeps late. Betty says nothing about having overheard a quarrel in the middle of the night. *It will be all right*, Kit tells herself as she walks to work. *We will find a way to make it right.*

But when she comes home for dinner, Trif is not there, nor is she there at supper-time. Kit goes up to the guest room to find Trif's clothes and her trunk gone, and a note neatly penned on a square of notepaper propped on the pillow.

Dear Kit,

I have been to call on Aunt Clara Bradbury, who lives here in Town, and she has been kind enough to ask me to stay with her a few days. I have removed to her house and will leave from there to take the Tuesday train to Bay Roberts.

Thank you for your kind hospitality.

Sincerely,
Trif Russell

She goes to the kitchen, wondering how much Trif said to the girl before she left. She's unsure how to broach the subject, but Betty says cheerfully enough, "So, Trif told me she was staying down with Aunt Clara for a few days. Is she coming back here before she goes, or going on home from there?"

"I ... I think she's going home from Clara's," Kit says, and Betty nods, taking it all in stride.

Kit does not ask where Aunt Clara lives, nor does she make any effort to contact Trif before Tuesday. On Sunday evening, though, she goes to George Street Church, where the revival meetings continue. Kit sits at the back of the crowded room and watches the ecstatic worshippers, hands raised in the air. She has almost satisfied herself Trif is not there when she recognizes Trif's hat, bobbing in time to the hymn music.

The sermon, highly emotional and quite devoid of any logical exposition, leaves Kit unmoved and irritated. She cannot understand why it elicits tears and cries of "Amen! Praise the Lord!" from the those around her, but several rows in front she sees Trif's hands raised to the sky as if she could pull heaven down, as if like Israel she could wrestle a blessing out of God.

She's always been this way, Kit reminds herself, rising to leave. She remembers the Salvation Army prayer meetings when they were girls, and the Adventist prophecy charts with the strange beasts that Triffie pored over with such avid interest. When they were girls, Trif and Kit were bound together by restlessness, by the knowledge that they sought something outside the life offered them. For a time they pursued it together, in the classroom and in books and in each other.

She is no longer sure if she and Trif are even looking for the same things, but their quests have diverged so widely they are like people on opposite banks of a river, shouting to be heard, barely able to make out each other's words.

A hymn is ringing out as she leaves the building, hundreds of voices raised in happy cacophony. *Will your anchor hold in the storms of life?*

That's it, exactly – she pictures Trif as drifting through all these superstitions and religions, but in Trif's mind it's just the opposite. She's found a secure harbour to anchor in, and Kit is the one cut loose and drifting.

Do I have an anchor? Kit wonders. She has, in some ways, travelled much farther from the small world of their girlhood than Trif has, going off to college, working and supporting herself, becoming an educated, independent woman. But if there is something out there in the empty, post-war, Ben-less world that will fill her with the same bliss that now animates Triffie as she dances and jumps around at this revival meeting, Kit has yet to find it.

Triffie

JACOB JOHN AND the children are waiting for her when she steps off the train. With them is Ruth, who has doubtless done most of their cooking and cleaning these last few weeks. Seeing her pretty young cousin holding the baby, Trif thinks, *What if I went away again, and left her with them? I bet it wouldn't take Jacob John long to find some comfort with Ruth – if he hasn't already.* Kit's secrets have planted darker thoughts in her head than she could ever have conjured on her own.

Jacob John looks pleased to see her, but Trif saves her kisses for the children. She has almost forgotten, in these weeks away, how fiercely she loves them and how that love anchors and grounds her. With Katie's plump arms around her neck Trif knows she can't go away again, not ever, not really. Not until they are grown up, at least.

They have supper at Aunt Rachel and Uncle Albert's house, and Trif tells them how Betty is getting on and answers questions about whether Kit is recovering from her husband's death, smoothing over the fact that she never set foot in Kit's house for the last several days of her visit. She brings out Aunt Clara as a trump card, and Albert is so pleased she has stayed with his sister that this opens up whole new vistas of conversation.

Finally, though, the time comes – the good nights, the chilly walk home to the south side of the Point. At the sight of the house Trif's heart leaps almost as it did when she saw the children. She has forgotten that she loves this house too, has made it her home, her own place. She cannot leave. Three weeks away have only shown her how rooted she is.

She goes in through the back door, through the pantry to the kitchen. She stands taking in the house, the shining black woodstove and the low wooden beams overhead. Jacob John lights a lamp. Billy is asleep in Trif's arms and needs only to be laid in his cot, but Katie must be persuaded to bed, and Trif has to tell her a story before she will consent to sleep.

Trif crosses the hall to the room she shares with her husband. She hopes Jacob John is still downstairs, but he is waiting for her, sitting on the side of the bed in his nightshirt.

"Good to have you home, girl," he says with a hint of a grin.

Trif moves toward the lamp. She always turns it off before taking her clothes off: to this day, Jacob John has never seen his wife naked in full light. *Did he see Kit naked?* she wonders. Thinks of the two of them, young and limber and beautiful, on a pile of old nets and brin bags. She reaches to put out the lamp.

"Leave it on for a minute, and sit down by me," Jacob John says, patting the bed beside him.

She sits stiffly, still in her skirt and blouse and sweater next to her husband dressed for bed.

"I missed you," he says.

"I wasn't gone half as long as you will be in a few weeks, when you goes to the ice," Triffie points out. She gets up to take off her sweater, hangs it on the hook behind the door.

"Not the same," Jacob John says. "Man goes away fishing or sealing, woman stays home and waits. Like when the boys went off to war – the women stayed behind. Always has been and ever shall be. Feels different when you're the one left behind."

"Well, you're getting a taste of your own medicine then." Trif puts out the lamp at last. For a moment everything feels the same as always, but it isn't. In the dark she unbuttons her blouse. She hears the bedsprings creak as Jacob John lies down.

She finishes undressing and sits on her side of the bed. His hand snakes across the quilt and touches hers.

Well, what else would he expect? They're man and wife; she's been away nearly a month.

That image of Kit and Jacob John in the fish store won't go away. Seeing she still won't lie back on the bed beside him, Jacob John makes things worse by saying, "So, it was good, then, having the time to spend with Kit?"

That *Forgetful* Shore

Triffie takes a long breath. "I don't want to talk about Kit."

She didn't mean to say that. She was going to keep the whole thing quiet, let Jacob John think with time that her friendship with Kit has just faded away, that they grew apart. But she can't. She won't live a life of secrets and lies like some people. If you don't tell the truth, what kind of person are you?

"No? Nothing wrong, I hope," Jacob John says, and it suddenly occurs to her that he too has been keeping this secret for ten years. It's not as if he doesn't remember doing – that – with Kit.

"She told me." Three words is all it should take.

"Told you what?" He sounds genuinely puzzled, and he's not a good liar. No, wait – she believed he wasn't a good liar, but obviously he is, better than she could have guessed. Is everyone but Triffie a good liar?

"About you and her."

Now it's his turn to be silent a long time, to give a heavy sigh. His hand doesn't pull away from hers, but grips it tighter in the dark. She still sits with her back to him.

Finally he says, "Ahh, Trif, that was years ago. We was youngsters."

"Oh. And that's all right then, is it? As long as it was years ago, and you were youngsters."

"No, I don't – I didn't mean it that way. It wasn't all right, but – it happened. A long time ago."

"So long ago, you'd nearly forgotten, had you? Forgot to mention it to your wife?"

"Oh, Lord, Trif. What man tells his wife if he's been with another girl long before they were married? Especially if –"

"Especially if it was her best friend?"

Jacob John is quiet again for a long while, so long she wonders if he can possibly have fallen asleep in the middle of this. He is a heavy sleeper, and has been known to drift off in company when people are talking, if the subject doesn't interest him. Finally she says, "Are you awake?"

"Of course I'm awake, Trif. What the hell was Kit thinking, digging up that old foolishness after all these years? Is she cracked, or what?"

"Maybe she is," Trif says, pulling her hand away from his. "She's lost her husband; she's been through a hard time. I'm sure she said a lot of things she didn't mean." Is this true? she wonders now. Did Kit say things she didn't mean to say, or things she had been longing to say for years? "But at least she

That *Forgetful* Shore

finally told me the truth, even if it was years too late."

"And what good did that do, eh? Are you better off, now that you know?"

"It's always best to know the truth."

"Right. The truth will make you free." It makes her madder than almost anything else, when he quotes scripture, like Satan rhyming off verses to Jesus in the wilderness. "Are you free now, then?"

"I wish I was." She gets up and walks to the window, pulls over the curtain. It's a moonlit night and the moon makes its path across the water. She loves this view, loves to look out at the calm cove and the moonpath that seems to lead to somewhere much farther and stranger than Bareneed.

"Ah, yes. You'd like that, wouldn't you? Is that why you wish Kit had told you the truth years ago – if she had, you'd never have married me?"

"Of course I wouldn't!" She turns back to him, though in the dark she can't make out his face, can't see the look in his eyes. "Don't you think it's been bad enough all these years, knowing you went around with her first and only came after me once she showed you the door? I already knew I was your second choice – now I come to find out there was more to it than I ever guessed. That you and her was –" She searches for the right word. "That you and Kit had relations, long before you and me was ever married. How do you think that makes me feel?"

"I'm sure it don't make you feel too good," Jacob John says after another long silence. "That's why I never wanted you to find out."

"It was her you wanted, all along," Trif says. "I know I was second best, but I never thought you'd be comparing me to her, all these years, in the bedroom as well as everywhere else. I'm sick to death of not bein' Kit Saunders, never bein' as good as her."

Again the silence. How did she ever wind up with a man so stuck for words?

"If that's what you think, Trif, you're crazier than I ever thought you was. And that's saying something." She hears the bedsprings creak again; he turns over, so that if she does get in the bed – how can she ever get in that bed? – his back will be to her.

"Well, that's a great comfort, I'm sure."

"I don't know what you want me to say, girl. If you haven't figured out after ten years that you're second best to nobody, I doubt I can give you much comfort now. I s'pose nearly every man got something in his past, some

foolishness he got up to when he were a boy. I never thought you'd drag that out to hold it against me after all this time."

Well, I only just found out, didn't I? If I'd known sooner, I'd have brought it up sooner, Trif thinks. But she doesn't say it; it's too much like one of her usual saucy comebacks, the kind that might lead to Jacob John laughing, turning over, pulling her into his arms.

"I'm going to lie down with Katie," she says.

"Please yourself," says Jacob John.

Triffie lies in Katie Grace's narrow bed, warmed by her daughter's small body, listening to the sniffling sound of Billy's breathing in the nearby cot. *This is my life,* she tells herself. *These children, this house.* A path of moonlight on the water might beckon her away, she might dream of Heaven's chariots and some golden daybreak, but the truth is she's here. Stuck here you might say, but also here where she belongs.

She listens for sounds from the other room, wondering if Jacob John will get up, will come in here or go downstairs. Finally she hears a sound: his deep, steady snore that used to keep her awake when they were first married, that now lulls her to sleep. Tonight it makes her angry. After all that's been said, he can go right off to sleep.

She, too, falls asleep at last. Images chase themselves through her tired mind and weave their way into her dreams – the two children, the house, the moon on the water. Joe Bishop leaning over a young girl with a schoolbook, a kindly image that has now been tainted forever. The girl is naked; she is Kit; she kisses the man who is first Joe Bishop and now is Jacob John, who lays her down on a bed of fishnets and brin bags and touches her body. The girl looks up into Triffie's face, her eyes laughing, mocking, triumphant. *I've won it all; I have everything,* she says, and her face changes again. Kit stands at the bottom of the stairs, angry and hurt. The room grows darker and darker so that Trif, at the top of the stairs, can barely see Kit's face. *The last time I saw her,* Trif thinks, *the last time ever,* though she doesn't know later if that's a waking thought or part of a dream.

She goes on sleeping in Katie's bed for the next few weeks, a treat the children accept without question. She returns to her own bed on the March night after Jacob John goes to St. John's to join the ship that will take him to the seal hunt. Back in her own wide, empty bed, she is unable to sleep. As one sleepless night follows another Trif reverts to her usual cures: prayer and books. Alone on her knees she tries to recapture that bright fire of the Holy

Spirit that enflamed her during the revival at George Street Church. She feels something – a sense of comfort, of not being entirely alone – but it's a far cry from the intense infilling of God's presence that she experienced there, and her inability to get back to that feeling hurts almost as much as the loss of Kit. She goes on attending services as always, Saturdays and Sundays, but no hymn or sermon or prayer can recapture what she felt then.

So she plunges back into books, and finds herself engrossed in Tennyson's *In Memoriam*, the poem Kit read to her in the bleak days after Will's death. Though the poem is about losing someone to death, she finds some parts of it more poignant, more fitting now than they were in that bleak summer after the July Drive. Tennyson's friend Arthur was to him what Kit was to her: the friend of youth, the one who understood and shared his dreams and aspirations. Lines drift from the page to haunt her dreams. One night she lies awake thinking, *For all is dark where thou art not,* and in the morning, over and over in her brain drum the words *And unto me no second friend.*

Kit is lost to her, lost as surely as if death had taken her. No letter comes, and Trif does not attempt to write one. Reading *In Memoriam,* Trif thinks that Tennyson had it easier. Surely death is the cleanest way to lose someone you love? Then the memories are forever pure and intact, not sullied by petty meanness. There is no book Trif can open, no spot on the Point she can walk, where there is not a memory of Kit. Everything is tainted – not just Jacob John and Joe Bishop, not just the schoolhouse and Abel Morgan's store, but the causeway and the church and even the Long Beach.

She goes down to the beach on those cold, blustery March days – takes the children down there sometimes to throw rocks in the water, chilly as it is, just to get out of the house and let fresh air blow on her face. One night when Katie and Billy are both tucked up in bed, Trif crosses the road in front of the house and goes down to the beach alone, her coat wrapped tightly around her, and sits on a rock in the dark, gazing out at the waves as they foam on the rocks.

> *And Love would answer with a sigh,*
> *"The sound of that forgetful shore*
> *Will change my sweetness more and more,*
> *Half-dead to know that I shall die."*

That *Forgetful* Shore

She thinks of the poet's forgetful shore, the River Lethe, and wishes she were sitting on that gentler shore instead of this wild one. Would she reach forward, take a drink of that sweet water? She has never realized how much memory can hurt.

Staring out at the water, lost in thought, she doesn't hear footsteps on the pebbled shore until they are close enough to startle her. She looks up to see a man's tall form silhouetted against the moonlit sky.

"Well, well. Trif Russell. Look at you, stuck out here on the rocks like a mermaid."

"I'm no mermaid," she says, recognizing the voice before she sees the face. Jabez Badcock has been gone from the Point for five years. When the war broke out he was up in Nova Scotia working, and then he joined the Canadian Army and went overseas. He's been back for several weeks now. The servicemen are slowly returning home in ones and twos: Ted Parsons and Ki Barbour have come back with medals; Cyrus Snow has written to Ruth to say he will be back by April and asking her to marry him before the summer fishery starts. Harry Mercer is back, the one Mercer boy to return unscathed. Every time a soldier or sailor returns, the people of the Point turn out to welcome him home.

Nobody remembers what train or steamer brought Jabez Badcock home: he was simply back one day, without ceremony. He lives in a house out on the furthest eastern tip of the Point, which used to belong to his uncle. It was once a nice, snug little house, but it hasn't been lived in for ten years and from all Trif's heard, Jabez isn't doing much to improve it. Even before the war he was well on his way to being an eccentric.

He sits on the cold rocks beside Triffie and pulls out a flask. He takes a long drink and passes it to her.

"What are you, foolish? I don't want that."

"You don't? What, you got nothing you wants to forget?" His voice takes on the sonorous tones it used to have in prayer meetings in the days when Jabez aspired to become a Methodist minister. "*It is not for kings to drink wine, nor for princes strong drink, lest they drink and forget the law. Give strong drink unto him that is ready to perish, and wine unto those that be of heavy hearts. Let him drink and forget his poverty and remember his misery no more.* I'm neither a king nor a prince, and my heart is heavy, so according to the Scriptures this is for me," he says, taking another drink.

"*And they sung a new song, saying, Thou hast redeemed us to God by thy blood, and hast made us unto our God kings and priests: and we shall reign on the earth,*" Trif counter-quotes.

Jabez throws back his head and laughs. "The one person on the Point I should have known better than to get into a battle of Scripture with!" he says. "Trif Russell, you've always been the only person I knew who was as haunted by God as I am. That Hound of Heaven, He's got our scent, haven't He?"

"I suppose so." To her own surprise, Trif tells Jabez about the revival meetings at George Street and the prayer meetings afterward, when the Spirit descended and she was slain and spoke in tongues.

Jabez nods. "I seen that too, up in Montreal one time – people laid out cold on the floor, shaking like they had fevers, babbling like maniacs – all in the name of the Holy Spirit."

"You never had it yourself, though? The baptism of the Spirit?"

Jabez shifts his eyes away from her, takes another pull from his flask. "I might have, I might not. I don't remember. There's lots I don't remember, lots I don't want to remember."

In the moonlight his profile is stark but handsome. He's always been a good-looking man, and in the years before he left the Point, Triffie knew there were many girls who wouldn't have minded trying to mend his broken heart. He looks older now, and harder, but he's still a fine figure of a man.

"That's why you took up drinking – so you wouldn't remember?" Trif suggests. She glances up at the lamp lit in the window of her house, calculates how long she's been down here on the shore. She should go up soon, check on Billy and Katie Grace. She remembers Jabez's stormy grief after Sadie Parsons died, and thinks it strange that he should still grieve after all these years. Sadie, as Trif recalls her, was a nice enough girl, pretty and good for a laugh. But even throwing an untimely death by consumption into the story she never seemed the type to inspire lifelong devotion on the scale of a Shakespeare tragedy.

Jabez laughs, as if he's heard her thoughts as well as her words. "Tell you the truth, Trif maid, I think I took up drinking to forget Sadie ... then I went overseas to forget things I did when I was drinking ... now I'm back and I got to go on drinking to forget what I saw over there."

"Were you wounded?"

"Bit of shrapnel in my shoulder is the worst I got. I knows there's plenty never got off so easy – I was sorry to hear about your uncle's young fellow,

and the rest of 'em. There's no justice to it, maid – them as wanted to live are buried over there in France, and some of us who didn't give a damn whether we lived or died came off without a scratch." Another pause, another drink. "I 'low you got your own things you'd rather forget."

"I s'pose I do. Don't we all?"

"Sure you won't have a drink?" He offers the flask again, and when Triffie shakes her head he puts the cap on, puts it in the inside pocket of his coat, and stands up. He offers Trif his hand and helps her to her feet, and for a moment they both stand looking at each other till Trif shifts her gaze out to sea.

"We got a lot in common, you and me, Trif."

There's such intimacy in his tone that she can believe there are women drawn to him, and she thinks for a moment he may be making a proposition. But when she looks back at him she can see that whatever he's got in his mind, it's not that.

Do they have a lot in common? On the surface, not much, she thinks. Trif Russell, pillar of more than one church, and Jabez Badcock, drunk and reprobate. But perhaps he's right. "You already said that," she points out. "The Hound of Heaven, and all that."

"Oh right, there's that. But there's more than that, far more…. Who's your father, Trif?"

She looks back at him, startled. It's a question nobody has asked her for years.

"You don't know, do you? But somebody knows. Ask Aunt Rachel – ask her what she remembers about my father, old Captain Josiah." And he turns around and begins to cross back up the beach towards the South Side Road, leaving Triffie alone on the beach.

She looks back out at the waves, at that forgetful shore. She knows what Jabez is implying, though she's heard only the vaguest of rumours about Captain Josiah Badcock, dead many years now. What would Aunt Rachel say if she asked her? It's not something Triffie can think about now, but she tucks it in the back of her mind for another day. Another piece of the past, another secret forgotten and buried.

She stands not on the shores of the River Lethe, but on the more prosaic shores of Conception Bay, and she knows now that she would not drink the waters of forgetfulness if she could. For every bitter memory there's a sweet one: the thought of Will lying dead on a muddy field calls up the memory of his head bent over the Royal Reader, a smile quirking his mouth as he says, "Read it for me, Trif, it's better when you reads it." The picture of Kit standing at the bottom of the stairs, her mouth twisted and angry, can't be separated from the memory of Kit and herself curled up in bed reading Shakespeare out loud. If she could erase the dark memories, she'd lose the bright ones as well.

She remembers Tennyson again – *'Tis better to have loved and lost / Than never to have loved at all* – and hopes the years will prove him right.

Triffie climbs up the beach and crosses the road, back to her children and her home.

Kit

Crossing the Atlantic
August, 1921

My dear Maggie,

I sit writing to you from a cabin on board the <u>Digby</u>, sailing across the broad Atlantic, bound for England. I find a thrill even writing these words, knowing that at last I am Outward Bound, setting forth upon such an adventure.

I think that our visit last summer was truly an <u>inspiration</u> to me, for I have taken some measure of Encouragement from seeing you, so Bold and Determined upon charting your own path in life, and realized that I must do the same. Things have happened to me that are out of my control – surely I would never have wished myself a Widow and an Orphan both, at the age of thirty! – but now I must take the good from the bad, and chart my own course. And so I have done, resigning my position at Spencer and applying to study for a B.Litt. at Oxford, just as we talked. So many things in my life have fallen out unfortunate, that I must always remind myself there have been a few Benefits as well, and take advantage of those.

The few benefits are not inconsiderable. Kit, though by no means a wealthy woman, knows herself fortunate to be as free from concerns about money as she is. Her St. John's house has been rented out, providing her with a steady income, and the house in Missing Point, left to her on her father's death two years earlier, has been sold to Ki Barbour. Thanks to Ben, she has a modest army pension, and thanks to Bishop Spencer School and her own frugal habits, she has savings from seven years of teaching. Not a fortune, by any means, but enough to make her an independent woman.

Nearly three years have passed since Ben's death. Two years since her father suddenly died of a heart attack. Kit hadn't expected this second blow. Her mother was the fragile one, the one expected to go first. Kit's plans had never included coping with a widowed mother.

She made her last trip to Missing Point the summer after the war, to bury her father, pack up her mother's things, and sell the house. Her mother, even more faded and fragile than before, made no protest about leaving the place where she was born, moving into St. John's with Kit. For the last year and a half of her life she lived with Kit, a querulous and often annoying presence in the house. Kit hoped that caring for her ailing mother would mold her own character, make her a better, more devoted daughter, but this has not happened. Still, she got used to the company, found herself more irritated by her mother in some ways and fonder in others. Kit cried when her mother passed away after a bout of pneumonia during the winter, but she'd be lying if she denied the renewed sense of freedom. No ties at all, now, and the future hers to do with as she likes.

The possibility of going to England woke something inside her that has been dormant since before the war. For the first time in years she feels excited, looking forward to a new adventure, as she was when she taught in Elliston or sailed into Halifax to go to college, or moved to St. John's to marry Ben.

It was Miss Shaw who gave her the idea of further study – and in Oxford, of all places. Miss Shaw attended Somerville College at Oxford in the 1890s, when the great university allowed women to study and write examinations, but not to receive degrees. In fact, the first women received degrees from Oxford just a year ago, an event Miss Shaw celebrated by returning, thirty years after the fact, to receive her own B.A. and M.A.

"The place is full of undergraduettes, as some people insist on calling them," she reported to Kit upon her return. "Of course the higher degrees

That *Forgetful* Shore

for women are still rare, but if you have the interest and the opportunity, there's no-one who would be better suited to the chance than you, Mrs. Porter." She always calls Kit Mrs. Porter, as does everyone at Spencer and, Kit supposes now, people she meets in England will do as well. It seems strange that her brief married life has left such an indelible imprint on her as to change her name, erase the memory of Kit Saunders altogether.

After landing in Liverpool and taking the train to Oxford, she arrives on a late-summer morning hotter than she's accustomed to. She stands on the platform of the station in Oxford, two trunks beside her, smelling the air. It tastes and smells different from at home; she is really in another world now.

Somerville College is like a dream of Oxford, with its brick halls and ivy. Kit, a mature woman with an education and years of teaching behind her, finds it hard not to stare and gawk like a small-town girl on her first outing to the big city. Anything might happen here; she is in a place where dreams can come true. Not just the dream of a higher education, but the dream of a broader, and perhaps even a deeper, life.

By the time Kit undresses for bed in the tiny room assigned to her, the day seems to have lasted forever. She has met with the Dean, taken dinner in the Hall and been introduced to faculty and fellow students. The majority of them are, of course, girls taking their B.A., but she sat at dinner with four other women who are reading their B.Litt., two a little younger than she and one at least ten years older. Two of them are, like Kit, school-teachers; the youngest, Miss Pennyweather, has just taken her B.A. and is staying on for further study. She intended to be married after the war, but her fiancé was killed on the Somme.

"We lost a great many men from my home on the Somme," Kit says, "at Beaumont-Hamel. At home they call it the July Drive."

"Oh, and where is your home?" Miss Pennyweather asks. "Your accent is hard to place – you're surely not Irish, are you?"

Kit, who believes she has erased all traces of her accent, explains where she comes from. Miss Pennyweather, despite her recent Bachelor of Arts, seems slightly confused about where Newfoundland is, but the other two women know all about it, and the older woman, Miss Stone, says kindly, "We heard a great deal about the bravery of the Newfoundlanders, during the war years."

"They were brave, indeed," Kit says, and, to get it over with, adds, "My husband was an officer with the Regiment; he fought at Gallipoli, on the Somme, and at Monchy and Gueudecourt."

"I'm so sorry, my dear. Was he killed in France?" says Miss Stone.

"No, he was discharged after an injury in 1918, and died of the 'flu only a few weeks after his discharge."

Now they are all feeling sorry for her, shaking their heads – one dark, one blonde, one grey. It can't be helped; her biography is short and simple, not intended to elicit pity, yet inevitably it will have that effect.

That night, before sleep, she sits on her bed looking out the window. She wants to write to someone about the day's adventures, but she has already written to Maggie and to Miss Shaw while on the boat, and mailed those letters upon arriving in Liverpool. The one person Kit really wants to tell the story of her sojourn in England to, the one person who would have burned with envy yet been truly glad for her, has not received a letter from her in nearly two years.

In that dark lonely time after Ben died, after she drove Triffie away, Kit composed one letter after another to her Posy, and tore them all up. She tried to put Triffie out of her mind, until she saw her again on that last visit to the Point. So strange to get off the train in Bay Roberts and not be met by Triffie, not step at once into that welcoming embrace. Trif attended Kit's father's funeral; she dutifully sent food over to the house as did most of the women of the community. She shook Kit's hand politely at the wake and said, "I'm sorry for your loss," but Kit could find no words to bridge the gap, and it seemed Triffie had no interest in seeking such words.

Soon after that visit Triffie's cousin Betty left Kit's house to be married, and Kit, though she liked Betty, was relieved to have this last tie severed. Trif is cut off from her; her parents are dead; the house on the Point is sold. Whatever Kit's future contains, there will be little of the past in it, nothing to remind her of the place she grew up, the people who were once her whole world.

Kit opens her trunk and finds her going-away gift from Miss Shaw: a leatherbound blank book. Kit has not kept a diary since she was twelve years old: she realizes now that she poured so much reflection into years of letters to Triffie, that she needed no other outlet.

Now she turns to the first clean page and pauses with her pen above the paper. How to begin? She cannot write "Dear Diary" or "Dear Journal"

like a schoolgirl. She sits with pen in hand until the urge to write, "Dear Posy," passes. Then she begins, without preamble or heading:

Today I arrived in Oxford, "that sweet city with her dreaming spires." If the spires are truly dreaming, I cannot tell, but I have been dreaming for years, all my life perhaps. What could be more surely a fulfillment of dreams than to be here, a student at Oxford University? Nothing. Which leaves only one question — how does one live within a dream fulfilled?

Triffie

"I SEE THE Church of England minister was here today," Jacob John says, coming in with an armload of wood for the stove. Trif is putting supper on the table, dishing up beans onto plates Katie has already laid out.

"Wasn't the first time, won't be the last," Trif says. "Katie, get the bread out of the warming oven and get your brother in out of the porch, make him wash his hands."

"I'll go get him," Jacob John says. He asks nothing more about the minister's visit; he must have met Reverend Spence on the road.

Since replacing good old Reverend White, the new minister comes every so often to reason with Triffie, to try to make her see sense and give up on the Holy Spirit, just as his predecessor used to try to make her give up the Sabbath, though Reverend Spence shows far greater fervour than Reverend White ever did in trying to correct her supposed heresies.

Sunday nights, now, whenever Jacob John can spare her and the pony, Triffie drives over to Clarke's Beach for the meetings there. Pastor Garrigus, a woman preacher from St. John's, came to Clarke's Beach to hold a revival. A congregation has sprung up there of people who, like Triffie, have received the baptism of the Spirit. Now that she's had a taste of real worship, worship with hands and voices raised as high as they can go, speaking in tongues and dancing in the aisles, she can't do without it. Hard to confine herself to the staid rhythms of the Prayer Book or the earnest Bible studies at the

Adventist Church. Since winter closed in it's been harder to get to Clarke's Beach, though two weeks ago she caught a ride in Eliza and Bertha Dawe's sleigh and stayed over Sunday night with Aunt Orpah Dawe.

Her association with the Holy Rollers, as Jacob John calls the Pentecostal believers, has caused a bit of talk around the Point, and it certainly seems to trouble Reverend Spence. Reverend White had known Triffie for years and after arguing with her a few times about the Sabbath and the state of the dead, he gave up and accepted her as she was. But this new minister feels an obligation to do something about a woman who helped raise up the Seventh-day Adventist Church and now worships with the Pentecostals, yet still holds her influential position on the Church of England Women's Association.

Today he came to explain to her that the gifts of the Holy Spirit, as described in the book of Acts, were only intended for the spreading of the gospel in apostolic times, and were not for the Church today. Triffie gave him back as good as he got – few Anglican ministers can quote Scripture to beat Trif Russell – and eventually he gave up on the Bible study and launched into a diatribe about Miss Garrigus and the other Pentecostals, and the woman minister Miss Guy who was left behind to shepherd the flock in Clarke's Beach. His diatribe degenerated into a complaint about how fewer people were coming out to church since the war, which trailed off into a whine about the difficulty of raising money for poor relief. With Christmas approaching people expect the Church to do something for the poor, but the money simply isn't there.

"Now, 'tis not that hard, Reverend," Trif says. "We need something like a sale of work. The children are having their pageant at the school before Christmas – why don't I talk to Mr. Bishop about putting off a sale the night of the concert? I'm sure he won't mind, and then I'll talk to some of the women and see what they can contribute. I'd say a nice few people would buy little things for Christmas gifts, and then we'll use the money, and maybe some of the goods that don't get sold, to make up a few boxes for the families that need it." By the time he left, the minister was calling down blessings on her name, forgetting that he'd come to warn her away from dangerous heresies.

She may be able to charm the minister, but Aunt Rachel is still angry about her joining the Pentecosts, and poor Aunt Rachel never got over the Adventists. Not to mention, the Adventists are mad at Trif too, now. She still worships with them on a Saturday morning, because the seventh day is the Sabbath of the Lord your God and will be until long after Trif Russell is laid in the grave, but a few of her fellow believers have harsh words for her.

Aunt Hepsy Snow has been barely civil to Triffie since Trif started going over to the meetings in Clarke's Beach. "What is it now?" she sniffs, when Trif shows up at her door to ask what she can contribute to the sale of work. "Are you preaching a new religion or campaigning for votes for women this week? I never knows what it is with you."

"Now, Aunt Hepsy, we may have our differences but that's no reason we can't pull together to do the Lord's work." Trif explains about the sale.

"The Lord's work? How can you be working for the Lord when you're dabbling in Satan-worship?"

"Call it what you like, I know the Holy Spirit when it touches me," Trif says. "But that's neither here nor there – I'm sure we can both agree that feeding the hungry and clothing the needy is God's work, can't we?"

"*And many will say to me in that day, Lord, Lord, did we not do many mighty works in your name,*" quotes Aunt Hepsy. "And what will the Lord say, Trif Russell? What will He say to those people?"

"*Depart from me, I never knew ye,*" Trif quotes back.

"Do you want him to say that to you on Judgement Day?"

"Of course not. Now, can you knit a few of your pairs of fancy mitts for the sale or what? Let's leave God and the Devil out of it altogether and say we're doing the right thing for our neighbours in need."

Aunt Hepsy she can at least respect, knowing the older woman speaks out of sincere, if misguided, conviction. It's a different matter with a woman like Clara Snow, who has always been petty-minded. She considers skipping over Clara's house in her canvas of the Point, but she's never been one to take the easy way out. She brings Katie and Billy along as a sort of bodyguard when she goes over to the north side to face Clara in her den.

Katie Grace is doing a dialogue with Clara's daughter Lydia in the concert. As Triffie sits down at Clara's kitchen table and her children are absorbed into the noisy crew of Snows, she hears Katie's voice raised above the rest, ordering Lydia to practise lines with her. Above the din, Triffie explains her errand.

"You must have some time on your hands, Trif, to be going around stirring up the rest of us to do good works." Clara hands her a cup of tea with such poor grace that some of it slops into the saucer. "Haven't you got

That *Forgetful* Shore

enough to do with your husband and youngsters and three churches to run?"

Trif bites back a retort to the effect that there are worse places to go on a Saturday morning than to church. One of the worst-kept secrets on the Point is that Clara Snow goes out to Jabez Badcock's ramshackle house at the end of the Point on Saturdays when Obadiah Snow is gone cutting and hauling wood. Officially, she goes to clean for Jabez, "but the Mister been inside that place and he tells me there's precious little cleaning ever got done there," Aunt Rachel once told Trif, with lowered tones and raised eyebrows.

Jabez is as much of an odd sock as ever. He lives alone, though there are always rumours about him and other men's wives, of whom Clara is only the latest. Triffie saw him once at the revival meetings; he was slain in the Spirit, spoke in tongues, and prophesied with great fervour, but never came back. Jabez fishes only when he pleases; he won't play the fiddle at dances or concerts but will sit for hours playing it on an empty stage head; he's drunk more often than he's sober. Triffie can't see the attraction, but for a woman like Clara, it's possible there's some romance to be found in a solitary, dangerous man like Jabez Badcock.

Clara's house is tidy, though noisy and crowded. She and Obe have six children. The baby currently squalling in the cot was born in April, nine months after the height of the fishing season; Obadiah Snow went down on the Labrador last summer, though Jabez Badcock did not.

Triffie does her best to ignore Clara's jibes and swallow her own dislike of the other woman long enough to get a commitment from Clara for a dozen crocheted doilies for the sale, which is also long enough for Lydia to get tired of practising the dialogue and Katie to stamp off in frustration. Prying Billy loose from the snarl of little boys in the yard, Triffie goes home, reasonably satisfied with the list of contributions she has managed to collect.

She puts in extra hours knitting and crocheting herself, on top of baking for Christmas, helping the children learn their lines for the pageant, and re-papering the kitchen and parlour. She is worn out by the night of the concert, but sits proudly to hear Billy recite a poem and Katie outshine the other girls in her dialogue. Then she slips out to the other room to set up tables for the sale, listening to the other concert pieces through the open doorway.

The performers are mostly schoolchildren, but near the end Char Mercer gets up to play the accordion and sing "The Boys from New-foundland" – hardly a Christmas song, but everyone gives Char, with his wooden leg and his Papist Irish wife, a bit of leeway. He's well on his way to becoming as good a singer and storyteller as old Uncle Jed was, and he often sings about the War, though he talks about it only to tell funny stories. He never describes the horrors of battle, or speaks of the death of his two best friends.

The older students continue the patriotic theme by getting up to close the concert with "God Save the King," and then parents crowd into the room to examine the items they and their neighbours have contributed to the sale. Trif, standing behind the table of fancywork, rejoices in one of her favourite sounds – the solid clink of coins falling into a money box, people contributing to a good cause thanks to her hard work.

When the crowd departs she's left to clean up. Reverend Spence thanks her as she hands him the heavy money box. As she sweeps the floor and packs the unsold goods in a box, she hears Jacob John and a few other men in the next room, putting back the desks that have been moved aside for the pageant.

She doesn't pay much attention to the men's conversation till she hears her own name. "You must have your work cut out for you keeping up with Trif," says Fred Mercer. "She don't stop, do she? If she's not getting up a sale of work, sure she's starting up another church."

Triffie hears, as Jacob John must, the implied rebuke in Fred's joke. Except for ministers, religion is pretty much seen as women's business in these parts, and it's certainly not unusual for a woman to be a churchgoer when her man is not, or to be more active in the Church than he is. A good husband is expected to keep his nose of out of his wife's religious business. But when it comes to her taking up with strange new sects or otherwise making a holy show of herself in public, well, a prudent man should keep a bit of a rein on his wife. Jacob John teases Triffie about her faith as he always has, but he makes no effort to change it.

"Nah, sure I don't bother her with that, she can get up to whatever old foolishness she wants," Jacob John says now, confirming her expectations. "The Good Lord got His hands full keeping up with Trif; I don't suppose He needs my help."

The other men laugh, but Obadiah Snow persists. "Even so, b'y, these Holy Rollers are a bit much. I heard the minister had to have a talk to your Triffie, and she still haven't stopped going over to Clarke's Beach for their meetings. She'll be raising up a crowd of them around here next, falling down on the floor and talking gibberish, saying it's the Holy Spirit. Sure you don't want the likes of that that going on in your house, do you?"

The men's rough laughter is quieter now, the challenge to Jacob John's authority no longer veiled. What would she do, Trif wonders, if he ordered her to stop going to the Pentecostal meetings? She believes on principle that St. Paul is right and she should be subject to her husband, but in point of fact she's rarely tested on this. She knows she is less than an ideal wife in so many ways. But she's never outright disobeyed him – probably because he gives so few orders.

Out in the classroom, a moment passes before Jacob John replies, and she feels the gathering tension, imagines the men looking at him for his answer. Finally he says, "Well, Obe b'y, here's how I looks at it. Some women, right, whenever they gets restless, you got to watch out for them. Woman gets restless enough, she's liable to be up to no good behind your back. But when Trif's gone out late at night, I knows she's only down on her knees prayin'. And if she gets restless, she just starts a new church. I 'lows I can live with that."

This time there are not chuckles but guffaws. Trif knows she ought to feel sorry for Obadiah Snow – or even for Clara, for Jacob John has said one of the things that's never said aloud, charged Obe publicly with having a faithless wife. Who knows if Obe might be the kind of man to make Clara suffer in private for that public shame? But what Trif feels is a swell of pride, or maybe gratitude.

She puts away the broom and closes up the box, then turns to see she is not alone. Joe Bishop has entered the room. He must have been in the other room, hearing the men's conversation.

"Grand concert, sir," she says.

"Katie's got your gift for recitations," he says. "She's a clever girl, she's coming along fast. All the children did well, really," he adds, then glances back over his shoulder to the men in the other room. "You've got a loyal husband there," he says, "as well as clever children. You're a lucky woman, Trif Russell."

"Well, thank you, sir," she says, and follows him out. She wishes she could burn out of her mind forever the terrible things Kit said about Joe Bishop, those awful lies. She's admired this man her whole life and now she can't look at him across the aisle in church or stood up in front of his pupils without thinking of those dreadful slanders. She watches him with the children when she's at the school for a concert or any other reason and has never seen a thing to back up Kit's accusations – but then, if Kit's story were true, this business went on before under Trif's very nose and she saw nothing, suspected nothing. Now she is saddled with suspicions, but tells herself over and over that it must be only maliciousness on Kit's part. It can't be true.

The men have finished putting the schoolroom to rights and Jacob John has the children collected outside the door when Triffie comes out. Joe Bishop locks up the school and says goodnight, walking away in the other direction as Jacob John lifts a sleepy Billy into his arms.

"You did a fine job tonight, Katie Grace," Trif says, taking her daughter's hand as they head back down toward the south side. She doesn't want to praise the girl up too much, to make her vain, but she knows what it's like to grow up without ever hearing a word of approval from anyone in your own house, knowing you're clever but never being told there's any value in that. She won't have that for Katie Grace.

As they walk home through the clear, cold night, Jacob John beside her, she ponders Joe Bishop's words. *You're a lucky woman, Trif Russell.*

She is not accustomed to thinking of herself as a lucky woman. Kit got the charmed life, while Trif got the blighted one, cursed by poverty and ill-luck. Never to go to school or become a teacher, never to leave the Point, married to a man she never loved. Awkward as that relationship was in its early years, it certainly hasn't gotten any smoother since the night she threw in his face her knowledge that he'd once made love to Kit Saunders. Not that they've spoken of it again – that isn't Jacob John's way, and Trif has said all she ever wants to say on the subject. But the knowledge is there, between them, never more so than when they're alone in the bedroom.

Tonight, though, she thinks of Jacob John cutting down Obadiah Snow in her defense. As they turn onto the road that leads down to the south side and she sees the bay spread out before them, she tucks her free hand into the crook of Jacob John's arm. Katie holds her other hand, chattering away with excitement, while Billy is almost asleep draped over his father's shoulder.

Jacob John glances over at her with a half-smile and tightens his arm a little, squeezing her hand against his side. "Now, what's that for?" he says, under the rise and fall of Katie's voice and the rush of the waves.

"The road is icy; I don't want to slip," Trif says.

"Fair enough, maid."

That *Forgetful* Shore

Kit

Charlottetown, PEI
April, 1923

Dearest Kit,

How exotic it still seems, even after two years, to be addressing letters
to you in Oxford! I am so thrilled that you are realizing your Dream
despite any difficulties. I know, better than most, that Dreams
fulfilled are not always what one expects them to be. When we were
girls in college it hardly seemed possible to me that there could be a
more Glamourous life than that of a Lady Reporter, working on a big
City Newspaper, a single Woman forging her way in a Man's World.

But the truth is, Kit, it is damnably hard and lonely, and there are
only so many society weddings one can report on. Even after crawling
my way up out of the social notes to human-interest stories and
interviews, I have had to face the harsh reality that I shall NEVER
be given a job reporting the "serious" news of the day – and even more
shocking, that I am no longer sure how badly I want it.

So, those Dreams fulfilled – to a degree – I have turned my thoughts
to other Dreams, things I did not even realize I wanted till I began to

pursue them. Thus I have two pieces of news for you, both of which will, I think, surprise: first, I am starting to write a Novel, and second, I am going to be married! ...

St. John's, Newfoundland
April, 1923

Dear Mrs. Porter:

It is my sad duty to inform you of the passing of one we both knew and loved well. Our dear Miss Matilda Shaw passed from this life on the 31st of March, after a severe bout of pneumonia had laid her low all winter. You will no doubt be touched to learn that in my last visit with her, your name came up. Nothing could have made her more proud than to know that one of her former students was pursuing higher education at that institution which she prized above all others. She truly gloried in your accomplishments, as she did in those of all her former "girls," as she still called us even when we entered our forties! ...

A letter from Maggie Campbell – soon to be Maggie Hamilton, wife of a wealthy businessman in his fifties – and another from her former co-worker Miss Smith of Spencer, sit on top of Kit's pile of mail this week. She reads through those two letters, flicks through the rest of the pile quickly – nothing interesting there – and lays aside the two letters to reread at her leisure. She remembers, years ago, laying letters from Maggie, from Miss Shaw, and from Trif side by side on her desk, weighing and balancing them, symbolic of different kinds of lives.

Ten years and a war separate her from those days. One correspondent's life journey has ended, ended as Miss Shaw would no doubt have wished, with a great funeral in the Anglican Cathedral at which fellow teachers and former students turned out in great numbers to pay tribute to her life of sacrifice and dedication.

Another life, Maggie's, has taken an unexpected turn. Marrying a wealthy widower? Turning from newspapers to novels? Kit hardly knows what

That *Forgetful* Shore

to think of Maggie's latest news, but she senses in the letter that same zest for life that she recognized in Maggie from the first time they met. However unexpected the choices, she is glad for her old friend.

But from that old balance, one factor is missing, one letter from her file. Four years after they last spoke, Kit still feels Trif's absence keenly. She has considered breaking the silence, of course. But though she can write learned papers on Spenser's *Faerie Queene* and attempt a half-decent sonnet, she cannot write this one simple letter. The words elude her, though they ought to be easy. *I'm sorry. I should not have said the things I did. You are part of my heart forever, as we always swore, and without you I am slowly bleeding.*

Looking again through her small pile of letters, Kit realizes that not only is Triffie missing from her correspondence, but the Point is missing altogether. She used to get other letters from there – from her parents, of course, while they were alive, and from her cousins and old school chums. Once, long ago, letters from Joe Bishop. Those dried up when she stopped replying. Most of her old friends have either moved away from the Point or stopped writing.

She's spent years trying to untangle herself from Missing Point, to cut all ties except the blood ties and the tie to Triffie, dearer than blood. With those gone, she might content herself that she has finally cut herself loose from the place she came from, a place she never wanted to return to. She sold the house and land she owned there, turned her back on it. She worked hard, in Halifax and later in St. John's, to erase every trace of the bay from her speech. Now, here in England, she has worked just as hard to wipe out the lingering traces of Newfoundland, to acquire that mid-Atlantic accent that makes it sound, not as if she is aping an English accent – that would be dreadfully pretentious – but as if she might be a well-educated person from almost anywhere. She wants to tear down and rebuild herself so nothing of the past is left. She wants to be seen not as a clever small-town girl made good, nor as a brave war bride widowed by the 'flu epidemic – nothing at all but a hard-working scholar and teacher.

She is within reach, now, of the Bachelor of Letters degree she has worked so hard for these last two years. Her research is on the *Faerie Queene*. After months of rigorous meetings with her tutor, Miss Jeffries – a rather intense woman whose minute scrutiny of every detail of her research used to annoy her, Kit has learned to become grateful for that level of attention. It helps her deal with the obsessive fear that she has made some dreadful mistake that will destroy all her painstaking work.

"You ought to have this published," Miss Jeffries says at their last meeting, handing back Kit's latest draft, copiously marked up with red ink corrections. "When you've brought it up to a scholarly standard, of course." That's as much praise as she's likely to get from the stern Medieval Literature don. It amazes her how being a student can put her, at thirty-two, right back into the classroom, eager for a teacher's approval as if she were a schoolgirl again.

Being a college student in mid-life has been, in some ways, an odd experience. When she first arrived at Somerville, Kit found it strange, as a woman who owned her own home for many years, to reduce her living space to a single bed-sit in a hall shared with dozens of other women. But she has come to enjoy the simplicity of college life, thinking of herself as a nun in a cell, a votary of Learning. She likes the college arrangement far better than the boarding houses where she lived when she actually was an undergraduate, a time that now seems very long ago.

She feels too old for many of the highlights of the life of an Oxford undergraduate, though she finds herself wishing she had attended Somerville, or a similar women's college, as a girl. She debates a few times, writes the occasional piece for a college magazine, but the Dramatic Society, the Going-Down play, the Bach choir, tennis parties and cocoa parties are the preserve of girls of nineteen and twenty. Kit and her closest friends – Miss Stone, Miss Pennyweather and Miss Harriday-Heath – lead a more sedate existence centred on essays, lectures and research in the Bodleian Library. She enjoys the buzz of activity around without needing to be intimately involved in it, feels as if she is at the centre of what Somerville and Oxford are all about.

Lately, though, Kit has had to think again of the wider world. She has applied for several teaching positions here in England; she feels nothing drawing her back to Newfoundland. This week she has two interviews, one as headmistress at a girls' school in Manchester, and another teaching English at a prestigious London school. Though the Manchester position would give her more responsibility and, incidentally, more pay, she covets the London position. She wants to live and work in the city that is, she believes, the heart of the world. To be a part of London life would be almost as good as staying in Oxford.

On a spring afternoon she lays aside her books and papers and goes to meet with the chairman of the board of governors for the London school. At first, the interview goes well. The chairman, Reverend Kensington, asks her

That *Forgetful* Shore

about her studies at Oxford, whether she has considered publishing her research. He asks her a little about her B.A. degree from Dalhousie, and about the classes she taught at Spencer. He asks about her future plans, and she says she wants to continue teaching.

She is by no means certain of this. While she loves the work, and the subject matter, Kit sometimes thinks she lacks the lively interest in people that allowed a natural teacher like Miss Shaw to follow the lives of her "old girls" for twenty years and more. But of course she does not say this to Reverend Kensington, and anyway, what's to be said? What other path is there for an over-educated female, but to teach? Apart from Maggie Campbell's choice – marry a millionaire and start writing novels – she can't think of another way for a woman like herself to live.

She wills her voice to show only eagerness, none of the ambivalence. But Reverend Kensington soon turns from talk of her career to what Kit thinks of as unnecessarily personal questions.

"So ... Spencer College is in ... St. John's, Newfoundland?" He pronounces Newfoundland the way the British do, swallowing half the letters as though the place doesn't matter enough to say the whole name aloud. "What brought you there?"

"It's where I was born," Kit explains.

"Ah ... born there, I see. In the capital? St. John's?"

"No, I was born in a place called Trinity. My family moved from there to a town called Missing Point. I went to grammar school there, and then into St. John's to attend Spencer myself, before I went to Dalhousie to take my B.A."

"And these towns where you grew up, they were – what? Farming villages? Fishing villages?"

"Fishing."

"Your father was not a fisherman, surely."

"No, he worked as a clerk and bookkeeper for my uncle, who was the local merchant." Back home it was a point of pride to have come from a merchant family, even the family of a small outport merchant. Saying the words in this setting, Kit realizes how provincial she sounds. The word "merchant" has an entirely different ring in Oxford than it did in St. John's.

"How very ... ambitious you have been, to come from such humble beginnings to a place at Oxford," says Reverend Kensington, nodding. The

That *Forgetful* Shore

words are more approving than the tone. "And you, Mrs. Porter, are – a widow, I presume?"

"Yes."

"The War?"

"Just after it, actually. My husband served from 1914 till he was discharged with an injury in 1918, but died in the 'flu epidemic a few months later." When she first came to Oxford, she thought it was necessary to get through the relevant information as quickly and efficiently as possible, to forestall the possibility of pity. Now she sees it differently; it's important, she's learned, to clarify that although her husband did not have the great good fortune to lay down his life for his country, he did serve and was honourably discharged, that his death might even be connected, however tangentially, to his war service. Such things matter more here than they do at home: everyone is passionately interested in what everyone else did during the war.

Now Reverend Kensington nods. "No plans to remarry?" he says. "You are still a relatively young woman, Mrs. Porter."

"No plans at all," Kit says decisively. She is prepared for this question: schools do not want to hire a woman only to have her disappear a year or two later to get married and have a baby. "I revere my husband's memory, and I am dedicated to my career."

Once the interview is over, Kit feels she has done well. When she tells her friends about it in the common room that night, Miss Pennyweather listens with bright-eyed approval, but Miss Harriday-Heath, whose father is a baronet, and the older and wiser Miss Stone both shake their heads.

"Oh, how very unfortunate," Miss Stone says when Kit recounts being asked to tell about the town where she was born, and what her father did for a living.

"Unfortunate? How do you mean?"

"Well, they'll have known you were a colonial from your C.V. and from your accent, of course – you can't help that," Miss Stone says, "but it's a question of *how* colonial you are. A clerk's daughter from a fishing village – that's perhaps a bit more colonial than a posh London school can stomach."

"But I'm going to be a B.Litt of Oxford University!" Kit protests. "What does it matter where I was born, or what kind of work my father did?"

That *Forgetful* Shore

The other three women exchange glances, but only Miss Stone says what they are all clearly thinking. "My dear Mrs. Porter, the very fact that you would ask that question demonstrates better than anything else that you *are* a colonial."

She looks from one to the other, helpless. Can they really be serious? Even Miss Pennyweather, whose father is a butcher, nods. "People say so much has changed since the war, and I suppose in a way it has – it's not as bad as it was in my father's day, but people still care what your family name is and what schools you went to and – well, you know. Class." She says the last word apologetically, like a mild curse, but the other Englishwomen in the room all agree. Kit, who once believed St. John's society was snobbish, is at a loss for words.

"But – but Reverend Kensington said I was ambitious," she protests. "To come up from such – humble beginnings." His words, repeated now in this room, suddenly sound quite different. The emphasis, she sees, is not on the rising up but on the humility of the starting point.

"I doubt Reverend Kensington believes ambition in a woman is entirely a good thing," Miss Stone says, "though in hiring mistresses for a girls' school, he is no doubt constrained to rub shoulders with more ambitious women than he would personally prefer."

They all laugh at this, united again by the common enemy of male prejudice. Kit tries only one more brief protest. "When I was interviewed for the Manchester school, they didn't ask all those questions about my background."

"Ah well, I'm sure it doesn't matter as much in the North," Miss Harriday-Heath says with a shrug.

Sure enough, a letter of offer comes from the school in Manchester. Discreet enquiries reveal that another Somerville woman has been offered the London post. The last draft of her thesis submitted, defended and approved, Kit takes her B.Litt. at a ceremony attended by her fellow scholars but not by a single other person she knows. Then she packs her bags for Manchester.

Triffie

"MAMA, I'M TIRED. And my pail's full. Can I stop now?" Billy's voice has an edge of whining to it, something Trif can't abide.

"That pail's no more than half full, and a big boy like you shouldn't be getting tired after a couple of hours of berrypicking," she snaps.

"Can we stop for our lunch soon?"

"We'll have our lunch when I say we'll have it. Now, back to work."

"I wanted to stay home with David," Billy mutters. But he says it low, almost under his breath, so Trif can ignore it. For the sake of her sanity, she does.

She has left two-year-old David with Aunt Rachel for the day while she took her two older children along with Ruth, Betty and their children to pick blueberries out past Country Road. Trif always enjoys a day out berrypicking; like most women, she thinks of it as almost a day off, despite being coopied over the low bushes for hours in the sun, combing for the small, flavour-filled fruit. She's a champion picker – not just blueberries but partridgeberries and even bakeapples in season. She always picks enough to have extra to sell at the Mercantile, and makes more jam than any woman on the Point. It's the one thing Trif can do that directly contributes to the family income, since she still refuses to take her children to Labrador for the fishing season. She puts heart and soul into berrypicking.

Children are not as resilient as grown women; they set off in the morning swinging their pails, laughing and carrying on, but it's nearly noon now. Billy, Ruth's two older boys and Betty's daughter Evelyn are all starting to complain. Ruth's littlest one, Lizzie, has given up picking and fallen asleep in the shade of a larger bush. She's barely four, and really should have stayed at home with the little ones. But you can't put too much of a burden on Aunt Rachel these days.

Betty and her husband Frank have been living in St. John's since they got married. This summer, Betty and the children are staying with Aunt Rachel while Frank goes fishing on the Labrador. When the fishing season is over, Betty and Frank and the children are moving to Nova Scotia, where Frank is going to work in the Sydney mines. Ruth and Cy talk about moving up there too, if the fishing doesn't get better. This sunny afternoon amid the berry bushes might be the last time she and Betty and Ruth go berrypicking together like they used to as girls, Trif thinks.

You can't say a word against Katie Grace when it comes to berrypicking. She's working as hard as the three grown women, barely lifting her head or saying a word. Betty nods toward her. "That one's some little worker," she says. "What is she, twelve now?"

"Just turned twelve in July," Trif says. "She's a grand hand for work."

"Mom says she's just like you were," Ruth adds. "Always with her head in a book so you'd think she wasn't good for a thing, but then you sees her put her hand to a job and you sees another side to her. Mom always said you was a dog for work."

Trif knows her aunt can offer no higher accolade. The words of motherly affection she was starved for as a girl never came to her, but for Aunt Rachel to call her "a dog for work" is equal to anyone else taking her in her arms and saying, "I love you, Triffie." You take what you can get in this life, Trif thinks, and you don't cast your mind back to what you missed.

If you think of anything beyond the day's work, you look to the future, to your children. She's proud to hear Katie praised as a good worker, but she doesn't want to hear that Katie is just like her. Katie will do better, go farther.

School starts up again next week, and Joe Bishop dropped by the house last night to talk to Trif and Jacob John about Katie Grace. "She's a smart girl," he said, "though I don't need to tell you that. I imagine you've taught her as much as I have, Triffie."

"No, no – she's gone far beyond what I was able to teach her," Trif protests. "Though I do still read Shakespeare out loud with her in the evenings, along with the Bible."

"Shakespeare and the Bible – Trif's right and left hands," Jacob John puts in. "I can't read more than a half dozen words in either one, but she reels off jeezly grand strings of 'em both, chapter and verse. 'Tis not half bad to listen to, in the winter when the evenings closes in early and there's not so much work to do."

"You won't get a much better education than you'll get from hearing Triffie read Shakespeare and the Bible," Joe Bishop assented. "But if Katie wants to go further in school and train for a teacher – then she'll need some extra tutoring, especially in Mathematics." The little school on the Point goes further now than when Trif went there; Mr. Bishop offers classes for the Prelimary Certificate to the older students, while two women teachers handle the younger grades. "I know she can do well in her exams, but I'd like to start working a bit more with her, maybe after school some evenings. You won't mind that, will you?"

Trif has expected this talk for years. When Katie was just toddling around, Trif imagined her heart swelling with pride; imagined, too, that she'd have to make her case to Jacob John, convincing him that somehow there had to be a way for a fisherman's daughter to afford an education.

She knows Jacob John well enough by now to know she will not have to persuade him on this point. "She's a clever one, for sure," he tells Joe Bishop. "If she could get on a bit in school, we'd be proud of her. I don't know where we'd find the money for her to go to St. John's, but I 'lows we'd find a way, wouldn't we, missus?"

"Of course we would, supposing I have to take up scrubbing other people's houses," Trif says. Why, then, this sick feeling in her stomach as she closes the front door behind Joe Bishop? Why feel dread on a night she should be celebrating?

Of course she knows why. The knowledge has lain there like a stone ever since Kit threw it at her, more than five years ago. She has never repeated it to anyone, never said a word to a soul. She's tried to pretend there's nothing to it, and most of the time she's able to believe that. But now, with Katie Grace before her, her little red-gold head bent over the berry bushes, Kit's words are as clear in her mind as if they were spoken yesterday. *Do you really want to risk not believing me, when Katie's the clever one, and Joe Bishop asks you can she stay behind for extra lessons?*

She can't keep silent anymore. To test it, she says to Ruth and Betty, who

That *Forgetful* Shore

are both nearby, "Mr. Bishop says he's thinking of keeping Katie after school for extra lessons this year. He thinks she'll have a good chance of finishing high school and training for a teacher if we can afford to send her to town."

"Well, that's no surprise," Ruth says.

"She's just like you, Trif, smart at her books," Betty agrees.

Nothing more, from either of them. Not that they were ever the ones to get extra lessons after school – dutiful but uninspired students, both her cousins. Still, they were young girls in Joe Bishop's schoolroom.

"Yes, she's a grand girl," Trif says. "I wonders about them extra lessons after school, though. I'm not sure I'm easy in my mind about it, if it's the right thing to have her staying after like that."

"Sure what harm could come to her?" Ruth says. "You got extra lessons back when you was in school, Trif – as much as Mom would allow, anyway. It's a sin you weren't allowed to go on farther."

Betty nods, but says, "All the same, you can't be too careful." Her face is turned towards the blueberries, her fingers picking swiftly and efficiently. Her eyes slide towards Trif's and then away.

Later, after the children have had their break for lunch and been set back to work filling their pails, Trif moves nearer to Betty. "You think I'm right," she says, "to have some doubts about Mr. Bishop keeping Katie after school?"

Betty is quiet so long Trif doesn't think she's going to answer. "I s'pose you'd know more about it than I would," she says at last. "Like Ruth said, you stayed after yourself the odd time. But … well, I don't like to say anything against anyone. It's not right to gossip."

"It's not always gossip," Trif says. She prays for victory over the sin of gossip, but not as hard as she does about her other sins, because you can pick up a lot of useful information from gossip. How would a small town ever function if people didn't know things they weren't supposed to know about one another? If you didn't know what people were up to, you'd make a right fool of yourself with the things you said, not knowing when to be careful. If you didn't listen to gossip, you might pass comment on how Clara Snow's youngest boy looks nothing like either of his parents but is the spit of Jabez Badcock. You might ask Isaiah Butler how his young one Elsie likes being in service in Carbonear and watch him stammer, if you didn't know the poor child was gone off to her aunt's house to have a baby. Trif considers gossip a useful tool, which may be why the Spirit hasn't given her deliverance over this particular sin yet.

Now she just says, "There's times things have got to be said ... otherwise more harm might be done." Hopes that will be enough to unlock Betty's tongue.

Again, the shifting sideways glance. "Did he ever try anything with you?" Betty asks.

Trif shakes her head.

"But you knows something. You must have heard." After a silence, Betty says, "Was it Kit?"

"Could be. Me and Kit don't keep in touch nowadays, but she said a few things in her time. I don't know what to pay heed to, tell the truth." Now that they're near the core of it, Trif feels sick to her stomach. She can't stand to hear this, but she can't afford not to. She gives up all pretense of picking berries and eases back onto her heels, then sits. Above, seagulls wheel and screech. She doesn't look at Betty, who is still picking.

"Well, I don't know much. He touched me a few times, nothing to talk about, you know, but it didn't seem quite right. But I'd never have said a word, only —" Betty pauses again. "You should talk to Amelia Snow."

"Amelia?" Trif remembers Amelia as a clever girl, very quiet. She certainly didn't go on to high school or to anything grand – she lives across the bay in Bareneed, married to a fisherman. Trif hasn't seen her in five years or more.

But Amelia's sister Helen goes to the Pentecostal meetings in Clarke's Beach, as does Trif whenever she can get over there. A while back a Pastor Vaters came through and had some revival meetings on the Point and some more in Bay Roberts, but the Spirit hasn't touched those places like Clarke's Beach, which still has the only Pentecostal congregation along this stretch of Conception Bay. The next Sunday night Trif makes an excuse, after the singing and praying and preaching and tongues, to go up to Helen Morgan, who used to be Helen Snow. She asks about how the family is doing, steers the conversation around to Amelia.

"Oh, you know, she's had a hard time since her little one's been sick – did you hear about that?"

Triffie remembers hearing that Amelia's daughter, a year or two younger than Katie, nearly died of scarlet fever last winter. The child lived, but she is very weak, an invalid, and Helen tells her that Amelia spends most of her time caring for her daughter. It's an easy enough thing to find an errand that will bring her over to Bareneed, to stop by Amelia's house with a couple of jars of jam – not just the blueberry, which anyone can get, but the bakeapple jam which is so much rarer, the berries being harder to find and more work to pick. Trif's bakeapple jam has won some fame on the Point.

"I was talking to Helen the other Sunday, when we were at the meeting," Trif says, when Amelia invites her in for a cup of tea. It's hard to get the conversation from their common acquaintance, Amelia's sister, to what she wants to talk about. Trif plots her course through Amelia's sick daughter and a promise to pray for her, to her own children, to the suggestion that Katie might have some extra lessons with Mr. Bishop. Finally she is able to lean towards Amelia, lower her voice, and say, "I hates to ask it, but it's on my mind, you know. I heard rumours, years ago, not long after I left school, about Mr. Bishop. I know he was a good teacher and all, but all the girls he used to keep after school for extra lessons – did he ever – you know? I mean, was there ever anything …?"

Amelia fixes Trif with a cool gaze, so much less awkward around this subject than Trif is. Her life has been hard, Trif knows, and perhaps it has stripped her conversation down to the bare essentials.

"Did he fool around with me, you mean? Of course he did. He done it with plenty of girls, you should know that."

Trif shakes her head, but Amelia clearly doesn't believe her. She shrugs and looks away. "I got more to be worried about than old stuff that happened years ago, Trif. All I know is, if my young one was well enough to still be in school, I wouldn't leave her alone in a room with Joe Bishop, no matter if he promised her a dozen scholarships."

That's all she will say; Trif knows better than to push her. She can't stop now; there are other women she has to talk to. Millicent Butler, now married to a Batten from Bay Roberts, will only say that she doesn't want to talk about it, but that if Triffie is going to spend as much time as she does down on her knees, she should say a few prayers for Joe Bishop. Effie Dawe is more forthcoming than all the rest, perhaps because she received a carefully worded letter rather than an awkward conversation over tea.

The letter took ages to write and Triffie thought Effie might just toss it in the fire. Instead she gets back three pages of perfect copperplate penmanship from Miss Dawe, now teaching in Grand Bank.

There is nothing I regret about my schooling, humble though it
was in that little schoolhouse with poor Mr. Bishop. Indeed, I have

endeavoured over the years to give my own scholars some taste of the fine education he gave me during those precious years of girlhood.

With all that said, I will confess that your letter awakened memories I have long kept buried. When I speak of our old teacher now I often think of him, as I just wrote, as "poor Mr. Bishop," for I firmly believe that that unfortunate man – who is, in essence, I believe a truly Good Man, and a fine teacher – has some manner of disorder or trouble in his mind, or perhaps in his soul, that causes him to do things that have the potential to tear down all the fine work he has laboured to build. In short, I may say that in my own experience, the damage done to my young spirit was balanced by the great good he did my mind by expanding it so. But I will not pretend there were no tear-filled nights as I struggled to come to grips with those so inappropriate advances.

I trust you will have the discretion to burn this letter. But as to the matter on which you requested advice – what you ought to do about your own daughter – I hardly know what to say. I believe with absolute fervour that any young woman who is capable of a higher education should avail herself of one if it is at all possible, and I doubt that could come to pass at all without the extra tutelage our old teacher has always provided so kindly. But if you ask whether I would leave an innocent young girl alone with the man of whom we speak – I must confess that unless God has wrought some great miracle upon him, to make him a better man ... then I would have Grave Misgivings.

Trif lays the letter on the table. Behind the flawless handwriting and flowery words, Effie Dawe's message is the same as Amelia Snow's. She sits and looks at the letter for a long time.

Unless God has worked a miracle. Trif is familiar with miracles. She has prayed for God to raise up churches, to heal the sick, to patch together wounded hearts, and He has always come through. But when it comes to this – to the safety of her beloved only daughter – she is not sure she can leave this in God's hands. He can be trusted, but can He do the job on His own?

If God is going to work a miracle, Trif Russell figures He may need her help.

224

That *Forgetful* Shore

Kit

"HERE ARE MY letters, Miss Edwards, but none of them is urgent. You may do them tomorrow morning if you wish." Kit hands a sheaf of handwritten papers to her secretary. Miss Edwards – a pretty young thing who was a student three years ago and came to work in the school office after completing a commercial course – smiles at her, her pretty bow of a mouth discreetly outlined and her hair in marcelled waves. Her skirts are as short as Kit's dictums will allow, though Kit herself still wears hers at the ankle, as befits the Headmistress. Students and office staff – and even some of the younger teachers – rush to embrace new fashions, but Kit, who would love to bob her hair, must present an image of timeless dependability. "Stagnation" is another word for it, but she carefully avoids saying that, even to herself.

Miss Edwards gathers her things – the two of them are the last people in the school, even the wildly disorganized Miss Cunningham having finally finished marking her papers and gone home. "Good evening, ma'am," Miss Edwards says with something approaching a curtsey, as she goes out the door.

Kit puts on her own coat, looks for a moment at a pile of correspondence and notes before deciding she will take none of it home tonight, and goes out, locking up the doors as she leaves.

St. Margaret's is a day school, so Kit does not live on the premises but rents a flat a few streets away. Sometimes she takes a tram home, but today she walks through streets in the dying hours of an April afternoon. There's little hint of spring in the air yet; it reminds her of April back home, damp and chilly. Many things about Manchester remind her of St. John's; there's no point denying this is not the England for which she crossed the ocean. There's little here of the glories of Oxford or London; it's as if she came all this way to recreate a life very much like the one she had in St. John's.

She's been here two years now, and has settled into her work if not entirely into the city. It surprised her at first how little the job of a Head-mistress was like that of a teacher; apparently she spent two years pursuing a Bachelor of Letters so that she could spend the rest of her life behind a desk answering letters, or sitting in meetings. Her greatest pleasure is her higher-form English classes, where she finally gets the rewards she always hoped to find in teaching. Coaching girls to take entrance exams for university, knowing that they have a good chance of actually making something of themselves, is worlds removed from huddling round the woodstove in a one-room outport schoolhouse, dragging the children of fishermen through one Royal Reader after another when almost all of them would rather be somewhere else.

Work keeps her busy, and it has its compensations. Her personal life, on the other hand, is virtually non-existent in Manchester. Her acquaintances are all connected with school, the mistresses on her staff and trustees of the Board, parents of students, all of whom must be kept at a cordial distance for various reasons. She attends church because not to do so would be unthinkable, but is not drawn to the life of the parish in any way; everyone understands that the school consumes all her hours and nobody expects much of her. Apart from reading, the only thing she does for her own pleasure is attend an occasional lecture or debate, telling herself she has an obligation to broaden her mind.

It's easy to see how one's mind, one's world, can become narrow and limited. Kit enters through the front door of the house where she rents the upstairs flat. She has books and time and space of her own, which she once thought was the definition of happiness. And she is not unhappy; it's only that these rooms, which she occupies alone, sometimes seem at once too large and too small. The empty chairs and half-empty bed yawn at her while the walls threaten to close in and trap her.

"Quite enough melodrama, Mrs. Porter," she says to herself now, flicking through the day's mail as she lays her umbrella, misted with the afternoon's

That *Forgetful* Shore

drizzle, near the radiator to dry. Pinned above her desk is a notice for the lecture she plans to attend this evening: something about Marxism, which intrigues her. She likes to learn about things well outside her area of expertise and has attended lectures on Theosophy, gardening and the archaeological discoveries in the pyramids of Egypt. Everyone she knows through school thinks the Bolshevik threat is a greater danger to the world even than the war was, but Kit also knows there are labouring men and women in the factories whose lot in life would be far worse than it is if not for the unions. She knows, too, that there are those in the city who think a Marxist revolution is exactly what England needs.

Her tea is a boiled egg and a sandwich of thinly sliced cucumber, eaten while reading *Barchester Towers*: she is working her way through Trollope. After tea she makes a note in her journal about the upcoming lecture: she tries to make her journal more a record of her life and activities than simply the outpouring of emotion it was at first. She has also kept up the habit of sketching in the margins, the kind of caricatures she used to draw in her letters to Trif. She notices, flipping through the pages, that her Oxford journal was full of sketches of her friends and fellow scholars as well as the tutors and dons, while the Manchester pages contain only a few sketches of students and co-workers, and many still lifes: the view from her window; a pile of crockery on her table.

Seven o'clock draws near. Kit lays aside introspection and changes from her severe office clothes to a slightly less severe skirt and blouse. For evening wear she allows herself a hemline an inch or two higher, though still considerably less daring than many of the skirts she sees on young women at tonight's lecture. One has, after all, an image to maintain in the community.

The visiting lecturer is a Cambridge man who has recently returned from a visit to Russia – or the Union of Soviet Socialist Republics, as he calls it. He explains the basics of Marxism and describes what he saw of the rule of the recently deceased Lenin and his successor, Stalin. Though he admits it is a harsh regime, he urges cautious tolerance of the Soviet Union. England, he says, should not cut all ties with Moscow as it is far too soon to tell how the great Socialist experiment will work out.

"But surely he's not advocating that sort of upheaval here," a man says afterwards. Kit is one of a group of people standing about in the hall afterwards. She goes to lectures because she is hungry for the kind of conversations she became accustomed to at Oxford, lively debates about books and ideas that were heady at the time and have now, in memory, been burnished to a higher gloss.

"Of course not." Julia Maynard, wife of a Church of England vicar whose daughter attends Kit's school, waves a dismissive hand. "It's all very well to talk Bolshevism over coffee, but do you think there's one person in this room who would mount the barricades and cry out for the blood of the upper classes?" She waves again, vaguely, indicating the assortment of middle-class people all chattering about the lecture. "Everyone here would have far more to lose than to gain from a revolution. We might be intrigued by socialist ideals on paper, but in reality? We'd run to the manor house and ask the squire to let us hide behind the battlements."

"But the people who would fight on the barricades are not the people in this room," another man said. "It's the factory workers and miners. The miners are already calling for a general strike, and where might that lead? That's what happened in Russia – a few intellectuals stirred up thousands of workers to action."

"And is that what we are – the intellectuals?" trills Mrs. Maynard, putting a gloved hand to her throat in mock horror at the idea of being either a revolutionary or an intellectual.

"Mrs. Porter certainly is," says the first man, who is a professor at the university. "Like a true intellectual, she remains silent listening to our babble. No doubt she forms her own opinions."

Kit smiles, trying to look enigmatic. "I think the workers in the factories have far more to gain by working through the system as it now exists, than by overturning it." Her comment draws a chorus of approving nods and harrumphs from her hearers. In her position, it's very important that any views she does express be mild and uncontroversial. Not that she actually is a Communist, but if she were, she'd certainly make every effort to keep it hidden.

Mrs. Maynard's green eyes flash wickedly at Kit. "Ahh, that's a very safe answer, Mrs. Porter. We'd hardly like to think you're teaching Marxism to our daughters, now would we?"

"I can assure you I'm not, ma'am, though the subject is covered in the history course – from a purely objective point of view, naturally." Kit smiles; she's not entirely sure what to think of Mrs. Maynard, who's been in the parish for less than a year and so is even more of a newcomer than Kit is. The two women are close in age and Kit admires Julia Maynard's keen mind and

That *Forgetful* Shore

acerbic wit. She also admires Julia's occasional lapses of judgement, even more damning to a vicar's wife than to a headmistress. Kit imagines if there is one woman in Manchester she might actually be friends with it is probably Julia Maynard, though her being the vicar's wife and the mother of a singularly recalcitrant pupil does complicate matters.

She knows most of the people in the circle, though she can't remember the names of two of them – both related to governors on her School Board. Only one person is a complete stranger: a rangy, rumpled-looking man in a knit pullover and heavy wool pants who stands next to Mrs. Maynard. He hasn't said a word so far and his casual style of dress makes him look a little out of place in this rather stuffy gathering.

Just as she's thinking that, Julia Maynard leans forward, tugging the man by his sweater-clad arm. "Mr. Lanski, is there anyone here you don't know? I'm being terribly rude – I ought to have introduced you round – you haven't met Mrs. Porter, have you? Mrs. Porter, headmistress of St. Margaret's school – Leopold Lanski."

He leans forward to shake her hand. His grip is firm as she says, "Pleased to meet you, Mr … Lanski." His accent as he says, "The pleasure is mine, indeed," confirms her suspicion that he is not an Englishman.

"So, what did you think of tonight's lecture?" she asks the newcomer.

He rolls his eyes. "It is very easy for those who are warm and well-fed to talk about socialism in the abstract. It sounds a bit different when the words come from men who are hungry and desperate."

"Like the factory workers and miners, you mean? Or the Russian workers?"

He smiles apologetically. His English is excellent, but his accent lends something exotic to his voice. "No doubt there is real poverty here in the North of England, Mrs. Porter. But what I saw in my home country before the war was far worse. It is true, people do reach a point where revolution seems like the only option."

He pitches his voice low and the rest of the conversation flows around them. Kit wants to know who he is, where he came from, if he's really a Communist and if so, why is he here rather than in Russia, building the new revolutionary society. She suddenly realizes she's far more keenly interested in the topic than she was a few minutes ago, and is honest enough to admit to herself that Comrade Lanski's rather intriguing face – not handsome exactly, but interesting, dominated by a crooked nose, a long, mobile mouth, and liquid brown eyes – probably has something to do with her sudden interest in Marxist theory.

"But of course, you have already said you believe in working within the system," he goes on. "Even if the system is rooted in injustice?"

Kit pauses a moment, collects her thoughts. "I have seen a great deal of good coming from collective action," she says. "Not just in factory cities like Manchester, but back home, among fishermen in rural areas," she adds, thinking of Coaker and the Fishermen's Protective Union.

"Ah yes. I was going to ask you where you had come from." *I vass goink to ask.* "I have not much of an ear for English accents, but I think yours is … what do they say? Of the colonies?"

She moves a step closer without knowing she's doing it. There's something electric in the man's presence. It reminds her of the long-ago morning when she came to the schoolhouse in Elliston and saw Ben standing outside. Of course, that's not the only time. She's felt the same magnetic presence, the same attraction from other men over the years, though she's moved in so many all-female circles that there haven't been many opportunities to be overpowered by the nearness of an attractive man. When there have been such opportunities, there's often been a complication, such as the man being someone else's husband. Which this man might very well be, for all Kit knows about him.

"Mrs. Porter, dear, we're about to get a cab – do you want to share a ride?" Julia Maynard lays a gloved hand on Kit's arm. Kit hesitates, and Leo Lanski says, "I had hoped to ask for the honour of seeing Mrs. Porter to her home, if that is not too bold."

"No, of course, thank you very much," Kit says to Leo, and smiles at Mrs. Maynard, who raises her eyebrows almost to her hairline and makes a tiny O of her mouth. Was Kit thinking just a few moments ago that this woman might be a friend?

Leo escorts her, not home, but to a nearby café. They aren't long into their conversation before he asks, "And is there, I should inquire, a Mr. Porter?"

He must know there isn't; wherever he's from, he's been in England long enough to know that a married woman would not be headmistress of a girls' school. "Mr. Porter died in 1918," Kit says, looking down at her coffee cup.

"Ah. I am sorry." He pauses, then adds, "I mean I am sorry in more ways than one – I presume your husband died in the war, and I served in the

That *Forgetful* Shore

German army. So when I meet an English war widow such as yourself – and I have met many – I feel I owe you an apology."

"You don't," Kit said. "As it happens my husband died after returning from active service. But even had he been killed in action – I would hardly hold an ordinary German soldier responsible for his death."

"Even had I been on the other end of the gun that killed him?"

"I would try not to," Kit says. "One would have an emotional reaction, of course – it's unavoidable – but logically, one can't blame soldiers for war. They fight for king and country, and follow the orders of their commanding officers." She thinks of the charge of the Light Brigade, of the charge at Beaumont-Hamel.

"That is surely true in my case," Leo says. "My father was Polish, and I grew up in what we called Poland, though it was not on the map at that time. I was conscripted into the German army and forced to fight against fellow Poles who were conscripted by the Russians. I never fought on the Western Front."

"Yet you apologized."

"I apologized for being part of the war. I claim the universal defense. We only follow orders – we fight for king and country," Leo says. "So the working men of one country slaughter their natural comrades, the working men of another country, in the name of wealthy kings who cares nothing for their lives. How long will this go on? Do you think we have learned anything from our war to end all wars?"

"You talk like a pacifist," Kit says, and he nods. "But if you're really a Marxist," she goes on, "don't you agree with Lenin – that revolution can't come without spilling blood?"

"It is true, you have caught me out." He laughs, then puts aside his cup and lays his large, bony hands on the table, palms down, fingers spread, so that she can't help but stare at them. There's nothing extraordinary about his hands but the gesture is strangely erotic; she can't look at those hands without imagining them on her skin, circling her waist, running down her thighs. She looks back up and meets his brown eyes, looking steadily at her from his long narrow face under a tumble of wavy brown hair. "But if bloodshed must come, should it not be in the cause of building a better world, rather than shoring up the old one?"

Kit pulls her thoughts back, startled to realize they are still talking of war, pacifism and communism. She suspects that his thoughts, like hers, are straying from the political to the personal.

But what kind of personal connection could there be between people such as this man and herself? She's managed to tease out during the conversation that he is a Polish Jew whose mother was born in England. After the turmoil of the war his widowed mother wanted to return to her own country. Leo accompanied her, read history at Cambridge and is now a lecturer at the university here in Manchester. He is also a member of the Communist Party, writes for Communist papers and dreams of sparking revolution in England. He is a man she might meet at a lecture, might even have a conversation with in a café – once only. A Jewish Communist rabble-rouser is certainly not someone Mrs. Porter of St. Margaret's could be seen with on a regular basis.

"This old order that you speak so lightly of sweeping away," she says, again pulling her thoughts into some kind of order, "I'm not so ready to dismiss it as you are. I think there is as much good as bad in it, and more good than I see in the Soviet Union."

"Ah, but the old order changes. It must – it is changing already."

"Exactly! Changing already, by gradual means. By the ballot box, not by revolution. England has already had a Labour government. Change is being built on the foundations we have already laid."

"Your faith is touching, and most of your countrymen share it," says Leo. "Even the poorest Englishman, the one who votes Labour government and puts his faith in the trade union – he clings to the hope of rising to a better position under capitalism, even as the capitalists do all they can to break the unions and grind the workers beneath their heels."

He really is a fascinating, frustrating man, and though she has to keep dragging her thoughts back from his lips and hands to his damnably incorrect ideas, Kit realizes that part of the attraction of the man is that her mind is as engaged and excited as her body is. She's about to reply with a spirited defense of capitalism when he leans forward.

"And now, where shall we go after we finish this coffee?" he says. "I have offered to walk you home, but I suspect you do not welcome gentlemen callers at such an hour – even if I were a gentleman, which of course I am not. My own lodgings are much humbler, but very private – and perhaps you will not need to worry about finding a way home until morning, hmm?" He lifts one of her hands in his and brings it, not to his lips, which would be oddly pretentious, but to graze, briefly, his stubbled cheek. The gesture

That *Forgetful* Shore

excites Kit so much she can hardly breathe. Really, it has been far too long since she has touched a man.

"Mr. Lanski, I'm sorry, but I think you have mistaken what kind of woman I am." She pulls back her hand.

He smiles, a slow, lazy smile that seems worlds removed from talk of revolution and bloodshed.

"Have I? You are a headmistress of a girls' school, an upright member of society and of the Church of England, a model of propriety. If either one of us has mistaken what kind of woman you are, Mrs. Porter, I don't think it is I."

Triffie

TRIF HAS NEVER been hunting, but she's heard men talk about it. Jacob John goes into the woods every fall with a few other fellows and they often bring home a caribou between them; jars of bottled caribou meat line Trif's pantry shelves, a treat in the cold months of winter. She imagines the hours the men must spend in patient waiting, squatting in the bushes, watching for a sign of their prey.

For two months now she has given that same attention to Joe Bishop, watching him in church, watching him walk down the road. She smiles and says hello to him as she always does, but defers the question of extra lessons for Katie Grace by coming to school herself to pick up the younger children, telling the girl to hurry home to do her chores. She sees Katie's face drop when Trif urges her home to make bread or beat the rugs and hears the echo of Aunt Rachel's voice in her own. She will not do that to her own daughter – rob her of life's chances, or the birthright of a sharp brain – but neither will she send her child unarmed into the lion's den. Sometimes you need more than prayers, more than good intentions.

She makes her move in the middle of October, as the evenings start drawing in and the chill in the air shifts from a nip to a bite. She makes an excuse to visit the man at home, because the schoolroom is no place for what she has to say.

She has spent these weeks turning things over in her mind, re-reading Effie's letter, remembering what Amelia said, what Millicent refused to say, what Kit said so long ago. Even Betty's words, mumbled and shamed. She has spoken to other women, none as blunt as Amelia or Effie or Kit, but she's heard enough.

She's turned over her own memories, too, replaying them, asking herself the obvious question, till she almost doesn't trust her own mind. Amelia Snow didn't believe her – didn't believe Trif could have remained innocent so long. She tries to call up memories of the schoolroom, of Mr. Bishop's hand on her shoulder, his voice next to her ear. Was there ever anything – did his fingers stray to the neckline of her dress? Did he lay a hand on her thigh while he helped her unravel the mysteries of Geometry?

Sometimes, lying next to Jacob John in bed, scavenging through the ragbag of memory, she almost convinces herself that she remembers such a touch, that she felt ashamed and buried the memory.

But in daylight, cooking porridge on top of the stove, she stirs the pot and brings up that memory, examines it again in the light of morning, and sees that it's false. There never was such a touch, such a moment. Joe Bishop never spoke a word to her that was out of line. And really, when would he have had the time? She was hardly ever alone with him – it was either her and Kit, or Kit alone for lessons that Triffie wasn't allowed to have.

There is no such memory; nothing happened. She has only hearsay evidence. But it will have to be enough.

"What a pleasant surprise, Triffie," Joe Bishop says when she comes to his door with a jar of pea soup and a loaf of bread. It isn't the first time. He is an unmarried man to whom they all owe a great deal, and the women of the community look after him. He is paid by the School Board, but he also gets paid in salt fish and jars of soup, in pies and loaves of bread. He says it's a pleasant surprise, but surely it can be no great surprise to see Trif Russell at his front door. He welcomes her into the kitchen and moves the kettle to the front of the stove.

"No, I won't be staying for a cup of tea," Trif says, nor does she sit down when he does. She stands with her arms crossed over her chest, as if she can hold herself together. Her heart hammers high up, almost in her throat. But she thinks of Katie Grace and it's like putting on armour. The whole armour of God, that she may be able to stand against the wiles of the Devil.

"Is there … something I can do for you, Triffie?"

"I got something to say to you, Mr. Bishop."

The room is silent except for a clock on the wall, ticking away nearly half a minute before Joe draws breath and says, "Go on, then. Say what you came to say."

She has rehearsed and rehearsed, like a recitation, but there's no rhyme or rhythm to carry her through this. "What you said – about Katie Grace. Her extra lessons."

He nods; a little tension drains from his face. "I meant what I said – I'm willing to do whatever I can to help her. She's a bright girl."

"I know that. You don't have to tell me she's bright, and I want her to have the chances I never had. But I don't want her staying after school for no extra lessons with you." She's usually careful with her grammar when speaking to teachers and ministers, but she can feel that caution slipping away under the wave of emotion rising inside her.

His eyelids flicker, and she sees her own fear reflected in his eyes. He's as scared of this conversation as she is, Trif realizes. That knowledge is power, like she's holding a good hand of cards. Not that she ever plays cards, that being a sin.

"Is it Jacob John?" Joe suggests. "Is he giving trouble about her getting an education?"

A tiny spark of anger flares at that: the spark that will ignite the flame. "Mr. Russell got no problem with our daughter getting an education," Trif says. "This is nothing to do with him – he don't even know I'm here tonight. This is between you and me. I came to say that my daughter deserves an education, but she don't deserve to be interfered with by some – some dirty old man."

Those last three words hit him like a punch in the gut, she can see. She feels punched too, like the air has gone out of her now that the words have been said. She's glad to let them hang in the air a little while she steadies her breath.

He's not an old man – forty-five or fifty, no more than that. He's always had a high forehead but the dark hair on it has receded back and back these last years till you'd have to say he was bald. But the fringe at the sides and back is not grey, and his face is less lined than Jacob John's, though her husband is a good ten years younger. Indoor work, she thinks; nothing is wrinkled but Joe Bishop's forehead and the lines around his eyes.

Those eyes widen, then narrow at her words. Not an old man. But "dirty" – yes, that hits him, she can see.

"I … don't know what you're saying. Are you accusing me of something?"

That *Forgetful* Shore

"You knows damned good and well what I'm saying," says Trif, who never swears. The word "damned" curdles on her tongue, but it feels right, all the same, sharp like a knife in the thick air of this room. *Damned*, no casual curse word but a very specific adjective with a meaning she won't take back. Nor does she use the careful grammar she's always reserved for conversation with her betters; she speaks as she would at home, in what she thinks of as her own voice. "I'm not spreading no rumours nor gossip – I'm talking about what I knows. What I've heard. Not from one woman, nor from two, but from plenty of others. I'm saying out loud what's been known on this Point for years but never spoken out loud. What you done to them girls."

"What girls." He doesn't even put a question mark to the words, just drops them into the room like two stones.

"Effie. Millicent. Amelia. Kit. And that's not all."

"What have they told you?"

"You know what they told me. You know what you did." She keeps her gaze even, will not let herself look away. Years of reverence and respect for this man fight inside her but she will not back down, because she has a daughter.

"I'm no – no child molester. I never –" She sees him searching for a word to say what he never did. He reaches into the language he knows best, books and poetry. "I never deflowered a girl, never violated anyone. I can't believe you would accuse me –"

"A girl can be violated without laying down on a bed, Joe Bishop. You laid hands on those girls, touched them, kissed them, said and did things that you know wasn't right for a teacher to say and do to a young girl. You call yourself a Christian man, and you can sit there and say to me that what you did was all right? Do you really believe that?"

Finally, he drops his eyes, breaks the connection between them. It's a relief not to be looking into his eyes anymore but she doesn't look away. When he looks up from staring at his boots, he'll find Trif Russell is still there. In her mind she's singing *I shall not be, I shall not be moved*. Like a tree planted by the waters.

He rubs his hands on the legs of his pants, as if he were Pilate or Lady Macbeth without the benefit of a bowl of water. "I don't say it was right, Trif. I know it was wrong. If you only knew – all these years, how I've tried –"

"Tried what?" she says, when he gives up speaking.

"To change. To make resolutions – to make amends."

"You tried to change. But you never did, did you? You didn't stop. It's still going on."

He nods, then shakes his head. "Not now – not – not for awhile. You can't think – I mean, your daughter. I would never lay a hand on Katie …"

"How is Katie any more valuable than Effie Dawe, or Amelia Snow, or Kit Saunders?" Trif says, raising her chin a quarter inch. He looks up again, to meet her eyes which will not be moved. "I'm sure you said about every girl you ever touched, that you wouldn't never do such a thing. You said yourself – you tried to do better. But you never did. I've talked to enough women to know you never changed."

He is still shaking his head, but no longer as if to deny her words. Rather, as if in disbelief, either at what he's become or at the fact that someone has finally challenged him. Trif is sure she's the first person on the Point to speak of this aloud. Some women protested silently, like Millicent, slinking away from the promised lessons. Others took what they could and got out of there, like Effie and Kit, carrying their scars. But no-one has said to his face in twenty years, *This is what you did, Joe Bishop. This is what you are.*

He tries to meet her eyes again but can't. He looks at the kettle on the stove, at the loaf of bread his accuser brought him. "Who are you going to tell?"

This is the part she has thought through most carefully, going over and over it in her mind. "There's lots of people I can tell. The minister. The School Board. Other parents."

"I should – do you want me to resign? Perhaps if I tendered my resignation, you wouldn't have to tell everyone … the reason why."

"And let you slink off to a job in some other school, some other cove?"

"I wouldn't –"

"Don't waste your breath on promises and lies. If you went away from here and kept it all secret, you'd bring the same thing down on another town, and leave us without a teacher. And you're a good teacher, Joe Bishop."

He looks at her like he's expecting more, but she lets her words lie there. Finally he says, "I promise, Triffie – if you don't tell, I'll put a stop to it."

"Prayers and promises won't cut it," she says. "All the resolutions in the world won't do it, you know that."

"Then what do you expect of me?"

"Short of a miracle from God – which I'll pray for, believe me – only

one thing ever changes a man," Trif says.

"What's that? Love?"

Trif snorts. "You're after reading too many books. The only thing on earth that changes a man isn't love – it's fear. And you're scared, I can see that. Scared of what I'll say, who I'll tell."

"You haven't told anyone yet, have you?"

"Oh, I'll tell people," she says. "Your secret's not safe with me. But I don't want you run out of town, neither. Here's what I'm going to do, Joe Bishop, and here's what you're going to do."

He looks up at her, and she's back in the classroom again, their roles reversed. She is up front laying down the law; he is wide-eyed, waiting to learn his lesson.

"I'm going to tell every woman on the Point who has a daughter in school," Trif says. "A good few have their suspicions already but they don't talk about it, they're ashamed. I'll lay it out in the open for them when their daughters turn – nine or ten. Is that young enough?" She allows herself one look of pure disgust, at the thought that a child of nine could arouse his desire. "I'll tell them that you have – a problem. That's how I'll put it, that you have a problem, you're a sick man, and you shouldn't be left alone with a young girl. And I'll watch you like a hawk. One finger out of line, one hint that you're up to your old tricks, and I'll tell the minister, the School Board, and every man on the Point. All those women I talked to, they'll back me up. Women like Effie Dawe and Kit Saunders are teachers themselves, well-respected. People will listen to them."

Joe looks at her like a man balancing on a single plank across a raging river. She wants him to have that look, to hold that tension for years, if need be. She has to keep him afraid, to keep the upper hand on him. Good teachers are hard to come by. If Joe is gone who knows what young fool they'll send to Missing Point, or even if they'll keep the high school going at all.

"Do you still want me to give Katie extra help?"

"Oh, indeed and I do. But not alone in the schoolroom. You'll come by my house in the evenings and tutor her in my kitchen, and you can do the same for any other young girls that needs the extra help too – or boys either, for that matter," she adds, an even darker suspicion crossing her mind.

She is not triumphant about her evening's work when she leaves Joe Bishop cowed and defeated in his house. Vanquishing an old enemy

might have brought some pleasure; there's no joy in bringing a hero to the ground.

There's no doubt he's a wicked man, but no doubt he's a good teacher as well. After turning it over in her mind for a few minutes as she walks home, Trif decides this isn't as strange as it seems. Everything in the world involves a balance of opposites: the sea brings life and death; fire warms and destroys; love makes people happy and drives them to despair. It's only a matter, Trif thinks, of caution, of keeping a dangerous thing within boundaries, to reap its benefits while shielding you from its dangers. Men build boats to take them out on the sea to fish, but also to keep themselves from being swallowed by the sea. Triffie has set up her own little defenses here now; it remains to be seen whether they will hold.

At home, she tells Jacob John she has been to see Joe Bishop, bring him over some bread and pea soup. "Did he say anymore about Katie's lessons?" Jacob John asks, his eagerness surprising her.

Trif realizes she'll need some explanation for this new arrangement. After a pause long enough to pour a cup of tea for herself she says, "He's going to give Katie some extra help. I told him to come do it here, in the evenings, instead of keeping her after school."

"Oh? And why's that now?" Jacob John's tone is as even as it always is.

"I don't like the idea of her being up to the school all hours by herself. Don't seem right for a young girl, to me, even though I wants her to get the lessons."

Jacob John often says Triffie worries too much over the children, and she expects that response now, but he only says, "Ah well. You'd know best about that, I s'pose."

That's all she'll say to him, but she is brimming to tell someone what she's done, and there's not a soul on the Point to whom she wants to confide this. She will speak to the other women with young daughters, but discreetly, measuring out her words. What she wants now is someone to whom she can tell the whole tale, including the heaving of her guts as she faced the man.

She sits down to her table with pen and paper. She could write to Effie Dawe – but no, not with the kind of honesty she needs. There has only ever been one person she can write to like that – the person who returned her honesty with betrayal.

That *Forgetful* Shore

Still, the words are there and they have to come out or they'll fester inside her. Knowing she'll never put it in the post, that she might even burn it, Trif takes the clean sheet of paper and writes:

Missing Point
October, 1925

My dearest Peony ...

Kit

KIT WAKES TO a rectangle of grime-encrusted sunlight spilling over the rumpled sheets that tangle her legs. In the disoriented moments between dreams and full wakefulness she's sometimes unsure where she is, but when she closes her eyes to block out the sun she smells sweat and cigarettes. Before she opens her eyes again to see the dirty window facing a brick wall, her other senses remind her she's in Leo's room.

This is the fourth or fifth night she's spent here in the months she's known Leo. They meet every few weeks, occasionally in public to attend a lecture and go to a café afterwards, sometimes alone here at his flat. It's rare that she takes the risk of staying out all night, returning home in the harsh light of a Manchester morning. It's an exotic pleasure to sleep beside him all night, to wake in the morning to hear him moving around in the other room, cooking eggs and brewing coffee.

Most of Kit's circle of acquaintances – still none of them can really be called friends, and she no longer has any great desire to make friends, now that she has secrets to guard – know of her unorthodox friendship with the Polish socialist. She has worked hard to make sure no-one ever suspects they are lovers. He has never been to her rooms, nor appeared as her escort at a dinner party or any such occasion. Surely if anyone suspected, the school governors would have had a word with her by now.

Kit likes the unorthodox arrangement. Living a double life adds spice to her staid existence as a headmistress. She loves being with a man again, especially one who combines passion and tenderness as Leo does, but she enjoys not having to fit him into her daily existence.

Leo is less content than she is, but then, he has a less contented nature. He is restless, not just for a workers' revolution but for more of everything in life. Mostly he complains, as he does this morning over breakfast, that he wants more of Kit: he wants them to live together, to be lovers every night, to wake up in the same bed and eat breakfast together every morning.

"That's marriage you're describing," Kit points out when he gets on with this.

"It doesn't have to be," he says, caught out for a moment, because he doesn't believe in the institution of marriage.

"What's the difference? If a man and a woman love each other, live together, share a bed all the time – how is that different from marriage?"

"Marriage is not about love. Marriage is about society, property, ownership." Leo leans against the window of his room, lights a cigarette. His cigarettes are European, strong smelling, and Kit used to hate them but has grown to like the smell. She occasionally indulges in a cigarette herself when she's at Leo's – she doesn't want the stink of tobacco in her own rooms – but she smokes Player's, which Leo keeps in a tin at his place for her.

"Marriage doesn't have to be all those things," Kit says.

"Of course it does. Yours was, was it not?"

Kit thinks for a moment. "I married for love," she says.

"Of course. You carefully fell in love with someone of the right social class, did you not?"

"You make it sound so calculated."

"You were conditioned, molded, shaped every step of your life – first to find a man, because society assumes a woman cannot be alone, and then to find the right type of man," Leo says.

"And what about now? Now that I'm a widow of thirty-five, sleeping with a completely unsuitable man?"

"Ahh, now you think you are old enough and independent enough to put the toe of your foot outside of society's rules." Leo laughs, sitting beside her at the tiny wooden table. The table is so small they can't both sit at it without their feet tangling underneath. "But still, so very cautious. It must all be secret, or you lose everything. And as for marriage – if I cared about marriage, could you marry me?"

Could you marry me? It's hardly the same thing as *Will you marry me*, is it? Not a proposal, but a hypothetical question, which makes it much easier to answer.

"I suppose I could, in theory," Kit says. "I might, if you wanted it. But everyone would disapprove. My family, my employers, society."

"Exactly. Because I am the wrong nationality, the wrong background, the wrong religion." Leo doesn't believe in God but insists that makes him no less Jewish. "Marriage is not for lovers. Marriage is for society."

"So in your ideal society – after the revolution – will anyone get married?"

"No," Leo says decisively, stubbing out the butt of his cigarette. "Lovers will be together if they want to, when they want, for as long as they want. Nobody will worry about a suitable match, and nobody will stay together because of religion or what the neighbours think. If you stop loving, you go your separate ways. And if a woman wants to be alone, she can be. No need for a husband—even a dead one – to make her acceptable." He reaches out to caress her hand, twisting her wedding band. He often plays with it like this, unthinking, as they talk or even as they lie in bed together, as if the ring is a fetter that still binds her, not so much to Ben as to a life she cannot share with Leo.

"We're fine just as we are," Kit says.

"You are fine. I am … stagnant."

"This air in this room, that's what's stagnant," Kit says, laughing to ease the moment, and crosses the tiny kitchen to push open the window and let some air in. She leans out – this window faces the street rather than a brick wall – and inhales. "Smell that air. It's May – how can anyone be stagnant in May?"

"It's May first," Leo says, with an odd half-smile. He takes the plates from the table and begins washing up at his narrow stone sink, three steps from the table.

"Of course – some sort of Communist holiday, isn't it?"

"Or a pagan fertility festival, if you prefer."

"We've already celebrated those rites, I think." Kit stays at the window, enjoying her perversely cheerful mood in contrast to Leo's gloomy one. That's one thing about having an affair with a moody, depressive Communist – it makes even the most cynical headmistress seem frivolous and light-hearted by comparison. And the fact that they have, in their own way, observed a few pagan rites during the previous night leaves her feeling happy – though fertility certainly had no part in it, both she and Leo taking a sensible modern approach to such matters.

"Then I will have to turn my attention to the other May holiday, to the plight of the workers. It's going to be called, you know – this week."

"The general strike?"

"Of course. The unions are meeting today." Everyone is talking about a general strike. Most people still find it hard to believe that the other unions will come out in support of the miners, who are already locked out for their insistence on "not a penny off the pay, not a second on the day." Leo doesn't sound at all stagnant when talking about the possibility of a strike; he lights another cigarette then turns back to finish the washing-up, still talking, making animated gestures with the dishrag. "How can the workers of this country stand it, Kit? Even your staid, respectable British – how can they bear it when the owners cut wages and increase hours at a single stroke? Less pay for more work? How can anyone go on believing that slow and steady, step by step, they'll win over the owners? It's revolution or nothing!"

"It might be nothing. The unions might not come out."

"Oh, they will. They will." He lays down the dishrag and stubs out his cigarette, barely smoked, on the edge of the sink. "I have to go to Party headquarters today, of course. I'm sorry."

"Don't be. The revolution must have priority." It's a Saturday; Friday nights and Saturdays are generally the only time they can find to be together, but the Party must come first.

Leo lacks the single-minded devotion to the Party Kit has noticed in some of his friends she's met – young Jewish intellectuals like himself, though most, unlike Leo, are English-born. These men allow the Party to control their jobs, their marriages, every element of their lives. By having a secret affair with a bourgeois schoolmistress, Leo is being, in his way, as defiant as Kit is. He's a true believer in the Red cause, but he's too much of an individual to march to the Party's beat in every parade.

The fact is, Kit thinks as she walks away from Leo's flat, she enjoys having a lover. She remembers Maggie Campbell at Dalhousie all those years ago, saying she wanted to be a round-heeled woman. "Perhaps you had the right idea after all," Kit thinks, and imagines writing that to Maggie, now Mrs. Hamilton, well-known author of improving storybooks for young girls. She still writes to Maggie regularly, but hasn't written about Leo to her, or to anyone. It's safer to have no confidantes.

The next day she hears nothing from Leo, which is not surprising. It's Sunday, her day to make an appearance in church, another symbol of conformity which Leo mocks without mercy. But the ancient liturgy soothes her, a different kind of peace than the kind she finds sitting at Leo's rickety table smelling his earthy cigarettes. Here, revolution seems impossible, unthinkable, though upon reflection she realizes the gorgeous English words of the service would not even exist without the considerable revolution of the Reformation, which involved quite a bit of bloodshed. The Church now seems solid and reliable, but perhaps the Communist Party will seem just as staid in four hundred years, simply a part of the background of society. Only it needs better writers, if that's to be the case. A Communist Cranmer, someone with the soul of a poet who can enshrine belief in words so lovely they are lodged forever, even in the hearts of those who no longer believe.

There's more here, Kit thinks as she goes forward to receive Communion, than she'll let on to Leo, more than simply keeping her job by an outward show of piety. She does feel something here, a connection, though she's sure it's not to God. She thinks of God as Triffie knew Him – insistent, persistent, creeping into every crack and corner of life, always teaming up with the latest snake-oil huckster in hopes of getting His foot in the door. If Kit ever believed in that God, she stopped a long time ago.

Leo calls himself an atheist – but a Jewish atheist; he insists that distinction not only makes sense but matters. Kit would never go that far; if anything, she's a Deist. An Anglican Deist. Perhaps that's what Leo means by his Jewish atheism: the ideas and even more, the words you worshipped as a child shape the person you become.

She wrangles ideas like this with Leo, who calls her a bloody hypocrite. She misses the opposite side of the argument, and amuses herself as she returns to her pew by inviting Triffie and Leo to an imaginary dinner party with God as the main topic of discussion. What would Trif make of Leo? One more thing Kit will never know.

The talk among respectable churchgoers after the service is all about the threat of the strike. Kit has become so accustomed to Leo's Communist rhetoric that she sometimes forgets how terrifying the threat of revolution is to the average English person. She's used to thinking of Communism as an idea, not a bogeyman – and perhaps, knowing as she does what a real Communist thinks, she's soothed by the realization that such ideas will never

That *Forgetful* Shore

take serious hold among the staid British populace.

The strike, however, goes ahead. Kit and the rest of Manchester wake on Tuesday morning to trams and trains that don't run and headlines that scream that the police have New Emergency Powers and that Everyone May Be Arrested! She walks to work instead of taking the tram, and passes a group of strikers picketing the tram stop, but otherwise sees little sign of unrest.

As the days pass, tension builds. The government brings in replacement workers to run the essential services. Out of a sense of loyalty to Leo and the cause, Kit continues to walk to work once the tram drivers have been replaced by strikebreakers. There are talks of the police and army making sweeping arrests, and Kit begins to feel uneasy about hearing nothing from Leo. It's not unusual for a week to go by without any contact, but this is not any ordinary week. When news comes, late in the week, of hundreds of Communists being rounded up for arrest, Kit is worried enough to send a messenger with a note to Leo's flat. There is no reply.

Then, suddenly, it is over. The Labour Party and the trade unions back down, ordering the strikers back to work – all but the miners, who remain out alone, with no support from their comrades. The government has broken the general strike, the great movement that was supposed to begin a revolution, in a mere nine days.

Three days after the strike ends, there's a note from Leo with nothing on it but a place and time to meet – a rundown café in his neighbourhood.

He tells Kit that he was arrested and questioned, but released without being charged just as the strike ended. He sits with his head in his hands, his coffee untouched, smoking one cigarette after another, ranting about the cowardice of the British, the weakness of those who mouth the slogans of brotherhood but collapse at the first sign of opposition. There is little Kit can say, except that she knew all along it would be this way. While part of her shares Leo's disappointment, mostly she is as relieved as every middle-class English person. It's terrible, of course, what the owners are doing to the miners, but does she really want revolution? Does anyone – even Leo, for all his talk?

"What am I doing in this country, Kit?" Leo grinds out another cigarette. "My mother was born here – so what? I am not English. I fool myself to think I could ever be part of bringing the revolution here. I need to be in my own place, among my own people. I need to be somewhere

where revolution is a real possibility. I should go to Russia, or home to Poland. Or even to Germany – now *there* is a country ready for revolution!"

"You know if you go to any of those places, you'll never be allowed back into England."

"But do I want to come back to England? For what?" He takes her hands across the table. "For you, of course, for love – but in the end, what is love in the face of revolution?"

"Still – you can't go home. Do you even have a home, anymore? Nothing is safe in Europe." She knows that Communists are being arrested all over Europe – in Russia, they are being arrested by other Communists, for being on the wrong side of Party battles. "I'm afraid of what will happen to you if you go home."

"Everyone goes home, Katerina. Sooner or later. Neither of us is going to lay down our lives to follow each other – so what are we doing here?"

Kit has no answer for this; she goes to his flat and they make love, not tenderly but with angry, tense passion, and then she lets herself out and goes home in the dark, taking a tram that runs as smoothly as England, carrying her back to her own quiet and respectable street.

In the months that follow, nothing changes. The miners remain out on strike, the dream of a workers' revolution receding ever farther into the distance. In November, when they finally go back to longer hours and lower pay, Leo is more despondent than ever, angry about the future both of Communism and of Leopold Lanski in England. He and Kit carry on as before, meeting and making love once every few weeks, but his moods turn darker and he talks more often of going back to Poland, or somewhere else in Europe. Kit tries to dissuade him, yet what does she have to offer if he stays? He does not suggest marriage, and she does not know what she could say if he did.

In the chilly grey winter of 1927, more than a year and a half after the strike, she begins to question her own future in Manchester. She gets a letter from her Oxford friend Edith Stone, now a headmistress in London, who writes:

Our English mistress has had the grave misfortune to fall in love and is now engaged to be married in the summer, which means that we shall be hiring again. Are you really as tired of administrating as you say you are? It's bread and butter to me but I do understand it's not

*to everyone's taste, and some are born teachers. If you would ever
consider leaving the North, and the status of Head, I would be
ever so pleased to offer you a position here. With your experience as
headmistress in an English school I think I could convince my
governors that your colonial accent is not the liability it once was.*

Kit lays the letter aside, wondering if she will discuss it with Leo. London
draws her, as it always has: she has done good work in the North, but she
longs to be closer to the centre of things, and she would like to lay aside the
reins of leadership in favour of more teaching, especially in a good school.

Another letter in the day's mail bears a Newfoundland stamp: unusual
these days, as she has few correspondents left at home. Ben's mother writes
at Christmas and on her birthday; Alice Templeman Penney sends the
occasional breezy missive. So does Kit's friend Maud Smith, still teaching at
Spencer, who is the author of this particular letter.

She writes about the school and about life in St. John's generally:

*I suppose it all seems very far away to you now, living in England,
but Times are Hard here ever since the War, and to tell the truth I
think you are better off out of it. I sometimes think of leaving myself,
joining my sister in the Boston States, but I can't suppress a twinge
of envy at you for having gotten to England and stayed there.*

Halfway through the chatty, breezy epistle a paragraph catches Kit's eye:

*We have a girl here this year from your hometown – I wouldn't be
likely to forget the name "Missing Point" having once heard it!
Katherine Russell – very bright girl, but of course her father is a
fisherman and although she's clever it doesn't seem likely the family
will have the money for her to finish this year, much less next year.
No doubt she'll soon be out teaching in some outport school without
even her Associate Certificate. We keep hearing that the Government
will tighten the regulations for teachers so that no-one will be able
to teach without a proper education, and with the founding of a*

University College I imagine the day will come when teachers will be required to have Degrees – quite a change from the old days! But it will be unfortunate for clever girls like young Katie Russell, who will never have the money to aim so high. Though it will be good to have them all better educated, I think we will lose some good natural teachers that way, people who simply had a gift for it regardless of how little education they had.

Miss Smith rambles on about the problems of education in the colony, the new university college, and Spencer itself, with brief digressions into her personal life and the lives of several common acquaintances. It's a good long letter, nearly five pages, but only that one paragraph lingers when Kit lays the letter aside.

Katherine Russell – little Katie Grace. Imagine her being old enough to be at Spencer! But she must be fourteen by now, finished school on the Point. It seems she's got Trif's brains, and that Jacob John has managed to do all right by her. For all everyone says the fishery is not good these past few years, they must have scraped up enough to send Katie off to school. What a shame if, as Miss Smith says, she won't be able to finish the year.

As she folds the letter and puts it away Kit thinks of Leo's words: "Everyone goes home, Katerina. Sooner or later."

Not I, she thinks. *I'm going to London.* She is surprised to realize that without talking to anyone or mulling it over, her decision is already made.

Absence that Afflicts my Heart

1928 – 1935

Triffie

ON THE FRIDAY that Katie Grace comes home from school, Triffie and little David drive the horse and cart over to Bay Roberts to meet her at the station. On the way back they stop at Parsons' Mercantile, partly because Trif needs a few items on the slate but mostly to show off her beautiful daughter, freshly back from St. John's with her Associate Certificate and the promise of a job teaching nearby in Spaniard's Bay in the fall. On the weekend she will tow Katie to three different church services with the same thought in mind. If pride is a sin, surely pride in your children must be the smallest of sins, the easiest for God to forgive.

The Mercantile is busy this afternoon, mostly with women whose husbands and sons are on the Labrador. Minnie Mercer is at the counter getting tea, molasses and liniment. "Are you getting any relief from the rheumatism?" Triffie asks, nodding at the liniment bottle on the counter as Minnie hands over her molasses puncheon to Skipper Wilf's granddaughter Abigail, who takes it to refill.

"No, I suffers something terrible," Minnie says. "This is the second year now I can't go fishing with Fred and the truth is I don't know if I'll ever be fit to make fish again, Trif maid." She sounds sorry; unlikely as it still seems to Trif, there are women who relish their summers at the fishery, look forward to the annual migration. Minnie seems really to regret not being well enough to go anymore.

On the other side of the store, next to the barrels of flour and oats and beans, Katie chats to Minnie's daughter Isabel and to Lydia Snow, her friends from schooldays. "Grand girl, she is," Minnie says, nodding in Katie's direction.

"She's a grand girl, and a good one too," Trif says. Personally, she believes Katie to be a sheer genius and a breathtaking beauty, though she recognizes a mother's bias may be at work in making that judgement. Katie did very well in her exams, taking first-class honours in several subjects. She is also, by any standard, a fine-looking girl; she has Trif's height with Jacob John's fair colouring and sandy hair. Trif wishes Jacob John could have stayed till Katie came home; he would have been so proud of his girl. But the ship that took him and Billy to the Labrador left before Katie's examinations were finished, so Jacob John won't see his daughter till the fall.

Abby Parsons comes back to the counter and hands the molasses jug over to Minnie. Trif has her list ready, but Abby says, "Mrs. Russell, Pop wants to talk to you." She nods toward the back room where Skipper Wilf sits smoking a pipe and looking over his accounts, coming out into the shop to talk to customers if anyone he cares to speak to comes in. Now that his brother Abe is dead and his son has taken over as a schooner captain, Skipper Wilf enjoys his position as the head of the family business. Trif has often exchanged a few pleasant words with the man while she's been in the shop, but she's never been summoned into the back room and she wonders if there can be something wrong with her account. This year they have been advanced more credit than usual because Billy is joining Jacob John on the Labrador, and Trif is always careful with figuring out how much her family owes and what's coming to them. She doesn't know what to expect when she goes into the little office.

"Have a seat, Trif. I got something to put before you," Skipper Wilf says. "Now you know poor Isaac Morgan who passed away in the spring, he was on the School Board, right?"

"Yes."

"I been talking to the minister about filling that place on the Board, trying to think who'd make a good job of it." In most towns the minister is also chairman of the Church of England School Board, but since the Point shares a minister with Bay Roberts, Skipper Wilf, as the town's leading merchant, chairs the Board, though he's expected to take guidance from the clergy. "We wants someone young, not an old fellow like myself or poor Isaac, maybe someone who still got children going up through school. Someone who cares

That *Forgetful* Shore

about the school and won't just be there to warm a bench. I got to thinking, what about your husband? You people have always been ready to take part and help out, and with your Katie starting up as a teacher herself, you're the kind of family we'd like to see represented on the Board."

"Jacob John? On the School Board? Well, I suppose so – I mean, he haven't got much education himself, but he's a great believer in his children getting educated," Trif says. "When he comes back in the fall you'll have to ask him, I s'pose, and see what he says. I can't speak for him."

"No, no, of course you can't, but I don't mind saying, Trif, if we were to get Jacob John on the Board I'd be hoping you would – well, not that you'd speak for him, of course, but that you'd be able to do your part, behind the scenes. I'd be hoping we could have the benefit of your wisdom as well."

The retort is so immediate Trif says it before she thinks. "If you want the benefit of my experience, you might do better off to put me on the Board myself."

There's a little silence in the room, broken only by the voices of the women and girls out in the shop. Trif takes a deep breath, inhaling the shop smell of cinnamon and cloves, turpentine and linseed oil. She considers laughing to make Skipper Wilf think she's joking.

"Well now, Trif, that's a new idea, for sure. I 'low it makes some kind of sense, but I don't mind saying I've never heard of a woman sitting on a school board."

"I don't know that I have either, sir," Trif says. "But we got the vote now, and they do say by the next election there could be a woman in the House of Assembly. I don't mean to be putting myself on that level, but I'm sure I could work hard and do a lot of good."

She wonders if Skipper Wilf has any clue that a few years ago she pulled his daughter-in-law Eliza aside and told her to keep a sharp eye on young Abigail, not to let her alone with Joe Bishop in the classroom or anywhere else. Triffie has kept her promise, spreading the story of the teacher's misdeeds only to those who most needed to know, but if she were on the School Board she'd be well placed to keep an eye on him, to put limits on his power. And who knows what else she could do? She doesn't really know how much power the school trustees have, but they must have something to do with making sure the children have enough books and slates and maps. Trif's heart races as Skipper Wilf leans back in his chair.

"Well, Trif, you've given me something to think about, I don't mind

That *Forgetful* Shore

saying. I'm going to have a word with Reverend Spence, see what he thinks about all this. I don't say he's ever heard tell of a woman on the School Board either, but I don't see how there can be a law against it, now that the women have the vote, like you say. We'll talk about this again, but don't mention it until then, all right?"

Out in the shop, Clara Snow is gossiping with Minnie while young Abigail fills Trif's order. Clara and Minnie stand in the doorway looking at the Katie and the other young girls, now standing outside in the sun. Clara gestures towards Katie and says to Trif, "Don't she put you in mind of Kit Saunders?"

Most people on the Point know that while Kit and Trif were once as close as sisters, they haven't kept in touch for years. Nobody has ever asked Trif the reason why; only Clara would be tactless enough to bring up Kit's name in this way. "Named for her, of course, isn't she?" Clara goes on. "Well, you'd best hope she won't get too big for her britches and think she's too good to come home like Kit did."

Rumours of Kit's splendid career have trickled back to the Cape, more slowly in the years since Mr. Saunders died and his wife moved away. The Parsons family, her mother's relatives, know a little about Kit's doings and have made a point to post occasional news notes in the Bay Roberts paper trumpeting her accomplishments. "And you never had no clue who helped out with Katie's school fees?" Minnie asks.

Trif knows, of course. She has known ever since the letter came from the headmistress at Spencer. She and Jacob John did all they could to scrape up the money for school, but fishing was poor that year and the price of fish even worse, and all the berrypicking in the world couldn't earn Trif enough extra money to be assured of keeping Katie in school that whole year, much less for another year after that. Katie went off to town with the knowledge that she could be recalled home at any time if the money to pay her board and fees ran out. She could have finished off two years of high school in Bay Roberts, but Katie had her heart set on the fine education she'd get from Spencer and the prospects of becoming a teacher. Trif dreaded bringing her home that Christmas and telling her they couldn't afford to send her back to town.

Then came the letter saying that an anonymous donor had volunteered to pay Katherine Russell's school fees. The headmistress could tell the Russells nothing except that the donor was an old Spencer girl who had a keen interest in helping a hardworking girl from an outport family.

Trif has written her thank-you letter half a dozen times, but it's not only the lack of an address that prevents her sending it. Each time, the letter of thanks turns into an angry rant, a tirade against the injustice of a life that allows Kit to play Lady Bountiful while Trif and Jacob John have to scrabble to keep from going further into debt to the merchant. Trif adds each aborted note to the box of unsent letters she's been saving for years.

That weekend she and Katie attend church three times, going to the Adventist service, Katie's favourite, on Saturday morning, then to the Anglican Church on Sunday and over to Clarke's Beach for the Pentecostal meeting Sunday night. They drop David with Aunt Rachel for the night before driving over to Clarke's Beach, since even Trif is willing to concede that church three times in a weekend might be a bit hard on a six-year-old. Jacob John says the poor youngster is after growing up in church, to the point that if he sits to the table and somebody passes a plate in front of him he thinks he's supposed to put collection in it.

Pastor Garrigus has come from St. John's to preach, and Trif loves hearing a woman speak the Word. The Adventists have a woman prophet but it's always men up front preaching, whereas the little Pentecostal congregation in Clarke's Beach has had as many women pastors as men. There's a Pentecostal Church starting up in Bay Roberts too, now, but Trif still goes to Clarke's Beach when she can. Her Billy loves these Sunday night services, got saved when he was just ten and now, at twelve, will stand up and testify as good as anyone. "The Lord's got His hand on that one," the Pentecostals often tell Triffie.

Trif hopes the Lord does have His hand on Billy – not just in the matter of being saved and baptized in the Spirit, but in the matter of protecting him during this, his first summer on the Labrador. Of course Triffie protested his going so young, and of course Jacob John trotted out the old reliable fact that he himself went fishing on the Labrador at eleven, as if that were any kind of a recommendation. Billy never even got to finish the school year, and while he's not as clever as Katie, he's an eager student at the subjects he likes, especially Mathematics. Triffie lost that fight, as she knew she would from the time she gave birth to a boy.

Katie sings along lustily on the hymns and listens attentively to her third sermon of the weekend, but remains in her seat when people stand to testify or kneel at the altar. Her lips are sealed while others around her prophesy and

That *Forgetful* Shore

speak in tongues.

"You don't take to the Pentecostal service like our Bill does," Triffie observes on the way home.

"No – but I don't mean to judge you, Mama. I've just never been able to believe that all their goings-on are what the Scripture means when it talks about the work of the Spirit. I've studied up on it a lot," she adds, knowing that Bible study carries more weight with her mother than anything else. "I started going to the Adventist Church in town this year," she adds. "I'm thinking I might get baptized."

Trif clicks the reins to get the little horse trotting a bit faster over the rutted road that leads back toward the Point. "Well, you got to go where the Lord leads you," she says. "That's what I've always done. If He wants you in the Adventist Church, that's where He'll put you. You likely won't be able to go on teaching in a Church of England school, though," she adds.

"The Adventists have a school of their own in St. John's," Katie says. "I don't want to stay on in Spaniard's Bay forever – I want to get more education. I'd love to go college."

"I'd love that for you, girl," Trif says. She doesn't bother stating the obvious, that she has no idea where the money would come from. Thinking of what she's just said about Katie teaching in Church of England schools, she tells her daughter about her conversation with Skipper Wilf Parsons. His warning not to say a word about it doesn't apply to Trif's own family, surely.

"Oh, you should do it, Mama! It's high time we had women on school boards, and who on the Point would do a better job than you?"

Reverend Spence pulls Triffie aside after the service a couple of weeks later and tells her that Skipper Wilf spoke to him about appointing her to the vacant seat on the Board. "I think the idea has some merit. I know you've always been a great supporter of our schools, but it is somewhat irregular."

"I know there's never been a woman on the Board before, but the times are changing –"

"Oh, of course, of course," says Reverend Spencer. "Very irregular, but we do live in a time of change and upheaval – to be honest, I was thinking more of your standing with the Church. Of course every Board member must be a Church member in good standing, and I know that your own religious affiliations have been – varied." He pauses, as if hoping Trif will admit she is a heretic and withdraw her name from consideration.

But now that she's had the idea, had a couple of weeks to chew it over, Trif isn't letting go that easily. She could do some good if she were a school trustee – and even if part of it is that, as Clara Snow has been heard to say, Trif Russell isn't happy unless she's running something, what's wrong with that? If God gives you a talent, Trif thinks, whether for making jam or organizing committees, it's a sin not to use it.

"I don't know what would trouble you about that, Reverend," she says now, looking him square in the face. "Sure I was baptized and confirmed in the Church of England, and I've got my backside on the pew every Sunday morning – when have you ever seen me miss a Sunday service?" She says nothing about the other baptisms, her baptism by immersion in a chilly lake with an Adventist pastor, or her baptism in the Holy Spirit at the Pentecostal Assembly. She gambles that in the face of her brazenness Reverend Spencer won't push it any farther, and sure enough he doesn't. He only says, "Well, there's no doubt you have the interest and ability, Mrs. Russell, but it is most unusual. And I did hear a suggestion that Mr. French might be willing to take the seat as well, though he is getting up in years."

The conversation trickles away with nothing definite being said. Trif talks of it to no-one but Katie, yet somehow word gets around the Point that there's talk of Trif Russell getting herself put on the School Board. Plenty of people are shocked at the idea of a woman – especially this particular woman – as a Board member, but all that talk is reported second-hand, few people wanting to confront Trif to her face about it.

"I told them, I said, why shouldn't a woman be on the Board?" Trif is surprised to hear this sentiment from Aunt Rachel, who has certainly never made any bold statements about women's rights and had not much to say one way or another when she was given the vote. But now she says, "It's always the mothers who send the boys to school when their fathers are trying to get them out in boat as young as eight or nine. Why shouldn't a mother have some say in her children's education?"

"Well, I've heard no more about it from Skipper Wilf, nor from the minister since he brought it up to me, but I expects any day now to hear Uncle Joe French got the place," Trif says. "Where is David, over next door? I should take him back over to our place now." Katie Grace is back home working in the garden while Triffie weeds Aunt Rachel's garden and lets her keep an eye on David.

"Oh, you know it's never no trouble to look after David," Aunt Rachel

That *Forgetful* Shore

says as the boy comes up the steps onto the front bridge. She reaches out to embrace him. "Leave him here all week – leave him here all summer, sure. He's the last little chick in my nest, aren't you sweetheart?"

David is big enough now to squirm away with a little embarrassment from her kisses. Aunt Rachel is far more sentimental and tender with her grandchildren and Trif's children than she ever was to her own when they were young, certainly more than she ever was to Triffie. But Ruth and Betty have both gone off to Nova Scotia now with their husbands and children, and Rachel has no-one but David left to spoil.

Aunt Rachel is over sixty now, and she's all right as long as Uncle Albert is around, but she seems lost when he's away. Albert stopped going to the ice this spring, but he reckons he has a few good years left in him fishing on the Labrador, and Trif determines to do everything she can for Aunt Rachel during the long months she's alone. She's offered, of course, to bring Rachel over to the south side with her, but Rachel won't leave her own house, and Trif can hardly blame her for that.

She's back at the Mercantile one day in late August, bringing in some blueberries she and Katie and David picked to sell, when she's again beckoned into the back room. Skipper Wilf looks up from lighting his pipe and gestures again for her to sit down. "Not everyone was happy with it, I'll tell you the truth," he says. "But Reverend Spence agreed with me and in the end most of the other Board members did too, though it's really only the minister's opinion that counts for much. You'll be joining us Tuesday evening in the schoolroom, Trif, for your first Board meeting."

Trif's steps are light on the road home that evening. She's gotten extra credit on her account for the blueberries – one more little safeguard against hunger and want – and she's won something no woman on the Point, perhaps no woman in Newfoundland, has had before. She has no idea how much power, how much say the School Board really has, but to sit there among those men, to raise a woman's voice to whatever questions they may discuss, is something to hold her head up about. And Jacob John will be proud of her – and doubtless relieved, too, since she knows he never would have wanted the job.

After the thrill of being appointed to the Board, the actual Board meetings are something of a letdown. Four old men – the two younger men on the Board are still down on the Labrador – sit about in the schoolroom and smoke; Skipper Wilf reads off lists of resolutions about teachers' salaries and plans to repair the leaking roof; and the Board members all say Aye. But still, Trif thinks, *it's a step*. At her first meeting she makes an effort to restrain herself, to say little and learn much with the thought that she may have more to say at the next meeting.

She's disappointed to learn that the Board meets rarely and leaves the running of the school almost entirely to Joe Bishop and the two young women who teach the lower grades. There's a second meeting in early October when one of the teachers falls sick and has to be replaced, but even then it's only a matter of lending their approval to a decision already made by the Church.

The few decisions have all been made and the meeting has been derailed by Uncle Ike Barbour reminiscing about how hard the old schoolmaster used to beat the boys back in his day, when someone knocks at the door. It's Abigail Parsons with a message for her grandfather. Skipper Wilf goes outside the door for a few moments. When he comes back in, he looks ten years older.

"We've just had a telegram," he says. "The *Sea Rose* never made port in Twillingate where she was supposed to, and there was a big storm up there last night."

The *Sea Rose* is one of two schooners owned by the Parsons family at the Labrador fishery this year; Ki Barbour is the captain, and Jacob John, Billy and Uncle Albert are all on board her. Triffie stands up suddenly as the men burst into questions, far more animated than they've been throughout the meeting. Skipper Wilf looks at her and says, "You go down and tell your aunt and the Frenches, Trif. We'll let you all know when we've got any more news."

At Aunt Rachel's house, Nellie French from next door is sitting at the kitchen table having a cup of tea, and David is asleep on the settee. Trif wishes for Katie's calming presence; somehow she thinks having her daughter here would make it easier to tell this terrible news, that the ship carrying all their menfolk may have been lost at sea.

As soon as Trif gets the words out, Nellie cries, "Oh, no! Oh, God!" and Aunt Rachel moves quickly from her chair. She goes, not to Trif but to her old friend, and the two older women grip each other's hands. Rachel and Nellie have been next-door neighbours for forty years. They have borne the worst together, losing their two boys in the war, sending their men off to the Labrador every summer and to the ice every winter. There is no news, only wild speculation and women's grief. As the news spreads, women come to the

That *Forgetful* Shore

door. The wives, mothers and daughters of the men on the *Sea Rose* gather to comfort and encourage one another. A knot of women forms around Rachel's kitchen table, voices and hands twining as they share stories of old shipwrecks, offer hopeful stories of survival against all odds. There is an empty chair but Trif stands by the door, unable to join the circle. There's something strengthening in the sharing of sorrow and worry, but Trif has never been able to do it – not with a group like this, rocking back and forth and keening, waiting for news to come in.

She tells one of Nellie's daughters that someone should stay over here with Rachel tonight, though that's really Trif's job. Instead she picks up the sleeping David, shakes him awake and stumbles with him up over the lane, across the Point to her own place, the only placed Trif can bear the thought of being right now.

The front bridge of Trif's house is cool but not yet cold in the early-October evening. She puts David down in his bed and then goes and sits outside. Across the road the Long Beach stretches out, the rocks worn smooth from the waves that beat against them year after year. *Like us,* Trif thinks, *like the women all along the shore. We sit here year after year and wait for word from the men, wait for the worst the sea can give, and whatever happens, we take it. We just take it.*

The sea looks calm enough tonight here in the bay but it's no difficulty to imagine the high waves, the screaming wind, the rocks that could tear apart a wooden schooner in minutes. Such things have been part of Triffie's dreams her whole life. They became sharper and clearer when she married a fisherman, and they have become oppressive this summer, since her eldest son went off to sea.

The sky darkens so she can hear the waves better than she can see them: there's no moon tonight, but that rushing sound of water on rocks is ever present. Triffie is angry – angry at Jacob John for encouraging the boy to go, for going himself year after year, angry at God, angry at the sea itself.

It's easiest to be angry at the sea, at this huge impersonal force that rules all their lives, that gives so grudgingly and takes with such abandon. She says aloud, "God, if you bring our Billy and Jacob John home alive out of this, no man of mine is ever setting foot in a boat again. No more fishermen in this family."

The next day word comes that the *Sea Rose* sank on the night of the fourth of October, in the waters off St. Anthony. Trif, Katie, Aunt Rachel and half

the women on the Point, it seems, crowd into Parsons' Mercantile to hear the telegram from St. Anthony.

Skipper Wilf stands up on a box and raises his hand. His son Ted is captain of the *Sea Rose*'s sister ship, the *Lily*.

"The first telegram is from the telegraph office in St. Anthony," Skipper Wilf says, raising his voice. "Ladies – ladies, quiet down now, it's not all bad news. *Sea Rose* lost, stop. Nine survivors safe with us, stop. Further news to follow."

"Nine?" The number is repeated over and over throughout the crowded shop. "Only nine! Nine saved? How many lost then?"

Skipper Wilf raises his voice. "The *Sea Rose* carried a crew of sixteen men. If nine men are saved, then seven are – lost." His voice breaks a little on the word. "We got no way to tell yet, who the survivors are. Not till another telegram comes from St. Anthony."

Over the panicked voices of women that break like waves in the room, Skipper Wilf raises his voice again. "I have a second telegram from my son, Skipper Ted, who made harbour in Twillingate. The *Lily* is going back to St. Anthony to get the survivors from the *Sea Rose*."

The second telegram arrives the next day, listing the survivors who made it to shore and are on their way home. Captain Hezekiah Barbour. Robert French. Arthur French. Nathaniel French. Jabez Badcock. Harry Mercer. Fred Mercer. Jacob John Russell. William Russell. The other seven men are not accounted for, presumed to be lost. The name of Albert Bradbury is not among the survivors.

Aunt Rachel stayed home this time, keeping David with her, rather than go to the shop to hear the telegrams read out. She can't bear it, she tells Triffie, so it's left to Trif to come home and break the news.

Trif, growing up in that house, in and out of it almost every day for years since she married, cannot recall many moments of tenderness or soft words between her aunt and uncle. In fact she can remember almost no conversation between them at all – Aunt Rachel spoke to the children, and Uncle Albert barely spoke at all. She can't remember ever seeing them touch, or kiss, or embrace. But Rachel cries with huge sobs that shake her shoulders and raw gasps of air, and when all her tears are gone she sits at the table staring down at the oilcloth with hollow, empty eyes.

What is she crying for? Trif wonders. *For the loss of the man she loved? For the loss of the only life she knew? For the years of widowhood lying ahead, with*

*husband and son gone and her daughters far away? If Jacob John were lost, what
would I be crying for?*

People come in and out of the kitchen all evening. Triffie feeds them and
gives them tea; Rachel sits quietly, accepting their condolences. She is not the
only one with a man whose name did not appear on the survivors list. Nellie
French has lost another son: John, too young to go off to the war that claimed
Isaac, is among the missing, leaving a wife and four children. The women of
the Point go from the house to house, sharing what comfort they can, until
long after dark. Lamps are lit, lights burning in windows for fishermen who
will never come home from the sea.

When Rachel talks, finally, it's only to Triffie, when the well-meaning
neighbours and relatives have gone and Katie, summoned home from
Spaniard's Bay to hear the news, has gone to bed next to her little brother in
one of the upstairs rooms. Tonight Triffie can't leave Rachel, can't go home to
her own place no matter how much she longs for it. She has to stay.

"I hated for him to go," Rachel says, looking not at Triffie but out the
window, though it's dark and there's nothing to see out there. One oil lamp
illuminates a small circle of tablecloth.

"I know, I know," Trif says. "I hated for Jacob John to go too." That's not
quite true: there was a time she used to be glad he was gone, though
she always worried about might happen to him. "And I never wanted Billy
to go."

"No, I was the same with our Will, remember?" Rachel says. "Much good
all my worrying did – better he should have died on a fishing boat than go
the way he did. Nothing good ever comes to those who go away from home,
Trif. I worries that much about Ruth and Betty and their crowd, you'll never
know. They goes off, they all goes off – only you had sense, Trif, you never
went away."

I wanted to, Trif thinks. If she'd had the chance to go, her aunt's worries
wouldn't have counted for anything. She doesn't say that; she says, "I went
away three summers to Labrador."

"Labrador!" The name sounds like something Rachel would spit out, not
fit to have in her mouth. "Everyone gone down on the Labrador. Albert went
to Labrador and now he'll never come home. Grace went to Labrador, and
look what happened to her! Will went to France, Ruth and Betty are gone to
Nova Scotia … nothing good ever comes from going away, maid. Nothing
good at all."

"Grace … my mother went on the Labrador?" Triffie has never heard this, not from Rachel or anyone.

"She went as cook on Josiah Badcock's schooner one summer – the summer she was seventeen. Came back home a disgrace to her family. And no, before you gets on with it, I don't know no more than that. It could have been any one of the men on that schooner or the old captain himself, bad as he was. I told her no good would come from going away and I was right … I was right about all of them."

With no warning, her sobs start again. She weeps with such abandon that Trif longs to comfort her, wishes she could put her arms around her and hold her aunt's weeping body against hers. They have never been close, yet now she is all Rachel has, the only one who stands by her. She takes one of Rachel's bony, weathered hands across the table and holds it between her own.

All over the Point that week, women weep and hold each other. Everyone is crying when the *Lily* comes into port and the survivors of the *Sea Rose* come down the gangplank. Ki Barbour comes off first, leading the half of his men who survived. He looks broken, this man who survived France and came back a hero, who took such pride in rising to be captain of a fishing schooner.

Trif watches Skipper Ki's face only for a moment before she sees, among the men behind him, the smallest of the survivors, and she breaks from the crowd to run forward and take her son in her arms.

Billy squirms and fidgets as she covers his dark head with kisses. Katie and David go to Jacob John and welcome him home, then it's all five of them together, the children in their parents' arms, Jacob John smiling at Triffie as if he's just come back from a great adventure and had a grand time. Even with the loss of Uncle Albert and the other men, Triffie cannot help but rejoice, cannot help thanking God that her husband and son are home, that her small family is intact.

Over supper in her own house that night, Trif lays down the law. What she promised God that night on the front bridge, she will fulfill. "No more fishing in this house," she says. "Not a man here will go out in boat, ever again. 'Tis tempting fate, and we've lost too much. I won't risk my boys in the boat."

They all stare at her, dumbfounded. What can they be, if not fishermen?

"I don't care, ye'll all have to learn some other trade," Trif says. "Billy, you stay in school, you got a good head on your shoulders and there'll be no more leaving school to go to the Labrador. You'll be back in that classroom tomorrow morning."

That *Forgetful* Shore

"Can I be a preacher?" Billy says, and now it's him that everyone looks at in surprise. He shrugs. "When we was out there in the dory trying to make her to shore I told God if he got me through it I'd be a preacher, and I means to do it."

Trif wipes away a tear with the back of her hand. "That you can, my boy. We'll find a way."

"Good enough," Jacob John says. "Katie's going to be a Seventh Day teacher, Billy's going to be a Holy Roller preacher – sure we'll make young David a Church of England minister and then we'll have the full set." They all laugh, even Triffie, and while they're still laughing Jacob John says, "But what are you going to do with me, Trif girl? What would I do, if I didn't go fishing?"

For that she has no answer. But she's made a promise to God, and God will have to help them figure something out.

Kit

...You will be most interested, I hope, in this position. Outside of a women's college, I recognize there are few opportunities for women to teach at the college or university level, but that will change; it must. What better place than here, where we are making all things new?

If that is not enough, then I will appeal to you bluntly: These are dark days in the Colony, darker perhaps even than they are in other places. We began this College in a mood of hope and optimism; we carry it on under a government on the point of bankruptcy, in a land where thousands of the people are destitute, and the rabble is ready to riot in the streets.

In such a time, what do we need more than an educated populace? Surely nothing but learning can banish the spectre of another Dark Ages?

It's an oddly passionate letter for someone to write inviting a person to apply for a teaching post. Kit certainly does not have a passionate relationship with this Dr. Paton – she has never met the man, though he has heard of her not only from contacts in St. John's but also from people in his home city of Manchester. But his passion for Memorial College burns on the page. And strangely, in reading it, Kit feels something not unlike the thrill of reading a love letter.

She has accumulated some love notes in her life – hasty scrawls from Ben in their courting days, tender and troubling letters from him while he was at the Front, and, in these last couple of years, a handful of notes from Leo – short, intense, and quite often, frankly indecent. All of them have stirred her in their different ways. Each, she thinks, was *fitting* for the woman she was when she received them, though of course if anyone among her London acquaintances ever read Leo's notes, "fitting" would hardly be the word that would spring to mind. But this letter from Dr. Paton, asking if she would be interested in a position at Memorial University College, touches another part of her entirely.

She thinks about it; at first she consults no-one. She wishes she could talk to Leo, but he is far away in Manchester, growing more and more frustrated with the impotence of the Party there and the unlikelihood of revolution ever springing up in English soil. How ironic if, after years together of Leo constantly threatening to return to Poland, Kit were the one to go home.

She hasn't been back to Manchester since leaving it, and Leo has visited London only twice. They meet during her school holidays, if Leo happens to be free from his lecturing duties then. To colleagues at her school, Kit describes her holidays as walking tours and brings back vivid word-pictures of remote Welsh or Cornish vistas where she hiked. In reality, though she and Leo take the occasional walk, those vistas are glimpsed mostly through the windows of hotels. They spend most of their rare time together in bed, having never tired of each other's bodies, which amazes Kit now that she approaches her fortieth birthday. After making love, they sit up late in bed at night, talking and arguing and laughing, then sometimes fall asleep in the early morning hours and wake to make love again at noon.

During those times together, Leo is the centre of Kit's world, but for the rest of the time, he is peripheral. He lives on the margins of her world, and she on the margins of his. At the centre of Leo's world is the Party, the hope of building a better society, the articles he churns out for radical newspapers. At the centre of Kit's world is her teaching, which she thoroughly enjoys

267

That *Forgetful* Shore

now that she is in an excellent school and no longer burdened with the duties of headmistress. Edith Stone is a good Head, and Kit is free to do what she does best – work with bright girls who actually care about learning, who have a hope of making something of their lives. Oh, there are dull and careless girls too, and she is stern with them while at the same time hoping to inspire them to care just a little about literature. But most of her energy is focused on the clever girls, the ambitious ones.

She sees herself in them – of course she does. But these are girls from well-off London families, and their ambition lacks that edge of desperate hunger that drove her and Triffie when they were the top students in the one-room school at Missing Point. Still, she is often reminded of her own girlhood. The endless pashes and raves of schoolgirls falling in and out of love with one another remind her of the notes she and Trif used to exchange, their teary farewells in each other's arms and promises of eternal loyalty whenever Kit left the Point to go to school in St. John's. They didn't know the language of English schoolgirls, never talked of having a pash or a crush. But being plunged once again into the intense emotional world of adolescent girls can't help but make Kit think of her own adolescence.

She has had two good years in London, likes her students, likes her fellow teachers. She would be happy to stay for several more years, yet that letter from Dr. Paton sits on her desk and draws her like a magnet every time she walks into the room. Finally she talks to Edith Stone, weighs the pleasures of her life in London with the possibilities inherent in a college position back home.

In the end, she makes her decision, and the letter telling Leo of it is the second one she writes. It, and her letter to Dr. Paton, go into the same post.

A week after the letters are posted – far too soon to have heard anything back from Newfoundland – Kit wakes at one in the morning to someone hammering at the door of her flat.

She goes to the door, wrapping her robe around herself as she walks, knowing who it must be. "What are you doing here?"

"A nice welcome for your lover," Leo says, stumbling across the threshold and into her room. He's drunk, and Leo is not a hard-drinking man.

"Lower your voice," she hisses, closing the door behind him. "Bad enough you come here in the middle of the night, do you want to announce at the top of your lungs that I have a lover?"

"Oh, of course, sorry. I forget that love is a shame that must be hidden."

That *Forgetful* Shore

"If you're a schoolmistress, yes, it certainly is. I can teach *Romeo and Juliet*, but I can't have men crawling up my balcony at two in the morning. What's the matter, Leo?" Although even as she says the words, as he moves awkwardly around the room and finally collapses into the wingback chair, she knows it's a stupid question. She sits down across from him on the settee. He looks exhausted, red-eyed, disheveled. He's not as drunk as she first thought – he's been drinking, but he's also genuinely distressed and that adds to the impression of mania. He sits now with his elbows resting on thighs, running both hands through his tangled hair.

"I got your letter," he says finally.

"Yes, I gathered," Kit says. "Was it really such a shock that you had to come tearing down here on the first train?"

"I never thought you would go."

"Yet you talk all the time of leaving me. Am I not allowed to be the one to move first?"

"You did move. Down here, away from me. That was bad enough. If you go back to Newfoundland we will never see each other again."

"If you go to Poland we won't either," Kit points out.

"I have told you I want you to come with me."

"And I've told you I can't. Anymore than you would want to come to Newfoundland with me – though that would be far saner than going to the Continent. It might even work, if we were married." She has her doubts about the position at Memorial being as freely offered to a married woman as to a widow, but a widow with an unemployed Polish Jewish Communist lover would be beyond the pale entirely. It's a safe proposal to make as he'll never say yes. Still, the idea of being with Leo in St. John's, making a new start in the new world, is not without appeal.

But of course he won't go. They argue for two hours till Kit insists they go to bed – not to make love, but to fall into an exhausted sleep in each other's arms. Despite her weariness she wakes at dawn, fearing someone in the house will deduce that a man has spent the night in Mrs. Porter's flat.

Leo stays in London for a fortnight after his abrupt arrival, though at Kit's insistence he moves into a cheap hotel. "I've still got a job here for three more months, and I need a good reference," she says. "I can't be seen to be a loose woman now."

Leo has left Manchester for good, it turns out, quitting his lodging and job there at a moment's notice when he got her letter, packing all his belongings into one small battered trunk. He says he is definitely leaving England, though whether for Poland, Russia or Germany, he isn't certain.

Kit again makes her argument about this being the worst possible time for a man like Leo to be in Europe. In Russia, even Party members are no longer safe – Leo himself has told her that, under Stalin, you can be a hero one day and in prison the next. In Germany, which Leo once believed would be the next home of a Socialist revolution, new powers are rising, violently anti-Communist right-wing parties. And his home country of Poland lies between those two old enemies like a bone between two hungry dogs. Leo is not a man to be cautious – even here in England he has been questioned by the police several times. In Europe, anything might happen to him.

Leo shrugs. "What is life, Kit? Something to hoard like a handful of coins, spending carefully, never losing a minute, so you come to the end with – what? Empty hands? I'd rather throw it away in one grand gesture."

"Which is exactly what you might be doing."

"Perhaps not. You may be a cynical Englishwoman, but I still believe in revolution."

They wrangle out their last days together like this, arguing about politics and class and the stupidity of each other's decisions. They do not talk about love or passion or how much they will miss each other, about the terror of knowing they may never see each other again.

On the night before his ship leaves they make love in his shoddy hotel room. It makes his rooms in Manchester seem palatial by comparison, but Kit will not have him back to her flat. "Proper to the very end," he says, but his tone is teasing rather than accusing.

"Proper? Really?" She sits up in bed naked beside him. "Is that how you'll remember me, the proper English schoolmistress?"

He grabs her wrists, pulls her arms out from under her so she is lying on top of him, her face inches from his. "That is how I will remember you," he says. "The proper English schoolmistress I loved, and will love always, as long as I live. How will you remember me?"

A sudden knot in her throat makes it hard to speak. After a moment Kit says, "I will remember you as my foolish Pole who was in too much of a hurry to die."

"Will you write to me?"

"Of course, if you write to me first. I won't know your address otherwise." She thinks of something, one thing she hasn't said yet. "If things

That *Forgetful* Shore

in Poland are – if it's not safe for you there. If you have to leave again – where will you go? Back here to England?"

"No, I don't think I would be allowed back to England. I might go to Russia, but I don't trust Comrade Stalin. Apart from all his other virtues, he hates Jews."

"Come to me. To Newfoundland. If you have to leave – please, promise me you'll come."

He reaches up to trace the line of her cheekbone with his fingertip. "If I am driven away by danger or desperation – it will drive me to you."

"I'll be your last resort, then." And because he said it, but she didn't, she finally adds, "I love you, Leo."

He leaves the next day, and Kit finishes up her school year, prepares for her move back to Newfoundland, trying not to wait for a letter from him. She doesn't receive one until September, when she is settled back in her old house on Gower Street in St. John's.

Lodz, Poland
September, 1931

My dear one,

How strange it is to think of you, a university Professor, a model of English Propriety, and I, the humblest and lowest of all, working in a factory, longing for you yet knowing our lives are like two lines parallel, never to meet.

My own new life is not the tragedy you imagine, though I have been obliged to take a humble position, but I think this is best for me. In Manchester, I often thought, those of us who were true believers in the Cause were hampered by being intellectuals, far removed from the real life of the workers. Here I am a worker as well as a member of the Party, and I feel I have a calling. As you have yours – only the fact that our callings keep us far apart, gives me a little pain just above my heart in the evenings when I sit alone and smoke, and remember you.

Your beloved,
Leo

Kit settles quickly into her new life, which feels like such a natural progression from her old life that sometimes she wonders if the ten years in England ever happened. But of course they did; those years have given her not just further book-knowledge but experience and confidence. Confidence enough to stand before a class of college students, young men and women so very different from her posh English schoolgirls with their light chattering voices. Here she hears everywhere the accents she grew up with, the slow drawl of Conception Bay North, the hasty lilt of St. John's, the dropped aitches of Bonavista and Trinity Bays.

Her new students are a shabby lot compared to the girls she left behind in London. Some of them, to be sure, come from good St. John's families, but many come from the outports, and while many are seventeen or eighteen, some are older, already with some work experience – usually teaching – eager to come back and get further qualifications.

Memorial University College is certainly no Somerville, no Oxford. The whole college, which offers two years of schooling in a handful of subjects, is a squat unlovely building at the top of Parade Street, sitting on grounds that are equally unimpressive. Groups of unemployed men forced to work for their dole are brought in to landscape and beautify the grounds, but they have precious little to work with.

There are no dormitories, not even a dining hall; students arrive in the morning for classes, go home for their dinners, and come back for the afternoon. The place is deserted by teatime. Yet for all the bareness of the college, there's a sense of energy and purpose here. It's different from the energy and purpose of a venerable institution like Oxford; here the excitement is not in being part of an ancient tradition but, as Dr. Paton said in his letter, of making all things new, creating an oasis of learning in what is, far too often, a desert of ignorance.

Kit is not idealistic about her home country. She wasn't sure she wanted to return, and even now that she's here, caught up in the venture of launching the college, she is not sure she can spend the rest of her life here. The Depression has hit Newfoundland hard; things are bleaker here even than she remembers them being in London. The price of fish has plummeted; men are unemployed all over the city; nobody trusts the debt- and scandal-ridden Squires government. As conditions grow worse throughout her first year at Memorial, Kit feels more and more that the

That *Forgetful* Shore

college really is an oasis, not of prosperity, but of hope in a colony that is becoming increasingly hopeless.

In the spring she writes to Leo at the address from which his last letter came:

St. John's, Newfoundland
April, 1932

Yesterday there was a riot here – a real riot, demonstrations turning to violence and the Prime Minister driven out of the Colonial Building – such an uprising as I never saw in England even during the General Strike. I did not join the protestors, but saw the crowd in the street as I hurried home. The air was electric, as if it might ignite any minute, and based on the reports I heard of what happened after I was tucked safely behind my barred door, it did ignite indeed.

Do you know what my thought was? If only Leo were here, how he would love this! I know how Revolution stirs your heart, and the thought that you might be present, light the match that ignites the powder, when a real Uprising comes.

It has not come here. The crowd rioted and broke windows and looted the shops, but today the sun has risen and there is no blood flowing in the streets. There will be – must be – changes in the Government after this, but not, I think, the kind of Radical ones you would applaud. We are, after all, still very English at heart …

Still, I wish you were here, and not only because you would enjoy a good riot!

Her first year at Memorial ends and, with no summer plans and nowhere she wants to be for vacation, Kit accepts the offer to teach during the summer session held for teachers who want to upgrade their education. She goes with a colleague for a few days to Torbay at the end of that term, and then another school year begins.

In her first class on the first day of the new year, Kit sees the name Katherine Russell on the roll and looks at the assembled group of scholars. She spots her at once, or thinks she does – a girl with dark hair and firm brows who reminds her of Triffie. But when she calls the roll, that girl answers to another name, and the young woman who says "Present" to the name Katherine Russell is a strawberry blonde with Trif's dark eyes and quick smile. She has forgotten how much Katie, as a child, took after her father.

It's a strange thing, to know this girl is her namesake. It had been one of their girlhood vows – we'll name our first daughters after each other – and Trif had obligingly complied. Kit was by her side, holding Trif's hand, closer than Jacob John or Trif's Aunt Rachel, when this girl was born. And yet she is a stranger, a name on a class list. Kit has not seen Katie Grace since the child was six years old, and here she is now, a woman of nineteen with teaching experience, beginning her two-year Arts course, paid for no doubt by the savings from her teaching and a hard-won scholarship.

It's not until the third day of classes, when the routine is well established and the students are beginning to know one another, that she sees Miss Russell break from a small knot of friends at the end of class and come towards her desk.

"Mrs. Porter." The younger woman puts out a graceful hand to shake. "I'm Katherine Russell – you know my parents, Triffie and Jacob John Russell?"

Kit takes her hand. The girl has little of Trif in her, except for her height and a certain confidence in how she carries herself. "Of course," Kit says. "Your mother and I were great friends when we were girls. I'm afraid we've rather lost touch – I hope she is well? And your father?"

It occurs to her as she speaks that they might not be well, that somehow, in the scattered news she gets from home, that someone might have missed telling her of Trif's illness or death, assuming she would already know. It seems condescending, but also true, to say that life is hard and short in a place like Missing Point. This realization makes the conventional words turn sour in her mouth and an unexpected lump rise in her throat.

But Katherine Russell says, "They're quite well, thank you. I remember my mother telling me I was named for you."

"Yes, you were," Kit admits, "and it looks as though your parents have every reason to be proud of you. You've been teaching for the past few years, have you?"

That *Forgetful* Shore

"Yes, in Spaniard's Bay," the girl says. It seems natural to fall into step beside her, to walk together to the women's cloakroom and sit for a few moments catching up on news of home and her family.

It's a pleasant talk, though bittersweet for Kit. Katherine says nothing about any rift in Kit's old friendship with her mother; the girl seems to assume that they grew apart naturally and lost touch when Kit went to England. Kit keeps the conversation light, but she feels like a hungry beggar snatching at scraps as she picks through Katherine's words for anything that will give her a picture of Trif, of her life now or what kind of woman she has turned out to be.

They spend a pleasant half-hour together before each has to go to another appointment. Kit imagines that after that there will be a special relationship between them, that she might become a mentor to the girl. But Katie Grace Russell – she is "Katherine" or "Miss Russell" in formal settings, but Kit overhears friends calling her "Katie" – does not seem particularly to need a mentor. She is an excellent, hard-working student, pleasant in class, active in the Glee Club and on the women's ice hockey team, a leader among her classmates. She is always cheerful and courteous to Kit, occasionally stops by her desk to give her some small piece of news "from home," as Katie calls it. She assumes Kit will be interested in the news that Aunt Nellie French has passed away, or that Lydia Snow is marrying Walt Mercer – and she takes the requisite moment to explain whose daughter Lydia is, who Walt's parents are, to put the puzzle pieces in place for Kit. Beyond that, though, they have little personal conversation, and Kit wonders at her desire to play a part in the girl's life.

By the end of the first term she's used to Katie's presence; she thinks of the girl more as one of her students than as Triffie's daughter. So it's something of a shock one day when Kit leaves class, walks through the cloakroom, and sees Katie, just ahead, pick up her pace and hurry towards an older woman sitting on a bench. The woman stands, Katie embraces her and says, "Mother!" and then, "Mrs. Porter! My mother's here!"

Reaching out a hand, forgetting propriety for once, Katie grabs Kit's hand and pulls her toward Trif. Amid the bustle of the girls coming and going to and from class, Kit and Trif stand face to face for the first time in over a decade.

Kit does a quick appraisal: Trif looks much as she always has. Her hair has far less gray in it than Kit's own, but her face is more weathered and

That *Forgetful* Shore

lined. She's grown a little stouter too: not fat, you wouldn't say, but curved and softened, as you might expect of a woman who's borne three children. Her gaze is as direct as always, and she doesn't smile as she puts out a hand to shake Kit's.

Katie steps back, falters a little. It's clear she expected a more joyful, less awkward reunion between her mother and her professor. For a moment Kit and Trif don't say anything at all, only eye each other, half greedily and half warily. Kit thinks of various phrases "….Good to see you …" "…You're looking well…" but it's Trif who breaks the silence, and as usual, she wastes no time on clichéd pleasantries.

"I nearly didn't come," Trif says. "I been thinking about it ever since Katie told me you was here, but I put it off. But we're in your debt, even if Katie doesn't know it. I couldn't put my mind to rest till I'd said thank you."

That *Forgetful* Shore

Triffie

THERE. IT'S OUT. She's said her piece. Trif prides herself on being a person who speaks the truth without fear – indeed, she's built something of a reputation on that. But speaking this truth, coming to say thank you to the friend she hasn't spoken to in more than ten years, makes her heart hammer and her mouth dry.

Kit, who hasn't said a word since she shook Trif's hand, now says, "You should know it was my pleasure to do it. But perhaps you want to tell Katie what we're talking about?"

Her voice sounds different, more layers of culture and education added on top of what she already had, like a room that's had wallpaper put on it so many times no-one could guess what the boards underneath looked like.

They both glance over at Katie, and Trif doesn't even try to quell the rush of pride she feels when she looks at her girl here in the college, looking like she was born to it. Trif herself may feel backward and old and dowdy next to Kit, but she has nothing to be ashamed of in Katie.

"I wanted to tell her long ago – I knew it was you – but I wanted to be sure it was all right with you. They told us it was anonymous."

"Only because it was – awkward. You know. After all these years."

They both begin, then, stumbling over each other's words, to tell Katie that it was Kit Porter who paid her school fees at Spencer, who made it possible for her to become a teacher and eventually come here, to college. Of course Katie earned her college money and her scholarship, but she would never have gotten this far without Kit, and Trif intends for her to know it.

"Really? It was you? I've so often wondered – wished I could thank the kind person who was so generous to me," Katie says. She looks like she wants to hug Kit, but Kit does not look embraceable, and Trif smirks at the awkward little dance her daughter and her old friend go through before Katie decides on seizing both Kit's hands in hers while she thanks her again and again.

"I was very fortunate as a girl, to be able to go on to school," Kit explains. "Your mother should have gone too, but she didn't have anyone who was willing or able to send her. I knew your parents would be willing, but knowing how hard times have been at home, I didn't know if they would be able. I wanted to help if I could."

Then Katie, her eyes filling with tears, excuses herself to go speak to a classmate, leaving Kit and Trif alone. "How long are you in town for?" Kit asks.

"Till classes are over and Katie's ready to come home for Christmas – what's that, three days?" Trif says. She's disappointed that Kit reverts so quickly to politeness. She wants to say something more, to needle her into a confrontation, as if there's something that can make up for years of silence. All their trouble came from telling each other too much, too late, she thinks. Sometimes silence is better.

"I'm sorry," Kit says finally. "I ought to have written."

"So should I," Trif responds, then remembers, *I did.* She thinks of the box of letters stored under her bed, all the things she wanted to say and had no-one to say them to, once Kit was gone from her.

"Well. It was a long time ago." Kit fidgets with her gloves.

Kit looks good. She always did, always the pretty one, and though you wouldn't call her pretty now. You might say handsome, or distinguished looking. She has good bones, and good bones last. Her hair is cropped close with a bit of a wave in it, and grey at her temples, but her face still looks young, unlined. Her clothes are nice too, probably top of the line for lady college professors. Certainly they're nicer than anything Triffie owns or has seen in Missing Point.

How easily it rolls off Kit's tongue, to say things are hard out home. Little she knows about it. "Hard" is not the word for it. Jacob John kept his promise about not sending the boys out fishing anymore, and for awhile he

That *Forgetful* Shore

even stayed onshore himself, working in the new sawmill on the Point alongside one-legged Char Mercer. Young Bill went as far as he could in the school on the Point, then finished up his Grade Eleven in Bay Roberts last year. He wanted more schooling, too, but there's no money for it. He's gone off to Sydney now to live with Betty and Frank and work in the mines. "You think the mine is any safer than a fishing boat?" Jacob John asks her, and Trif feels her heart like a stone inside her. But what can you do when people are lining up to take the dole to feed their families? It's a miracle to have one child in college, and Katie has put in years of hard work to get here.

Last year Jacob John got laid off at the mill and in the spring he told her he was going fishing again, no matter what she'd promised God. As a matter of compromise he was going to fish inshore, as a shareman in Fred Mercer's dory; Fred's wife Minnie is no longer well enough to join him in the fishery, and neither Fred nor Jacob John wants to go back on the Labrador any more. This past summer, for the first time since before Katie was born, Trif worked on the flakes, hating it as much as she did when she was a young wife those summers in Battle Harbour. But if that's what it takes to stay off the dole and keep food on her children's plates, then she will do it.

She thinks now of those hours splitting and gutting cod, a pitiful few cod, too, for the sad price the merchants were offering. Thinking of the smooth feel of Kit's hand when she took it a moment ago, the old envy rushes back, like a salt taste in her mouth. Trif prays for charity. Actually, what she prays is: *God, you got me into this, get me out of it.* She felt the Holy Spirit like a kick in her arse, telling her she had to go see Kit, put things right. At least, put her part of it right. Thank her for the money she sent for Katie, and apologize for her part in the rift.

"Well then. Will you come over and see me while you're in town? My address is here –" Kit pulls out a card and passes it to Trif.

Trif sizes up the card. "Very high class," she can't resist saying, and sees Kit's shoulders stiffen.

"Well then," Kit says. "The invitation's open. I would like to – catch up."

"What do you want to hear about? Who's dead, who's moved away, the price of fish, who's on the dole? There's no good news out home." Trif realizes she's crossed her arms in front of her and forces herself to uncross them. She tries to keep resentment out of her voice.

"Katie has done a good job of keeping me up to date on what's happening on the Point. It's – good to feel like I'm back in touch again."

Trif nods. She's going to make an excuse and get out of there, end this awkward encounter. "Anyway. I don't know if I'll have time to drop by while I'm in town, but I just ... wanted to say thank you. I should go find Katie."

"Yes, of course." Kit holds out her hand again; their fingers brush briefly. Trif turns away.

"Triffie ... wait. P-Posy ..."

The old nickname sounds odd, false, in Kit's new voice. But it's enough to make Trif turn around.

"I'm sorry," Kit says. "No, really. I am. For – everything. I was a fool – to say all those things, and then never write or anything. I'm sorry."

The silence that follows is not silent: girls pass through the corridor talking and laughing, but it feels to Trif as if she and Kit are standing on the Long Beach hearing nothing but waves. "I was as foolish as you," she says at last. "I went off half-cocked, took off and never wrote or nothing. And you were right – about himself. Dear Pedagogue." Another old name that sounds strange, saying it now.

"You'll have to tell me all about it," Kit says, and for the first time she sounds like herself, like Kit, like Peony.

The odd thing is, Trif doesn't tell her all about it. About Joe Bishop, and how she threatened him and made him toe the line, how for years Trif would have him tutor youngsters in her kitchen in the evenings, even after Katie was gone on to Spencer. She determined, before and after she got on the School Board, that no child, boy or girl, would be done out of the extra help they needed if they were clever enough. But she also made sure there would be no more of Mr. Bishop having them alone in the schoolroom after hours, either.

It's a good story, but Trif doesn't tell it, and Kit doesn't ask. Trif does go to Kit's house for tea the next day, while Katie Grace is going around with a few of her friends, Christmas shopping. The two women talk for hours, catching each other up on the past ten years, regaining something of the old intimacy but never straying too close to the subjects that divided them.

What's to be said, anyway? Trif could tell Kit the whole story of her victory over Joe Bishop, has written it all out in a letter that was never sent. But if they started talking about that, there'd be the other thing too, that old business with Jacob John, and the truth is Triffie's ashamed to talk about that. Ashamed of how angry it made her, ashamed that she ever threw it in Jacob John's face the way she did.

That *Forgetful* Shore

She can remember the hurt she felt when she first heard it, the way you look at a tree cracked off the stump and remember the big windstorm that took it down. But you don't feel the wind in your face when you're standing there, years later, staring at the tree stump. There's only a memory, and that's all Trif feels when she thinks of young Kit and young Jacob John, little more than children really, in each other's arms. She remembers her own rage at hearing it, but can't remember why she was so angry, why it mattered so.

Once Trif believed that you couldn't mend a broken relationship without thoroughly picking through the rubble, examining each of the shattered pieces, gluing them back together with painful care. She would have thought the whole thing had to be hashed over, discussed, repented, forgiven. Like a Catholic going to confession, she thinks now, rhyming off everything you did wrong, asking for your penance. But it's not like that at all.

Instead, she and Kit between them pick up the damaged thing, their friendship, and although there are pieces missing – ten years apart, things they don't speak about – they just pick it up and lay it between them and start using it, pour something new into it and hope it holds. They begin talking about their lives now, and about Katie Grace, the thing they have in common. They go on from there, without any great reconciliation or explanation. And it feels right.

Kit

HAS ANYONE, KIT wonders, ever gone home after many years without pondering the phrase "You can't go home again?" Or to attempt a more classical allusion, can anyone bathe in the same river twice?

All the experts agree that one can't. Go home again, or re-bathe in the river. Neither is possible, so Kit schools herself to expect neither. She approaches this visit to Missing Point with no preconceptions, no expectation that anything will be the same, least of all herself. She tries to think of it, in fact, as visiting an entirely new place, a place with perhaps some historical interest, like Shakespeare's Birthplace in Stratford-upon-Avon. Not exactly Kit's birthplace – she was born in Trinity – but certainly the place that shaped her more than any other. There is always one place that one longs and fears to return to, and for Kit it is the Point.

Four years after her return to Newfoundland, she still hasn't gone back.

She's come, finally, at Trif's insistence. Triffie, Jacob John and the boys all came into town for Katie's graduation from Memorial. The two-year course has taken her three years, because she took a teaching job in between her first and second year, to save a little more. This last year she boarded with Kit, and the whole family comes to stay for Convocation weekend.

Like other families from around the bay celebrating the convocation of their hardworking sons and daughters, Triffie and Jacob John looked dowdy, frightened, a little dazed, but beneath their lowered eyelids was a pride they fought to keep under control. One of their children has managed to escape a life of incessant toil; one child has the chance for an easier life and may raise the rest of the family from grinding poverty.

Looking around at the graduates, Kit wonders how realistic these hopes are. Many of the young men and women convocating come from well-off families and will no doubt have the chance to follow in their parents' footsteps. But the fishermen's sons and daughters like Katie Russell, those who scrabbled their way to a college diploma by sheer toil and bloody-minded determination – what are their chances? In the Newfoundland of 1935, with more and more people on the dole, fish prices still dropping and fewer jobs available all the time, Kit fears that for many of them all their struggle will only earn them what so many already have – a ticket on a boat going to the Boston States. The Depression is bad everywhere of course, but Newfoundlanders are driven by the eternal hope that things will be better somewhere else.

Young Bill is home from Nova Scotia for the occasion, and both Kit and Katie show him around the college, taking special care to introduce him to Dr. Carew and show him the room where the engineering students study. Kit sees Bill's narrow face brighten: the boy had no interest in being a teacher like his sister, Trif told her, but he had a great head for facts and figures. Despite the fact that his childhood ambition was to be a Pentecostal preacher – and, indeed, apparently he is a fine lay preacher – it's the engineering classes that attract him. Kit has already made the offer that if Bill wants to put his savings from working down in the mine towards college, she will help in any way she can, including the free room and board she gave Katie.

Trif has urged Kit for a long time to come back to the Point. Now she says Kit must come back with them after Convocation. Jacob John adds his voice to Trif's. "Sure you knows you wants to come back, see how it's all changed, how modern we are now," he laughs. "They got electric lights on the street in Bay Roberts, you wouldn't know the place."

Kit dreads seeing the people who watched her grow up, who will never look at her without seeing the ghost image of the awkward young girl she once was. For some people, like Triffie, the presence of those people is a constant, and Kit supposes because Trif has watched those same people change and grow old, too, her life is part of a closely woven whole. Whereas Kit's life is patchwork, pieces disconnected, and she will land on the Point as a woman out of joint. People will spend a fortnight exclaiming over how she has changed, or else how she hasn't changed a bit.

There's also the more practical consideration of putting herself under the feet of Triffie and Jacob John for two weeks at a busy time of year. Jacob John fishes inshore in summer, and young David, whose mother will not permit him to go out in a fishing boat, helps his parents make fish onshore. "Don't mind that," Triffie said when Kit said she'd be afraid to be underfoot. "Sure with our Bill home, he's going to give Jacob John a hand out on the flake too, and they won't need me. I'll have a vacation myself, right in my own home."

Kit wonders, too, what it will be like to spend day in and day out with Triffie and Jacob John, living under their roof. She and Trif have corresponded regularly for the past two and a half years, but there are still many things left unsaid between them. She wonders if the fabric of their friendship is strong enough, after everything that's passed, to survive a fortnight of each other's company.

She sizes up Jacob John over Convocation weekend: she can see in this weathered, work-toughened middle-aged man the shadow of the boy she knew, but it's a shadow only. His green eyes still squint at her in that measuring way he had, of taking somebody in before making a saucy remark. Kit thinks of her own image as she sees it in the mirror each morning: thin, graying, prim, reserved. There is no hint in that picture of the girl who pushed Jacob John up against the wall in Abel Morgan's store and made him laugh with surprise and delight; no hint, either, of the schoolteacher who made love to Ben Porter on the desk in her classroom, or of Leo Lanski's secret lover. All of that longing is tamped down and tucked away, and she is confident Jacob John sees nothing in her to remind him of the past.

Stepping off the train in Bay Roberts, Kit is hit with a wave of memory: the smell, the sight, the sounds of an outport town. She is stepping into a different world, and she realizes that Jacob John was joking when he talked about her coming back to see all the changes on the Point. Fred Mercer meets them with a horse and cart to drive them across the causeway, and as they drive onto the North Side Road, Kit thinks that Missing Point has changed far less than she herself has in sixteen years.

The boats tied up at the wharf might be the same boats that were tied there in 1920, and the houses along the North Side Road are the same too. The sawmill and the coal and salt works are new, ugly buildings offering a brazen promise of prosperity that so far has not been fulfilled. Houses and

That *Forgetful* Shore

boats look weathered, as if they haven't seen a lick of new paint since the war.

Even the people look the same, just older and more worn, like their boats and houses. Gray hair where once there was black or brown or blond; more lines on faces. Children she barely remembers have grown into men and women while she was away. Missing faces, too: Trif's Uncle Albert and Aunt Rachel, both dead now; Trif's cousins, moved away to Canada. Many people have moved away, looking for the prosperity that has always eluded the Point.

Beneath all these surface changes, the Point still feels like a place untouched by time. In St. John's, there is a change in the air. During the war years and even for a year or so after the war, people spoke as if the future held great things, as if Newfoundland were about to become a player on a world stage. As if the staggering sacrifice of the troops in the Great War had bought the country a place among nations.

Now, after years of depression, after the country squandering its independence and the Commission of Government rushing in to save the day, the mood in St. John's has soured. Every new enterprise, even the College itself, feels these days like a lick of paint over peeling despair. Underneath it all is a sense that Newfoundlanders are a people perhaps forever unfit to govern themselves.

The mood on the Point is different. There never was, as Kit recalls, any of that heady optimism here, and so there is none of that headlong rush to despair to follow it. Fish is low and times are hard; people are out of work and on the dole, but the cycle of good times and hard times is familiar. Rather than highs of optimism and lows of despair there is only a constant patient endurance, a sense that the weather and the price of fish and even wars and governments are in the hands of the Almighty. Ordinary people must just get up every morning and get on with the work.

At night, in her bed in Trif's house, Kit wonders if there is any accuracy at all to her observations. Is she making sweeping generalizations about a place she hasn't lived in twenty years on the strength of a single afternoon and evening back home? What does she know, really?

Kit determines not to analyze the Point while she's here: she wants to talk less and listen more, perhaps even to learn something.

Mostly, she keeps that resolution. Jacob John and his sons are busy at the fish, Jacob John in the boat and the boys onshore. Triffie would rather her sons never touch a codfish, but she knows in the present climate that's impossible and tries to be content with their promise not to go out in a boat. While they work down by the water, Kit spends much of the day up on the hill with Triffie and Katie. The small vegetable garden Kit remembers up here above the house has become much larger: with times getting harder Triffie has broken new ground, growing more crops so they owe less to the merchant. Weeding the potatoes, carrots, cabbage and turnip takes a good bit of time, and on nice days it's a grand place to work, with the warm breeze blowing in their faces and the whole south side of the Point spread out below them.

If Katie is not with them, Kit and Trif talk more freely. Kit tells Trif all about Leo, including the fact that she hasn't heard from him in over a year. Trif, still rock-solid in her own convictions of sin and righteousness, listens without judgement to Kit's tale of her Communist lover and her fears about why his letters have stopped coming.

She wonders if Trif even knows anything about Communism beyond a distant Red Menace she might hear of on the news, but she finds that although Trif has not yet read *The Communist Manifesto* – "I keeps meaning to get my hands on a copy," she says – she has read a number of articles about socialism and communism. "It's lovely, of course, just like Jesus and the apostles – or Tolstoy for that matter, no wonder the Russians like it so much. But how far are you ever going to get with a philosophy that expects people to be better than they are?"

"The Church expects that," Kit points out.

"But the Church allows room for sin and repentance, and the gifts of the Holy Spirit too, though you may not make much of those," Trif says. "I don't gather there's any Holy Spirit of Communism."

"You still put a lot of stock in God and the Holy Spirit," Kit observes.

"More than in guns, which is what Stalin seems to put the most stock in," says Triffie.

Triffie's faith, which has meandered through several different churches and come out in a way that allows her to attend them all without any apparent discord, is still beyond Kit's grasp. But it no longer irritates her as it once did. After Leo, maybe she's gotten used to the fervour of a true believer. Perhaps that made her more tolerant of all kinds of faith, and the strange places it might lead. Or perhaps middle age just makes everything easier, less intense and more bearable.

This seems a likely thought, except for the nights when she lies awake

That *Forgetful* Shore

imagining where Leo might be now. On those nights, as she now tells Triffie, she knows that the pains of middle age are just as sharp as those of youth. "I loved Leo, but there was no way for us to make a life together," Kit says. "Now he's gone, and I'm afraid – scared I'll never hear from him again, scared of what's happened to him."

"It's a hard thing, loving anyone," Trif says. "It nearly always ends up hurting, but I don't say you'd want to miss out on it. *Better to have loved and lost*, like your man Tennyson said."

When Trif is not in the garden she works in the house, baking and scrubbing and sewing. She dresses from top to toe in clothes she makes herself and sews as much as she can for the rest of the family, again to save on money and credit. While Kit stays there they eat fish at least once every day, but Trif varies the meals when she can, once making a stew out of moose she bottled the previous fall.

Kit has forgotten – or never really known, perhaps – just how hard this life is, how close to the bone, how dependent on the earth and the sea and human toil. By cutting the Point out of her life for so many years she managed to forget how harsh it was, but also how beautiful. She was homesick for the place when she first left; a part of her still belongs here as it does nowhere else.

Among the visits Kit makes to old friends, she spends an evening at the home of her cousin Ted Parsons, visiting his wife Eliza in what is doubtless the most comfortable house in the community. Ted, who is down on the Labrador, owns not only the shop and schooners the Parsons family always owned, but also the new sawmill. "We got to try other things," Eliza tells Kit, "make money off of something besides fish. There's no future in fish alone."

Looking around at Eliza's simple furniture Kit sees that while this is luxury compared to Trif's house or the homes of most fishermen, it is still spartan compared to homes she visits in St. John's. She remembers the old resentment the fishermen feel for the local merchant, making his fortune off their bent backs. But she also knows that the plummeting prices of fish hurt the merchants too, that men like her cousin face hard times.

"Have you been up to visit the school?" Eliza asks. "It's come a long ways since we were in it. Mr. Bishop did a lot for that place in his time."

"Triffie took me up to see it," Kit says. She doesn't attempt to convey to Eliza, whom she barely knows, the heart-clutch of mingled fear and nostalgia she felt when Trif unlocked the door and let her in to the empty classroom. Nor does she say anything about what Joe Bishop, who retired last year after nearly forty years of service, has or hasn't done for the young people of the Point.

But Eliza won't let the subject go. "I saw him in church this Sunday – it's a shame you weren't there," she says. "Plenty of people would have liked to see you. Perhaps you'll get out next week? Anyway, when Mr. Bishop heard you were visiting Triffie, he said you should come by to see him. He's very crippled up with his arthritis and I think his heart is weak. He's not old – not sixty yet – but he's worked himself into the ground for that school, he has. And he'd love to see you."

Kit mentions the invitation to Triffie that night. "Yes, he said the same to me in church Sunday," Trif says. She doesn't turn around from peeling potatoes.

"You never told me."

"Truth be told, I didn't think you'd want to see him. After everything."

"Do you think I should?"

Trif pauses in her work, but still doesn't look at Kit. "Hard to say, girl. There's something to be said for making things right, but there's a good bit to be said for leaving sleeping dogs lie, too."

"Some help you are," Kit says, but she knows Triffie is right. There are times no-one else can tell you what's right or wrong.

She goes up the next day to see him. There are only four days left to her visit, and she doesn't want Joe Bishop hanging over them. A stout middle-aged housekeeper – a Dawe, by the look of her, though Kit can't say offhand which one – lets her in and announces, "Mr. Bishop, that's Mrs. Porter to see you." Apparently she has no trouble placing Kit.

Eliza is right – he looks old. A few wisps of gray hair cling to a bald pink scalp; the hands gripping the arms of his chair are gnarled with arthritis. He looks nothing like the commanding figure at the front of the classroom; she can hardly even imagine his presence next to her, both sinister and attractive, one arm sliding around her while her head bent over the book close to his.

"Mr. Bishop," she says.

"Mrs. Porter – Kit Saunders, I feel inclined to say." Even his voice is thinner, though there's something there of his old timbre. "Of all my old students, none has had as impressive a career as you have."

"Well – it's kind of you to say so, I'm sure."

That *Forgetful* Shore

"Not kind – true. An Oxford degree? A professor at Memorial College? Hardly accomplishments to be sniffed at."

"No – no, they aren't. I have worked very hard for everything I've achieved."

He waves a hand towards a chair, high and straightbacked. He's received her in the parlour, the same rarely used room that most families on the Point would have ushered him into when he came to visit. The parlour was for the minister and the schoolteacher; the kitchen was good enough for everyone else. "I shouldn't keep you – standing." His breath catches a little. "Do, please, sit down."

"That's all right, Mr. Bishop. I won't be staying long – I'd rather stand."

For the first time he looks at her with something other than a beatific smile, as if taking her measure. Whatever he was hoping for out of this visit, it's not meeting his expectations.

"I wish you would. Sit down," he says, his thin voice high and querulous.

Kit stays on her feet, her hands clasped behind her. It strikes her that her pose is not unlike the one she would take for giving a recitation in the schoolroom, in days of old.

The conversation staggers and almost falls, but the old man makes an effort to pick it up, asking Kit about the college and her work there. Reflecting that the man did give her the best possible teaching for his place and time, despite the harm he did, Kit tries to be gracious.

But before much time has passed he brings the conversation back to the little schoolroom in Missing Point. "You've gone on to do great things, Mrs. Porter," he says. "Studying at Oxford, teaching at college. I've never done anything very great in my life – just been a simple outport teacher. But I like to think my greatest accomplishment was planting seeds – yes, making it possible for young people like yourself to go farther and do more."

"Yes, sir," Kit says dutifully. "As Newton said, sir, we stand on the shoulders of giants."

He likes that, smiles and straightens his own shoulders. He likes thinking of himself as a giant. "Yes, I look at a woman like you and think, there is my greatest accomplishment, there is my legacy – to know that I made all this possible, and that the leaders of today are grateful to the teachers of yesterday, to those of us who placed their feet on the path of success."

The man sounds like he's writing a book – or making a commencement address. Slowly it dawns on Kit what he wants. He's waiting for her to thank him.

The disparity between what he wants and what she wants hits her like a fist below the ribs, and without thinking she lets out a short, sharp laugh.

"You find it funny? That you would thank an old teacher for helping you along the way?"

"No, sir … that is –" Kit collects her thoughts. This man is old, possibly dying; should she be kind? Perhaps Kit should say the words he needs to hear and go away. Let him rest in peace.

"Of course, sir, like any student I'm grateful for having had good teachers. But you might perhaps appreciate why it's difficult for me to thank you."

His eyes are mild and blank. Perhaps his memory is gone – perhaps he really doesn't know what she means. Certainly he sounds innocent as he says, "Why would that be, Mrs. Porter? Do you think you could have gotten so far in life on your own, without my help?"

The insolence of his frail voice snaps the fire inside her. "I could have done quite well, sir, without your inappropriate advances. As, I'm sure, could a number of other young ladies."

His bushy white brows draw together and his eyes narrow. "Are you raking up old scandals, Mrs. Porter? You're as bad as your friend Trif Russell, holding a man's youthful mistakes against him. Have you no sense of proportion? Would you hold a grudge all these years – when the mistake was so small in the light of all I did for you, for all you girls?"

"Really? What about girls who gave up on schooling when they could have had more, because they didn't want to sit with you in the classroom after hours and have you pawing all over them? Or girls like me, who didn't even know it was wrong, didn't know what was wrong with them at all till they were grown up?"

The picture of Katie Grace's face, round and sincere, rises before her, and her stomach churns. She's never dared to ask Trif what happened in later years, whether Katie was safe from Joe Bishop. "Do you know what's ironic, Mr. Bishop? I came here today because you wanted to see me – because I thought you wanted to apologize, to make your peace. I didn't begrudge you that. I would have forgiven you, if you'd asked it. But to come here and find that you expect to be thanked, that you were waiting for me to go down on my knees and say what a blessing you were to me – that's unthinkable."

That *Forgetful* Shore

"Is it? Is it? There are plenty of women not as proud as you or your friend Mrs. Russell, plenty who aren't vengeful, who have fond memories – they've told me, they've thanked me. They are better women than you are, Mrs. Porter – you were too proud as a girl in the schoolroom and you're still too proud today!"

He lifts his stick, shakes it in her direction as if warding off a dog. Kit takes it as a cue to go. "I'll take my leave of you, Mr. Bishop. If there are so many students who are ready to forget what you did and thank you for your kindness, you'll have to be content with their gratitude. You won't need mine."

She walks out of the parlour, past the kitchen where the housekeeper is trying to pretend she's not eavesdropping, and out the front door. Anger fuels her steps as she walks down the Neck Road and takes the turn down to the south side of the Point.

She imagines she'll tell Trif about the visit right away, but she arrives back at the Russell house to find supper on the table, and she's caught up in the whirl of family activity till the dishes are done, Jacob John and the boys go to Fred Mercer's shed to mend nets and visit, and Katie Grace is at Lydia Snow's house for the evening. Trif brings her chair and her bag of mending out onto the front bridge, since it's a warm night, and Kit comes with her, sitting beside her as they watch the sunset paint the waters of the bay a hundred different colours.

"Our Bill was talking about college again today – I think he's really giving it some thought," Triffie says. "I'd be some glad if he never had to go down in a mine again."

"I hope he comes to Memorial," Kit says. "There's something in him that's too bright to be kept below ground – I think he could do well if he got a bit more education, and I mean it about him coming to board with me."

"You're some good to offer, and you might think I'd be too proud to accept so much help." Trif finishes the torn shirt she's mended and picks up a pair of young David's pants with the backside split out of them. "My eyes aren't good enough to be doing this kind of work in the dim light anymore," she says, but does it anyway. "I never thought I'd take handouts from anyone, even from you – least of all from you – but it's different when it's for your children. I'd do anything to see them better themselves. I don't know what David is likely to want yet, but he'll be staying in school till he gets his Grade Eleven, s'posing we have to go on the dole to keep him there."

"You won't have to do that," Kit says. "I know – I understand why it's hard for you to take handouts, Trif. But look at me! I'm not rich, but I'm comfortable – I've worked for years for decent wages and never had a soul to spend money on but myself. And I haven't even got anyone to leave it to! You're the closest I've got to family, and if I can't use what bit of money I've got saved to help Katie and Bill and David, what's the good of money at all?"

Trif nods. "Like I said, I'm not too proud to accept help if it's for the children."

"What about for yourself? I know you won't take money, but – what if you came in to visit me in town the odd time, once or twice in a year, times when you weren't too busy at home? I'd pay for you to come in – it'd be a treat for me to have the company. Maybe someday we could even take a little trip together." She thinks of all the things she could do for Triffie with her modest savings, things like a trip to Boston or Montreal, that would be small for Kit but life-changing for Triffie.

She expects refusal, but Trif just shrugs. "I don't know, Kit. It's hard, with times like they are, to see further ahead than the next bill to be paid. But I wouldn't say no to a change of scenery now and then, that's the truth."

The sunset colours have faded and the sky is twilit now, dark enough that Trif has to put aside the mending and pick up her knitting, which she does so automatically that she never looks down at her fingers. The click of her needles makes a counterpoint to the rush of the waves on the beach, that same sound that provided the background to a hundred late-night talks they had shared in their youth.

"So how was it – going to see old Joe Bishop?" Trif finally asks, and Kit tells her, as simply as she can.

"He said something about you – twice," Kit remembers as she finishes her account of the afternoon's brief visit. "Said I was as bad as you, holding a man's old mistakes against him. So – you must have said something to him, after all."

"Indeed and I did, once Katie got to an age where I was worried about her." Trif pauses, though the knitting needles continue their rhythmic clicking. "You were right to tell me, Kit, for all it made me mad. Something had to be done, and I did it. It's a long story, but – well, sure, I wrote it all down, it's best if I show you –"

That *Forgetful* Shore

They are interrupted, just then, by Katie Grace coming home. She perches on the railing for a few minutes to talk and then goes inside, and just behind her comes Jacob John.

"That's himself now, back from mending nets and jawing with the men," Triffie says, laying down her work. "I wonder the boys aren't with him – off with them Mercer boys, no doubt." She goes into the house; she doesn't need to say that she's going to put the kettle on. Kit knows the pattern by now, after nearly two weeks in their house. Whenever Jacob John comes in, whatever time it is, Triffie puts the kettle on and makes him a cup of tea.

He moves slowly up the lane, so that Trif is back out and sat down in her chair, waiting for the kettle to boil, by the time Jacob John climbs the steps.

He nods to Kit; he's been warmly polite to her ever since she arrived, like you would be to any old acquaintance. But his eyes move at once to Triffie as he says, "Bill and David are down on the Long Beach with Fred's boys and a few other young ones – they got a fire built down there. I told Bill to keep an eye on David and make sure they was both home by ten."

Sure enough, when they stop talking to listen Kit can hear the boyish laughter and shouts drifting up from the beach, and see the flicker of their fire.

"They shouldn't be at that foolishness – they both got to be up early in the morning. And I don't trust Fred's young fellows, nor Char's neither – young Bob drinks, and I wouldn't be surprised if he got the younger ones into it too now."

"Stop worrying, missus. Young fellas got to have a bit of badness in them, and Bob's like all the Mercers – full of foolishness, but he won't do nothing too stunned." Trif rolls her eyes and Jacob John, who's standing behind her and can't have seen her face, must be able to read her expression without seeing it, for he says, "Sure you're not worried about our boys getting into no trouble down there. If there's any foolishness going on our Bill won't stand for that. He's as likely to have 'em all down on their knees havin' a prayer meeting as anything."

"Proper thing," Trif says. "Be glad I raised him right."

"Anyway, if they're not back up here by ten thirty I'll go down to the beach and haul 'em up myself," Jacob John promises.

"Yes now, I 'lows you'll still be awake at half-past ten. You'll be snoring fit to raise the rafters by ten. Come inside now, that kettle must be boiled, and it's getting chilly out here."

Trif laughs as she gets up to go into the kitchen, and sort of bumps Jacob John as she walks past him, a movement both careless and intimate. He laughs too, follows her into the kitchen. Kit goes in after them, and there's something in that shared gesture and that unromantic touch that tightens Kit's throat.

She pauses for a moment on the bridge, hearing their voices fade into the lighted warmth of the house. The rise and fall of voices blurs past the point where she can pick out the words; she hears only the tones of people who have talked to each other for so long they sound like people in church, singing hymn tunes they have known all their lives.

She goes inside, joins them for their cup of tea. Jacob John says goodnight and goes up to bed. "I'll be up in a few minutes," Trif says, as she has said every night since Kit has been here. The two women sit together at the table, finishing their tea.

"What did you mean – you wrote it all down?" Kit says. "About Joe Bishop?"

"I got something to give you. I've been thinking ever since you came about whether I should give it to you or not, but they were meant for you – at first they were, anyway – and I want you to have them."

Trif crosses the room and goes upstairs. She comes back with a biscuit tin, a lovely red one with a hinged lid and a picture of Buckingham Palace on the cover. She lays it down in front of Kit, who opens it to find letters – three or four dozen, at least. Every one in an envelope with *Mrs. Katherine Porter* written on it, but never an address or stamp.

"I went on writing to you," Trif says, sitting back down, folding her hands in front of her. "Not right away – but a few years after. When I had – things to say, that I couldn't imagine telling anyone else. The whole story is in there about Mr. Bishop, and a lot of other things besides. I s'pose I was really writing to myself, but I couldn't do that – like a diary or anything. It only made sense if I put your name on it."

Kit opens and unfolds the first one. The date is October 1925, and it begins:

My dear Peony – I will never forget what I did today – I say that now, and yet I know how time passes, and one does forget things. So I write this to you, with no hope that you will read it – why should you care for such things now?

That *Forgetful* Shore

Kit looks up. "Can I take these back with me?"

"They're yours," Trif says. "They served their purpose for me – writing them kept me sane, I 'low."

"I wrote, too," Kit says. "I did write in a journal – but I was thinking of you, all the time. Can I send it to you, when I go back to town?"

"If you like," Trif says, "I'll be glad to read it. Or maybe you can save it for if I comes in to visit, like you said. Later on in the fall when the fishing's done. If our Bill goes to college I'd like to come in for awhile, if you'll still have me. We'll have plenty of time, then. Plenty of time for everything."

Epilogue

MISSING POINT, 1955

When the young minister leaves, Trif Russell, a legend in her own time, sees him out the front door and stands looking out over the Long Beach. This morning the house was full of neighbours, but she hooshed them all out when the minister arrived, told them to leave her alone till suppertime.

Katie came out last night when Trif called her, and stayed the night. This morning she drove back to St. John's to pick up her brothers at the airport. Bill arrives from Toronto and Dave from Boston at noon. Before they come, Trif needs just a little time alone with Jacob John.

She shuts the front door and turns to go into the parlour. There's a funeral home on the Point now but every time Trif has been to a wake there it's felt wrong, as if she were visiting the dead in a museum like that big one Kit took her to in New York. Home is the place for birth and death. Trif sits down on the chesterfield, looking at the pine box where Jacob John, rarely still in his life, now lies motionless.

It's not like she needs to say goodbye, really. They were never great ones for saying sentimental things. Last night Jacob John dumped an armload of wood in the box by the stove and said, "That's it, girl – I'm going to turn in for the night."

"Good enough, I'll be up in a few minutes," said Trif, who was reading and finishing her tea.

She heard his tread on the first two steps, then on the third step she heard a noise like the wood falling into the woodbox, only louder. A tumble, a thump and a short sharp cry. No "I love you darling," no farewell. He was dead before she got out in the hall, and though she dropped to her knees in shock and cried, "No! No!" over and over, a quiet part of her brain thought he would be glad to go this way. If he could come back for a moment, surely he would lay a hand on her shoulder and say, "Better this way, missus. Who wants to be wastin' away in a bed for months and months?"

She heard his voice in her head saying that, so clearly that she's mostly convinced herself he actually did say it. Despite what she believes about death being a sleep and the dead knowing not anything, she also believes that Jacob John somehow lingered just a moment, just long enough to tell her he didn't mind going this way. Not to say goodbye or thank you or to say he loved her, no, nothing like that, but to set her mind at rest. So she wouldn't be brooding on it. "Your only problem is, you broods too much." She hears that too, but that's something he actually did say, over and over again.

It's quiet and restful here, and she's content to sit beside him. It's not so different from the evenings they used to sit together in the kitchen, her always with a book and Jacob John always at some little thing he could be making or mending, something to keep his hands busy. His hands are folded now. He's finished his work and done, and Triffie needs just a little while to get used to the idea. Not to get over the ache, but to learn to live with it.

She sits there until the light in the room changes. Sunset will come early this November evening. Soon Katie and her husband and youngsters will be here, and the boys with them. The Adventist minister, a Salvation Army officer, and a matched pair of Pentcostal pastors came this morning to offer their condolences, though it's the Anglican minister who will have the job of burying him, as Jacob John would have wanted. Tonight the neighbours will come with food and comfort and memories of funny things Jacob John said and what a hard worker he was. She will feel, as she always does at such times, alone in the crowd, unable to be touched by the comfort that others share so easily.

When she hears the back door open she doesn't get up to answer; everyone will know where to find her. Slow heavy footsteps move through the kitchen and a tall frame fills the parlour door. Jabez Badcock stands there, his gray hair windblown and his fiddle tucked under his arm. He's a strange sight, not usually the first person to show up at a wake, but it seems fitting he should be here. He might, after all, be family. In a way Trif feels like the

That *Forgetful* Shore

old drunkard has always understood her, though they've exchanged no more than a few dozen words in twenty-five years.

Jabez crosses to the coffin. He takes off his shabby cap and lays it over his chest as he looks down at Jacob John, then intones, "*Remember now thy Creator in the days of thy youth, when the evil days come not, nor the years draw by when thou shalt say, I have no pleasure in them.*"

"Well, Jacob John was spared that," Trif says. "He always had pleasure in his days, right up to the end. And how much mind he paid to his Creator I was never sure, but he was good to his fellow man." Being born again as many times as she's been herself, Triffie used to be contemptuous of those who said they needed only to live a decent life to get to heaven. She could lead a Bible study to show you that you needed to repent and believe on the Lord Jesus to be saved. But now she hopes there's something to that humbler creed, which Jacob John surely subscribed to. He used to like that poem about Abou Ben Adhem, may his tribe increase, the fellow who couldn't say he loved God but loved his fellow man. Jacob John would get Triffie to read that out sometimes, when she was in a poetry-reading mood. God couldn't ask for a better citizen in heaven, and the thought of eternity without Jacob John somewhere nearby seems bleak.

Jabez goes to sit in the corner of the room, lifts his violin, and begins playing a mournful tune that, after a moment, Trif recognizes as "She's Like the Swallow." She hums along with the haunting notes: *I love my love, and love is no more.*

More voices and footsteps at the back door, and suddenly the house is full of people, neighbours and friends and church people coming in twos and threes as if they've been bottled up outside, just waiting for Triffie's dictum of "everyone out until suppertime" is lifted. "You may want to be alone but 'tis good to have people around you," Minnie Mercer says, kissing her on the cheek and putting a cherry cake on the table. Other women bring food and lay it out, even Clara Snow who brings a plate of cold sliced ham, presumably because she knows Trif won't eat it.

Over and over, people ask Trif what she's going to do now. Go live with Katie in St. John's, or move away with one of the boys, or stay on in the house alone? The answer is none of those, but people will find out her plans in her own good time. "I'm not staying on here another winter," she does tell Millicent Batten. "This place is not fit for living in year-round anymore, and I'm not putting the money in to get it done up with electricity and indoor plumbing at my time of life. We'll keep it on for a summer place, that's all 'tis fit for now." More and more older homes on the Point are like that, boarded up in winter and left to rot or, if families can afford it, visited in summer by men and women who have moved away to the mainland or the States.

"I 'low you're right, girl," Millicent says. "You gets to a point in life when 'tis not fit to be going out to the outhouse or hauling buckets of water from the well."

Under all the talk Jabez Badcock continues to play the violin, sweet and eerie tunes drifting out from the parlour where everyone goes in briefly to pay their respects to Jacob John before drifting back into the overcrowded kitchen. It's strange to have people in the house without Jacob John to tell them a few stories, get them all laughing. After awhile Char Mercer comes in with the accordion and joins in with Jabez. Trif hears Charlie singing "The Prisoner's Song"; the bleak words wind their way in and out through the mourners' conversation. *Oh, I wish I had someone to live with, for I'm tired of living alone.*

Katie and her husband Wayne and their children arrive with Bill and Dave. Neither of the boys have brought their families; Trif's lucky they are both able to fly down themselves on such short notice.

They all take Trif in their arms, one by one, and she holds her sons, drawing strength from their broad shoulders and strong bodies. Neither of them is a fisherman, as she decreed, but both are strong men, men their father was proud of. For the past few years they have brought their growing families home for summer visits, and offered to bring Triffie and Jacob John to see them. Jacob John never wanted to go; he was content to stay on the Point and let them come to him.

Triffie had no such reluctance to travel. In the past ten years she has gone into St. John's to visit Katie, and to stay with Kit while she was still teaching at Memorial. She's gone to Boston and Toronto to visit the family, to Montreal and New York with Kit. Last year Kit sent her tickets for their greatest adventure together, a trip to England and France. For that, they flew in a plane, an experience Triffie didn't particularly enjoy but is glad to have had.

To her surprise, Jacob John didn't object to these jaunts of hers. "You'd never get me up in a plane," he told her before the trip to Europe, "but it tickles me to think of you and Kit flying across the ocean – you always was

That *Forgetful* Shore

one to enjoy a bit of gallivanting. Enjoy your travels, missus, and don't worry about me. A man don't die from eating bread and butter for a few weeks." Lately Kit has talked about a trip to Italy where she can paint watercolours. Trif has no interest in painting, but now that Jacob John's bread and butter is no longer a concern she can imagine herself sitting in the Italian sun, reading a book with her feet up while Kit paints.

She follows her daughter and sons into the room where Jacob John lies, where the mournful music fills the air. They gather around the coffin and Trif stands back to give them room, leaning her hand on the wooden doorframe, like she sometimes used to lay a hand on Jacob John's shoulder, an apology she couldn't or wouldn't put into words. She loves this old house, this place where she came as a reluctant bride, where she bore her children and cried over losses and was angry and stubborn and loved. This place where she prayed and cursed and worked like a dog for forty-five years. The house and Jacob John are tied together in her mind, almost as if they were one and the same. She will come back here as a visitor – summers on the Point are always grand when you're not working your fingers to the bone – but it will never be her home again, not after tonight.

People come and go. Trif minds the company less than she thought she would. They don't know it yet, but it's her farewell party as well as Jacob John's, and these people, like the house and the Long Beach and the sea, are part of her. She will leave them behind, but she'll never fully let them go.

She steps outside the stuffy kitchen to get a breath of fresh air and goes around to the lane just in time to see a car pull up in front of the house. The passenger who gets out is a tall, straight-backed, gray-haired woman. An old woman, like herself.

"You foolish thing," Trif says. "Didn't I tell you on the phone last night not to bother coming up for the funeral?"

"You didn't think I paid any attention to that, did you?" Kit snorts, lifting her overnight bag out of her cousin Ted's car. "I bought your ticket to come down just like I told you – I just decided to bring it to you rather than send it. Flew in this afternoon, took the outport taxi to Bay Roberts, then called Ted to drive me over." She looks at the lighted windows, music drifting out into the night air. "What are you having here, an Irish wake?"

"Close enough. He would have enjoyed it – he always liked a good time," Trif says.

They stand together for a moment, looking not at the house but out at the sea as Ted Parsons drives away with a wave. Trif puts her hand on the old fencepost and Kit lays her own hand on top of Trif's. The steady rush of waves on the shore is a counterpoint to the music coming from the house and Trif wonders for a moment what it will be like to live away from that sound. Kit tells her that in North Carolina, where she's lived since retiring, they won't be all that far from the ocean. But the beaches there are sandy and Trif imagines it will sound different.

She recites softly:

The sound of that forgetful shore
Will change my sweetness more and more,
Half-dead to know that I shall die.

"You will," Kit says, her hand squeezing Trif's more tightly for a moment, "and so will I. But not just yet. We've got a bit more living to do."

"I'm glad you came," Trif says, and they turn to go into the house together.

That *Forgetful* Shore

AFTERWORD

Anyone with a passing knowledge of the geography of Conception Bay will recognize that the fictional community of Missing Point, located across the causeway from Bay Roberts and at the other end of Long Beach from Bareneed, sits on exactly the same point of land as the real town of Coley's Point. My reasons for putting a fictional place in such an obviously real location are that the flimsy disguise of a false name allows me to take a little license with geography, with history, and most of all with people. Missing Point is very like Coley's Point, but different in a few significant ways, and by giving it another name I felt absolved for making those changes.

On the south side of the real Coley's Point, at the same spot at the head of the beach where Triffie and Jacob John's house stands in fiction, stands a 150-year-old house built by my great-great-grandfather, Abraham Morgan. In this house many years ago, my cousins found, and showed to me, a collection of postcards from the early 1900s. All of them were addressed to the same woman, Abraham's daughter Emma Morgan, a teacher who worked in various Newfoundland outports between her graduation from Spencer College in 1907 and her marriage in 1917. The postcards came from family, friends, and former students all over the island, but a small subset of them – just over a dozen – came from a woman named L. Martin.

In the postcards, Miss Martin and Miss Morgan addressed each other by pet names – "Puggie" and "Muddles," and L. Martin made such flowery protestations of her love for E. Morgan that my cousins and I at first assumed the postcards were written by a man to a woman he loved. But they were, in fact, written by one woman to another, and made use of the conventions of romantic friendships of young women in that era.

I know only a little about the life of Emma Morgan, and nothing at all about her correspondent L. Martin, not even her first name. I have far less than half of their correspondence – only the postcards from Puggie to Muddles survive, not the replies, nor the longer and more private letters that the postcards allude to. It's hard for a writer's imagination not to be stirred by that kind of circumstance, and as a result I ended up exploring not the real lives of two real women, but the fictional lives of two women who lived at the same time and in a similar place, whose friendship was as intense and as important for them both.

Visit www.thatforgetfulshore.com for more about the background of this story.

One final note about the parallels between real life and fiction. A few real people appear very briefly in this fictional story: R.A. Hubley, Victoria Booth-Clibborn Demarest, Alice Garrigus, Sophie Guy, Eugene Vaters, Ethel Dickinson and Dr. John Paton. But all the major characters are fictional. Just as Missing Point is a sort of Platonic shadow of Coley's Point, so the career of Joe Bishop in the Coley's Point school parallels, at least in time, the incredible career of a real man, James Norman, the beloved and respected schoolteacher in Coley's Point for over 40 years. (One of Coley's Point's most famous sons, Ted Russell, credited Mr. Norman with awakening his lifelong love of learning). But while the two men lived and taught under similar circumstances for many of the same years, I want to emphasize that there is not a hint of a suggestion that James Norman ever shared any of Joe Bishop's more unsavoury qualities. In fact, the desire to make a distinction between the two men was one of the reasons I felt the need to change the name of the town.

While as a novelist I'm interested in characters like Joe Bishop who manage to do a great deal of good and a great deal of harm simultaneously, as a Newfoundland writer and educator I'm keenly aware of the debt we all owe to real life heroes and heroines like James Norman, Emma Morgan, and thousands of other teachers in one-room outport schools. These men and women kept a love for learning alive against overwhelming odds. The tremendous flowering of Newfoundland literary and cultural life we benefit from today would never have happened without the dedicated efforts of the teachers of our grandparents' era.

Trudy J. Morgan-Cole
St. John's, 2011

QUESTIONS FOR DISCUSSION

1. Midway through the novel, Kit reflects that she and Trif are equal in every way, except in social class. Is she right in believing that all the differences in their lives are due to class differences, or are there other factors that come into play?

2. What do you think of Triffie and Jacob John's relationship? Did you find the way it developed believable? Satisfying?

3. In the prologue of the novel, Triffie tells the minister that her twin sister died at birth, then thinks, "Tryphena and Tryphosa; Peony and Posy. It explains everything. Half of a whole, a piece torn away." What do you think she means by this?

4. What did you think about Joe Bishop's character and his role in the story? Do you think Triffie should have exposed his wrongdoing once she knew about it, or did she handle things in the best way possible?

5. Who was your favourite character in the novel? Why?

6. Who was your least favourite character? Why?

7. For much of the novel, Triffie resents Kit for having the life that she, Triffie, wanted. Do you think she overcomes this resentment? If so, why and how?

8. How did you feel about the ending of the novel? Would you consider it a happy ending? Was it what you expected?

ACKNOWLEDGEMENTS

I am grateful not only to all those who helped and supported me while writing this book, but to the many scholars and writers whose research enabled me to depict history as accurately as possible. The howling errors and anachronisms that remain are, of course, entirely my own. In addition to numerous authors of published works I would like to thank several individuals for taking the time to answer my questions: Dr. Trudi Johnson, Dr. Garfield Fizzard, Dr. Elizabeth Murphy, and Linda White, all of Memorial University; Jennifer Lambert of Dalhousie University, and Maura Hanrahan.

The helpful staff of several vital institutions deserve gratitude: this book would have been far more difficult to write without the people at the Centre for Newfoundland Studies at Memorial University, the Newfoundland Collection at the A.C. Hunter Public Library, the Provincial Archives, the Road to Yesterday Museum in Bay Roberts, Starbucks on Kenmount Road (the customer with the raspberry mochas thanks you), and, of course, the modern-day Maggie Campbell for the generous use of her name.

A book is only half-finished when it leaves the writer's hands; without a great publisher it rarely makes it into the hands of readers. Thanks to the wonderful team at Breakwater Books who believed in this book from the earliest stages, sometimes even more than I did. Particular thanks are due to my sharp-eyed editor, Marnie Parsons.

I am grateful as always to the Strident Women for support and encouragement and especially to Jennifer Morgan and Tina Chaulk for reading and critiquing the manuscript. Most of all, thanks to my long-suffering family: my parents, Don and Joan Morgan, always my best proofreaders and historical fact-checkers, and to Jason, Chris and Emma for putting up with me when I'm in the middle of writing a book – and at all other times.

TRUDY J. MORGAN-COLE is a writer and teacher. Her previous works of historical fiction include *By the Rivers of Brooklyn*, *The Violent Friendship of Esther Johnson*, *Deborah and Barak*, and *Esther: A Story of Courage*. *By the Rivers of Brooklyn* was a finalist for the Best Atlantic Published Book Award 2010 and the Silver Medal Winner of the Ippy for Best Regional Fiction 2010. Trudy lives in St. John's with her husband and two children, and teaches English, writing, and social studies to adult learners.

GR
JAN - - 2012

Liv
nov2014

BW
OCT - - 2018